Beacon

A Robot's Odyssey

By Stephen Fenech

Stephen Fenech

Fourth Edition © Copyright 2024

Portfolio Visions Books
ISBN 9780995261143
Digital ISBN 9780995261150
Toronto Canada
© Original Copyright 2017

To my parents: Alfred and Doris, who brought me into the world and helped me navigate its strange nuances, to my brother, David for his selfless, tireless efforts in editing the first monstrous draft of the manuscript, to my friends at Kidcrit Writer's Group for helping me polish my automaton, and to my sister, Marthese, whose genius of the craft helped me make my robot's coding more user-friendly. Without all your help Beacon could not have been activated.

You are all beacons.

Cover Art by Stephen Fenech

Stephen Fenech

Beacon A Robot's Odyssey

Message from Dr. Anne Morrison:

Descendants of Earth:

As you face a brave new world, it is my hope that our story will form an integral link to that lost part of your heritage, that it might facilitate a legacy. I am done with secrets which have governed my entire life. Unlike my predecessor, I wish to be completely transparent, so that you will know what I know. Rather than tell you about the scattered but quintessential steps of our story as a factual account, like some dull historical text, I have chosen the form of the narrative to help you feel the emotion of the events—to truly *know* the paragons and malefactors that have moved these events along. Emotion, after all, is something which underlines your humanity and continues to forge your path.

I have chosen not to use Galactic Clock/Distance Standards—GCDS to describe distances and measures of time within the body of the text. For the sake of fostering a more poignant grasp of what life was like before annexation, I will use Earth's own units of measurement. For any non-humanoids reading this compendium, you may cross-reference the conversion charts in your supplementary appendices to find and automatically replace those units with their equivalent GCDS values. I wish you all calm horizons...

Anne Morrison
Wardeness

Stephen Fenech

Table of Contents

Prologue: Blue Wind
1759 CE

Wind. The key to success or failure. Drifting on an endless swell of troubled ocean, the HMS *Blue Wind* yawed and swayed, rolled and pitched, as if attempting to balance the lopsided hearts of her crew. Like their ship, each waited with his own brand of apprehension, dragging it around the dimly lit decks like an ill-fitted pendant, like a ball and chain. But despite the topsy-turvy water, the salt air remained still.

And the enemy was out there, *somewhere*. If only the cursed fog would lift, just some, it would give them at least a little warning. But alas, they were doomed to wait on the edge of the silent storm, wait as it brewed towards the inevitable confrontation. Powerless to act, powerless to do anything but keep waiting, they had allowed dread to seep through their trembling bones like gouts of sap.

Out of the ethereal limbo, the air nudged back to life. When the breeze invaded Captain Percy Morrison's open tunic, it jolted him back to reality.

Stern of comportment, unwavering in resolve, Morrison's adroitness bespoke pragmatism. Of his own accord, he'd achieved success on the high seas through resourcefulness and cunning. A row of King's medals attested to that.

Many of his peers in His Majesty's Royal Navy agreed that 'Morrison embodied his own honorific statue.' A few among them insisted that the real thing deserved to be set upon a high plinth in Buckingham Palace or London's Hyde Park.

If only he stood there now in its place, strolling the park's colourful gardens hand in hand with his bonnie dearest. A world away at present, she understood that the sea was his life. And war, his curriculum vitae.

Yet this—this presented something beyond even the scope of

9

his long career.

Shivering, he pulled his cloak tighter about him. These gusts were gone as quickly as they came, though long enough to remind the captain how bitterly cold the air and how bitterly hopeless his predicament.

The *Blue Wind* had been marginalized, sustaining considerable damage in the brutal skirmish with those French bastards. Outnumbered four to one, outgunned equally so, her enemies' hectoring had taken a severe toll. The *Blue Wind*'s continued survival had been bought at too heavy a price, in sweat and blood.

One in three from Morrison's crew had gone down to Davy Jones's Locker. And with the mainmast blown to smithereens, the crew had been forced to rig a jury mast.

Amazingly, they had survived the onslaught. Exchanging broadside for broadside, the *Blue Wind* narrowly escaped the funnelled gauntlet perpetrated by those ruthless swine, trying so tenaciously to hem her in. By ramming the closest barque, Morrison's ship had secured a bit of a lead, forcing the other vessel out of the immediate battle to lick her wounds.

But the remaining three ships trained their culverins, ready to unleash a torrent of hell. Death reared—moments away.

That's when the unthinkable happened. In place of wind, fog swept in from all directions at once, shrouding them from their foes' sights. Of a thicker make than the captain could ever recall, it surpassed even the roiling pillows, which sat obstinately on the North Sea off his coastal home near Dover. *A fog so thick you could cut it with a knife,* the old maritimers would say over their spilling pints. As a child, Morrison had been told such a fog meant the Devil himself had come to roost. This fog proved worse.

For out there, the French still pursued his ship, listening with the Devil's own ears. They would not let their quarry go to ground uncontested. Such was the code of the sea. They knew it and followed it to the last. So did Morrison—that's what made him a survivor.

He'd ordered the crew to man the oars and follow a random pattern that would hopefully befuddle the French while putting some much-needed distance between the *Blue Wind* and her hunters.

For the last three days, the desultory sailors' quiet rowing continued unabated in scheduled rotations, assuring that the ship remained hidden within her cloak as she drifted upon wayward tides.

But for this confounded dead air! Despite the crew's best efforts, exhaustion would only be kept at bay for so long. The captain ordered them to respite, lest they be too weary to fight when the need arose again, as it surely would.

Battle was a horrendous terrifying prospect, straits to be avoided at all costs, but waiting on the edge of imminent combat evinced far worse. It had a gnawing effect. Time felt an eternity ere the ship had knifed the Atlantic under full canvas, late of Folkestone. Now, listlessness had settled on his crew like a pall.

Hearing an anchor chain rattle in his head, Morrison straightened. As he surveyed the forlorn decks, he knew he required a diversion as much as his crew. But what?

They all needed to adhere to hope. If wind was the key, then hope was the keyhole. He had to make it available for his crew's sake. Once that guttered, his men would look upon the battlefield with dead eyes.

At odd intervals, through the drifting skeins, a window opened briefly, revealing an empty horizon. This marked one of those moments. Seizing the opportunity, Morrison grabbed his sextant for the fifth time that day. He plodded onto the forecastle and took a measurement, making sure the lads saw him do so. He dropped the instrument to his side and mouthed a silent curse.

Morrison turned to the closest deckhand, busy coiling a rope nearby. "My Ex-O," he instructed. "Be a good man 'n summon my first mate, quietly now."

"Aye-aye, Cap'n, right away Sir," the sailor replied as he eased the corded figure-eight down to the planks and hastened

11

away.

Morrison adjusted his tricorn and stared out over the odd swell of the waves. Save for the caesura, they became lost in oblivion on either side, mere yards beyond the ship's waist. Without looking, he sensed when his Ex-O came to stand beside him.

"Seems we have sailed off the edge of the world, Mr Blythe," the captain said softly to the fog in front of him. "In naval combat, foul weather is an equalizer."

"That indeed, Captain, but we both know how close to the dragon's den we lay if not in its very bosom. We've exchanged broadside for blindside."

"Caught between the hammer and the anvil," the captain agreed.

"You summoned me, Sir," Blythe gently prompted.

"Yes, I noted something—curious." Morrison turned and handed his first mate the sextant. "Tell me, Blythe, what do you make of this? Point it twenty degrees amidships towards that window in the mists." Blythe took the instrument and did as instructed.

"Take a reading."

After a moment, the first mate replied. "Looks normal, Captain,"

"Now, raise it in line with the masthead."

"Captain?"

"Oblige me. Raise it incrementally. Observe the reading as you do, slowly now," Morrison cautioned.

Blythe followed the order, raising the instrument five degrees, ten, fifteen, thirty. He never made it to forty-five. Dropping the instrument, he turned, open-mouthed.

Morrison felt the corners of his lips curve up into a thin smile. He regarded his Ex-O in fierce silence.

"But that's—impossible," Blythe stammered. "It would mean…"

"Precisely," the captain finished for him.

"Could the surface of the ocean have changed angles by six

degrees? We should have felt it, if not be floundering for it."

"I've already checked it five times this day."

Blythe inspected the sextant closely for a moment before handing it back to his captain. "Perhaps the instrument itself is broken."

"It's the third astrolabe I've used," said Morrison.

"And each showing an identical reading of five degrees off-kilter?"

"Aye, except for one difference." Seeing his officer's frown, Morrison said flatly, "With every measurement, the vector's angle increases." He allowed the other man to grasp the import of his words.

Blythe gaped.

Another murmur of that same chilling breeze punctuated Morrison's startling revelation. It also caused the fog to veil the brief gap once more. Exactly as it had done for the last three days, the wind returned long enough to remind the *Blue Wind* of her stalemate. The captain waited for it to die.

When it didn't, a tingling sensation took root at the base of Morrison's spine. Blythe's widening eyes mirrored the captain's shock.

Morrison opened his mouth to issue the order for the proper lay of the sails when something equally vexing caught his notice. The wind did not come from any lateral direction, but an anomalous *stormless* downburst from above. Flapping and clapping, the sails buffeted uselessly as the wind descended straight down from the sky.

"Ahoy, Cap'n!" the lookout called down from way up atop the crow's nest, his voice sounding strange in what had escalated to a keening wind. "Something strange happenin' above yonder moonraker."

"Aye-aye," shouted another hand as he climbed the foresail rigging. "I see it too!"

Morrison and Blythe quickly followed the sailors' pointing fingers, triangulating above the foremast's skysail, skyscraper and

13

finally past the topmost square sail called the moonraker.

The captain tried to comprehend what they all saw. A conical aperture had opened up in the mist directly above them. It swirled, turning the mist at its fringe in a counterclockwise rotation, roiling faster and faster as the cyclonic orifice widened and heightened. The wind grew stronger too as it funnelled down, creating a longish chop to the sea.

Morrison bit his lower lip. *What new devilry is this?*

When the vertical squall contacted the water's surface it spread out from the *Blue Wind* in all directions, pushing the curtain of fog further and further back. Ten yards, twenty, forty, one hundred yards, two hundred. And then...

Morrison spotted *them*.

One by one, emerging from the shroud's unveiling periphery, a barque and schooner appeared off the *Blue Wind*'s starboard flank, another schooner off to port and the barque they'd previously rammed astern. All four French vessels had effectively stalked them the entire time within the vaporous cloak. The *Blue Wind* was trapped.

"Battle stations!" Morrison roared. "All hands on deck!"

No sooner had the French ships caught sight of their quarry than their ship's bells clanged in angry chorus. Cries went up. The French immediately brought their vessels about in the strangely reborn wind.

"Damnation," the captain spat. No doubt, the French had already trained their guns on their target like hunters wetting their chops at the hasty entrance of game.

Seconds later, they confirmed his notion. The air erupted with the report of cannon fire. Burning potshots unleashed with thunderous cracks. They streaked towards the *Blue Wind* in vicious volleys, leaving trails of fire in their aerial wake.

BOOM, Splash, *BOOM*, Splash: the constant barrage of red-hot cannonballs striking the ocean on all sides of Morrison's vessel created an infernal wall of fire and water. A blustery wind and confused wake exacerbated their collective hell, throwing

14

everything into further chaos. The charred smell of smoke and sulphur reigned everywhere.

Miraculously not a single shot of the merciless cannonade struck the *Blue Wind*. Morrison would try to keep it that way as long as possible. But the sounds, smells, and light of pitched battle, and the rampageous expression of nature at its worst clashed and tore at the fabric of his mind.

Still, Morrison kept his wits as he brought his crew to task. Chin high, his movements precise, he impelled them to act. "Helmsman to the wheel, turn her about. Take evasive action. Everyone, snap to, man the guns!" he shouted in a titan's voice. "All guns—double-shots! *Fire at will!*"

Across the teetering decks, all hands scrambled to their stations, hearts trip-hammering, faces creased with mortal fear tempered by anger and determination. Arms extended like rapiers, Blythe and the other officers raced from bow to stern and back, pointing to assets and directing sailors with specific orders.

One blast, loaded with chain-shot found them true. Stays snapped and the mizzentop spars crashed to the poop deck.

Despite the grievous harm, the captain drew some relief—the *Blue Wind* had begun returning fire, blasting back with impunity. An injured leviathan, raging on as she fought for her life. Stern satisfaction coursed through his veins. Aye—the crew had risen above their fear, resolute that they would not go to the depths lightly.

They sent this firm message to the French by striking back hard and true. Besides training her periers and cannons on her attackers, swivel guns loaded with grapeshot were brought to bear.

BOOM, Splash, *BOOM*, Splash. CRACK!

Having more targets gave the *Blue Wind* a small advantage, but the French ships too caused considerable damage. They set the afterdeck ablaze. Flames licked up the mizzenmast and clawed at the sky. Falling detritus burned several crewmen. Three had fallen. Two more had taken flak from musket fire and a sixth, his trusty boatswain, Pullen, was killed instantly when the bowsprit blew off the bulwark and impaled the ill-fated man.

Meanwhile, the tumultuous swell and stormy gale, the very breath of pandemonium, levelled the battlefield. The handicaps facing the *Blue Wind* as she struggled through the heavy seas, also wreaked havoc with her enemies.

But the French were persistent if nothing else. All four ships surged through what became mountains of water, moving relentlessly towards them. The gap closed. The waves heaved against the sides of every ship, making the sea swell one moment before draining it down to her barnacles the next.

The pervasive reek of ash, smoke, and gunpowder wafted everywhere. Even without such bedlam, the incessant combat, fusillade for fusillade, writ the *Blue Wind*'s doom. It was only a matter of time.

So engaged with the exchange of battle and death, no soul present could've fathomed what unfolded high above the immediate mêlée. The uppermost tip of the conical cavity had risen unhindered. Driving upwards, it pierced the heavens to reveal a circular patch of blue sky.

Only when the Sun shone down through the opening did heads, including Morrison's, crane up. He squinted as the light of the orb intensified the colours of the savage theatre, momentarily blinding the combatants. Something seemed peculiar about the Sun itself.

The captain afforded it but a brief glimpse before returning his gaze to the battle. Once his eyes adjusted, they bulged.

The trajectories of the enemy fleet's latest potshots suddenly skewed mid-flight, as though the flaming cannonballs had decided for themselves to drastically change course mid-volley. The attack ceased.

Even more disturbing, the watery expanse between the *Blue Wind* and her rivals began to churn and roil, moving in a more distinct circular motion.

Morrison wiped salt spray from his eyes to make sure they weren't deceiving him. They weren't. *Good—God.*

A maelstrom was forming!

It quickly ensnared the *Blue Wind*, jarring her at the waist. She swept sideways. So too did her antagonists. The French schooner closing in from port heaved around them in a sublime arc, suddenly forced along the renegade curve. Several of the French crewmen were flung off her deck and cast into the sea. The vessel collided against the side of the compromised barque astern. Their caterwauling crash sent shards of wood pitchpoling in every direction.

Both ships married, rocked, and pushed violently as one. With their lines entangled and knotted, the pair careened towards the remaining two adversaries. In seconds all four ships impacted with such a gut-wrenching thwack and squeal, it sent a shiver coursing through the *Blue Wind*'s decks, straight into the hearts of her staggered crew.

Now, a mere seventy yards off the *Blue Wind*'s starboard side, the four vessels clasped one another amidships as if in a tight transfer mooring.

Morrison clutched the railing in a white-knuckled grip and gawked as the quadruple collision rent and splintered wood from each of the four vessels. Bulwarks grated. Lines snapped. Sails rent. As the ships unintentionally cannibalized one another.

The spiralling centrifuge pushed the vessels further away from the *Blue Wind*. And sucked them down.

The maelstrom deepened. Its massive concave depression placed the four French ships dead centre in the throat of its vortex.

The captain's fear ratcheted up several notches. He didn't need a sextant to confirm what his eyes refused to believe. The *Blue Wind* rode a full thirty degrees above the French ships, at an impossible angle, yet as incredulous as it seemed, she didn't founder. By sheer velocity alone, she glided true as if glued to the inner curve of a bowl made of water. Insanity reigned as the swirling hole in the sea reflected the tapering maw in the clouds directly above it.

Through the heavenly gap, Earth's star beamed down on the

17

scene of destruction, its light intensifying with each passing moment. Abruptly the arena's water ceased its movement stilling into a mirror. The ocean's surface took on an emerald cast, an impossible colour of such brilliance... all sound stopped.

Morrison tore his gaze away from the deadlocked battle to glance up, sight swelling, hands seizing the railing in a death grip.

Tinged emerald around its corona, the Sun—blazing Orb of Creation itself—streaked towards them. Expanding as it fell, Beacon of the Almighty, Herald of Armageddon. The fireball ignited the clouds, filling the sky in seconds.

No sun, the captain realized.

Everything went WHITE.

!!—!!

The blast's concussion surpassed any imaginings Morrison held from the worst parts of the Bible. It singed the air in electrical seizure—an unearthly resonance amplifying the brutal onslaught of light and sound in a phantasmagorical release.

Lucky for the crew and captain of the *Blue Wind*, its energy focused straight down on top of the melded French ships.

They didn't have a chance—to be pulverized. The *Blue Wind*'s opponents were instantly incinerated as the fiery projectile passed through them and into the water on which they floated. So intense was the orb's power that it tunnelled down through the watery depths without exploding at the surface. Had it done so, the *Blue Wind* would have been vaporized too.

Seconds after it passed, the watery tunnel collapsed in on itself, causing a massive implosion that stole the air from Morrison's lungs and sent a monster wave hurdling outward, towards the *Blue Wind*.

Again, luck was with them: the initial impact wrenched the ship ninety degrees on her centre axis, aligning her bow with the approaching rogue wave.

The *Blue Wind* cut it head-on as it struck. From decks to keel beam, the ship's wood buckled. Iron screamed under the unnatural strain. But she rode the tidal wave well, summiting its crest and into the immense trough left in its wake. She crashed. And resurfaced, incredibly still in one piece.

Within moments, the angle of the depression ebbed and the sea returned to relative normality—with one difference. Narrow columns of steam began to plume, breaching the surface around the impact site. They whistled like banshees as they shot towards the true-blue sky above.

Braced against any available rail or rope, the crew watched the geysers, their clenched faces vacillating between terror and relief. For several moments no one moved.

With his sleeve, the captain wiped cold sweat from his brow, trying to wrap his mind around the preternatural occurrence. Unsteady footsteps behind him drew his attention. He wheeled to find his Ex-O.

Visibly shaken, Blythe staggered up: face pale and scratched, uniform drenched and torn, hands and lips atremble.

Somehow, Morrison found his voice. "Mr Blythe, report." His own words sounded strange to him, devolved.

"Frankly Sir," Blythe croaked as he steadied his carriage against the rail, "I wouldn't know what kind of a report *to* make."

"How's my ship, Mr Blythe? And what of the crew?" Though he could not fault his first mate's condition, the captain knew he had to get this man focused, despite what they'd just been through. That was essential to restoring order.

Blythe's voice cracked a little as he spoke. "We lost five more souls, Sir." He glanced over his shoulder before returning his eyes to Morrison. "Another two probably won't last till dawn, some ten others injured." He cleared his throat. "As for the *Blue Wind*, she's hurt plenty but hasn't broke deep. She'll sail true for you, Sir."

"That is good news, all things considered, but—" Morrison blew out his cheeks.

"You hate to lose a single man," Blythe finished for him.

Morrison swallowed. "May God watch over them." His thoughts circled to Pullen to avoid what troubled him most about the inexplicable event.

"Indeed, He will, Captain, for was it not His hand that smote down the French curs? We were in a hopeless situation, and in earnest I, well I began to pray, Sir. This was, I believe, a boon from the Almighty."

"No, Mr Blythe," Morrison said slowly as he descried the remnants of the anomaly, "I don't think so. This was no godsend. No random event either. And I cannot be sure it is over."

The captain faced his first mate and studied his measure. "I believe the Devil Himself has come back to roost."

Blythe chewed his lower lip and stared. A few awkward seconds passed with only the sound of the steady wind, the creak of loosened timbers, and the soft whistling of the steam plumes to fill the silence between the two officers.

At length, the Ex-O gave him a resigned nod.

Morrison broke the moment with a rare smile. He tapped his sextant against the side of his lapel once, twice. And handed the instrument to his first mate. "Before you initiate the more pressing repairs, see to the dead and wounded. Then, I want you to take our exact heading and bearings and include any other anomalous findings or observations from the crew—any findings."

He paused and gave Blythe a long look before continuing. "See if any flotsam survived our foes' timely demise, anything we might salvage towards facilitating our own repairs or to help us understand what the hell happened. I'll be in my quarters."

Blythe inclined his chin. "Captain."

"Carry on then." Keeping his eyes averted from the event horizon, Morrison strode to his cabin where he immediately sat at his bureau, impatient to start what was sure to be a rather lengthy entry into his logbook.

The convalescing sea outside churned and simmered for the rest of that day.

1: Anne
2039 CE

Dr Anne Morrison could tell by the static and hiss at the other end of the phone line that the call came from somewhere remote.

"Hello, I'm trying to reach Professor Morrison." His accent was British and he spoke eloquently. "Is this she?"

"Yes."

"The name is Blythe, Henric Blythe of Blythe Aerospace—out of Southampton," he clarified. Not that it needed any clarification; she immediately recognized the name of the shipping magnate turned world-renowned inventor and uber-rich entrepreneur.

"What can I do for you, Mr Blythe?" Anne asked.

"Professor, it has come to my attention that you've acquired a very old logbook." Anne's mind raced. "I cannot begin to tell you how valuable it is to me, and for that matter, how significant you are. I'd like to meet with you at once to discuss a matter of profound importance—to us both."

Anne exhaled, her eyes dropping to the stack of exams cluttering her desk. "Mr Blythe, it's an honour, but I'm sorry, I'm not sure I'd be a good fit for you. Besides that, my schedule here at the University is filled for the next two weeks at least. Tell you what, I'll call you back this afternoon to work something out but I can't stay on the line. I'm already late for a lecture I'm giving."

His laughter made the line's static spike briefly. "Professor, the Dean has already graciously covered you and approved a leave of absence—after I made a certain donation towards a new wing on campus. He saw no reason for you *not* to assist me in my research." Blythe fell silent. The line's hiss swelled.

"Research?" Anne swallowed, her eyebrows pulling together. "What kind of research?"

"Tell me, Professor, what would you say if I could help put you exactly where you crave to go?" Blythe paused before continuing, pitching his voice low and even, "And use your field of expertise to lay that most vexing question to rest? You know, the one that has been haunting you these last few years?"

He knows. Anne held her breath, a cold sweat trickling down her spine. Still cradling the phone to her ear, she sat on the edge of her desk. "I'm listening."

"I have a limo waiting for you in your staff car park to take you to the airport."

"You want me to get on a plane to Southampton?" she asked, unable to mask her incredulity.

More laughter. "No, Professor. I need you on one of my long-range helicopters to rendezvous with my flagship, *Stormwatcher*. We are currently en route to *the* coordinates."

2: Stormwatcher
Anne

The horn's resonating blast made every head look up. The familiar squelch heralded a ship-wide announcement. A gargle of static followed the oscillating whine of a microphone coming to life.

"All hands ready. Winch is hot. Prepare submersibles—probe launch in T-minus ten minutes. Set chronometers. Mark... *now*."

An abrasive electronic suffix rang off the *Stormwatcher*'s superstructure, signalling the end of the message as the PA switched off. A flurry of activity followed as the crew made ready to carry out their respective assignments, in what became a well-rehearsed program, all except the *Stormwatcher*'s chief researcher.

"Fuck, I thought we had more time!" Anne Morrison shot her eager understudy, Wayne Clarke, an exasperated look.

He flashed her a Hollywood smile that made his dimples show. "You know how it goes with this company, Boss. We're late *before* we even start."

Running a hand behind her neck, Anne studied the laidback twenty-five-year-old's comely features, framed by a shoulder-length mop of brown hair.

After a moment, she released a lungful of air. "Okay, drop the prelims and get this sensor array aboard that tub before they sink her."

"Aye-aye Boss," Clarke replied, pulling out a series of 16-pin connector cables from a metallic box slightly larger than a briefcase. The LED on the unit's display panel immediately dimmed, signalling that the array now ran on battery power. With the case under one arm, the wiz-kid left the lab at a brisk pace, leaving an unhappy Morrison staring at his back.

Her pained grimace didn't mask the fact that Anne was still an attractive woman, having aged gracefully into her mid-forties—handsome with high cheekbones, chiselled features and bright blue eyes that spoke of an inherent no-bullshit approach to everything she tackled better than any words. But her words could all be soldiers; every syllable, a bayonet if the situation merited such.

Her chestnut hair, salted with a streak of white was currently wound in a ball and held in place with a black scrunchie behind her head. A pair of fitted blue-grey coveralls flattered her athletic figure. Despite her exhaustion, her mind was as sharp as ever.

It'd been a struggle trying to maintain the integrity of her work around the demanding schedule imposed by the suits back at the office, the *military-industrial* office, but she swallowed the pill in exchange for the chance to see the fruition of her life's work at this most crucial stage, especially after so many failed attempts.

"Don't worry, Doctor," her new assistant, Tasmin said as she took a step closer. "They'll wait. You still hold the trump card here. You're the one who discovered *the Glass*."

Anne studied the pretty blonde's freckles and allowed herself a thin smile. "Actually, Tasmin, that's not right, or fair. It wasn't my discovery, not really."

"What do you mean?"

"Believe it or not, it started as a historical search through my family tree while I was still an undergrad."

"Really?" Tasmin said, eyebrows arching in apparent surprise.

"Yup," Anne affirmed, her eyes dropping to the paper cup half filled with black coffee, long gone cold. She reached for it anyway and took a sip before turning her attention back to her assistant. "My search didn't pull up anything too interesting, except that I was related to a decorated British captain, one Percy Rigmund Morrison, unknown to the masses, but quite famous in nautical circles. *God*, this coffee's ice!"

"I can make a fresh pot," Tasmin offered.

"No, it's okay," Anne chuckled. "Nothing a quick nuke can't fix, and we should both be here when the show begins."

Tasmin followed her to the small microwave set to the inner wall of the lab. Anne opened the door, placed the cup inside and set the pad to ninety seconds. "His life became a pet project between my first and second PhDs. When I completed those, I sent a query across the Pond to England, trying to dig up some more info from my great-great-great-great-great-grandfather's closest relatives."

Anne's focus shifted from the rotating cup to Tasmin. "Despite all that *greatness,* my inquiries went unanswered, so eventually I put the matter to rest. That's when the package arrived, delivered Fed Ex to my department office back at MIT."

Tasmin leaned in. "Where you taught astrophysics and quantum mechanics, right?"

"Yeah," Anne laughed, "the light subjects. Well, I freaked when I opened the package and found the original leather-bound logbook of my near 300-years-gone ancestor, worn to shit—a real museum piece." Anne quickly described the riddle of the blast from the sky, which wound up turning the captain's hopeless situation on its heels.

"That piqued my interest even more. I searched the Net to verify any similar accounts of the phenomena described by Captain Morrison, placed phone calls, consulted astronomers, astrophysicists, historians. Even curators at various museums. But always no dice. French historians took affront at the notion that a single British vessel sank four of theirs. One of them hung up on me."

Beeeeep!

Anne opened the door to the microwave, reached in and brought the cup to her lips. After a small taste, she went on, "There just wasn't any info out there that might've corroborated the captain's story. Nothing except for his account, and the coordinates he faithfully logged."

"Where we're parked right now," Tasmin put in.

Anne dipped her chin as she closed the oven door. "Time has a funny way of making pivotal things happen when you least expect them, pulling cosmic forces, aligning the planets—something like that. Call it fate or divine intervention, I stumbled upon the true discovery when I least expected it. Just as I was leaving my office to give a lecture one day, I received that pivotal phone call, which made this whole production possible."

"Blythe," Tasmin guessed.

Anne nodded. "That's when matters snowballed into our current avalanche—but that logbook was the real owner's manual. Like a beacon, it marked the path to all these scientific surprises, each one more astounding than the one before. Blythe had me whisked away by limo and chopper from my former life." She tilted her head towards the closest lab station. "He set me on this quest."

"One that seems to get stranger and stranger the closer we get to our goal," Tasmin observed.

Anne inclined her chin and swallowed more coffee. "Ironically, by unlocking my past I inadvertently began turning a key to the future."

A static-charged voice gargling out of the ship's com broke the moment. "Boss? Clarke here. Sensor array made it aboard the submersible. It's good to go. I'm heading back now." Another fizzling punctuation sounded. Then silence.

"Speaking of which—" Anne moved to the lab's angled window, pockmarked with water droplets from a recent rain shower. The forecastle crane slowly lowered the probe into the swell. "God willing, we should get some serious results, now."

3: Descent
Anne

As soon as the robotic envoy sank out of view, Anne's eyes fixed on the ship's prow where waves, two metres high, heaved past the anchor chain. Grey clouds blanketed the sky overhead and erased the horizon, giving the entire seascape a dreamlike quality.

The *Stormwatcher* had been her home for months now. Anne remembered those first few days aboard the impressive ship, steaming east across the Atlantic to the site as she got up to speed.

She was sure the *Stormwatcher* would prove nothing more than a retrofitted cargo freighter. But when the chopper touched down on the helipad, she found a massive state-of-the-art research vessel with all the latest top-of-the-line scientific equipment money could buy. And Blythe had plenty of that, making the Fortune 500 and becoming a household name like Bill Gates or Steve Jobs.

Thoughts centring on Blythe, the operation's instigator and prime mover, Anne left the lab with Tasmin in tow, a tablet hugged firmly against her chest with both hands. They headed for the scientific tub's main control room.

Anne's first big shock came when she learned that the industrial tycoon-turned-philanthropist was directly descended from the first mate on the *Blue Wind*—hence his knowledge of the right coordinates. She immediately felt better about everything, knowing that they had a shared stake in the matter.

Despite his peculiar mannerisms, Blythe was a handsome watchful man on top of his game. Experienced in several business arenas, he seemed content to delegate and not micromanage his 'little' empire. Her boss clung to his ideals and his health with fervency, looking an even fifty, above average height, with a modest build.

Anne's relationship with the man became symbiotic in every sense. She had the brains and he had the resources. Anne used those resources to their fullest capacity. When she reached an impasse, she didn't hesitate to approach Blythe and demand more equipment or a specialist to overcome it. They had an understanding that as long as she justified her reason for the added expenditure, she'd get it within the week.

So, when she asked to have a government-owned mapping satellite retasked to maintain a geostationary orbit with Ground Zero, she had only to convince him of its worth. And it was done.

After the ship's sonar and infrared scanners had garnered nothing, correlating data streams between satellite and onboard pulse emitters and sonar imaging equipment gave Anne her first major discovery. There was something down there all right, revealed through refraction and reflectivity at a depth where no light could or should exist—except artificially.

Moments later, they reached the control room. Clarke met them at the entrance, offering Tasmin an uncertain smile as he swept his arm low, gesturing for her to go first.

The tech-crowded enclosure had started to gather bodies, several of them already busy at various control stations with heads-up or VR displays. Those seated communicated through wireless headsets affixed to their matted crowns. The sound of electronic beeps and blips and quiet conversation broadened the din of whirring servos and fans.

"How long before we see anything?" Tasmin asked over Anne's shoulder.

Instead of answering her new assistant, Anne tilted her head in Clarke's direction.

"Well, that depends on how angry we make it," the understudy replied with a devious grin. "Tethered to the *Stormwatcher* by the same reinforced umbilical securing this one, our first sub went down with an innovative digital camera."

As Clarke carried on, Anne moved over to a coffee station and poured herself a fresh cup from the carafe. She listened in silence as she returned to the pair, remembering all too well that first submersible's slow descent into the black.

It had dropped at a rate of one metre per second, relaying

readings back to the surface as it plunged. A sudden increase in water temperature denoted the first threshold it crossed. Shortly after, the high-sensitivity cameras began registering increases in both luminescence and the electromagnetic—EM band.

"That first probe found the aura of light, little more than a kilometre above actual," Clarke explained. "It was tinged emerald and continued to manifest out of the event's heart, before finite lines of an image took shape, pretty much like a pre-digital photo being developed in a dark room."

Tasmin bit her lower lip thoughtfully. "What did it look like?"

Clarke steepled his fingers as he pondered the question. "Sort of resembled a massive electronic eye, complete with corona and pupil. Solid enough, semi-transparent, basked in a lambent nest, suffusing it from inside. It looked like an engine nacelle, but one made from the finest Venetian glass." He nudged his chin at Anne. "Right away, Doc believed, and I agreed, we were looking at some kind of vessel."

"A vessel—you mean a ship?" Tasmin exclaimed.

Clarke's engrossed eyes and brisk nod bespoke earnestness. But Anne knew he was having fun with the poor girl. Still, she found his attraction to Tasmin a tad comical and didn't interrupt.

Anne kept her smile to herself, but her postgrad smirked openly as he carried on. "Inside it, we made out something even more bizarre—a definite form—the only part of the object not transparent. Looked like a pair of stacked beetles facing each other, but joined at the head, Siamese-like, with multiple legs protruding outward. Kinda reminded me of an ancient rune, etched in the wall of some cave. But its structure appeared only in silhouette and wasn't comprised of rounded curves like any insect. It had linear edges and symmetry. Something mechanical."

"That wasn't the biggest mystery," Anne reminded him.

"Right." Clarke glanced in Anne's direction. "The ship sat in the middle of a shallow but extensive crater. The depression resembled a melted glass ashtray, extending well beyond the probe's scopes. It was impossible to tell how far it spread.

Darkness swallowed the nimbus further out."

"The Glass," Tasmin supplied, tilting her head to one side and pulling her blonde locks absently. "That's why I'm here, actually,"

"Your background's chemistry, right?" Clarke asked.

Tasmin's chin dipped slightly. Her hand left her hair and returned to her tablet.

"Then you're definitely on the right boat."

Anne leaned in between the pair. "We couldn't fathom how the seabed had been so chemically transformed, melted and fused at temperatures we guessed beyond anything possible on Earth, or in it."

Clarke wagged a finger and chuckled. "Hell, we couldn't begin to ascertain any of the implications of the discovery, except one. Doc struck gold."

As Anne sipped her coffee, her understudy's recounting took her back to that first moment. She had seen meteorite impacts before. Even the monstrous impacts in Tunguska, Siberia and Chicxulub in the Yucatan didn't produce results like that. If it was glass, it was something she'd never seen in her life. According to the probe's sensors, the hardness of the substance's constituents went far beyond the crystallization of diamonds.

Even then, she harboured a sinking feeling, like engaging in something she shouldn't, like turning the key that would open Pandora's Box.

"So," Clarke continued, bringing Anne back to the moment, "the submersible started a sensor sweep on all bandwidths and spectrums, which didn't reveal a helluva lot until its external strobes scaled up to bear down on the object. When this secondary light source intensified, seeking full luminosity, the vessel transformed. It changed colour, solidified, and began pulsating."

Anne cleared her throat. "But then, just as the strobes clicked over 73% luminosity, the monitor went black. The LEDs on the remote panel controlling the probe all winked out."

"And just like that." Clarke snapped his fingers. "The sub was a dead stick."

Tasmin's eyes darted between Clarke and Anne, who only nodded at her postgrad's appraisal.

"We had to pull the defunct craft back up to the surface," Anne said.

"Figured a reciprocal reaction to the strobes caused the malfunction," Clarke supplied. "But sheer proximity to the target added another factor."

Over the rim of her coffee cup, Anne watched her new assistant blink. She counted two breaths before answering the silent question in Tasmin's eyes. "When we played back the entire visual and sensor recording, we found our rover's cause of death—an energy surge—a brief localized EM spike. It came from the vessel."

Clarke pinched the bridge of his nose and snorted. "That it did. Running the numbers of the sensor log's data stream, we detected something even more puzzling—and chilling. The probe was utter scrap, but for a moment before it went belly up, it revealed an aura of sound. Not static, mind you, like random background noise generated by the energy discharge. It had the definite focus and wavelength of a pattern. The vessel was transmitting—a radio signal."

"That signal turned our whole world upside down," Anne put in before Clarke got too carried away. "As you know, Tasmin, it brought in the military. That's why the entire op is shrouded in such a veil. Geez, practically overnight, they isolated the whole venture, spidering all over the globe to retain experts deemed key to the investigation."

Clarke laughed. "Well, when you retask one of Uncle Sam's satellites, Boss, can't expect him to look the other way."

Anne bowed her head in agreement. "Over the next four months, we tried again with half a dozen more probes." She exhaled her resignation. "But at the exact point as the first, they all died. Meanwhile, from across the globe, the scientific community's cavalry charged in. Astrophysicists, oceanographers, radio decryption analysts: they all wanted to join the show."

As if on cue, Anne's phone chimed. She reached over her console, picked it up and examined the text message. It came from Blythe, a single word, 'GODSPEED.' She texted him back with a decidedly British vernacular, 'STEADY ON.' And added a smiley-face emoji.

"Me too," Tasmin confessed as she moved to stand beside Anne.

Anne put her phone down. "But *this* show can't have an audience." She lifted her gaze and smiled at the sheepish look in the chemistry major's eyes.

Tasmin shrugged and waved the tablet in her hand. "Hence the gag order I had to sign."

"We all signed NDAs," said Clarke. "It's a requisite for permission to come aboard the *Stormwatcher*." His pupils flitted to Anne. "And for those already aboard."

"Our military liaison insisted," Anne said. "I resent that kind of coercion, but admittedly, the non-disclosure agreements force anyone who knows anything about the discovery to keep it out of media circles."

"Otherwise, activists and fanatics would converge like vultures on the kill," Clarke said.

A coldness seeped down Anne's spine. "That new radical group emerging out of the university system notwithstanding."

Tasmin shivered, eyes widening in understanding. "The Apocs—God help us. A leak like that would turn what we're doing here into a flipping circus beyond *their* lunatic fringe."

"Couldn't have said it better myself," said Clarke.

"Though, I can't really blame any dissidents," Anne conceded. "Anyone with a free-thinking mind would either fear or fantasize about the discovery's implications—including the Teslas and Einsteins—y'know, the good guys." With that, she tipped back the rest of her beverage.

Anne liked to consider herself in the latter bracket. She'd witnessed firsthand how an innocent family tree project spiraled up exponentially, and at times out of control, into the most incredible find of the twenty-first century.

"Yeah, the new faces keep cropping up," Clarke agreed. He ogled Tasmin again, making the girl blush. "Just ahead of you, a German cybernetician named Bernhardt came aboard."

Another shadow crept over Anne's mood at the mention of that name. The appearance of the mechatronics authority, Dr Clas Bernhardt seemed an odd choice at first. Then it disturbed her.

Ping, ping, ping, ping. The soft proximity alarm drew Anne's regard to the monitor. The screen revealed what the probe's cameras distinguished.

Anne was confident that the latest submersible on loan from NASA—a nautilus prototype initially designed for the Enceladus Mission—would be more successful than its predecessors. Along with a better calibrated sensor array, it utilized the latest quantum nanotechnology for its casing and circuitry, which would hopefully protect it from the devastating EM effect of their new acquaintance down in the deep end of the pool.

The control room had since filled to capacity, standing room only, so visual and data feeds had to be patched through to various labs all over the ship. Anne sat down in her designated swivel chair and pulled it up before the main monitor, anticipation building with each increment of depth the sub attained.

The LED depth reading flickered across the panel below the monitor like a tiny green sprite taunting her about an impending bane. Time slowed. Beads of sweat trickled down the centre of her back as the submersible neared the event horizon where all the other probes had failed.

The lumen indicator, which had been locked at 0.000 began to climb steadily up. Anne's pulse quickened. Moments later, the familiar emerald glow lit up the screen. Out of the intensifying aura, the vessel finally re-emerged, like an apparition returning from the netherworld.

Anne had memorized this view, having played back every frame of the other recordings a thousand times, trying to glean some new clue to the conundrum.

EVENT HORIZON BREACH: 30 METRES
STROBE GUN LUMINOSITY: 70%, the probe relayed on the monitor.

EVENT HORIZON BREACH: 20 METRES
STROBE GUN: 73%.

"C'mon. C'mon," Anne mouthed. She held her breath.
EVENT HORIZON BREACHED
STROBE GUN: 75%. The value continued to climb steadily to a full 100% luminosity without further interruption. All at once, the control room erupted in a flurry of cheers and hugs and quips like, 'Leave it to the folks at NASA.'

"Thank you, baby," Anne said quietly to the sub, patting the monitor like a mother pleased with her child. She looked up across each shoulder at the grinning faces staring back, and her expression softened. "Well done everyone. Well done."

As she turned back to the screen her placidity hardened. The moment of relief gave way to the crucial task at hand. After more than six months of waiting, plagued by the same EM hurdle, which stymied every probe since the first, Anne would get to see an uninterrupted live feed, up close. Much to her relief, the NASA prototype continued to work flawlessly as it drew up to the enigma.

Her eyes scurried across the screen, tracing every contour, comparing this new image to the one she'd committed to memory. She knew in an instant that something *had* changed.

As the submersible ceased its descent, levelling off and switching to a neutral buoyancy hover mode, the intercom suddenly lit up like a Christmas tree. All the other PhDs, spread throughout the ship's various niche labs tried to key into her at the same time.

Anne ignored them, concentrating on the panels of LEDs indicating the real-time stats and scans that her new sensor array read off the vessel: Spectro-Analysis, Ambient Energy Co-Variant, Temperature Median, Harmonic Acoustic Reverberant Co-efficient. She scanned them one by one, mentally processing their import as she scrolled down the list. They all seemed to be in the green, functioning normally and within expected parameters.

But when she found the radio emission LED her eyes stopped short and did a doubletake. Her heart followed. That LED spouted gibberish: blinking asterisks and dashes, half-completed numerics and finally a steady stream of zeros.

What the— "Wayne," she called in a deliberately cautious tone, "I think one of the sensors might be fucked."

"Which one?" he called from his station, four metres away.

"Radio emission."

A pause. "That's funny. All the sensor's servos and solenoids read five by five. If that puppy got fried, the kill would have triggered across the board."

"Hmm, no gutter." Anne peered past the jumble of people until her eyes found and locked on Clarke. "Maybe it's an internal connection break with the processors up here on the ship."

Clarke's eyebrows dove down. "Maybe," he said, his tone doubtful.

As Anne brainstormed, she chewed the inside of her cheek like a chipmunk in fast forward. "Can we verify the watch-file from your end, maybe run a diagnostic?"

"Sure Boss, the watch-file is no probs, but for a proper diagnostic we'd have to haul the tub back to the surface to do it, and aft—" Clarke's voice dithered on his lips.

"After—?" Anne pressed.

He hesitated a moment longer. "Y' know, Anne, all five audio-based sensors run on the same grid, so they can correlate common data in real-time. Ergo, if one fails it'd bring the other four down along with it—weakest link and all that."

"Tandem computing, shared-grid multiplicity circuits. Yup, know all about that."

Clarke gave her a thumbs-up.

"So, you don't think it's a malfunction?"

A slow smirk ambled across the postgrad's face.

Anne found it contagious. "Okay, impress me."

"Let me try something before we bring in the big guns. It'll be a long shot, but you never know. I'm gonna widen the range of the sensor's amplitude and sweep emulator."

"Good idea. While you're at it, get it to key on a few bands we haven't tried—carrier waves and such. If we can still coordinate with the satellite subspace frequencies, do it. See if that turns up anything."

Anne faced her monitor again. Her anger at herself for not considering this possibility right away was tempered by the reprieve of tackling the problem head-on—and having the best tools and minds to do so. Clarke might be young, prone to an occasional bout of puppy love but he was truly gifted with electronics and worked on her team.

While the postgrad made the necessary adjustments to his board, patching a few peripherals to the console with external cables and adapters, Anne scanned the other panels. Exactly as she figured, they all gave readings that made sense. She busied herself inspecting the macros generated by the watch-file's report when Clarke's voice ripped her out of her private little world.

"Doc, I found something!"

Anne's head whipped around. "Talk to me, Clarke."

"The reading shows we got something strong, really, really strong. I'm talking ten-to-the-power-of-a-gazillion strong. Turns out there is no EM pulse at all, not really anyway. The magnitude of the radio signal is what fried the other probes."

Anne rose out of her swivel chair and walked through the sea of standing bodies to Clarke's station.

"When I enlarged the scope of the sensor to broadband it told me right away, our boy down there is fine and dandy," said Clarke. "We were too close is all. The computer just couldn't process the data—the range we gave it was far too localized. It would be like trying to use an oral thermometer to measure the heat in a rocket engine during take-off. When I zoomed out and dampened the sensors, the readings began to make more sense. See."

Using his finger, Clarke indicated the corrected LED display, which now gave proper numeric values on the signal's parameters. He stole a peek up at Anne's face.

When she nodded, he continued more excitedly, "So, I zoomed out to see the outer limit of what we thought formed part of the EM band. It extended outward alright, but only as far as the crater's edge. It just ended there, which seemed bloody strange as there should've been some kind of decay like a fading light, but there wasn't."

"Go on," Anne prompted.

"So, I repo'd the dish. Pointed it up to an inclination, a micron shy of ninety degrees—and found no degradation, *no* falloff— none. It's focused, straight-up, and infinitely strong like a laser beam. I still couldn't tell what kind of signal we were dealing with, so, I did as you suggested and, Boss you were right. It *is* a subspace transmission, heading way out into interstellar, if not intergalactic space—satellite's sensors confirm it."

Anne froze.

Clarke continued to talk, but his voice suddenly sounded muted, as though coming down a distant corridor. "That radio signal started transmitting when we engaged our first sensor sweep. The vessel must've had some kind of trigger that reacted when we spotted it with the strobes, maybe some kind of photosensitive sensor of its own—fits the facts anyway. Whatcha think, Boss, did I just earn my PhD? Doc?" The postgrad fanned his arm in front of Anne's face. "Earth calling Professor Morrison?"

Anne snapped out of her daze. Working moisture into her mouth, she tried to keep her voice in measured tones. "You're assuming that it only began transmitting that signal up there when we lit it up with the strobes. But remember the logger stream? That signal didn't gear up from zero when we first picked it up. All we did was open the door to something already going on in the next room. It flew at full strength then, and hasn't dropped one scintilla since."

For all his electronic genius, Clarke's expression registered blank. He gulped, "What are you saying, Anne?"

"I'm saying, it's quite possible that that thing's been sending a signal into space since it arrived here almost 300 years ago. The power of the emission is staggering, beyond anything on Earth— maybe infinite. And it's going somewhere."

A sudden sore patch announced itself over Anne's left temple. "Okay, it may not be an electromagnetic pulse in and of itself, but it's riding along a similar divergent beat, that is by its very nature electromagnetic, yet it varies in amplitude and repeats itself, *like* a radio transmission."

She sighed and pressed her lips into a tight line. Clarke blanched and his jaw fell open, every trace of his former jock swept away.

Tasmin who'd been hovering over Clarke's other shoulder paled too. Her voice dropped to a whisper. "What do you think it is, Doctor?"

Anne kneaded her temple, then the base of her neck, where her soreness had migrated. Throbbing eyes found her assistant. "If I were to guess, the pattern indicates some form of beacon and judging by a non-existent decay rate, might travel a limitless distance—provided the source of the transmission remains uninterrupted. And that's just what we can surmise from the facts so far. Beyond that, we're speaking strictly in a speculative paradigm."

Clarke leaned back in his chair and raised an index finger. He flicked it in time with his words like an attorney making a series of points in a trial. "It's been transmitting this beacon—this message if you will—into interstellar space, *steadily* for 300 years." He glanced at his monitor, then back to Anne. "But for what?"

"Closer to the point," Anne corrected, "to whom?"

The question hung in the air unanswered, the implications simply too haunting to be given voice. They all stood there like defendants awaiting the jury's verdict when a sudden commotion from the control room door brought them back into the anxious moment.

Behind the sea of heads, a desperate-sounding, thickly-accented German voice called out, "*Dr Morrison, Dr Morrison.*"

The crowd parted and a breathless man stood before Anne. The German cybernetician, Clas Bernhardt, his chest rising and falling accordion-like as he struggled to get his breathing under control. His face looked as white as his beard, his fear palpable, and infectious.

"What is it, Doctor?" Anne asked. She braced herself, digging fingernails into her palms.

"Trying to reach—from cyba lab, veren't answering hails," he finally managed to say.

"Take your time," Anne said, waiting for the man to get his breathing under control.

"Something has begun." *A guilty verdict*. The hairs on Anne's nape stood on end. Her throat felt suddenly dry.

"What?" she croaked.

Rather than tell her, Bernhardt reached around Clarke's shoulders and gripped the joystick controlling the probe's main turret camera. With shaky hands, he hastily panned and tilted the camera's lens. Then zoomed and focused on the opaque form Clarke likened to Siamesed beetles.

Anne needed no further explanation. Whatever that black thing was, it now plainly moved, revolving like some morbid amusement park ride. The image on the monitor clearly showed that the beetles' appendages had fanned out and burrowed forward, using what looked like an arsenal of razor-sharp fan blades and drill bits—all ablur as they spun. The beetle began cutting its way out of the glass sarcophagus that had entombed it for centuries.

Anne's stomach plummeted. She really had opened Pandora's Box. The question now: what would happen next?

4: Baron
2104 CE

Baron Fieldbank watched as Dr Anne Morrison took the stage. An immersed look creased her facial wrinkles as she approached the podium to formally open the ODS symposium, the first for the *whole* group. Brought into this soundproof, tightly guarded auditorium, all of the world's best minds sat down and waited.

The doctor's famous pet robot hovered nearby for all to see. As per usual, Beacon would not say a word and let Morrison do all the talking. The ebony automaton had learned English the first day they hauled his sorry ass up from the Atlantic, but acquiring all the nuances of humanity proved to take the mechanical xenomorph substantially longer. 'That's a work in progress,' Morrison often quipped.

The professor had named the alien robot, *Beacon,* citing a specific reference her ancestor made in his logbook. The late Captain Morrison had first likened the robot's arrival to a 'Beacon of the Almighty.' Since Anne made the discovery and was in charge, the world simply accepted the title. Baron thought it was a clever name, symbolic and poignant to humanity on several levels.

"Welcome, my colleagues and fellow scientists," Morrison greeted, "and thank you all for convening on such short notice."

She straightened her notes and adjusted her wireless microphone. "Up until now you've all worked in your separate task groups, but as our CEO, Mr Blythe assures me, the time has come to bring you all up to speed together. As a race, we have reached a pivotal crossroad. The traffic light at that intersection is Beacon."

No doubt there. Beacon formed part of Baron's life and pretty much that of the entire scientific community now. About time he got used to the idea. The Moderns bestowed the alien robot with their new-age endearment—bunch of flakes the lot. They'd make the hippies from two centuries ago seem like a bunch of Neo-Nazis in comparison with their, 'Beacon has ushered in a new era of enlightenment and peace for the children of the universe' bullshit.

At least the geek squad took a small liberty to make the robot look a little less intimidating, crudely painting a large yellow smiley-face over the upper half of his raven torso. Otherwise, the mechanized monster would've scared the shit out of children and adults alike.

The robot's body looked like two beetles facing one another, vertically joined Siamese-like at the head. In a sick way, the two bodies appeared frozen in mid-collision, flailing appendages fanning out in seizure. Baron quickly dismissed his bizarre cartoon image.

But *bizarre* underscored the robot's full history and all the discoveries that followed first contact. A case of bringing to light one mystery only to sink knee-deep in a greater quandary, finding another beneath its bed and so on.

Baron hadn't been assigned to Operation Deep Salvo—ODS until several years following the initial disclosure. He wasn't even born when Beacon first surfaced, and in an older era, he might be nearing death right now, if Beacon's *Glass* hadn't intervened, or more precisely the latent energy infused in its structure. The robot introduced the world to this exo-element that had splashed down with him so long ago.

With plenty to spare, Beacon showed the world a method of harvesting its energy to bolster everyone's physiology by genetically infusing the population's gene telomeres. The next step came in the form of logic gates, created from the conjunctive manipulation of DNA and gut bacteria to craft biological computers.

This new generation of microscopic biotic devices travelled around their host body, cleaning arteries and destroying all viruses, cancers or degenerative diseases before they manifested. Yes, increased longevity was an undeniable boon of Morrison's discovery. God, she herself was pushing 120, yet looked and acted in her early fifties.

But apart from living longer fuller lives, which everyone on the planet benefitted from, the technology offered other advantages for those closest to the magic.

Baron was one of the recipients because of his skillset and aptitude with complex systems, chaos theorem, and causality. He had his own PhD, three years into his first post at Caltech when Blythe brought him into the loop. The tycoon's first video call had spun Baron's world upside down.

On Blythe's insistence, Baron didn't have any contact with Morrison or Beacon for several years after that. "I need my teams to work independently of each other," Blythe cantered on in his annoyingly melodious way. "Trust me, Baron, it's all connected."

Baron would have told him to go fuck himself if the money wasn't so good. As irksome as the mogul could be, Blythe offered him an outrageous salary for examining all sorts of empirical data. Baron spent the next few years plugging the magnate's data into various algorithmic models to plot outlandish scenarios involving chaos protocol and xeno-stratagem—heavy stuff to be sure, but a challenge.

His contributions to ODS intertwined with the jobs of a dozen strangers assigned to one of several specialized task groups. At least, in Baron's case, they all got along, sharing similar sentiments about the program and almost identical stories of how Blythe brought them on board.

Baron's indoctrination had been long and tarrying but it put someone like him, accustomed to connecting dots to the spaces between, in the ideal niche, merging several fields of study into a completely new science.

Baron's cadre worked off-campus, their time divided between running experiments out of the Kennedy Space Centre, JPL, and back in his more familiar haunts at Caltech. On occasion, task groups shared information, correlated and reintegrated it into their respective models.

But now that all the groups met in one room, including Morrison and Beacon, a louring cloud crept over Baron. And he was willing to bet he wasn't alone in his circumspection.

From all four corners of the planet, with research in hand, came the entire bunch of PhDs, some held in fields even Baron, with his own eclectic schooling, couldn't grasp. Along with a security detail, they shipped in to Blythe's monstrous 300-storey World Sciences Centre. This ultra-modern ODS skyscraper, soaring over Phoenix, Arizona, had been popularly dubbed the 'Tower of Babel'. Lots of that today, with the amassed brain power in this think-tank.

"As you all know, there have been many revolutionary discoveries instigated by ODS," Morrison said as a giant screen slowly descended from the ceiling behind her. "The human race continues to benefit from our infrastructure projects, environmental equilibrium, medical breakthroughs. Positive social reform all over the globe keeps improving the quality of life for the masses."

As Morrison went on, still images and short B-roll clips filled the screen behind her, matching her subject matter perfectly.

"It has flowered exponentially and unabated for decades now, exactly as computer technology did in the previous century. The betterment of everyone's lifestyle, indeed our very longevity continually edges us towards immortality. Beacon stands at the centre of all this. He wards the crossroad."

From his seat in one of the middle rows, Baron observed her with his prosthetic eyes, set firmly in his sculpted face. He felt more storm clouds gather at the way Morrison said, *crossroad*. She was right of course. Beacon had been responsible for the so-called Golden Age the human race currently enjoyed. And no one was more grateful than Baron himself. He'd be blind without his prosthesis, derived from that same Glass. This cure-all had been used in myriad applications, including the ground-breaking lenses adorning the Hubble II space telescope.

Baron had lost his eyes, his *real* eyes back at the university after a flare bomb went off in his face. It happened during an Apoc protest, which escalated into a full-blown terrorist attack.

Shortly before *Stormwatcher* pulled Beacon up, this radical group of activists known as the Apocalyptic Sedition—*Apocs* for short, emerged. They'd declared a veritable Jihad against the entire civilized world, launching a global-wide campaign of terrorism, sabotage, and strikes to advance their cause.

Problem being, no one understood their cause. Baron was convinced they themselves did not know, except that somewhere in their convoluted mantra sounded an off-key note of intolerance to any differences, ethnic or otherwise. The Apocs proclaimed anathema towards any society that functioned and flourished, free from suffering and repression—the true marks of equality.

Mostly comprised of failed firebrand students who went rogue and turned to anarchy as a vent for their frustration, the dark-minded purists used Beacon's arrival as an excuse to ramp up their destructive cause. The robot epitomized their worst fears and therefore garnered their greatest malevolence. So, towards Beacon or anything associated with the robot, the Apocs concentrated their most vicious attacks.

"Beacon has gone on loan to NASA and the European and Japanese Space Agencies," Morrison went on, recapping from behind her podium. "Under the robot's guidance, they learned to exploit general relativity, harnessing gravity and magnetism for practical purposes like interstellar travel.

"Integrated into our spaceships' existing multiple-burst nuclear fusion drives, this augmentation has led to a new revolutionary hybrid propulsion system, dubbed MANIFOLD for short. FTL—Faster than Light travel—has become a reality.

"Many sorties have been sent to the asteroids between Mars and Jupiter, and into the Kuiper Belt to mine essential ores and minerals not found on Earth. Innovative manned probes, equipped with ram scoops have visited Neptune and collected various gaseous elements from the ice giant's upper atmosphere. For the first time in human history, we have leapt beyond the Solar System to the far side of the Oort Cloud, taking the first Humans into interstellar space. With our new Manifold Engines, trips once measured in centuries can now be done in weeks."

Baron eased back in his chair and viewed the documentary-style presentation with a grain of salt. The slew of shots and clips of manned probes landing on Jupiter's moons: Io and Europa provided a very stimulating show, but instinct warned him that Morrison's inspirational summary would lead to something sobering. While he digested the cosmic slide show, he'd keep a toehold on terra firma.

"The missions brought back several new elements to add to the Periodic Table," said Morrison. "With these new exo-elements, many more developments can now be made on Earth with greater efficacy."

When a giant blue **O.O.S.** logo dissolved up from black to fill the screen. Morrison dropped her head, causing a wisp of her chestnut hair to fall forward. She combed it back over her ear and raised her head again. "I've always known the Glass surrounding Beacon's vessel was special, even before I met the automaton. It isn't just some random effect. But an important clue to unravel the conundrum surrounding his arrival and determining our future course of action.

"The Glass, unlike anything found on Earth, burned so hot when it first arrived that the seabed around its aura hadn't just transformed, it winked out of existence.

"When it cooled, I'm guessing a nanosecond after impact, nothing could cut it. Even diamond-head drill bits lost their bite within seconds. Lasers and heat proved equally ineffective. The stuff is formidable, harder than diamonds."

The **O.O.S.** logo faded out again and the slide show resumed, this time showing a series of stills depicting everything concerning the Glass, from its discovery aboard the *Stormwatcher* to its retrieval and eventual technological implementations.

"The Glass, which formed the crater where we found the vessel," Morrison narrated, "bore the same molecular properties as the vessel itself. After Beacon became communicative, he identified the Glass as a form of solidified plasma. There is latent energy within it that had to be harnessed before any cutting could be done. Maybe no diamond-head would score it, but my trusty robot had the means.

"Beacon modulated his cutting tools to the specific resonance of the plasma within the Glass. For the robot, it proved as simple as tilling a hot knife through butter, harmonizing the vibration frequency of his hotter knife to ply and part the Glass—to capitalize on its myriad applications, including our farthest-reaching instrument, the Hubble II."

Her statement sent Baron's mind back, almost four years ago to the events following that announcement. It had taken three years to complete the Hubble II, launched in a series of missions from Cape Canaveral and constructed in space. Enormous, it dwarfed the ISS—International Space Station, which was eventually integrated into its structure permanently, *siamesed* as it were, like Beacon. Forthwith, the ISS became known as the H2S or Hubble II Station.

The Hubble II was equipped with a monstrous lens, meticulously cut from the Glass and fully programmed by Beacon himself. The lens fed a plasma energy beam, already part of its internal matrix, sending it outward into space.

"Since its inauguration," Morrison explained, "the media has ascribed the Hubble II's energy beam to an X-ray—a super component X-ray."

She paused and took a drink of water from a clear bottle set on the podium. "And they are right, in that it can penetrate any obstacles in the cosmos, seeing beyond them to literally any point in known space. But in truth, the plasma of the Glass behaves exactly like gravitational waves. Unlike light, electromagnetism, or other forces, an energy beam rendered from the lens substrate moves through space without any conceivable interference. Dust, debris, gas, glare, magnetism, gravity, even the intergalactic medium—all are superfluous before it. They lose all presence, if they occur between the lens and the determined focal point."

More brilliant interstellar images of nebulae, superclusters, binary pulsars, and fermi bubbles filled the screen behind the speaker and robot, along with a collection of captivating views of the station itself.

"The Hubble II observatory is equipped with highly sensitive laser interferometers," Morrison said. "It can see over immeasurable distances while staying atop any baseline shifts, self-adjusting from the most infinitesimal nudges, including the stretch and compression of spacetime by gravity ripples.

"As a result, the H2S can look farther into space and further back in time than ever before, giving new insight into such things as dark energy, protogalaxies, displacement fields of quasars, baby photos of black holes—basically the whole damn infrastructure of the Milky Way and beyond.

"Because the entire system is drag-free, the station can automatically fire thrusters to maintain exact pinpoints, necessary to present clear images, even from as far as one gly. Not just still images but live video feeds as well. We are now able to study the Universe in unprecedented ways, listening as well as seeing. By adjusting the Hubble II's focus, strength, duration, and direction, the instrument can send back images from virtually anywhere in the night sky."

Baron listened to Morrison's explanation with more than his ears. On the surface, it sounded concrete and admittedly impressive, but her disclosure convinced him this too led to something direr than his earlier prediction. He remained equally sure that *her* 'something' still wouldn't provide the whole truth.

Morrison paused and cleared her throat. "We have not done all this for the sake of pure science, mind you. We harbour a more pressing agenda, and it is time to make all of your efforts more cohesive to that effect."

5: Second Symposium
Baron

The slide show sequel ended and a giant blue **O.O.S.** logo dissolved up from black to fill the screen. Baron's eyes adjusted as the houselights brightened to full.

Just as she had done at the first forum two months before, Anne Morrison prefaced her presentation with a recap of general news and progress. But this time she dug deeper.

"As some of you know," Morrison went on, "the radio transmission into outer space was reciprocal. It bore very similar properties to that of a laser beam with infinite focus and no spread or degradation. But it wasn't any laser, or radio signal—well, not any more. Beacon's presence notwithstanding, the two-way transmission confirms a positive answer to the fundamental question about other life *currently* present in the Universe."

Morrison hesitated and checked her cue cards. Was she bracing her audience? More than at their first meet and greet, Baron's premonitions piqued. He sensed a much stronger storm front heading his way this time. The clouds pressed in, grew leaden, and rumbled.

"That reason carried with it a warning. As Beacon explained it to me, the race who sent him here was doomed itself. Known as *Dovan*, they were planetary refugees, forced to flee their world from a nemesis so great none made it out of their system. Unable to make a stand, the Dovan cast Beacon from their midst to act as a life buoy, a diminutive ark that would carry a record of their existence, and proffer advance notice to any other species that might find themselves facing the same annihilation. They found us. They chose us."

The sound of shifting seats and hushed murmurs trickled throughout the sealed auditorium. The air of unease mushroomed as others realized which direction Morrison's speech was heading.

"The Dovan's tech was advanced enough to send the vessel containing Beacon across the gulf of space, but not adequate to

49

prevent their own extinction. Dovan—their homeworld—was obliterated."

Baron swallowed, as he compared the images of Morrison's cosmic PowerPoint to her dire revelation. The mental image formed an equation in his mind: too little = too late.

"I'm sure none of you would argue that above all else Beacon serves as a learning and teaching machine," Morrison said. "His makers designed him to prepare any race he encountered for the threat that might one day loom over them."

A dark-haired woman seated next to Baron dropped her com-pad, drawing his notice as it clunked to the floor. When she leaned forward to pick it up, she bumped shoulders with him. The woman quickly scooped up the device, her face flushing red as she turned and mouthed *sorry* in his direction. He smiled and shrugged before facing the stage again.

"The Dovan surmised that, if given their knowledge base concerning their adversaries, we might potentially expand on it, find and exploit some weakness in their foe's armour—succeed where they had failed. They were on the right track with their technology but in the end, they ran out of time. As both their literal and figurative *deus ex machina*, Beacon shipped out, but the Dovan's adversaries wiped the senders out."

Morrison's voice fell silent. In its place, a din of white noise scaled up, emanating from the auditorium's speakers until it engulfed the entire room. Her voice rose above the static-charged rumble. "What you hear is a recording of the dead background noise still transmitting from the Dovan homeworld. This formed the incoming portion of the original transmission we picked up before we switched it off."

Muted gasps filled the room.

"For all you geneticists," Morrison said as the alarming recording faded out, "the evolution of the Dovani tech could be likened to chromosome pairing. Using this analogy, perhaps what the Dovan sought in their final days was a stab at hybridization—a kind of polyploidy. Beacon was the Dovan's final hope in seeing the fruition of their quest to stop their nemesis."

Morrison tilted her head to one side and scratched her crown, an adjournment no doubt to frame her next bit of bad news. After a moment, she resumed. "As for the Dovan's adversary, it may be called an empire for at its heart that's what it is—a ubiquitous inexorable race of dark-minded beings, spanning countless systems across hundreds of galaxies. Yes, you heard me correctly: that's *galaxies*—plural. As we form the dominant species of this planet, the beings of this empire are the dominant species of our Universe."

Baron tried to wrap his mind around the concept, and failed. A sharp inhalation drew his awareness. The woman who had bumped him earlier chewed her lip nervously, mirroring his sentiment.

"The empire's name is simply unpronounceable but the Dovan referred to them as *Garaxian* in their tongue, which literally translated means *Ice Demons.* In light of ODS' invested interest in quelling their potential danger to us, we'll refer to them as such henceforth."

Morrison took a deep breath and chocked her arms on the podium. "The Ice Demons—ID for short, are humanoid, flesh and blood like us and the Dovan, bi-pedal, seeing with eyes, breathing oxygen with lungs, but that's where the similarities end. With functioning body temperatures of minus-forty degrees centigrade and organic antifreeze for blood, these *Overlords* endure temperatures and geochemically extreme conditions that would be fatal to most other races after prolonged exposure."

"Extremophiles," Baron blurted before he realized it.

Anne grinned. "Exactly right, Dr Fieldbank. And space being so cold, they consider it their rightful domain." She looked over her shoulder briefly. When she turned back, her grin straightened. "That's partially how they spread so quickly and completely. If a virus could be considered powerful for its resilience to environmental or industrialized stressors, then the scourge of the Overlords is an unstoppable super strain.

51

"The hardy sentients that make up this empire—or *Imperium* as Beacon called it are tenacious. And sadly, immortal too—not gods by any stretch, mind you, just evolved so biologically perfect that, once born they simply do not die, unless met with some lethal trauma, like a bullet.

"The Imperium follows a simple equation: if opposed by a substantial threat, they engage it, taking great pains to learn. Once they grasp what they need to quell an opponent, they obtain it. And strike back with impunity. Through the law of averages, they've become immune, ultimately rendering themselves implacable."

Baron's turn to shift in his chair came. When he settled back, the woman beside him reached over and gently squeezed his hand where it rested on the armrest. His artificial pupils met her genuine orbs, and they shared an uneasy smile.

Miss Doomsday's voice broke their connection. "No matter the cost in lives or resources, the Imperium pays it to maintain their position. The benefit of having so many: strength in numbers. As ruthless as it sounds, their system works. According to Beacon, the ID's expansion has accelerated beyond that of any other race. The core of their society has grown exponentially, reaching an impregnable echelon."

Baron gulped as the auditorium lights dimmed to half-brightness. *She wasn't just digging deeper this time around; she was digging an open-pit mine for fresh graves.*

"Equally cold and methodical in thought as they are in body," Morrison elaborated, "they abhor individualism, principled only by one frigid and unwavering belief that 'the Universe remains consummate with *their* natural state, including all who dwell within its repository.'"

Despite the relative darkness in his section, faces revealed the full spectrum of reactions: curiosity, fear, doubt. Baron felt a melange of all three.

"If a species can adapt to the edicts within the Imperium's manifesto," Morrison said, "they are tolerated, integrated as an undercaste, with one caveat. By submitting, they are in point of fact surrendering their species forever. There is no going back—tantamount to striking a Faustian Bargain.

"The only choice the Demons offer a potentially compatible race is this: genuflect or genocide. If it is the latter and the species cannot adapt or worse, poses a threat, the Demons exterminate them en masse. The ID believe to do otherwise would elicit 'an abnegation of their purpose and that of their Exarch'—the Imperium's supreme ruler."

Morrison exhaled and stepped back from her soapbox. She threaded a hand through her hair. "They considered the Dovan 'antagonistic to the natural order.' This same disparity fuels the Imperium's campaign of annexation, assimilation, speciation, and xenocide. No matter how you look at it, they're an intergalactic holocaust."

She returned to the podium and shuffled her cards before glancing over at the silent robot hovering beside her. "According to the records Beacon has shown me, the Garaxians have a staggering armada of ships, fleets of fighters, bombers, interceptors, bulky dreadnoughts, and *beyond*-massive capital ships."

"How 'massive,' Professor?" someone called from the back.

"As unbelievable as it sounds, their capital ships are larger than your average dwarf planet or planetoid," Morrison answered. "They would swallow Ceres."

Baron did the math in his head. That dwarf planet hiding in the asteroid belt spanned over 950 kilometres in diameter!

"With the help of the Hubble II, you'll see such ships for yourself, today in fact, but bear with me for a moment. The capital ships I describe are equipped with devastating weapons that can destroy stars, create singularities, or charge swathes of vacuum with lethal plasma, frying anything in its path."

Morrison let out a long breath and fanned back a stray lock before continuing, "In the absence of any humanity, or *dovanity,* without an iota of compassion, the Demons excel in forensic propagation, owing to their godlike technology. They use this superior tech to convert worlds as well, terraforming them to sustain their biological requirements. That often means radically dropping the temperatures."

"How is that done?" a climatologist Baron recognized asked.

Morrison lifted her shoulders. "By any one of a hundred different techniques, Dr Bowen. From launching super gravimetric grenades to knock a planet to a more distant orbit around a star, to collapsing the star itself, to thinning a planet's atmosphere by bleeding it into space, to triggering a permanent ice age by hastening positive feedback loops.

She leaned forward again on strutted elbows. "They all draw the same axiomatic result, making yet another world that can support the Imperium's expansion. If a species on that planet can acclimatize, the Demons subvert and tolerate them to co-exist. If not, to the ID, such is the natural order."

One sceptic sprang to his feet and shook an accusing finger at Morrison. "This is fear-mongering—plain and simple," he berated. "There isn't any proof, Doctor, other than your robot's unsubstantiated account concerning these Dovan. Even if we had evidence, we wouldn't stand a bloody chance against such an enemy."

"A valid point," Baron said under his breath. He couldn't blame the peevish speaker for his reaction, faced with something so completely beyond anyone's scope, or the whole human experience for that matter.

"You are right to think that of course, Professor Grant," said Morrison. "Given how much you have all been told up until this juncture. But I intend to show you something which will resonate otherwise."

Grant brusquely sat back down and folded his arms. Morrison ran her tongue across her upper lip as she pondered. And Baron felt the first smattering drops from the brewing tempest. He smelled everyone's fear like ozone fronting the impending storm.

Time stretched.

Morrison tipped back a swallow of water from her bottle and

sighed. With a thud, she parked the vessel back on the podium and steered her visage towards the audience. "Speaking of resonance, Beacon's communication skills were rudimentary at first but he interacted with me in such a way to quell any misunderstanding. For the sake of brevity, he'd been designed to get the Dovan's point—and the fundamentals of their tech—across quickly and succinctly.

"For all my own nuances, and granted they are plenty, I guess I made a good listener," she added astride a faint chuckle.

Baron saw the truth in that. Anne Morrison provided the perfect host and vessel for the mechanical emissary to teach and learn from—to plant his directives. Anne was the ultimate sounding board, a symbiont round peg. Her forte, really.

"So, when Beacon urged me to utilize the Glass to construct the Hubble II," Morrison said, "I didn't flinch. Through our revolutionary space telescope, we now have all the proof we need."

Baron grimaced. In his mind, lightning forked and thunder clapped. The speaker's final revelation loomed on the tip of her tongue. It threatened him with hailstones the size of meteorites.

"So yes," Morrison went on. "The Hubble II has truly opened up space like never before. But it also substantiates Beacon's caution about the ID. Targeting various coordinates, the H2S has tracked real-time feeds of their monster ships moving through space, exactly as Beacon described. I have several clips to show you, but would like to begin with the one I consider most poignant."

Morrison turned to Beacon. A moment later the auditorium lights dimmed to complete darkness. When pitch black swallowed the yawning space, a video image of an M-class planet, much like Earth, appeared on the screen before Baron.

"This was recorded by the team aboard the station's ISS pod, roughly a month ago," Morrison voiced over the clip. "I must remind you this is classified above top secret."

Baron's mouth fell open as an overwhelming armada of Imperium ships entered and filled the frame, including nine of the gargantuan capital ships.

Suddenly, the central ships erupted with brisance as they simultaneously fired enormous energy weapons—what looked like emerald-coloured plasma surges. Each power mass hurled towards the planet like a hypernova's death ray. A split-second after impact, they engulfed the entire globe in an aura of the same green hue and brilliance. A few moments later, the nimbus dissipated, leaving the planet stricken white, leaning towards the cooler spectrum— exactly like a drained corpse.

Morrison coughed in the darkness. "That's not ice you see— but hardened plasma. An infrared thermographic plugged into the feed confirms the average temperature on that inhabited world radically dropped by 137°C after impact, all of its inhabitants, dead, their planet, sterile."

Beacon said nothing. There was nothing to say. Everyone in the auditorium, including Baron, just gaped at the derailing feed looping back over and over again.

Small wonder the world hadn't been told the entire story. *They couldn't*. Otherwise, Beacon's Golden Age would come to a screeching halt. Only a select few were cursed with this much of Morrison's foreboding tale. And Baron was one of them.

Wishing to God he could rewind all the life events that led him to this unwanted discovery, Baron suddenly felt like an anchor cut from its line and plummeting to the bottom of the Marianas Trench.

6: Amalgamation
Baron

"Dr Fieldbank, with your background in causality, I find it intriguing that your knowledge extends this far into astrophysics. Tell me, what do you know about the properties of the boson?"

Baron tilted his head to the side and fixed Dr Morrison with a stern look. She'd been going on about newly discovered astral phenomena and he was growing increasingly impatient.

He knew Morrison had been there from day one, witnessing the impossible become reality, so if anyone sympathized with Beacon's plight, it would be her. The robot's cause became her cause. She saw the big picture and even if it looked grim, if not harrowing, demonstrated the strength of character to acknowledge and face the consequences head-on.

Morrison parsed the disturbing truth of the matter and dared to take the next instinctive steps, correlating and interpolating all the data that the mechanical emissary had to give her. Ultimately, Morrison chose to act post-haste upon the information and make those steps firm ladder rungs.

She gave the cursed ones like Baron a sense of purpose, maybe even hope. The human race would boldly take all the necessary steps to prevent its annihilation. She became a breakwater for the entire planet.

That image quelled Baron's ire now, preventing him from voicing his agitation during this third general assembly of the ODS think-tank. In the weeks leading up to the confrontation, something he remembered from that second symposium began to gnaw at him like a splinter in his mind. Not one to dance around an issue, he demanded a private audience with Morrison and Beacon.

Baron was a little amazed, and more disturbed by the swiftness at which the higher-ups granted his request. They ushered him into a secure boardroom where he now sat across a heavy oaken table opposite the stoic figure of Morrison, with smiley-faced Beacon floating innocently over her shoulder like a big simpleton child.

"So, the boson?" Morrison prompted.

Baron blew out his cheeks. "Only that it has no spin, no electric charge, and the particle allows multiple identical particles to exist in the same place and quantum state." He paused and levelled his gaze at Morrison. "But Doctor, discussing the boson is not what I had in mind when I called for this meeting. These are hardly normal endeavours or normal times. From my 'causality-prone' point of view, I can't help but notice how expert your attempt to fish my questions into a specific net before I can ask them otherwise. So, let's drop the charade." He glanced at Beacon before locking on her. "The Demons are still out there, so the most important question here is what the hell are you two gunning for?"

Morrison feigned surprise. But when Baron pressed his lips into a tight line, her shoulders slackened. "Frankly, I'm a little embarrassed by my transparency."

"Don't be, Doctor," Baron soothed. "I'm just connecting the dots—that's what you pay me to do. But I got to say, you're full of even more riddles than this robot of yours."

"Please, call me Anne," she said with a winsome smile. "To answer your question, we seek a bridge or more accurately a ladder. And you're right, Baron, there is more to this than what I mentioned, a lot more. Beacon already has a plan, utilizing the latest and best of our existing technologies. He's enhanced and combined them with the Dovan's vast trove of research already accumulated on the Imperium. Coffee?"

"What? Oh yeah, sure, cheers," said Baron, remembering himself. "I take it black."

"Like me." Anne leaned forward in her chair and made to get up but Beacon stopped her, already gliding to the beverage station in the corner of the room.

"I...will—get...it," the automaton said in his mechanical E.S.L. voice. "Continue ...please."

Anne smiled up at the automaton before training her eyes on Baron. "It's been like filling in the missing pieces to a jigsaw puzzle with surrogate bits, so, we have no guarantees, but Beacon employs a full faculty of quantum-mechanical techniques to do it. Progress has evinced admittedly slow since the amalgamation of the task groups, but it has begun in earnest."

Baron jutted his chin. "Then let me be plain, Anne. We're going about this the wrong way. All of our efforts have been fastened on a plan to stand against the possibility of an ID threat, assuming our little speck of a planet is still hidden. Maybe I'm missing something but nobody seems to have taken into account that there's been a radio signal beaming back up there for the last 400-plus years."

"We've already established—"

Baron silenced her with a wave of his hand. "You forget who you're talking to, Doctor. That signal didn't head to any extinct race, at least not the entire time, as you led us to believe. Someone up there must've received it by now. And I'm willing to bet my ridiculous salary it's the Demons. If they haven't already, they're going to act on what they heard. Then, I don't think Earth is going to be the best place to plan your next vacation."

Before Anne could reply, Beacon returned, two large ceramic cups clutched in a single metallic hand with twelve splayed fingers. And that was just one arm fanning out of his umbrella rack's worth.

"Ah, thanks Beacon." Fingers trembling, Baron took one of the steaming mugs and brought it to his lips while the robot's upper torso rotated. His arm extended like a crane gimbal over the width of the table to offer the second mug to Morrison.

She took the cup and immediately rested it on the table's oaken surface. "Cheers."

The rich aroma and taste eased the tension in Baron's neck and shoulders as he carefully sipped the hot brew. Lowering his cup to the table, he sought Morrison's notice. "We all saw what those bastards did to that planet. So, no more bullshit. What's really going on?"

Anne raised her hands in a placating gesture. "Please Baron, that's been the primary impetus behind everything we're trying to accomplish here."

Baron folded his arms. "Really? Then please enlighten me."

"You're right. It was an ID tracer signal from one of their core worlds tight-beamed to Earth. It formed a link, initially established by the travelling plasma surge itself, the same wave Beacon's vessel rode in on, the same mass that formed the Glass over 400 years ago. As soon as the plasma cooled, the dynamo of our own electromagnetic field, generated by Earth's core has kept the link in place. Much like a relay station, it generates enough energy to power the conduit core to core."

"Like the energy beam of the Glass?"

Anne shook her head. "No, this is something totally different."

"Even across such vast distances?" Baron asked unconvinced.

"It's not linked through normal space." Anne reached for her cup and drank. "Or beneath it, in hyperspace, but furrowed in a kind of hybrid abyss we have named *subhypra* space. It is essentially dead space, or the space between proto-dark matter clusters as they occurred before our Universe was conceived. It's the state of reality before the Big Bang. This void is both residual and inherent to the infamous boson—hence my reason for broaching the subject to you just now."

A flash of chagrin stole over Baron, heating his earlobes. He could only stare in silence.

"But it is also benign," Anne continued, putting her cup down with a hollow thump. "The plasma can tunnel through normal space, tapping these subhypra conduits as it passes. The channel left behind acts as a kind of express conveyor for radio signals, energy beams, perhaps even the passage of ships."

"That doesn't sound good," Baron murmured truthfully.

"No," agreed Anne. "It doesn't."

"So, it confirms the Imperium knows we're here. What's next?"

Anne's eyebrows pulled close together. "Our plan all along has been twofold: escape and entrapment. Our new quantum technologies in spacecraft design, our medical developments, priming the human race for the rigours of extended space flight: that all falls under the first bracket."

"And the second?" Baron prompted before taking another swallow.

"The second part is much more complex and formidable. That's where your field of expertise is being applied, along with the various teams we've assigned to specific parts of the project. It's not enough to escape the predator, absconding with false hope only to be hunted to our doom another day. We must neutralize the threat itself."

Baron scoffed. "That's all fine on paper, Anne, but have you looked through the Hubble II lately? At last estimates, between their core and fringe worlds and, oh yes, all those armada ships causing a goddam traffic jam across space, we're clocking the ID numbers somewhere in the neighbourhood of sixty *trillion*, and that's just what we can see. It doesn't even include any species annexed to their cause. Doesn't that strike you as a little bit of an uphill battle?"

Anne cocked her head to one side and gave him a knowing smile. "I think the more appropriate question is how does that hill strike you?"

Baron took the hint and surrendered a chuckle. From all the task group reports he signed off on, Anne had become used to his signature *uphill battle* remark. She'd come to understand the way he rolled well enough to know he never backed down from any uphill battles—his verbal pretext before he buckled down to task.

"Professor?" she said at length. "Have you ever heard the Biblical tale of David and Goliath?"

"Which one?" Baron laughed sardonically, "*the* Bible's or the apocryphal shite in the Apocs' Vatican III Reform?"

"I think we both know which one," Anne replied in an even tone. "Look, I know how this must all sound and quite frankly I don't blame you for your scepticism, but you must trust that we're focused, and making significant milestone progress. We just don't

61

have all the pieces yet. Beacon has—"

Baron stopped her short. "Quite frankly, Anne, I'm a little suspicious of his part in all this." He tilted his head in Beacon's direction. "Your robot seems a little too smug, considering he brought this peril down on our heads. For all we know, he's the one who's been sending the signal up there in the first place. *Hey boys, hound found another planet—come and get it.*"

Anne rolled her eyes.

"No seriously, I excel in my field for a reason—that's why you hired me. It's my job to question a complex system when there's nothing on the other side of the equal sign. So, I'd question the word of the alien who crashed our party, who's bending over backwards to help us when most of the truth surrounding him, and I know it exists, is hidden in one big quagmire."

Beacon's seeing-dome panned back and forth between Baron and Anne, but the robot chose to remain silent while the doctor vented.

Baron went rigid, making no attempt to hide his bitterness or his unease. "You call him Beacon after your Gramp's reference, inferring he's a 'beacon of hope.' That's based on the supposition that he's our saviour, but I can just as easily draw the exact opposite conclusion from the same empirical data."

"And what's that?" said Anne with a touch of asperity.

"That he's a pariah, our enemy's beacon, a Trojan horse, and the very harbinger of our destruction."

For a moment Anne looked her age. She rubbed her temple with her fingers and took a deep breath through her nose.

"Dr Fieldbank," she replied in a more formal tone, "his makers designed Beacon with a very specific purpose. Beyond the irrefutable scientific proof to back up absolutely everything he's divulged, my own heart tells me it's an altruistic drive that guides him. He was unaware of the signal's transmission until the Enceladus probe awakened him fully, the day we brought him up to the surface."

Baron opened his mouth to voice a rejoinder but Anne stopped him with a pacifying hand gesture. "Wait, hear me out. He terminated the signal from our end, negating the radio part of the transmission as soon as he became cognizant of it, close to a century ago now. It hasn't been the full 400 years you believe. Unfortunately, the plasma conduit through which the beam travelled remains. That is science beyond our scope, and Beacon's. Unless our planet stops spinning, it can never be switched off. Earth's core feeds it."

Baron chewed the inside of his cheek while he studied her measure. This was something new.

Anne placed her hands on the table. "Now consider, even if the signal which rode through the conduit had been terminated centuries earlier, it left Earth intact and complete, like an arrow already loosed from the bow. The linked energy between the two cores would see the transmission delivered, provided its target remained intact at the other end. As for your current doubts about Beacon's intent, he needn't have told us any of this about our fate. What would have been the point if he planned to doom us anyway?"

The question floated in the air unanswered, but Baron felt himself stir. What Anne said made sense. "Beacon could've turned around and told us to go fuck ourselves once he surfaced," Baron said.

"But he didn't," Anne concurred before turning to the robot. "You're our beacon now—and I trust my robot."

"Christ Anne," Baron complained, "You're beginning to sound like one of them Moderns." But even as he said it, he considered that maybe Anne had pegged the robot true. Beacon was the Dovan's last flare of hope; he may be the only lighthouse for humanity. At the very least, he proved an invaluable resource towards Earth's evolution, towards its survival—the robot's prowess with a decent cup of joe notwithstanding.

Baron surrendered a lopsided smile. "Of course, when the Moderns do get wind of this association, they'll begin hailing it as the second coming of Jesus Christ. Hey everybody Mechanical

Messiah on hand. Download your salvation today!"

Anne laughed and the tension in the room began to ebb. But Baron wasn't finished. He exhaled. "I can't help but feel more than ever that we're standing in the dark here, in the middle of a minefield, taking potshots with theory." Baron paused and checked himself. "Coming from an authority on chaos, I guess that sounds a bit hypocritical."

Anne's grin joined his. "Not at all."

The moment passed and Baron concluded in a more sombre tone, "Working separately as we are, we're only marginalizing ourselves. I need more control over the full designation of resources. It would definitely help if I could plug into the *full* blueprint, from on high, allocating those resources myself, quantifying and qualifying all the systemic logistics to complement the encyclopaedia's worth of psycho-babble my brain spits out."

"I think --- it is—time --- to do—just that," Beacon said.

Baron's gaze shifted to the robot. "Sorry?"

"Baron," Anne said, drawing his attention again. "Longevity has served me well, and the human race even better, but enhancements can still only work with a person's given physiology. I am 123 years old, with a clean bill of health I might add, but my days are still numbered."

Anne eased back in her chair and twirled a pen between two fingers. "Each successive generation will benefit from a longer lifespan—if we survive the potential holocaust. Your life might last significantly longer by the time you finally kick. Maybe you'll lap me by another century. I'm not saddened by my departure as I've enjoyed a most fulfilling career, making a profound difference in the lives of others. That has been its own reward."

"What are you saying?" Baron asked, but he already knew the answer.

Anne suddenly lost interest in the pen and her regard found Baron. "For the last decade, I've been fraught with doubt but hope as well, sorely pressed to find a suitable replacement—someone I can trust to continue my work after I'm gone. I think that person should be you."

Baron blinked. "What?"

"I've looked at many potential candidates for some time now, but you've been at the top of a very short list since you joined us. After what you said this afternoon, I know beyond a doubt you are indeed my replacement. You question the system but more importantly, you ask the right questions—the hard questions. You excel at lateral thinking, random quotients, peripheral intuition and integration—and I like you," she added with a wink. "But more than that, Beacon has just given you his sanction, and we both know where I stand on that front."

Baron thought of a thousand objections, but given his background, he also knew that each one could be quickly dismissed. He had a sudden urge to vomit, but thankfully that too passed. Genuine excitement replaced it. He now possessed the means to summit his most ponderous hill.

Reining in his elation, he found his voice. "I would only succeed you, Doctor."

"Well," Anne chortled, "I'm not dead yet, and before my wits grow completely addled, we still have work to do. In the meantime, I want you to delegate your task group's management to another and take control, overseeing the entire project, and I do mean the *entire* project. I'm going to give you access to all resources so you can answer any of your questions about the system. You've earned that right. From now on you'll report directly to me and Beacon."

Baron bowed his head and took it all in with the solemn eyes of a knight receiving benediction.

Anne didn't break stride. "I'll send out memos to all ODS staff informing them of your promotion to Assistant Director. Keep closer tabs on my Big Eye in the Sky and report any anomalies you find. I know you're the right man, who'll parse what to look for. I think we should ship you up there on the next shuttle—if you would consent to go that is."

Baron knew she referred to the Hubble II. He had never been off-world and didn't relish the idea, but it did offer him the chance to escape his ex-wife, who'd make an Apoc sound sane—guess Beacon couldn't fix everything.

He nodded briefly, stood, and turned to go, all the while trying to wrap his spinning mind around what had just happened. Anne stopped him with a raised hand.

"One more thing, Professor. I feel in all fairness and for the sake of fostering complete trust between us right from the start, there's something you should know." Anne turned to her mechanical counterpart. "Beacon?"

"There are—some --- missing fragments—in my–memory circuits—like—-—blind spots—which I left mes—unable to recover --- I do not know what—caused them --- Diagnostics—have verified futility --- may result in --- potential lack of—definitive response to—future queries."

"Beacon's been tampered with," Anne translated astride a cough. "But has no memory of the intrusion. It happened at some point while locked in stasis. He wants you to know that if he comes up no dice on any of your questions it's not an attempt at further subterfuge. He has unwittingly been handicapped."

Baron's eyebrows reached for his crown. "Looks like you have some competition in the riddle department after all, Anne." Then, turning back to Beacon he placed a hand on the robot's ebony torso. "I'm sorry to hear of your disability, Beacon. But equally relieved you're honest enough to share it with me from the get-go. It's just something we'll have to work around."

"I think," Anne declared as she stood from her chair, "the three of us will get along just fine."

7: Hubble II
Baron

Four hundred kilometres above Earth, Baron gazed upon his blue planet with a mixed sense of longing and nostalgia. As he caught his reflection in the circular window, he replayed the pivotal moment when he simultaneously became an astronaut and Morrison's Number One.

Baron could never have prepared himself for the experience of being in orbit for the first time. Beacon's developments with inertia dampening had freed him from what would've been a tumultuous affair with nausea. Motion sickness was a curse of the past. Sadly, homesickness was not.

He swore he'd get used to it, but life in space proved too lonely and too removed from the environment that made him human. Sure, he had peripherals, available on a whim. Attached to his temples through a series of nodes, they generated a virtual cinema within his brain. With all synapses firing, the experience felt so real to all five senses, at times he often mixed up realities. It may have only been virtual, but it sure triggered the right chemical responses in his brain.

The rec library's selection included sedation programs, sports and adventure simulations, and on those really lonely days sex programs with a virtual partner or two. He refrained from the latter as it probably would've killed him. Morrison might be chronologically old, but he was no spring chicken either. In the end, he avoided them, and not just the extreme versions, as they were all just so much plastic diversion and artificial joy.

Baron's real pleasure came from plugging coordinates into the main guidance console and manning the Hubble II's central lens beam himself. Apart from experimenting with the latest tech, including the subhypra kit Beacon sent up with him on Baron's inaugural trip to the station, he spent hours examining any system in any quadrant of any galaxy—including those about to disappear forever beyond the cosmic event horizon.

Alas, he didn't have enough time or freedom to explore for the sake of pure science. In this theatre, most of the Hubble II's time focused on tracking the movements of the ID.

The H2S team had christened the station's main lens 'Morrison's Big Eye' and monitored it 24/7. Shifts of men and women watched continuously for any anomaly that might be deemed an untoward advance. They plotted and forecast fleet movements, alerting Baron whenever they felt the slightest cause for concern.

It freed up Baron's schedule to concentrate on the many other facets of his charge, including the continued analysis of his chaos models, which he'd established with his former team back on Earth. Yup, he definitely had his work cut out for him.

One morning during his tenure, a resounding thought occurred to Baron. The infamous radio signal had already been transmitted and terminated, but with the damage done, the recorded data of the stream itself got eclipsed by more pressing demands.

He called up the relevant package on his cabin's terminal and examined its derelict data strings more closely, assigning mathematical prediction algorithms to the represented values, whether he considered them gibberish or not.

Baron quickly discovered something more to the signal after all, an inherent and cloaked element tied to or rather meshed into the stream. Previously missed it would seem—something Beacon had overlooked, chose to ignore or *hide*. More than just a transmission tight-beamed from an ID core world to Earth. Baron's premonitions started to assert themselves at an alarming rate. He couldn't contemplate and theorize anymore. He had to act.

On an encrypted communiqué sent directly to Anne and Beacon, he asked that the terminated radio signal be reactivated for a time. Naturally, his two consorts questioned the move, but Baron convinced them of its warrant. And so, it happened.

Baron repo'd the Hubble II, lining its plasma ray to marry with the reenergized signal—directly into the subhypra conduit.

The manoeuvring of the lens to align with the focal point of the radio beam was an easy task. The synthesis of the two energy sources so that they acted as one was not. But Baron drove himself to the task and wouldn't relent. Uphill battles.

Poring over streams of figures recorded during first contact and comparing them to the live stream, a subtle disparity between the two surfaced. He'd been up, working solid for 19 hours and almost missed it.

Strictly a binary code divergence, but it meant at some point, between the first detection of the cypher in the signal and when Beacon deactivated it, someone, or something manipulated the outgoing torrent—from their end. Strangely, it gave credence to the robot's claim that the signal originally targeted the Dovan. But as Baron postulated, had been redirected to the Imperium.

Working fervently now, Baron isolated the rogue character-string and attacked it with a life's worth of chaos algorithms, stripping it down to its lowest common denominator. His hunch tested right—a hidden code. After further deciphering and translation, using the Dovan's stored data on ID technology, he found his prize: an intelligence command cryptogram, a response activator. Which meant...

ODS had a spy in its midst.

When had someone infiltrated their initiative? Before Beacon deactivated the signal? Or upon its recent reactivation? Regardless, one thing grew abundantly clear: he couldn't tell *anyone* about this, not yet. Who could he trust? Had Beacon played them all along, stalling for time while his masters made ready to annihilate Earth? Seemed plausible but Baron had his doubts. Then again, had that been what the Mechanical Messiah counted on?

It drove one mad to think in these endless loops, like studying one of those illusions that changed perspective every time you looked at it, exactly like applied chaos theorem.

No, he'd keep his mouth shut for the moment, lest he wind up admiring the Earth from outside the station without a pressure suit. Volunteering to work the graveyard shift on his own—citing a special diagnostic maintenance test—Baron cleared the control room of other bodies. His staff seemed happy to oblige.

Once alone, Baron locked access to the main console and took the CPU off the network. Only now could he concentrate on the task at hand, getting to the base of the mystery first. Baron plugged his deciphered strings into the command interface, which controlled the newly synthesized radio/plasma transmission and channelled the foldback up through the lens and into the heavens.

So instantaneous came the response, it staggered him into the backrest of his chair. Inhaling fiercely, Baron pulled the chair closer as rows of data marched across the screen in front of him. And filled it. His translation program ran in auto mode, already filtering and recording the data, which had to be decrypted twice: first from ID into Dovani, and then from Dovani into English. On a celestial scale, it happened so fast, as though the transmitter sat in the next room and not on the other side of the galaxy.

Baron might've patted himself on the shoulder for tapping into Goliath's technology, if he wasn't so bloody scared. Hyped to the max, he couldn't sleep if he wanted to—even the sedation program in his wrist pad wouldn't work with the amount of adrenaline coursing through his body.

His gut told him to cut the connection, or more to the point, gear it down to a standby mode. His plug-in told the Dovani driver, which instructed the ID program out there, to stop transmission, and it did. Looking at what he uncovered so far, he found all sorts of military intelligence concerning the Demon armada and their homeworlds, sciences, stellar cartography, fleet weaponry. Reports of every kind occupied the display, including flight paths, coordinates of intended waypoints, and protocol.

Such a hacker. He felt his smile stretch at his self-deprecation. But it contracted again when he began feeding the Hubble II's guidance control with a series of six-string numeric sets he took to be stellar coordinates.

The lens tracked in towards the first set of coordinates. Sure enough, a Demon core world appeared on Baron's screen, glistening white on the hemisphere as it faced a knot of blue dwarfs in the system. Pinpoints of lights, which he resolved were cities, dotted the planet's dark side. Another numeric set revealed a capital ship cruising above an asteroid field, a young yellow sun blazing just behind. Following that, a frame filled by a fleet of dreadnoughts holding station at some interstellar waypoint before a nebula's iridescent blue and magenta gas clouds.

On and on it went and a very haggard Baron found it an almost relaxing way to wind down from his stigmatic discovery. Until he stumbled upon something rather odd.

At the bottom of his coordinate list, he came across a single *seven*-string set. His brows dovetailed into a quivering chevron. The last or seventh numeric in this unique filament relayed the value of 0.00000000.

That particular code denoted either a source marker or a destination plot: a 'ground-zero.' Taking the value of zero as his x-axis, he plugged the remaining six coordinates into the lens controller and waited for it to track in. When it locked on the final image and relayed it to the monitor, Baron mentally processed the scrolling stats at the bottom of the screen.

His heart slipped gears. Staring in stolid disbelief, he remained transfixed by the image on the monitor, until the morning shift personnel entered the control room.

"Hey Doc," an approaching female's voice called to him. His assistant, Taryn. *Oh God.* Baron snapped out of his trance and scrambled to clear the image in front of him.

"What you got there?" Taryn asked innocently. *Too late.* She leaned in over his shoulder.

Baron craned his neck and through bloodshot prosthetic eyes, met his assistant's warm gaze.

"Trouble," he croaked.

8: Plan B
Baron

Silence. The anti-grav generators supporting the missile train on a cushion of air two metres above a single-beam track made no external sound. Nor did the train as it streaked across the barren landscape. Except for one: the sonic boom trailing far back in its wake.

But all the passengers aboard were oblivious to this, well out of earshot before that particular whip cracked.

The train began ramping down from its top cruising speed of Mach 1.8, 150 kilometres outside of Phoenix. In so doing, it would attain subsonic speeds before reaching the city's 100-kilometre transonic perimeter.

Moments later, a cheery voice sounded on the train's PA system. "Ladies and Gentlemen, this is your conductor speaking. We have just crossed into the outer zone threshold dictated by local bylaws and will shortly arrive at Phoenix Central. Please ensure that you take all of your personal belongings with you when you leave your cabin."

The all-too-familiar announcement brought Baron out of his dream. Bleary eyes sought the cabin's digital clock. Another ten minutes or so remained before the train covered the final 100 K to the station.

He glanced out the window where a polarized view of the southwestern desert flashed by. The sandy expanse should appear a warm orange, but the darkened windows cooled the spectrum, making it look unnatural... alien. *That word again.*

After pondering options all night, this transformed desert scenery made him believe it was for the best, all good things and such.

Luckily, he could count on Taryn to keep tight-lipped about this shocking development. In a way, it was good having her in the loop, to monitor things from the station and help him with any post-logistical work he might need on the ground.

Under normal circumstances, Baron would've waited for the

next supply shuttle or passing space yacht to break atmo, but this couldn't wait and he wasn't about to transmit from the station, encrypted or not. No, he had to double-time it to Morrison. So, after leaving Taryn with some simple but imperative instructions, he inserted his body into an emergency escape pod and jettisoned down to the Canaveral Landing Field. It had been a quick commute from the field to the missile train station in Orlando, and an even quicker connection from the Florida depot to HQ in Phoenix.

Baron steered his mind to the task at hand, grateful that the train had to slow down this far out from his destination. It gave him time to gather his thoughts and prepare the professor for the bad news. Hard to imagine the fucking Apocs had it right all along.

Looking down, he tapped a curved biofeedback control pad saddling his wrist. It beeped and an LED flared to life, signalling its readiness. From the menu, he selected the **ABL** or AUTO BIO LEVELS icon, which would help see him through the worst of it.

Shame seeped into Baron for activating the macro, but in light of what had to be accomplished this day, he needed all the help he could get at his disposal. So long as he didn't linger in that mode, he would be okay. Everyone knew the danger of prolonged ABL, something akin to drug addiction.

A split-second after hitting the RUN code a spike of euphoria entered his body through the nano-prods housed beneath the saddle. A moment later, the program achieved a perfect balance, infusing him head to toe. All of his senses sharpened and his thought processes aligned to their most efficient synapses. Expressed as a percentage, Baron's mindset and physiology now registered 100.

Anne would know he rigged up and filter his report accordingly, but Baron had no choice. He had to be that thorough, that concise. Anyone in a high-stress position used these devices regularly: soldiers in combat, lawyers in the courtroom, even space yacht pilots on long hauls.

Apart from optimizing his physicality, the wondrous device also served as his secretary. Baron told it to send his GPS coordinates to the central interface. Authenticated with his DNA signature, that one command activated a slew of logistical subroutines. A chauffeured pod would be waiting for him when he left the station and his hosts would be sent a message signalling his ETA with real-time updates. It made reservations for his preferred hotels and restaurants, instantaneously activating and coordinating credit lines to that effect.

Although it seemed impossible to get more efficient, it did take away the humanity of it all. Such technology proved the human race's greatest ally. Also, its greatest curse, thanks to Beacon. For better or worse, Baron would side with the 'guiding light' the robot's name represented—given what little time they had left.

The train pulled into the station, coming to a stop without a whisper of inertia. Suspended in the air, it waited for the station's umbilical conveyors to snake out from the platform and form a seal with the carriage doors.

"All passengers may disembark. Thank you for using Bullet Net—faster and safer than flying." Light instrumental music followed the recorded message.

Lifting a small metallic briefcase from under his seat, Baron stood and followed the other first-class passengers out the exit and onto the semi-enclosed bridge. As he crossed the limbo chasm, a wave of dry heat brought the fragrant scents of desert flowers. He breathed deep, feeling alive as he marched into the main concourse and hastened to the tram-island where five white pods awaited.

An LED sign on the side of one of the bean-shaped vehicles had his surname, FIELDBANK labelling it. The pod's gull-wing door opened as soon as his shoe touched the island. He ducked in.

Even as Baron secured his briefcase and settled into the black leather bucket seat, the door sealed behind him and the pod pulled away. It magnetically converged with the tramline. And zoomed away.

No matter how many times Baron confronted, dealt with, or interacted with Morrison's robot, he always felt the same trepidation, the same stigma. Any contact with the mechanical enigma reawakened some atavistic prelude to fear. Nothing for it.

Despite all the tangible and intangible benefits Baron had witnessed firsthand, he now knew, and surmised Beacon did too, that Earth had just been handed an expiry date—without the Apocs' help.

Moments later, Baron's pod arrived at Blythe's massive monolith, the World Sciences Centre. After a brief pause, the pod automatically attached itself to a track running up the side of the building. It began to rise with increasing alacrity. The pod would take seconds to zip him up to the rooftop observatory crowning the skyscraper.

Baron did have one small consoling and somewhat selfish thought as the roof of the city fell away beneath him. The Apocalypse wouldn't happen in his lifetime.

Three hundred storeys later, the pod married itself to an access door and the entrance swished open. The pod's hatch followed suit a second later.

Case in hand, Baron climbed out and walked into a sun-drenched foyer where Beacon awaited him, his ebony torso infused with orange dusk light.

"Hell-O, Doc-tor—Field-bank," the robot hailed.

Baron surrendered a curt nod to the giant black beetle. "Hello back, Beacon, been a while. How's it going?"

"The-inquiry-of all—instances - to the——interrogative applied to, *'it'*-as a precept to-the general condition-of the lab-and observatory———the progress-of my latest-experiments——— and/or-the status-of your-deferred request—I would-describe-as-——- marginal," Beacon's innocuous voice droned.

Baron exhaled. *Typical response.* He always thought Earth's first alien encounter would be with some squishy green thing, not a morbid-looking machine with discombobulated syntax and semantics. "Where is Professor Morrison?"

"Anne is-in the-telescope—command pod," the robot said. His airborne carriage drifted two metres to the side, giving Baron an unobstructed view of Anne's location. "As usual."

Despite the situation, Beacon's lilt of sarcasm brought a smile to Baron's lips. *He's definitely improving.*

But Baron's emotions tangled. He wanted to laugh one minute and cry the next. Now that he was here, about to break the worst news of his life, his knees started to give. Exhaustion? Had the ABL program short-circuited? *Now I know how Atlas felt. Should I shrug too?*

With Ayn Rand, the famous author and philosopher occupying his mind, Baron marched on leaden feet to the telescope command pod or TCP. Just a glorified name for a redundant backup to the Hubble II in case some major malfunction fried the motherboards, or the whole damn H2S station went up.

In moments Baron arrived at the pod entrance and entered his access code on a side panel. As the door shushed open, the insectile shadow of Beacon crept up behind him. *If the Toaster doesn't hear it from me, he'll hear it from Anne in a jiff.* The pair moved inside the room.

When the doors sealed behind them, leaving them in relative darkness, an anti-static mist sprayed down from nozzles set in the ceiling. Baron bunched up his nose as the oddly sweet smell of ozone wafted past, rendering the bubble and its new occupants 'clean.'

The pod's inner sanctum mimicked the main control room back up on the Hubble II, but it had its share of Christmas lights and three-dimensional holo-monitors, along with walls filled with the regular assortment of LED screens.

Baron found Anne sitting on a swivel chair by a rectangular metal table, an electronic tablet in one hand and a cup of black coffee in the other. No stim programs for this lady. Old school to the core.

Anne looked up, her eyes warming as they approached. "Hello Baron," she greeted. "This is the first time the three of us have shared the same physical space for what, a year now?"

"About 14 months," Baron corrected, trying to keep his voice steady.

"So, what's up? How's your research in the heavens?"

"Hell, actually."

"Take a seat," she said more seriously. "Tell me about it."

Baron rested his briefcase on the table, pulled out an empty chair and sat.

"Can I get you a coffee, or are you running one of those ABL stim programs?" *Nothing gets by her.*

"I think we both know the answer to that question."

Anne gave him a coy shrug.

Unsure how much he should divulge, Baron adjusted his seat. "As you know, we've randomly ascertained the movement of various ships in the Imperium's armada, plotting potential targets and such. Well, everything has changed now, perhaps for the better, but there's a caveat." He matched her facial stance. "You want the good news first or the bad?"

"I could use some good news," Anne confessed.

Baron went on to explain about his breakthrough from the night before, leaving out the bit about his suspicions concerning the potential spy.

"That's wonderful," Anne remarked when Baron finished. She carefully placed her tablet and coffee mug down on the table and leaned forward. Elbows propped on its surface, she rested her chin on folded hands and gave him her undivided attention.

Baron knew Anne well enough—she was bracing for his grievous disclosure. On any other occasion, his impasse might land on a technical or logistical side. But in light of his recent request to reactivate the signal, taking the H2S CPU offline, and then using an escape pod to get on the ground fluttered the red flag loud enough.

"So, the bad news," Baron said as he rolled his chair closer to the table. "The last coordinate I plugged in was a seven-string set. When the lens tracked in, it revealed an image of an enormous plasma surge, like the ones we saw decimate that first M-class planet way back."

Anne prompted him to go on with a tilt of her chin.

"I know you're familiar with the Doppler Effect—to determine whether a celestial object is moving towards or away."

She gave him a thin smile.

Baron cleared his throat. He hated being the bearer of terrible news, especially to his most esteemed colleague. "Well, before I left the H2S, I had one of my assistants plug the Doppler co-variant into the image coordinates I found, utilizing keyframe markers to capture a series of stills. I could then visually track the surge's movement through space, like a zoom lens going wide in stages from a telephoto position."

"And?"

"It confirmed what I suspected. That plasma surge is heading straight for us. It's bound for Earth."

Anne's breath caught. "Good God."

Over Baron's shoulder, a voice asked, "Have you double-checked your initial analysis, eliminating the co-variant from the equation string?"

Baron spun on the robot. Beacon had spoken—like a human.

"To keep up appearances, Baron," Anne soothed across from him. "Beacon has spoken all this time with that cumbersome mechanical voice to make the general public more accepting of his presence, and to mollify those furtive Apocs—somewhat. We're in private quarters now, so there isn't any need. And it seems you know more than both of us about this impending doom."

"You're just full of surprises, Beacon," Baron said, wondering if the robot fully grasped the irony beneath his import. Regardless, it would have to wait.

Guilt mired Baron when he turned back to Anne. Crow's feet and number elevens trembling, mouth pulled down, she'd never looked so vulnerable as she did right then.

Baron reached for her arm and gave it a gentle squeeze. "Hey, Anne, it won't hit us for another century or so."

"Dr Fieldbank?" Beacon again. "I've noticed one thing you overlooked in your calculations."

Baron's apprehension resurfaced. "What's that?"

In answer, Beacon glided over to a console a few feet away. He extended an interfacing prod and inserted it into the closest jack. The board flashed to life as the robot's appendage rapidly dialled the disk-shaped peripheral back and forth.

Baron knew what he was about. Beacon was inputting the necessary command functions to give him a direct uplink with the Hubble II. As instructed, Taryn would be up there in the control room, awaiting such a signal. They all lapsed into silence as Taryn acknowledged and executed Beacon's directive. Fifteen minutes later, the robot announced, "I have it. Come, take a look."

Baron and Anne stood and joined Beacon by the interface. The robot backed away as Baron drew up to the overlarge monitor above the console.

A series of images divided the screen into nine equal squares. Each tile depicted the same massive discharge surrounded by interstellar space and carried a string of sixteen numbers attached to the top of every frame. The last string of numeric figures on the bottom right square counted down at an alarming rate.

Baron had produced a similar display the previous night in orbit, so he already knew its significance. He narrowed his eyes and turned to face his two companions. Anne compressed her lips into a frown and shook her head. Where was the robot going with this?

Before Baron could frame his question, Beacon explained, "Through inflation dichotomy, spacetime itself stretches and thins, owing to dark-matter/dark energy tugging."

Baron gulped, feeling a clawing sensation in his gut. "Ergo?"

"Ergo, velocities of matter in motion fluctuate," the robot elaborated. "Barring gravity-assists, they can radically change over great distances. Along its present trajectory, with the added Coriolis effect, the plasma surge you discovered currently hurling towards us—is accelerating."

Baron reached for his wrist pad and turned the stress-suppression program up to its fullest setting. Facing the monitor again, he stared in grim silence, riveted to that last frame tile and its cold countdown to doom.

Behind him, Anne broke the disturbing quiet. "Well, Beacon, I think it's time we ramp up our other initiative."

9: Resa
5104 CE

Stricken—it cast a ghostly emerald-white light through every window and viewscreen on the bridge of the *Inner Peace*. Three humanoid crew members piloted the ship, arranged in a neat triangle with two seated up front and one further back.

Since the command centre was otherwise dark, the light filled the entire enclosure with the same ethereal glow, giving the occupants an eerie, almost sinister pallor. The nimbus of the planet below had aberrated their usually neutral features.

Neutral defined the Tolkane, articulated by their blank expressions and achromatic dispositions. But their blankness did not indicate emptiness; rather that of thinking creatures being quiet. They were just as emotional, as quick to anger as the next humanoid race. The Tolkane simply hid it better.

Apart from being able to communicate telepathically, they could align their minds and work synergistically to solve problems. Limited to a short range, but when amongst their own they chose to bypass speaking aloud. They preferred to project their thoughts, using a wiry three-centimetre-tall antenna they'd all been born with. The diminutive node protruded from their forehead, immediately above their right eye. It accounted for their vacant facial expressions, their outward blankness.

As for their inner blankness, the Tolkane conducted themselves like prisms, vassals open to the ambient energy flowing through the cosmos, ever ready to reach tangency with its eternal aura and infinite memory.

They championed their own brand of *Wu Wei*—of knowing when to act and when not to act, to *do without doing*. This ability to drift along with the current of time, aligning their purpose with the natural flow of the universal continuum, was not their own. But they saw its value and adopted it.

In the grand scheme of existence, the Tolkane always followed the path of least resistance. Rather than breaking down any obstacles, they flowed around them like water in a river. It's what kept them alive in the overwhelming swathe of the Garaxian Imperium.

All living creatures awoke to the light of a sun, except the Demons. Their cold light gathered from an inherent spectre of war and negated all others, holding sway over the entire quadrant. The way of the Demon dictated the way of the Universe. But not for all.

In no way did the Tolkane side with the Imperium, but neither did they give their Overlords cause for suspicion, lest they be regarded as a budding hazard. No, to the Garaxians, the Tolkane served a purpose—like bacteria helping in the decomposition of an expended adversary. So, the Demons tolerated the pacificists but continually monitored them.

Tolerance ingrained the Tolkane mantra and the same held true for their sublime ship. The eponymous *Inner Peace* embodied her namesake in every meticulous fibre of her construction. She had been built with the kind of understanding and love that a master craftsman bestows upon his magnum opus. The prototypical vessel was a sleek white cutter, streamlined and beautifully seated on a single triangular mono-wing. It gave the ship a look of stalwart resolve like a giant metallic eagle.

A cross-section of the main hull might be likened to a rounded infinity icon and it housed the forty members of her crew in comfort, with some of the latest technology to make it all possible. Four powerful engines adorned her body, two aft and two amidships. The engines all ran on the same plasma, or an allowed derivative, which the Ice Demons used to move their massive fleets from system to system.

Even if the Tolkane wanted to use the pure stuff, they couldn't. The molecular structure of the *Inner Peace*'s hull wouldn't handle the stress of that much siphoned energy; it would instantly rip the spacecraft apart. The Imperium ships could handle it because the same latent plasma comprised their hulls, a technology that made the Garaxians so daunting and devastating. The ID loathed sharing any of their tech with undercastes, but when it came to pure plasma, they hoarded it with extreme prejudice.

A muted klaxon sounded, signalling that the *Inner Peace* approached optimum perigee for insertion into the ghost world beneath them. The ship's navigation computer waited for the co-sign to release helm to manual control.

One of the crew members who sat up front, a smartly-shaped brunette named Shyce turned and projected her thoughts back towards her captain, 'We cut main thrusters thirty seconds ago. Braking in one minute. Telemetry looks good.' Concern painted her bladed features and otherwise beautiful dark eyes. 'What's the story with this one, Sir?'

Captain Yaemin Resa, a statuesque man with a square face and salt-and-pepper hair, rubbed the base of his small antenna for a moment before projecting back in kind, 'She's S-class alright—Stricken to the core. Looks like they went in with the plasma. The world didn't stand a chance. Sun looks unaffected, yellow—young. The size, amount, and proximity of the orbiting asteroids indicate the world had a single moon—must've been shredded in the displacement field when the plasma hit.'

Used to his grey noncommittal demeanour, Resa's crew understood his 'greyness' inside and out, which wasn't to say that he was unaffected, indifferent, or plainly *not there*. Resa was a reticent man who comported himself well and strove to remain task-orientated, keeping emotion out of any situation. He just concealed it better, locking it in his mental vault. Of that, or his probity, his crew had no doubt. If anyone embodied *Wu Wei*, it was Resa, whose taciturn methods and gravitas drew the unbridled loyalty and respect of his entire team.

'What about the former inhabitants?' Shyce asked, tilting her head up to a console directly above her.

'Extinct. No extirpation, as far as we know, and we don't know much. I checked on the Box when we landed on Korian III. Information was scarce at best. Just a footnote really that the ID annexed it. Nothing to say these *Hu-mans* survived the attack or got off-world in time, but you never know.'

Shyce dropped her gaze back to Resa. She gently bit her lower lip and gave him a solemn nod.

Who would know? Resa's mentor probably knew. Knew the

whole verboten truth, or most of it anyway. Something his guru had deigned to keep hidden from him for the same reason the captain kept such meandering secrets un-projected to his crew: safety.

"Give me a scan and run the numbers," Resa said aloud, his voice cracking a little from underuse. "I want to make sure we're alone out here before we go in. I needn't remind you this one's been quarantined for more than three thousand years."

Shyce coughed. "With all due respect, Captain, why *are* we out here? There are so many other S-classes with decent tech to salvage. That's why they're S-class now, Sir."

Resa leaned back in his chair and gripped his armrests. "Yes, but this one's different. There's a private party involved and he's funding the entire expedition out of pocket." *Private* was one way of putting it. Resa never met the man in the flesh; the captain only ever dealt with either an avatar on a viewscreen or one of the Funder's associates. "He's not looking for any random tech. It's something very specific, extremely rare and invaluable. This isn't salvage. It's search and recovery. He's the one who sprung for all the retrofits and upgrades on the *Inner Peace* back on Ursula Minor—some of which you lot are now enjoying."

"Can't argue with that," Shyce said with a coy smirk. She faced forward again. "My new private quarters have all the luxuries of a starliner suite. That's something I won't part with any time soon."

Resa half-smiled. "The *Inner Peace* left UM's dry dock, a new ship. She's been reincarnated."

"New or old, this whole business is not our way," Shyce pointed out. "It goes against the natural flow."

"At the moment, that appears to be the case," the captain conceded, "but great changes are afoot. We must strive to flow with them. Like our ancestors of old, trying to reach ultimate Zen, something down there may very well light our future course." *And everything we know.* "Freeing us into uncharted, *unpoliced* space."

Shyce swivelled in her seat and sought Resa's eyes. "At what cost? This is more than uncharted space. It's forbidden space. And technically, we're flying blind out here."

"True enough." Shyce's co-pilot, Brenor murmured in a nervous tone. Head tilting up, he reached for a console attached to the ceiling and adjusted a seated dial one quarter-turn. His hand dropped and he shifted forward again.

Resa's fingers idly brushed the armrest consoles. "Trust me, people, this is no blind, on-a-whim op. I wouldn't have agreed to it otherwise. I have it on good authority that what we do today will garner positive consequences. Might even instigate a fundamental shift in the karmic wheel, enough to finally break the cycle—and that is our way."

Shyce pursed her lips and evaded his stare. "Sounds big—too big."

"I know what you're thinking," said Resa. "Had the same feeling when I talked to the Funder, but I did do my research, downloading an entire precept pirated from the Imperium's annals to cross-reference what he pitched." He tilted his head towards the window. "A 'Human' population thrived down there, and much further back in time, on another world, a race called Dovan. Their fates are linked, sharing secrets of a quintessential path to our own destiny."

"As I said, Captain, too big," Shyce reminded him.

Resa lifted a finger. "Perhaps, and although the Funder didn't tell me the entire story—" *Neither did my mentor.* "—I'm convinced that the Stricken down there is hiding something, really important."

Shyce frowned. "So, what *is* down there? What are we looking for?" Judging by her tone, and Brenor's, Resa wasn't the only one feeling the awakening of some primal terror.

"Honestly girl, I don't know," he admitted. "The entire surface is probably sterile. The trace gases in its lousy excuse of an atmosphere might support some resilient bacteria, but other than that, it's essentially a dead planet. I received another packet from the Funder, sent subspace. We picked it up just as we dropped out of warp into the system. I'll take a peek at it once we finish mapping."

Resa paused and studied his pilot's face.

Shyce blinked several times, then swallowed. "I don't trust

this situation, but I trust you."

He gave her the most reassuring smile he could feign, then looked out the window again. His attention fixed on the blighted world rotating below. "There's a reason the Demons kept this particular Stricken in quarantine for so long. I intend to find out why." After a moment, his eyes returned to her. "So, how about those numbers?"

Shyce pivoted her chair until she faced ahead. Her dark mane drooped as she leaned over her console. "We're currently holding perigee along an equatorial parking orbit," she reported. "We can go in when we're ready. Scanners are online and traffic is... clear. Atmospheric is... as you described, barely nominal. Surface temperature... below the line. I'm reading -57°C. We'll need the suits. Brenor already launched a pair of cradle buoys into high geosynchronous orbits above opposite poles. The sentries will cover our 360. We'll know if anyone's out here or decides to crash our party after we land."

Satisfied, Resa said, "Good. Let's get this done. When you're ready, Shyce, if you please, take us in."

Shyce nudged her chin over her shoulder. "Copy that." One hand on the double-grip yoke, the pilot coaxed the lever forward, applying a hair's breadth of thrust.

The *Inner Peace* responded like poetry, rolling to port and pitching forward as her angular nose dipped towards the planet. Like a bird of prey about to sweep down on its quarry, the ship assumed an insertion tack.

Shyce added her other hand to the yoke's second grip and leaned back in her g-seat.

Then, in a flare of brisance, the *Inner Peace* shot down towards the ghost world.

10: Shadows and Ghosts
Resa

After a series of systematic high-altitude flybys just inside the planet's atmospheric envelope, the scan-map computer spat out an accurate, to-the-metre, grid reference. But the entire map failed to turn up anything conclusive.

Except that nothing had escaped the plasma. Apart from the lingering remains of the cities' tallest buildings, trying to poke their way out of the Glass, the same uniform glaze covered the entire surface of the planet.

"I'd better take a closer look at that packet now," Resa announced as he made for the gangway.

"Captain?" Shyce called over her shoulder, stopping him midstride. "Are we chasing tech here, or ghosts?"

"Maybe both," he replied. "Maybe both."

Resa wasn't one to tinker with perchance. If the packet didn't offer a satisfactory answer, he'd break radio silence and call the Funder directly, and if the patron refused to respond, Resa would refuse to land the *Inner Peace* until he did.

A short walk brought the captain down to the first deck corridor and into a tiny alcove that served as a private workstation. He projected his desire for privacy to the ship's computer.

Hushed servos sounded as the CPU responded to his request, sliding a tempered glass door across the threshold behind him and locking it.

Effectively sealed in the suite, Resa sat before the computer screen and punched in a series of command codes, which allowed access to the contents of the encrypted packet. Moments later, it opened up and the familiar avatar of the Funder's face popped up on the screen.

"Hello, my good Captain," the prerecorded clip began. "I suspect by now that you've completed several passes and mapped the entire world—to no avail. Befuddled, you finally decided to open my packet and see if I might lend a hand."

Though only an avatar's face and voice, Resa flashed with indignation at the Funder's smug look and supercilious tone. Just because he was their patron didn't give him a license to be patronizing. The captain took a deep breath and let his ire pass like so much thruster exhaust.

"As a matter of fact, Captain, I can." Resa felt his node stand up in surprise. "If you recall when you set down on Ursula Minor, we added some tech to your, shall we say, quaint apparatus."

The singsong quality in the Funder's voice ebbed, taking on a more earnest tone. "I apologize for not informing you of everything before you left the world. But the mission had to be done delicately—without all the facts—to protect its secret from unfriendly ears. As you are well aware, to possess such tech, illegal *ID* tech, would be tantamount to broadcasting your death warrants on the Box. Ergo, ignorance has served as your ally."

Resa lifted a hand to his collar and unfastened the top two buttons. Despite the twinge of ominousness, he received the warning with solemn acceptance.

"Unwilling to let this oversight undermine the success of your mission, I dug deeper into my own resources from my end."

The Funder's avatar leaned in towards the screen. "I value your ship and crew too much, Resa, but hold you in the highest esteem. Since you left Prime Dock, my own investigations have turned up an invaluable benison."

Resa straightened in his chair. His throat began to throb with a dry ache.

"I've attached a string of command codes to this packet,' the Funder disclosed. "Enter them into the ship's new scan-map computer. They will activate a wide-spread short-range signal generator that will key on the specific energy signature of the item I seek. Again, for the sake of secrecy, I had to limit the strength of the emitter, so no tertiary scanners could lock on to your broadcast from orbit."

Movement in Resa's peripheral drew his regard to the left as one of his crew members strode past.

"If it's still down there," the avatar said, recalling Resa's attention back to the monitor, "it should begin emitting a corresponding signal. You can then track it directly from the spherical grid you've undoubtedly generated by now. I don't know where it may rest exactly or if it will turn up at all. But if it does, rest assured you will recognize and know how to retrieve it. I always get the best people for a reason."

The comment triggered Resa's memory of the Funder's associate, Jro, captain of the *Maelstrom*. The shady go-between remunerated him for the covert op upfront when his ship rendezvoused with the *Inner Peace* back on Ursula Minor. The Funder had always isolated himself from his ventures, 'to protect his other interests from priers.' His associate was the exact opposite, divesting himself of nothing. Jro gave Resa the impression he wanted to commandeer the *Inner Peace* and go on the mission by himself.

Towing a considerable cache of formidable weapons and cutting tools, Jro drove a bulky all-terrain rig seated on eight massive balloon tires down the cargo ramp of his own vessel and up the ramp of Resa's ship.

There in the cargo hold, he gave Resa and crew a quick once-over demonstration of everything, his scar of a smile never reaching his calculating eyes. Without saying anything indicative to the effect, the man seemed to bleed evil into the air around him. Resa was glad to see the back of him.

Still, the trace of unease lingered, suffusing the *Inner Peace* long after Jro had departed, indeed long after Resa's ship broke atmo on Ursula Minor and moved into an escape attitude for a jump. Resa felt his vessel tainted by the Funder's associate.

"I wish I could be more helpful," the Funder's voice cut in again. "But information is scant and outdated. The *Inner Peace* is probably the first ship to arrive in the Sol System since that world's annexation."

Resa nodded to himself, his trepidation rising another notch.

"Since we last spoke, I also managed to acquire a satellite

imaging profile of the planet, before the Demon's annex. It's attached to this packet. Try matching its macros and latitude-longitude vectors with your own topographic grid reference. I've gone through it and may have the most plausible coordinates for you to begin your search. Activate the new scan parameter and keep it focused on no more than a five-kilometre radius."

The avatar sat back, looked across his shoulder, and exhaled. After a pause, he shifted forward even closer than before. "Captain, I don't need to tell you to move slowly down there—and to watch your back. Much is at stake here for both of us. Good hunting."

The image on the screen cut to black, signalling the packet's end. After downloading and reallocating the macros in the attached files, Resa deleted the contents of the entire packet and marched back up to the bridge.

11: Stricken
Resa

The milky-emerald starkness of the Stricken's surface stretched out before Resa like a vast ocean flash-frozen in time. Apart from a glimpse of thin wispy cloud high in the atmosphere, nothing moved. The veneer coating the planet made it look embalmed in polymer or translucent glass.

The striking hand gathers all flame. This wasn't just seizure or annihilation. It was overkill, plain and simple. The world had been simultaneously entombed and suffocated.

A full two hours had elapsed since Resa told Shyce to bring the ship down in the middle of what resembled a series of industrial flats. From the moment the engines began cooling, cycling down to a droning idle, the captain planted his boots by the forward bridge window to start his vigil.

With her landing struts settled firmly atop the white wasteland, the *Inner Peace* faced the skyline of a small city. Most of the buildings and bridges lay beneath as much as five hundred metres of latent plasma, but some of the tallest structures were only half-submerged and one exceptionally tall spire might still be considered a skyscraper.

Towards that monolith, their instruments honed in. Somewhere inside that giant tombstone, an unwavering countersignal reciprocated the signal the *Inner Peace* broadcasted.

Resa started the clock as the massive eight-wheel rig the Funder had provided alighted off the cargo ramp. It trudged ponderously towards the skyscraper looming in the distance. With its balloon tires absorbing the uneven terrain, the impressive behemoth carried the bulk of the weapons and tools cache and half the ship's forty-person crew.

His scrutiny flitting periodically to the bridge clock, the captain remained fixed with pupils pressed to the glass as the rig arrived on-site and his crew set to work. When he swayed back a little, a wraith of his own haggard face reflected in the window.

The deep circles under his eyes reminded him of his weariness and his worry.

And for good reason. The first set of coordinates the Funder had given him proved to be the right ones. Initially, Resa wasn't sure if he should feel relieved or disturbed at the discovery, but distress won the tilt. As soon as he plugged in the command codes, the CPU's display changed into an entirely different operating system. A new interface overlaid the specific grid references, enlarging and enhancing them.

In the middle of that map, a tiny red dot blinked up at him.

Interpolating helm control with navigation, Shyce steered the ship in a beeline towards that beacon, flying as low and as slow as possible under muted jet propulsion. Although grateful for her caution, Resa knew they would have to speed things up when they landed if they wanted to get a lockdown or even a proper fix before the day ebbed completely.

Erring on the side of caution himself, Resa made Shyce touch down a kilometre away, before dispatching a pair of scouts aboard an anti-grav sled. When the signal proved authentic, not just a bogus lure, he consented to sending in the full team to commence retrieval operations.

The remainder of the crew, including Shyce, Brenor, and himself would stay back to monitor the cradle buoys and keep the ship's engines warm—in case the rig squad needed an emergency evac.

So far, the skies were clear, but when the sun sought escape over the horizon behind the city and the shadows cast by the tower lengthened, reaching out towards his ship, Resa felt trapped. It had become one big waiting game—a game he had no desire to play.

Unable to mollify his apprehension any longer, Resa opened up a channel to the drill team. "*Inner Peace* to rig," he transmitted over the com. "Report. What's your status?"

Pico, the rig's straw boss answered a moment later. "It's down there all right, Captain, though not inside the building as we first thought but about 30 metres outside of it. I have the main phase-drill and scope in centre-vertical position over actual, point zero-zero. We'll scope first, then rotate the tools from short yield to big gun depending on how effective the excavation effort goes with each. I'll keep you posted if we need to ratchet up."

"Understood, Pico. Sounds good," Resa lied.

"Oh, one more thing, Captain. It's trivial but some of the crew examined the tower up close. Plasma's so thin against its exterior, they think they can cut through easily enough. They didn't of course, just looked inside. They spotted a hardcopy city map on an interior wall, which they captured and cross-referenced with the Funder's spherical grid."

"And?" Resa prompted.

"It's a match, Sir," Pico said. "Found photos too. For what it's worth, we now have an idea of what this place was like before the quarantine. I'm sending you a copy. The city we're in was named *Phoenix*."

"Great, I'll update our files. Resa out." The captain switched off the com.

As Resa moved to retrieve the attachments Pico sent him, he noticed Shyce staring at him.

"What is it?" he asked.

"About to ask you the same thing. You look like you've already seen your ghosts."

"It's getting dark outside and I don't want to spend the night here if I can help it. I sense shadows, true enough, but also a light in the distance, if that makes any sense. Somehow, the very name of this place offers a clue. It means something, but for the moment that *something* eludes me. Damn subliminal really."

"Do you want to abort the op?" Shyce asked innocently. "Regroup further out of system? We could monitor the cradle buoys from beyond the fifth planet out and try again later."

Resa weighed that option for a moment before shaking his head. "No, we've already activated the corresponding signal. Just have to place my faith in the karmic wheel on this one. Proceed as planned."

93

"The wheel might turn our way, Captain, but wheels can break. I for one will feel a lot better once we get off this rock and back into or—!"

Blinding light seared reality. Shyce's voice cut off as a thunderous crack split the air. The floor of the bridge bucked, launching Resa and Shyce off their feet as the ship's hull jarred.

When the seizures and light finally waned, Resa scrambled to his feet and rushed to the window. He refused to acknowledge what his eyes were shouting at him.

The planet's shell had cracked, fanning out like claw marks from the spot where Pico had parked the rig seconds ago. Ambits of white light emanated from the centre of the massive fissure, spilling up into the darkening sky—its aura more pronounced in the world's departing terminator. No sign of the closest crew members either, and Resa knew why. The blast had obliterated and vaporized them in a sudden expanse of pure plasma.

Resa's skin crawled. Only the Imperium's lifeblood could cause that white horror, but how? *Half my crew are gone.* It took several moments before Shyce's desperate pleas registered in his ears.

"Abort? Captain! Do we run?"

Mustering his wits, Resa worked up moisture in his mouth. "No!" he fumbled at last. "Any move might trip another blast." *Half gone.* "And we can't abort. We must wait. See if there's any more fallout or aftershock, or if any secondary alarms triggered as a result. Hostiles might already be coming to investigate," he added. Resa paused at seeing his pilot's haunted visage. He smiled with his eyes and set his jaw in a determined cast.

Shyce recovered immediately. She bit her lower lip and pondered. "If the trap was recently planted, it's been sprung, so as far as whoever set it knows, we all went up in the smoke."

Not all: half. "We can't take that chance. The nature of the attack indicates a munition with energy-proximity sensors— warding against certain power signatures. The explosion didn't go off until long after the rig arrived onsite, so, it wasn't anything physical like a pressure-sensitive land mine that set it off."

Resa retreated into himself, falling into a rapid-fire thinking pattern, which he knew made him look catatonic. His inner projection began calculating their best odds, the quickest way to pick up the pieces, move past the disaster, and bridge to their most viable solution.

Moments later, he re-emerged from his trance and nodded to his pilot. Relief banished the ghosts from her eyes. Shyce let out a breath. "You have a plan." It was a statement.

"I do," he confirmed.

Shyce lifted herself off the floor. "Good call to park us further out," she said, clearly trying to sound positive.

"We'll know soon enough." Resa wasn't convinced of anything anymore. *Half dead.* "One thing's certain. Even though we need to lay low and keep our wits, we can't afford to, and we can't abort. If we do, whoever set *that* will only strengthen their defences so that next time—well, there won't be a next time. We have to finish this."

"Understood," Shyce acknowledged. Her tone said she did not relish the idea but accepted it all the same. Straightening her shoulders, she asked, "What do you need us to do?"

"Send in a sleigh on remote. The plasma should have already cooled enough to drop one into that fissure. I want eyes onsite and get me an actual from our eyes in the sky. Did they see anything?"

Shyce moved briskly to her station and sat before her console. After punching a few keys, she paused and looked up. "The cradle buoys remain in perfect halo. Both read green across the board: they say everything's quiet up there. It's still our party."

"Bad choice of words," Resa admonished, sharper than he intended. "We just paid for it in blood."

Shyce's face coloured. "Sorry, that was inappropriate."

Resa joined his pilot at the console and placed a hand on her shoulder. "I'm angry at myself, Shyce. It's your captain who should be begging forgiveness, putting you all in such peril."

Half dead.

95

"We all knew the risks, Sir. We'll see it through."

Resa allowed himself a thin smile, but Shyce's loyalty and conviction tore at his heart. Striving to justify them, he added gravely, "We're going to do this. We will succeed. Now, let's get that sled in there, a-sap."

This was madness. Every gut instinct cajoled the captain to abort. Except one. At the heart of all his doubt, grief, and fear, a driving absolute superseded all, some voice beyond primal, which insisted *not to*. And Resa listened.

Within the hour, the sleigh had returned intact with no further mishap, and some startling but problematic results. As expected, they found no sign of the rig or any of the ill-fated crew members that had gone out on it.

At ground-zero, a strange enigma emanated an ethereal afterglow, suffusing the surrounding latent plasma with a more intense emerald hue. It lay roughly 500 metres below the surface, directly beneath the rig's grave. The explosion had left a 120-metre-deep trench in its wake, but that still left a full 380 metres of latent plasma separating their target from the base of the surface furrow.

They'd lost all the heavy artillery when the rig went up so they couldn't blast or even cut straight down, not with the tools they had left. Resa explained to his crew that if they wanted to bag their prize in the same century, they had to up their game somehow. Pooling their minds to the task at hand, a course of action quickly became apparent.

Someone would take a supply of the Funder's tools and cut into the nearby building where the plasma had only coated a wafer-thin barrier. Then, the building itself could be used as a natural conduit into the plasma crust, all the way down to the former ground level where their goal awaited. At worst, they would have to cut a 30-metre lateral traverse towards their target.

When it came time to make the hard call, Resa would not let anyone else go back out there in such a compromised state. No one on his team could be called skittish, but after losing half their peers in the recent catastrophe, the crew was still understandably shaken. He needed them frosty and objective. The captain determined to go alone, travelling light with the bare minimum of tools.

But even as Resa began suiting up in the cargo bay's marshalling area, Shyce appeared and quietly, purposefully, strode past him to the storage rack. She immediately unhooked one of the environment suits.

Resa marched up beside her. "Just what do you think you're doing?"

"I know what I'm not doing," she replied as she inserted one leg into the suit, "so don't even think about trying to dissuade me. You're *not* going out there alone. I pilot the *Inner Peace* well enough. I think I can handle an AG sled. Brenor's holding down the fort. And besides, you're going to need an extra pair of hands when we get down there, if you still want to get that thing up here and off this godforsaken rock—in the same century."

Resa opened his mouth, about to order her to desist, but the look in her big eyes stopped him. His single antenna coiled in. Resa had known Shyce to be headstrong, wilful, and dedicated to the cause, but something more surfaced in that look.

At this most inopportune moment, something unsaid but no less wondrous passed between them, which made the captain feel strangely buoyant. It was something Resa swore he'd follow up on if they ever got out of this mess. Still touched by the revelation, he reined in his emotions and turned his thoughts to the task at hand.

"Whatever you do, Shyce, follow my lead. And when we get close, no scopes on that thing—that's probably what triggered the upheaval. There's nothing to say it won't happen again if we repeat it. Should I become compromised, under no circumstances are you to make some foolhardy attempt at rescue. You run—okay? Your number-one priority is the crew. Swear."

Resa's command drifted in the space between them as Shyce donned her enviro-suit helmet. Even then, through its faceplate, her solemn eyes studied him a moment longer. With a reluctant nod, she croaked, "I swear."

12: Reception
Resa

Unlike the Funder's rig, which could only plod along the glossy surface on awkward balloon tires, the anti-gravity sled sailed swift and true as a wisp to their target at the base of the crater's trough.

As darkness fell, the ambient temperature plummeted to more than a hundred below, stirring up a maniacal wind. Because of the depleted air pressure, it lacked any punch, but its demented skirling gnawed at Resa's nerves as the gusts swept across the altered surface of the world.

His suit compensated for the environmental shift automatically, but it did nothing to quell the captain's trepidation. He had wanted off this Stricken before night fell and now that wouldn't happen. Luckily, with Shyce at his side, things moved like clockwork once they disembarked from the sleigh. He was suddenly grateful for her company.

Rendered jagged by the blast, the veneer of crenulated plasma clung to the tower's wall like some artificial parasitic growth. With only thirty or forty centimetres to contend with, they quickly cut a two-metre-by-two opening through it and the glass window it enveloped. Then, boosting the output of their headlamps, they moved inside.

Resa only allowed himself two quick pans of the room, to record its function with his helmet's camera and make a mental note of the way they came in. Judging by the telltale mix of clerical materials and scientific apparatus, the room had served as some kind of laboratory office. On any other S-class salvo, Resa might have given it a closer inspection to indulge his curiosity, and his salvage rights, but not this one. It was going to be a long way down.

From the room, a dark corridor led them further into more windowless rooms and finally a staircase shaft. The way down evinced slow and onerous, encumbered with their backpacks full of various tools. Trudging carefully, they followed an interminable series of switch-backed staircases. The descent felt a bit dizzying as each one looked identical to the one above it—with one exception.

At intervals they came across corpses strewn out in ones and twos on the landings and stairs, some clutching their necks, faces contorted in masks of death.

"Gatch-*ameh*," Shyce breathed.

"When the ID cover a planet, everything beneath suffocates and becomes preserved in sterile vacuum," Resa explained.

"They look like us," Shyce remarked. "Only, without our nodes."

Resa gestured with a slow sweep of his arm for them to continue. Down they went in a seemingly unending spiral with nothing but the sound of their breathing, footfalls, and the blips of their suit-stat indicators to occupy their minds.

After several minutes, Resa paused and adjusted his pack. Shyce murmured something, which he didn't quite catch. But when she caught him scrutinizing her, she didn't repeat it. Instead, she looked down at her sensor pad. "Two more flights, Captain, and we'll be there."

They escaped the stairwell and entered a room that looked almost identical to the one they'd left 380 metres above them. Using the room above as a template, they simply reversed their course through the gloomy corridor and found an exact replica of their entry point.

It *was* an exact replica because this one too had been cut—? On the far side of the room, a section of the window was missing. Beyond it, a tunnel had been excavated, through solid plasma, a traverse close to 30 metres across. It led to a strange vessel imbued with a brilliant emerald glow. Silhouetted black against this aura stood a strange insectile form.

The thermostat regulating the internal environment of Resa's suit did nothing to quell the ice congealing in his marrow.

Turning to his companion, Resa projected, 'Looks like we found my ghost, Shyce. And I don't like it, not one damn bit.' The pilot didn't refute him. The two Tolkane lapsed into frozen silence, gawking across the mysterious chasm, at the conundrum stationed at its terminus.

If the mechanical husk was aware of them, it showed no outward response, at least none Resa could discern, given the vessel's aura behind it. That light suffused the entire tunnel, spilling out into the opened room where Resa and Shyce now stood. It rendered their headlamps superfluous so they switched them off. *No scopes.*

Shyce found her voice. "That's obviously what we're looking for—has to be."

Resa nodded.

They lowered their backpacks to the floor and slowly approached the black enigma. As soon as he'd laid eyes on it, Resa knew he was staring at a robot. They drew closer. Halfway across the tunnel, the captain noticed the strange face painted yellow across its ebony torso.

"It's not broadcasting, whatever it is," Shyce reported. "I'm not getting any kind of reading, nothing. It looks intact, but no energy signatures at all. It's one lonely piece of dead tech."

"Let's hope it stays that way. Quick, deploy some lifter-bots. Let's try and get this heap back up to the surface."

Shyce retreated to her backpack and retrieved a set of four metallic spheres, each the size of a large fist. When she returned, she placed them on the floor of the tunnel at equal points before the robot.

With a few flicks of her control pad, she activated them. They immediately rose into the air and began orbiting the object's torso, communicating with one another, reading and relaying the dimensions and mass of their charge, the location of their controller, the ambient gravitational factor, and the enclosure's dimensions.

A second later, the android slowly lifted into the air. It tilted back, easing into a horizontal position to hover like a parked AG sled, while the spheres circled its suspended form on slow varying ellipses.

"Use smart tech to move dead tech," Shyce said. "God, I sound like a commercial."

"Nice. C'mon, let's go."

They walked back out the short tunnel and into the room where their backpacks lay. They wouldn't need those any longer so they left them, heading straight for the stairwell. The lifter-bots trailed a few steps behind, keeping their charge afloat.

It would be a long climb back up the stairs, but it quickly proved easier without the extra gear to hinder their passage.

Another gnawing doubt outspooked Resa's concern over putting this critical part of the mission behind them—something he couldn't shirk or begin to contemplate until they got away. Eyes lowered, he walked ahead and remained silent, doing his best to hide his anxiety from Shyce.

But halfway up, just as he rounded the landing, she caught his troubled frown through his faceplate and grabbed his arm. "What is it, Sir?"

"That tunnel, that's what," Resa replied gravely. "It didn't dig itself. Someone or something, *somehow* has been here before us." *They may still be in the building. Unless this dead tech isn't so dead.*

As Resa, Shyce, and company started forward again, the captain wanted to add the creeping sense of déjà vu the gatcham thing they carted instilled. Best to keep that to himself. He already had more than enough to fear on this operation without adding conjecture to fan the flames of his crew's fright. And too much blood. *Half gone.* But even that must wait: he'd make time to grieve his lost crew members later—if there was a later.

When Shyce announced that they had reached the surface, Resa joined her in a sigh of release. But their reprieve was stillborn. Through a steadily increasing garble of static on their com-links, a panicked voice surfaced through the chatter, shouting.

"*Zhhhhh*—C-a-a-aptain—*zhhhh*—r-espond-d-d-d!" Brenor. "This is the *Inner Peace*! Captain?"

"Resa here. What's going on, Brenor?" *Nothing was ever*

easy.

"Captain? Finally! You okay? Where are you? What's your ETA?"

"We're fine and en route. We'll be back on the sleigh in a minute. We have the precious cargo. Repeat, we have the PC. We'll need some prep time for the acquisition. Once it's secured, estimate back to the ship inside ten."

"Negative," Brenor countered. "We're coming to you."

A pit formed in Resa's stomach. If Brenor believed it crucial enough to risk the perimeter, it was their worst fear realized. Resa didn't countermand the co-pilot. Brenor's tone brooked no argument. Resa would get his explanation in due course, but he already knew it would stink.

Seconds after he and Shyce emerged from the building, with their PC in tow, night became day as the *Inner Peace*'s floodlights washed the entire crater in a brilliant swathe. The cargo ramp splayed open before the ship touched down.

They ran towards it, abandoning the hovering AG sled where they had parked it.

Resa and Shyce tore up the ramp, which began to close as soon as it sensed contact with their boots. Their payload and its lifter-bot escorts slid neatly in behind them. Airborne before the cargo hatch finished sealing, the *Inner Peace* blasted upward with a punch of vertical thrust. Then, under hard burn, the ship raced south as fast as her screaming engines would go.

Ripping off his helmet, Resa sprinted up to the bridge, leaving the discarded helmet to crash against the cargo bay floor in a series of clamorous protests. The captain barely heard them. Already gone.

Resa found Brenor glued to the helm. Before the winded captain could ask, an anxious Brenor confirmed his fear. "We got bogeys inbound."

"Weapon or ship?"

"Weapon—and it's ID."

"Is it tracking us?"

"Negative, it's heading to the landing site. I dropped a sponder before we came to get you, but we have to get far enough down the planet's surface before we can break line of sight."

Resa smiled inwardly. "Good thinking. Where are they orbiting? Maybe we can get a fix and a firing solution on them—send a salvo their way."

"They're not."

Resa's node shot up. "What?"

"They're not in orbit," said Brenor.

"You're saying they're here on the Stricken?"

"Yes, that's exactly what their attack vector suggests," the co-pilot declared.

Shyce had since joined them on the bridge, eyebrows diving down as she listened to their animated dialogue.

"But why didn't the CBs pick it up?" Resa asked. "We had a perfect halo with the cradle buoys before we even broke atmo."

"They did," Brenor explained, "for about a second or two, before the sentries were destroyed."

"Explain."

"Everything was quiet, skies clear, full 3-60 serenity. Then, about eight minutes ago the cradle buoys started going nuts. They had enough time to monitor the trajectory of the attack, but not enough to engage evasive thrusters. Just a moment to recognize the danger and send us their warning."

"So, what were their last words?"

"The Stricken has its own halo. The launches came simultaneously from two separate SAM sites at either pole."

Resa chewed his lip as he considered Brenor's revelation. "Still, we should've had more warning, provided the buoys didn't malfunction. They should've sensed the hostiles on the ground. Hell, our own flybys would've told us as much."

"The hostiles weren't on the ground," Shyce calmly chimed in. "But beneath it. My guess is that the Imperium's outposts remained hidden until they launched the attack. That's why neither the ship nor the CB's sensors picked them up."

She sidled up beside Resa. "The ID probably dug in shortly after they blasted the planet and trenched deep ever since, waiting to see who'd show up." Shyce paused and took the seat opposite Brenor. "Given the sudden nature of the attack, I wouldn't be surprised if the Demons knew we were here as soon as we jumped into the system."

"It's a gatcham ambush!" For a Tolkane, Brenor was hysterical.

"Okay, okay," Resa placated as he pressed a hand on Brenor's shoulder and leaned in over the co-pilot's console.

Resa had to think fast. With no time to join minds, he scanned the digital map generated on their initial flybys, and a potential escape plan took shape.

"Keep this flight path," Resa instructed. "Stay low on this heading." He pointed to the map. "When we reach the cordillera on that southern continent, change course to match its lay. Drop speed and zigzag through them. They'll help cover our rear. We'll never outrun the ID on this tack, so when we're close enough to the equator, drop-fire a couple more sponders. Then, I want an emergency ascent 90. We go straight up into the debris field of that former moon.

"And after that?" Brenor asked, regaining a modicum of self-control.

"I don't know," Resa confessed. "I'm making this up as I go."

Far away, within the Garaxian subterranean polar base, eyes of pure ice observed. The ID Halo control room's holographic viewscreen painted the pallid figures within it in an ethereal pastel-blue glow. They looked like living corpses with bulging elongated orbs. These white pupil-less slits angled up forming a V from a set of nasal gills that flanked mouths set in permanent frowns.

Their cadaverous faces, bearing features between insectile and reptilian, focused on their assigned duties. Fixed and expressionless, they constituted an asexual race, leaning towards a male gender in appearance with masculine attributes, but essentially, they had no genders, and no hearts—the very concept of emotion anathema, a single impetus drove them: conquest.

The late Dovan called them Garaxians, but all the curs allowed to subsist under the yoke of their omnipotent Imperium referred to them as Ice Demons.

The tactical officer scarcely breathed as he monitored the holographic image of the Tolkane ship speeding southward. He tracked the miniature 3D icon of the vessel, reproduced in the frozen air before it. The Demon regarded it impassively, almost drone-like, but his hands moved with mercurial speed at the controls to relay the ship's changing coordinates to his superior.

So, when the target drastically changed course, instigating a sudden ninety-degree vault straight up, he triangulated the deviation and imparted the information without a second's hesitation.

His commander stood at the back of the room, ready to receive and respond to the tactical development.

The atmosphere was always tense with the Garaxians, but at this moment an even greater air of imminence prevailed. Still, they kept calm, knowing how crucial their roles to the hierarchy of their kind.

The Exarch himself had given the directive and would be waiting for the progress report. He would take the dimmest view of any lack thereof, or any delay for that matter. They all knew never to question authority. To do so would warrant permanent elimination from the Universal Crib.

With the Exarch, the commander now communicated. Secrecy had been rendered superfluous when they eliminated the Tolkane cradle buoys. Otherwise, the surveillance satellites would have revealed the presence of the Garaxian battle group, which had moments before amassed in the system. They would need the small fleet soon—to its fullest efficacy.

No, until they captured that ship, their theft recovered, all other considerations came secondary, so the channels remained open and unencrypted. A matter of quintessential importance hinged on the officer's decades-long reconnaissance in a millenniums-old wait.

Now, the wait was over.

The trap had been sprung, but the commander never suspected for it to happen on his watch. Even more puzzling: the incursion had been instigated by the Tolkane bacterium. Perhaps the time had come for their homeworld to be annexed. Regardless of the outcome, he knew this would be a day of days.

"Analysis?" the commander demanded.

"Estimation based on tactical trend logarithms indicate a 98% probability the *Inner Peace* will break atmosphere and hard-burn for the accretion disk generated by the former satellite's remnants. Once there, it will deploy similar evasive tactics with decoy transponder drones before attempting to make the most suitable jump out of the system."

"How long before that can happen?"

"Three and a half minutes," the tactical officer answered.

"This is a most profound and delicate matter. The Exarch made it clear—no annihilation. Where is the battle group?"

"Holding station at the designated waypoint, midway between the fourth and fifth planet. Their ships can skip into orbit above the Stricken in forty seconds."

"Dispatch a squad of interceptors immediately. Have them provide the Tolkane ship with a proper reception."

13: Fisher
5314 CE

This leg of the journey had been painfully long and arduous, and matters indicated the next leg would be no different. Except maybe worse. Hectored by one problem after another, putting out one brushfire just in time to detect and deal with the next seemed to be the way of life for the six-person crew of the *Skow*.

Limping across interstellar space, they addressed each obstacle with a measure of tenacity, balanced with humour at how impossibly bad their lot had always been.

They held no illusions about the ways of the worlds. After all, the Universe was a very cold place, dotted with the occasional inferno of a burning sun—well actually, several billion to the billionth of them. The lights of those orbs helped the warm-bloods connect the dots of their own frail reality.

But the *Skow*'s crew accepted their modest bundle as they inched along at their snail's pace. Regarding each new test as a challenge kept them sane in the frigid carnival of space and politics.

And none knew that lesson better than the *Skow*'s Tolkani captain, Roland Fisher. If ever there was a 'Non-Garaxian' able to navigate the miasma of control between the Overlords who created it and the cattle they policed and prodded, it was Fisher. A man apart, guided by a loose sense of principles and morals that hinged on survival, open to extreme measures and extreme solutions, which included ship and crew. The captain was tough on them, sure, but never assigned a task he himself wouldn't undertake.

Fisher instilled a rare sense of loyalty in his small posse, simply because he strove never to hide the truth or his faults therein—and there were plenty. He didn't refute them. Rather proudly, he owned them.

Neither a handsome man, with a nose repositioned by squatter camp fights and eyes weathered from everything else, nor particularly clean-kempt, sporting a faded-grey loosely fitted overcoat that draped over an equally dull pair of brown trousers. His tousled hair styled itself on the whim of a situation, usually of the nail-biting variety, and always made him look in dire need of a haircut.

His coyote's smile made up for all of that. In combination with his dishevelled unshaven look and his dishevelled unshaven attitude, it made him a magnet to the opposite sex.

Though the kind of women he most often attracted displayed psychotic inclinations. The little souvenir he bore from his left eye past the corner of his mouth to just shy of his jugular was proof of that. But the scar also instilled in him a sage's ability to read and navigate people.

As a result, Fisher held more than positional power over his crew; he exuded such personal power, they were drawn to his esoteric persona like moths to a light. They followed wherever that light led them. And now, it led them through a patch of isolated space. An expanse quarantined by the Ice Demons.

Luckily, the Imperium rarely noticed captain and crew. Even Fisher's own people regarded them as inconsequential, except perhaps as objects of disdain.

As for Fisher's ship, the *Skow* was neither fast nor pretty, shaped like a snub-nosed pregnant seal. A common model, built as economically as possible to maximize payload at the expense of aerodynamics and fluidity. And for that reason, she was also a discontinued model—rare enough to be considered a collector's piece.

The massive intake manifold located just below the ship's nose resembled a drunken mouth. Two cigar-shaped external thrusters rode the tips of an overhanging delta wing, affixed to the back of the central fuselage.

Without the nacelles, the ship would resemble an unimpressive rock, smoothed and rounded over time by water and wind.

The only exception to the ship's drab look was her fresh paint job, thrown in free of charge back at the shop on Ursula Minor as part of the upgrade package the Funder had insisted on and paid for when he contracted ship and crew. Along with her registration number, she bore her shiny new name proudly on the side of her hull like an aged woman trying to reattain her youth with a smear of blush.

But even her proud name had been marred when they landed on Korian III for resupply. Some punk—probably an Apoc wannabe, had thought it funny to scratch out the *'S'* with a phase-ray. It now read: *kO W.*

Fisher was rightly pissed about the defacement until he saw the humour and irony behind his ship's rechristening. So, he left the alteration. It would make his ship less desirable to potential pirates—well most of them anyway.

The ship's other upgrades were strictly internal. Apart from a commendable med-lab, they included the absolute minimum of refinements: a better sensor array, low-grade weaponry, and lower-grade shielding.

The cradle buoys and escape pods stuffed inside her guts marked the only real visible improvements the captain could acknowledge.

Her true beauty lay in her *invisible* improvements. The *Skow* (or **kow*) had been retrofitted for stealth—that's Stealth with a capital *S*. Her upgrades in that department glowed—simply top-of-the-line, state-of-the-art, here's-mud-in-the-Demons' eye kind of stealth, with double-backup redundancies.

That tech calibre alone would fetch more in salvage than Fisher's entire ship—technically her line of work—if they ever fell prey to a competitor. The trick was not to. Still, not the kind of ship anybody living under the yoke of the Imperium would want, should they find themselves in a sudden firefight.

Better to leave the dogs asleep. Stealth is best when you're outnumbered and outgunned one hundred percent of the time. And given the circumstances of the *Skow*'s latest gig, Fisher was happy knowing he had it at his disposal, in case he needed it later, or quite

111

soon for that matter.

Fisher glanced at his Allianthan pilot, Jonus Baines. "Give me the skinny version, Baines."

"Running silent, Fish," the pilot replied. "If these charts are accurate, our present skip-string will de-spool directly into the central cluster of that former moon's debris field, provided there's no gravitational anomalies generated by the Stricken."

"Yeah well, we are dealing with pirated charts. It looks crowded. Will she hold together in there?"

"So long as we don't collide with any of the bigger chunks, we'll be jumping *limbo a' limbo*." Baines studied his captain for a moment. "You do know how risky this one is, eh Cap?"

"Too well, but this is the backwater course the Funder demanded we take to get the gig in the first place. He insists we have to keep under the radar and out of the shipping lanes."

"Backwater is one thing," Baines persisted, "but this—" the pilot stopped short when the captain shot him a sideways look.

Fisher had already considered everything and didn't want to rile a fifth ear. Baines, perceptive as ever, nodded. "Ah yeah, well, the next part will be the trickiest, but after that, we'll be good. Any of the smaller chunks'll just bounce off her big ass. Once settled, I figure an hour to recharge the core and we'll be gone, clear to the other side of the no-fly zone."

"Good, and after that, Centauris X, right?"

Baines dipped his chin. "We can make the rendezvous in two, maybe three jumps, but those should be easy. Like I said this is the tough one."

"Just keep us invisible, and incommunicado. I needn't remind you how much we're pushing the envelope on this one."

"Since when did we become a courier ship anyway, Fish?" Baines asked.

"When the price became the right one," Fisher said. "Funder's in a hurry. Apparently, he's been waiting a long time to get this packet there, but couldn't trust anybody with a decent boat or legitimate connections to take it across. The ID would've noticed them before they could say, 'We're dead.'"

Fisher allowed himself a grin. "The Demons will take one look at us and write us off as a rogue asteroid or blob of space junk. We're no threat—the Funder knows this. That's why he took our bid. Pat yourself on the back, Baines. We're a bona fide commissioned mail ship now, even if the *Skow*'s just doing his dirty work for him."

"I imagine Doc will want to have a look around. It is a Stricken after all."

"Dr Cholla?" Fisher shot Baines a look of mock chagrin at his mention of the Korian. "Always loves a mystery, that one. Well, he'll have whatever *sciencing* time it takes us to respool and make tracks. We're not tourists here, only passing through. *Only passing through*," he repeated in a lower tone to test his certitude. "Deliver our payload to the Funder and be done with it."

While Fisher chewed the inside of his cheek, Baines tilted his chin up, gaze lingering expectantly—a clear indication he knew his captain hadn't finished.

"But," Fisher continued. "While we're here, no harm in seeing what else we might find. Maybe turn up a glimmer of profit."

Baines smiled.

Stephen Fenech

14: Tourists
Fisher

The energy discharge which exalted the *Skow*'s successful skip into the debris field dissipated into darkness as quickly as it birthed. A moment later, the ship's inertia dampeners kicked in, suppressing its forward momentum and slowing the spacecraft down.

The *Skow* coasted with the odd bit of rocky debris no bigger than a star helmet banging against her hull with a rambunctious but harmless thud. She slowed to a dead stop with the last audible sigh of pressurized gas releasing into vacuum.

"Holy Shi—moly!" Fisher gasped, staring out the forward bridge window. Through the languid jumble of tumbling rock, the desecrated planet loomed before him. Its white sheen resembled that of an ice planet, but the captain knew better.

He was looking at the residual polymer blanket of an expended plasma expulsion suffocating the entire surface. Outside that shell, the atmosphere would have, over the years, dissipated until vacuum reigned. But beneath the surface all the inherent gaseous, volcanic, and tectonic forces metastasised, so perfectly contained, the planet literally ate itself alive. Broiling in some parts, flooding in others, the world had no chance to relieve any pressure until it had reached equilibrium, matching the air 'quality' outside.

Within the bubble, anything not winked out of existence by the brunt of the plasma charge would be dead within a week, after the scant reserve of contained air became toxic. Such callous and forensic exercises in extermination never failed to send a shiver down Fisher's spine. Sickened by it, he forced himself to look away.

"Okay, pad the shields a bit," he croaked. "Manoeuvre us into position for the next jump, and turn our eyes on: full stealth mode. We may have a big butt, but we're gonna keep it a quiet butt. I don't want to hear so much as a far-ar-r$_{rr}$…"

"Fart," Baines finished for him.

"Right, I've got a—"

A flashing com-link interrupted Fisher. It came from the med-lab. *Always loves a mystery.* The captain tapped into the com. "Yeah Doc, you get an hour. We're not going down if that's what you were about to ask."

Dr Lore Cholla's wizened and gentle owl face appeared on the viewscreen, the round but not quite portly man pushed back a pair of half-bottle spectacles with one stubby finger.

"Captain, I found something." *Already!* Fisher was genuinely surprised. "I won't need an hour and… what I found is not on the surface."

Fisher knitted his brows. "Where?"

"Turn the ship's eyes towards the sun, five kilometres off the starboard nacelle. It will be obvious."

Fisher and Baines exchanged a brief look. "Do it," the captain instructed.

Baines accessed the controls and trained the *Skow*'s lenses in the direction of the sun. Sunlight blasted the panorama, washing out all detail from the image. He dialled down the iris and the image calmed, revealing the expected jam of moon debris, rotating on their own errant trajectories, all silhouetted against the dazzling backdrop of the sun's corona. Even with this filtered image, Fisher could not detect anything unusual, just asteroids doing what asteroids did, right across the entire scope of the monitor.

Fisher must have looked as baffled as he felt for Cholla let out an exasperated breath. Through the com-link, the doctor's face flashed with impatience as he transferred control of the external camera from Baines' station to his.

"Hey—?" Baines protested.

"Look," Cholla said.

When the camera zoomed in, Fisher and Baines flinched.

"Goh—rate Scott!" the captain exclaimed.

"Two outdated expressions—within a minute," Baines said, a bemused smile playing on his lips. "This is serious."

116

The captain scoffed, "Can you blame me?"

Baines had been with Fisher, or *Fish* as his crew came to call him, for most of his career. He experienced his captain's penchant for profanity and colourful metaphors from early on. Fisher's habit had gotten him blacklisted by the holier-than-thou religious crusaders who made it their mission to patrol the cosmos spreading 'the Word.'

The *Word* to them stemmed from an amalgamation of several archaic religions, the dogmas of which somehow fused over a few millennia, their ancient origins lost since time out of mind, at least to the common folk who made up your average, or above-average sinners.

Fisher, being one of them—Baines another, knew only that some guy named Jesus fell into cahoots with some rotund fellow named Buddha and along with Muhammad and a few other celebrities formed a splinter religion and the very first God Squad. Their Word took the best aspects of all faiths, but when broken down to its lowest common denominator, it preached, 'Be good.'

One time when the crusaders' patrol took them to a squatter camp on Alliantha, Fisher happened to be there finishing a delivery. Coincidentally, the same camp where Fish eked out the first twenty-five years of his sorry existence.

They found him double-fisting hard liquor in the middle of a more drunken escapade. When Fisher spotted one of the Squad's highest religious leaders, a Tolkane by the name of Cardinal Wisdan, he mistook him for a competitor who had recently tried to swindle him. Fisher confronted the bald pontiff and let out such a litany of creative expletives it would have made the Devil himself blush. Wisdan did more than that.

Having some pull with the local administration, the Cardinal had the captain arrested, locked up, his shipping license revoked, and worst of all: his ship impounded.

When Fisher finally sobered up and realized the predicament that he had landed himself in, he tried to explain his error to the magistrate, but the official ignored him. At Wisdan's behest, the magistrate gave Fisher a choice: to serve penance in the cell for the rest of eternity, or to atone for his transgression by undergoing a behavioural modification procedure, which would ensure 'he never uttered another moral trespass again.'

The choice was simple and the results, interesting. Whenever Fisher had the urge to rant on in his usual diatribe, an implant in his brain would suppress his intended curse and he'd say something much less offensive or very outdated. So, in the face of danger, fear or exasperation the captain voiced less effectual expressions such as *Holy Moly* and *Great Scott* when what he really meant to spill was *Fuck Me*.

It became the subject of endless amusement for the *Skow*'s crew. But now, staring at what had excited Doc to such an extent, even Baines' expression lost all humour. Fisher's own face probably elicited that sobering effect.

Wreckage: unmistakable and incontrovertible bits of hull and junk littered the entire grid Cholla had highlighted for them. Fisher's mind raced as he did the math in his head and used his aptitude for abstract thinking to literally and figuratively put the pieces back together.

"Do you see what I'm talking about *now*?" the Doctor asked stiffly over the com.

"Twelve small ships, maybe fourteen," Baines confirmed. "One is definitely Tolkane, but the others?"

"Is that even possible?" Cholla asked. "Could it be true that someone found a way to take out, not only one but a small fleet of Demon Interceptors?"

"That's just up close, Doc," Baines said. "Look a little further out. There's… Jesus, Fish, I think I see the remains of a few battlewagons, and a fucking dreadnaught to boot!"

Fisher chewed his lip. "If that's the case, then at some point in time, a legitimate threat *to* the Overlords existed. But just by seeing this, our danger curve soars. If word of this ever got out, the sh-poo wouldn't just hit the fan, it'd smother the room, home, and entire planet, with some to spare for a pretty moon. There's a reason why the Demons didn't clean up this mess."

A sinking feeling swallowed Fisher, forcing him to recall the tragic story of Vorancia, the late LUW President—the final nail in the undercastes' coffin. A lesson prefaced by Fisher's own experiences as an orphaned kid back at the squatter camp on Alliantha, growing up with all the other pooled humanoids at the site. A lesson drilled into his skull: nobody opposes the Imperium, *nobody*.

It became Fisher's code, one he lived by since his trials and travails began in that refugee camp and later aboard the myriad mercenary ships he landed on—the key being, he still breathed for it. But now, for the first time in his life, he had broken that code.

"Tell me we're alone out here." A cautious timbre fretted the captain's voice.

"That's what the *Skow*'s eyes and ears tell us," Baines reported.

"Alright, we can afford to get a little curious then. Take us in closer, but slowly Baines—manoeuvring thrusters only. Keep spooling the main engines and get Bliter to watch our back. He can man the *Skow*'s sensors. I want you completely focused on the remnants of that Tolkane ship. That's the black sheep in this muddle." Fisher stabbed a finger at the monitor. "Take us *there* first."

Baines gave him a quick thumbs-up. The captain turned back to the com-link. "Doc, get your butt up here."

The *Skow* let out a sigh as Baines siphoned compressed air from the ship's main pressure tanks and channelled it into sets of tiny vents near the aft port nacelle. The manoeuvre coaxed the ship's hull to pivot on its centre axis until the *Skow*'s snub nose trained perfectly on their goal.

Firing three controlled bursts from the stern exhaust vent, Baines nudged the bulky ship forward. It slipped into a glide, crossing the debris-littered gap quickly and with uncharacteristic grace. As she neared her target, the *Skow* fired reverse gas thrusters sunk in her prow. The vessel coasted to a full stop, just over the wreckage of the Tolkane ship.

"Light it up," Fisher instructed. "Let's see this for ourselves."

The narrow beams of the *Skow*'s spots kicked in, illuminating bits of wreckage as they crossed into the beams' fields. Several moments passed before something, almost indiscernible in the roaring aura of the sun framing it, caught the captain's notice. Unmistakably, a piece of the Tolkane ship's hull drifted beyond the main cluster. Fisher pointed to the elusive bit on the screen. "See this? Draw it in close with the tractor beam."

Baines locked on to the four-metre-long portion and engaged the beam. The target immediately drew up, settling into a static hold 20 metres before the *Skow*'s nose. Close enough that Fisher no longer needed the cameras so he looked out the window. Written in shiny black letters across the curved fragment, the ship's name read:

Inner Peace.

"Run it through the Box, search the Tolkane registries. I want to know where the fuzz it came from and why it's here."

"I can answer that."

Fisher jumped and spun. Saul Bliter, the *Skow*'s raptor-eyed navigator and general crewman raised a hand and smile in defence. "Sorry, Captain," he laughed. "Didn't mean to startle you. I stepped in during your retrieval—didn't want to interrupt."

A rush of blood filled Fisher's ears at the stocky man's smirk. "Why aren't you at your post?"

"I am—monitoring by remote." Bliter raised his forearm and presented the wrist pad saddled there.

The captain relented. "Okay, tell me."

Bliter fanned a hand through his dark hair and raised his com-pad for Fisher to see. "The *Inner Peace* left Hagen's Shipyard on Ursula Minor after a retrofit. Departed on a private sortie, roughly two hundred years ago. Mission unknown. Reported missing by some Tolkane Funder shortly thereafter. Fate of ship and crew: unknown."

Fisher crossed his arms. "How do *you* know this?"

"I was with Doc when he first uncovered the scrap pile. Trained a peripheral infra-red camera myself while he spoke with you over the com. That's when I noticed the name on the bit and ran the identification. When I found the info, to save time, I came up immediately to tell you in person. This isn't the safest place to linger discussing history."

That mollified the captain and he tilted his chin forward. "Quick thinking, but Ursula Minor?" A sudden realization made him gasp. "That's the same yard where we got our fix-up."

"Hate to say it but infra-red revealed something more—an active power cell."

Fisher gulped. "Active?"

Bliter turned to the pilot. "Baines, flip that fragment 180 degrees. Something's attached to the opposite side."

Fisher gave him a cursory nod. Baines angled back to his console and did as Bliter ordered. The curled piece of hull scrap pivoted. There, attached to the underside of the fragment, previously hidden in the shadow of its concave shape, sprawled the unmistakable figure of a robot, apparently magnetized to the hull bit. It looked like a poised mechanical spider.

Fisher felt as if he just jumped off a ledge, a very high ledge, with no going back. He could only freefall and see what the Tolkane fates had in store.

"Bring it into the cargo bay," Fisher said bitterly. "We're already dead just for being here. Might as well find out why."

"Captain?" Cholla chimed in over the com. *What now?* "Since you're already going to open up the *Skow*'s bay doors to space, might I suggest we retrieve another find?"

"What? There's another one of these things?"

"No, Captain." The doctor paused. "It looks to me like an escape pod. And it appears intact, lodged within a cleft cut into one of the asteroids. If we lock on with the tractor and—"

"Forget it, Doc. We take the fragment and get the f-heck out of here."

"It's a Tolkane pod," Cholla pressed. "May give us some more clues about the robot—and what happened here."

"Too risky—might be a trap," Bliter warned over the captain's shoulder. "I think we should quit while we're ahead… while we still have heads."

Fisher studied Bliter for a moment before looking at Baines. The pilot only stared back, his blank expression giving no opinion one way or the other.

"Ah, Fuh-*darn it*." The captain struggled with his quelled expletive a moment longer before the inhibitor kicked it back inside. Pragmatism replaced profanity. "How are the engines, Baines?"

"Vigour's back. Ready for a skip-string on your command. Full jump capability in five."

"—minutes," Fisher acknowledged with a dip of his chin. "Okay, we'll try and bring both targets in, if we can. But don't dally, and don't jump, unless things get piping hot. Skips only until we're well clear of the unfriendly zone." The captain shifted his scrutiny to the com-link monitor. "Doc, you get one shot only. Scoop the trash and go, understood?"

Over the com, Cholla beamed, head bobbing. Bliter grimaced.

Fisher half-shrugged in the navigator's direction. "Can't please everyone."

When the crew had stowed the hull fragment, its robot passenger, and the escape pod safely in the cargo bay, the *Skow* aligned herself on an escape vector, adjusting attitude and telemetry for her next skip.

A moment before she winked out of normal space into hyperspace, the robot in her cargo hold lit up like a Christmas tree as it came back to life.

When the signal screamed across the vast chasm of interstellar space, it marked the beginning of the end. But the Garaxian capital ship receiving it was oblivious to any of this at the time. The same held true for its Demon crew and commander. But the electronic message carried a highest priority tag, originating from the Garaxian homeworld, from the seat of the Imperium's Exarch himself.

The transmission interfaced with the ship's systems, which had no way of denying it access. When the communications officer saw that part of the signal was a live AV packet, he relayed it directly to the Garaxian commander of the monstrous vessel. A two-way channel opened and the Exarch himself materialized on the holoscreen.

"Commander?" he droned like a funeral dirge.

The commander bowed reverently. "Supreme Master."

"Were you not the same Garaxian assigned to the polar base on Earth at the time when the robot was extracted and destroyed?"

"I was, My Lord, but that occurred more than 200 years ago."

"Did you not report that the closest interceptors met with lethal force in the moon's accretion disk when the *Inner Peace* self-destructed, obliterating the robot and ultimately our chance to unravel the mystery surrounding the veiled threat—a matter I regard to be most poignant and delicate?"

"I did." The commander could not feign the resignation in his voice. He knew where this discussion led. Remembered too that he'd ordered the destruction of the second wave sent in immediately after the demise of the first. The months-long search through the field did not uncover any trace of the robot.

"How then, Commander, can you explain that the cradle buoys left in the abandoned system picked up the energy signature of your obliterated robot not two hours ago?"

"I—cannot," he replied truthfully.

"Then, Commander," the Exarch's voice seethed like acid. "Since the duties of your office have proven beyond your capabilities, you are no longer fit to command your vessel or any other. Your entire fleet and crew have been attainted and made inconsummate by your incompetence. So, they too have no place

123

in the Imperium. I consider you and those you command, warm-blood. I must exact the appropriate penance."

The commander understood, bowed, and said no more.

Moments later a command protocol that formed the bulk of the Exarch's communication told the capital ship's engines what to do.

The plasma explosion that detonated the massive engines obliterated the ship and blazed with the light of a thousand suns before winking back into blackness a second later.

The resulting shockwave, however, continued to expand, causing a chain reaction that took out more than a hundred heavy cruisers, cutters, and interceptors, every last ship in the former commander's battle group. The event affected all the in-system planets, the closest with catastrophic repercussions in the form of earthquakes and tsunamis.

Penance was served.

15: Maelstrom
Fisher

When Baines announced that the *Skow* had safely jumped into Centauris X space, completely clear of the no-fly zone, Fisher felt no relief. His guard was up and he broke into a cold sweat, or rather reactivated it. The sweat actually began immediately following their first skip when Cholla reported that the robot in their cargo hold was functioning.

Not wanting to take any chances, Fisher ordered the bay sealed and off-limits until after their rendezvous with the Tolkane cutter, *Maelstrom.*

He had Doc monitor any activity with the deck's surveillance camera, but so far, thankfully, the robot played nice. There were a few anxious moments when it first rose from the hull fragment it surfed in on. The robot hovered in the middle of the bay and stared up at the camera as if deciding how to take it out. Or take the crew out.

But then, to Fisher's relief, Mr Gearbox floated back to the curved scrap, pivoted into a horizontal position and hunkered down again. When all its telltale lights dimmed to darkness, its smiley-face tattoo gave Fisher the impression it was satisfied with the arrangement.

Smile or not, Fisher wasn't about to let his guard down, assigning a motion/energy detector to the surveillance feed. The *Skow* would know if the robot started up again. The captain left it at that, having more pressing matters to attend to.

After the first few skips had taken them safely outside the quarantined patch, Fisher made Baines change his flight plan. Rather than following the Funder's prearranged course, Baines deviated, taking an ancillary route. He also staggered the detour, executing shorter and more frequent skips.

It would take the *Skow* substantially longer than if she jumped outright, but when she finally did arrive in Centauris X space, her engines wouldn't be as exhausted and could be respooled in a fraction of the time.

Fisher rubbed his neck and exhaled. Now that they arrived, he felt a sudden urge to break away and make a run for it. But as much as he wanted to abort, his gut told him not to. And he trusted his gut if nothing else. Working moisture into his mouth, he turned to Baines. "How far are we from the rendezvous point?"

"Under standard burn, we'll get there in eleven minutes," the pilot said. "Coordinates are set."

Fisher chewed his lip. "Make it twenty. Is our partner broadcasting yet?"

"Yup. She's waiting for us and… hailing. Do we answer?"

"No," the captain decided. "She'll be able to see us with her scopes if we do. These stealth upgrades have to be worth something. Might as well make full use of them. The *Maelstrom* will know we're here when we decide to let her know. Till then, let's play to our anonymity—just another Allianthan heap passing through the sector. We're back in regulated space after all and traffic should be plenty."

"Understood," said Baines as he carried out the order.

The plan was to rendezvous with the *Maelstrom* in a local void, thus avoiding any chance witnesses. Their exchange would take place in the upper mesosphere of a local gas giant. But it also meant that lightning perturbations in the planet's ionosphere would impair the visual acuity of the *Skow*'s sensors when she drew close to the Tolkane ship.

As the *Skow* closed to a distance of 120 kilometres, Fisher ordered Baines to cut the engines. The ship coasted freely, Fisher's trepidation mounting with every kilometre.

Although the cutter sat right where she was supposed to, the roiling mass of gases had obscured the details of her specs. Furthermore, there seemed to be an unusual number of asteroid bits scattered amidst the coalescing gas clusters.

Ten kilometres short of their target, Fisher instructed Baines to slow the *Skow* further and surf her through a melange of noctilucent clouds. At five hundred metres, the ship came to a dead stop, hovering between a pair of fortress-sized cumulonimbus clouds.

"Lock cameras and remove our cloak," Fisher instructed. "Let her see us."

Baines did. Nothing happened.

Out in the distance, the *Maelstrom* hadn't moved. As though the ship remained completely oblivious to the *Skow*'s presence.

"Unless, that's what they want us to think," Fisher said aloud. *Asteroids—or fragments*?

Before Baines could ask his captain what he meant, the ombre mass of grey and yellow clouds billowing past the cutter's hull cleared. When it did, Fisher's head cleared—of all blood.

"Abort!" he cried. "It's a gh-*da*-Demon Interceptor. The *Maelstrom*'s destroyed. Quick Baines, get us the fhhhh—" he scrunched up his wrinkles, then let them spring. "!—*outta* here!"

Knee-jerked, Baines fired up the engines and aligned the *Skow* for the furthest, most elusive jump the ship could muster.

The black sky above them suddenly filled up with ID interceptors and cutters skipping in, one and two at a time, trying to block the *Skow*'s escape.

"Evasive!" Fisher commanded. "And cloak us!" *For all the good it will do us now.*

A moment later, the more-than-deft Baines found a gap.

And the *Skow* winked out of the sector.

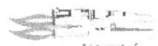

"Guess life just got a lot more complicated for us, eh Cap? Captain?"

Fisher didn't respond to Baines' question. The captain had retreated into his own private world as he stood staring out the bridge's port window. He contemplated the incredible chain of events, which led him into this predicament, and what he must do under the circumstances. What he would do.

At length, Fisher spoke. "I don't think they got a fix on our exact position, ergo our trajectory but they sure knew we were there. And even with the stealth upgrade, they saw us reactivate it, so they'll be looking for that first. We'll be safe for a while yet, unless…"

"Unless what?" asked Bliter.

"Nothing," Fisher answered. He faced his pilot, staring up at him. "Great on the evasives, Baines, as always. Now, let's see if it got us any extra points. I won't launch sponders—trick's too old. Bet that's what the *Inner Peace* tried. Besides, the Uglies are crafty buggers. They'll trace the drones back to us, and if that happens, space'll get a lot smaller. No, we'll keep them intact, and make a run for it, big butt and all."

"Where to?"

Fisher met Baines' searching eyes. "I'm thinking we try a one-night stand. How far are we from the Junkyard?"

Baines nibbled his lower lip and lifted his eyes to an overhead panel. "Eight or nine."

"Jumps—right." Fisher idly scratched his nose. "Break the last four into two or three skip-strings and ply them along an erratic jibe. That'll make it more cumbersome if they try scanning for residuals. It's a good bet the Junkyard's our only option, apart from surrender, and we all know how that'd pan out. How's our guests?"

"Robot's apparently in some kind of standby mode and we extracted the two Tolkane from that escape pod," said Baines. "Way past induced torpor. Deep-frozen. No vitals, but we won't know if they made it until Doc tries to revive them. Anyway, we transferred them into the cryo-tubes as you instructed."

"Good. Keep 'em on ice until we get our bearing. If the coast is clear we'll thaw them. Doc's right. Maybe they *can* shed some more light on this cluster f—ull. In the meantime, I'm going to take a look at that packet—now that the delivery's off with no foreseeable payday in our dim-at-best future."

When Fisher paused and ran a finger down the contour of his scar, Baines grinned. "Yes, Fish?"

"We spooked Big Brother something fierce to merit so many armada ships homing in on us. Makes me more than a little curious to find out what that might be. And that packet is as good a place to start as any. Might recover the balance of funds owed us after all. I'll be in my quarters."

Baines turned back to his console and plotted his captain's flight plan. Bliter and Doc exchanged resigned frowns.

Fisher paid them a cursory glance as he strode off the bridge. His crew knew as well, the ride was about to get a lot bumpier.

16: Junkyard
Fisher

The lunar cave entrance offered the six crew members of the *Skow* a good view of their ship—just before she winked out of the system. The *Skow* had faithfully served most of them as home and transport for the last eleven years. And now she was gone.

Fisher let out a sigh, which caused his helmet to briefly fog as he trained his eyes on Baines.

Sitting in the driver's seat of the small rover, the pilot looked up from his com-pad and swivelled his torso around his seat, as best as his bulky EVA suit would allow. Through his helmet's visor, an unmistakable grin spread across his face. "She's away, Fish. Plan B is officially in effect."

Apart from the pilot and himself, the crew's blank faces revealed they had no clue what Plan B could be.

"Give them the abbreviated version, Baines." Fisher prompted.

"Our um, ghost ship will loop a bit," the pilot said. "She'll figure-eight across three systems before performing a full shutdown. Auto Evasive is engaged so the *Skow* should reach her destination before going to sleep. Then, it's a cold lullaby."

"That's great!" Bliter admonished in a fury, shaking features going red-purple. His eyes bulged, then narrowed like stifled combustion. "What about us? If I knew how you guys would debauch the job, I never would've told you about it. We're stranded down here with no hope in hell. Even with the suits' air recyclers and bio-regulators, we'll just sit here and fucking rot with the rest of that junk floating up there."

Bliter stabbed a gloved hand up at the metallic graveyard, nicely framed by the irregular walls of the cave mouth. Crowded with so much space junk: dead, stripped-to-the-bone ships, useless cargo, and the odd frozen-solid corpse, the *Yard* saturated the night sky.

Baines' expression darkened. "Cheer up, Bliter, before you give yourself an aneurysm. Your head explodes inside that thing, we'll call you Blister."

Everyone laughed. Except Bliter who regarded the pilot with a tight look of fracturing ice.

Cholla cleared his throat to intercede. "We appreciate the heads-up on the job, Bliter, but you've only been with us six months. Fisher never would have let us down here on this rock if he didn't have a viable plan." He turned to the captain. "You do have a plan, don't you?"

Fisher shrugged, knowing how positively comical the gesture made him look in his puffed-up EVA suit. After a moment, he nodded. "I do, Doc. I do."

"Can you enlighten us then?" Bliter said, temerity fretting his voice.

"For now, we sit tight and wait," Fisher said. "It won't be long, kiddos."

The crew fell quiet and waited with what struck Fisher as feigned calm, their suited body parts moving idly, visors tilted up, eyes tracking wayward bits of the floating debris parade. Fisher chewed the inside of his cheek and breathed. And breathed.

After several protracted minutes, three ID interceptors winked into view, very close to where the *Skow* had been before she skipped away.

"Right on cue," Fisher observed.

The ships did not linger very long—a few minutes to recognize and dismiss the residual trails of the three decoy-sponders. As the captain expected, they found the *Skow*'s true trajectory and jumped out of system once more."

"Cavalry's gone," Baines confirmed. Fisher turned his restrictive helmet and exchanged another foolish grin with his pilot.

"But once they find her, the Demons will blow her the fuck up," Bliter snapped, his frustration mounting again.

"Nope, I don't think so." Fisher craned his neck to the littered heavens. "Sure, they'll capture her after she powers down, board and search her top to bottom—hopefully not too brutishly—but they won't destroy her outright."

"How can you say that?" the crewman fumed.

Fisher lowered his gaze and met the navigator's stare. "Because, Bliter, what they want is no longer aboard the *Skow*."

"The packet?"

Fisher shook his head and gestured to the open bucket hold at the rear of the rover where the robot and the two cryo-tubes stretched out politely. On such short notice, Baines had fashioned a makeshift gurney out of the same piece of hull scrap the robot used as a security blanket.

"And besides," Fisher said, "if I know the Demons the way I know the Demons, they'll let the *Skow* sit right where we parked her." *If we were still aboard, they'd have tortured and killed us without a second thought.* "Oh, they'll set a watch of course, from a distance. They'll linger there forever if they have to, waiting for us to come back for her, but they won't destroy her."

"So, that's it then, for the *Skow*?" Bliter asked, the uneasy timbre in his voice unmistakable. "If she's history, so are we."

"I didn't say that either," Fisher replied evenly. "I thought for a while that maybe the Imperium was interested in our undeliverable packet, but when I gave it some juice and opened it up, all I found was a series of command protocols and a few executable files to access and unzip more data in its CPU."

"Anything in the database?" Cholla asked.

"It's written in a language I've never seen before, like some kind of runes," Fisher said. "Maybe it's an archaeological record log, but whatever the device is, it doesn't work—benign. I copied some of the files and ran them through a translation program over the Box, but no dice. In fact, the only thing about it I know for sure is that it's called, *Dovan*."

"How'd you figure that out, Fish?" Baines asked.

"Cause it's written on the casing, in English," Fisher laughed.

"Maybe I could take a look." Doc ventured. "Might still be connected to all this."

"I'll let you," the captain agreed. "I brought it along for that exact reason."

"Um, one small problem," Bliter said, his voice dripping with sarcasm. "We have no Box, we have no ship, and, oh yeah, we're stranded on a *fucking* moon!"

131

Instead of getting angry at Bliter's outburst, Baines and Fisher erupted into an uncontrolled bout of laughter, which caused their microphones to gargle with static. When the captain finally brought his mirth under control he turned to Baines. "I think it's time we woke up the twin."

"Copy that, Captain." Baines applied his mitted hands to the rover's double-toggle control levers and engaged the transmission. The rover spun 180 degrees on its centre axis so that it faced the abyss within. Then, with a lurch, the vehicle vaulted forward and proceeded deeper into the thicker darkness of the cave. Fisher took one last look over his shoulder as the Junkyard became obscured in a grey cloud of stirred-up moondust.

Bliter grappled Fisher's arm and stutter-baulked. "What are you *doing*?"

"I'm starving," Fisher said jovially as he removed the navigator's hand. "Evidently, we'll need some less-cramped shelter pretty soon."

"Nothing like stating the obv-i…" The navigator's complaint trailed into silence. Something further inside the lunar cave materialized. Something big, metallic, reflected the twin light beams generated by the rover's headlamps.

As the vehicle plodded towards it, pushing deeper into the cavern, everyone, except Fisher and Baines, had their mouths open, rendered dumb. The rover's headlamps revealed another ship, but not just any ship. A vessel identical to the *Skow* in every last detail.

Except one. The insignia painted on the side of her hull read… *Skow II*. Fisher was a bizarre one.

The captain had not exaggerated. It *was* a twin to the ship they had all watched skip out of system not an hour before.

Parked neatly on a relatively flat expanse of cave floor, the inert *Skow II* sat lucidly like a sleeping beast resting her big butt on her haunches. Three triple-strutted landing gear assemblies, one beneath her stubby nose and two further back, nearing her aft section, supported the vessel.

Without hesitation, Baines drove the rover beneath the surrogate ship's nose. Directly below its central intake manifold, he brought the stout buggy to a blunt stop.

A laborious process followed as Baines tapped into the hermetically sealed bubble of life, accessing the right encrypted access controls on his com-pad. His thick gloves kept hampering his efforts, but eventually, the pilot lowered the ship's ramp behind the landing carriage. He immediately drove the rover around the strut, up the slope, and into the ship's cargo bay.

Once the bay door sealed behind them, Baines climbed down and walked over to a wall-mounted control panel, while the rest of the crew remained seated in the rover. It took a while longer: first light, then pressurized air, and finally heat brought the ship's internal environment back up to a nominal level.

"*Skow II* is officially capable of supporting a warm-blood's sorry ass again," the pilot announced. The others hastily alighted from the vehicle and formed up.

Fisher removed his helmet first. His nose bunched up as he inhaled the stale, slightly acrid air, but it would do. Knowing that it would only become cleaner and more breathable with each passing moment, the captain dipped his chin at his cadre. They removed their helmets.

"Okay, might as well keep the same quarters you had on the *Skow*," Fisher said before turning to Gars Brumbal, his heftiest crew member. "Before you settle in, Tank, stow Mr and Mrs Freeze in a cryo-storage locker and unload Mr Gearbox same as before. After—" Fisher stopped himself midsentence when he noticed Brumbal and most of the others staring at him, smiling wide and slowly shaking their heads.

"What?" Their attention made Fisher feel uncomfortable and he turned to Bliter, busy fidgeting with the gloves of his EVA suit. The crewman's flushed face and evasive eyes did little to hide his chagrin.

"How is this even *possible*?" asked Cholla, drawing Fisher's scrutiny.

"Let me explain, Doc," Baines offered. "As you undoubtedly know, the Junkyard is precisely that: a heap of ship parts, floating aimlessly, but corralled by the vaster-than-usual Lagrange point between this moon and another. Mind you, the point's more of a pen in this hood."

The doctor nodded before turning to the others. "Both moons are tidally locked, orbiting the same gas giant. The gravitational forces governing all three celestial bodies are aligned in syzygy, so precisely balanced there's virtually no tidal variance or drift, nor has there been since the mini-system formed."

Cholla removed his mitts and unzipped the front of his enviro-suit without breaking his explanation. "That's why so many merchants who've acquired odd bits of space junk, fragments of starships and the like, find it such a suitable spot to deposit wares they no longer desired to cart around the galaxy. Bits are tagged with adhesive decals but otherwise abandoned, hauled around the gas giant, merry-go-round fashion while clenched in the perfectly-equal grasp of the two moons. There's no risk of theft as the chances of anyone finding anything useful are slim at best."

"And even if they did, well, good for them," Baines chortled. "But, since Fisher's bit of junk wasn't a bit of junk, we couldn't just leave it floating out there with the rest of the melange."

The pilot removed a glove and couched it in his armpit. "So, Cap had me take it one step further. After scanning from orbit with seismic radar, we uncovered this subterranean cavern—a long-extinct lava tube."

Baines removed the other bulky mitt. "I used a couple of mini-nukes to tap into the wall of the closest crater. That way, our makeshift garage remained hidden from on high. It's just another natural fissure." He raised his hands, presenting both gloves like evidence. "And the rest is history."

Cholla listened intently, chin bowing and lifting throughout Baines' explanation. But once the pilot finished, he pulled off his spectacles and rubbed the bridge of his nose. "Okay, the crew understands that, but—" he seated his glasses again. "—what I first meant was, how did you acquire the second ship?"

"Right," Baines chuckled. "Um, Fish and I commandeered it off some no-life pirates trying to do the same to us, bout a year before you came onboard. Now, *that* was a shitstorm, Doc, even for Fish. But our ever-resourceful captain saw its rainbow, specifically the precise location of our attacker's life support modules."

Baines threw Fisher an appreciative smirk. "See, unlike the pirates, Fish understood all the nuances of his own ship better than anyone. Proved it that day, knowing exactly how and where to hit them with countermeasures."

The pilot took a deep breath as he dropped his mitts to the floor and began unfastening his suit's belt-lock. "The pirates drew first blood, pounding the shit out of us, but they didn't expect us to return the favour. Fisher paid them back with interest, sending a couple of attack missiles to distract them and soften up their ship's shielding—at its most vulnerable chink. When a brief gap opened up, we made a surgical hit with a phase-cannon blast."

An audible click and sigh accompanied the unfastening lock around Baines' waist and he shimmied the suit's lower half to the grating. With the boots permanently married to it like hip waders, he had to unsheathe his legs from the pile he made. "An effective combination one-two punch into her underbelly, which quite literally knocked the wind out of her. The pirates didn't know what hit them, till they froze and imploded in vacuum."

"Cap always struck me as a fighter on the ropes," Cholla said. "He takes a beating, but comes back swinging."

Fisher smiled inwardly as he looked on but did not comment.

"So, what happened next?" the doctor pressed.

Baines began pulling the top half of his spacesuit up and over his head. "After all their ship's air vented into space, she was ours for the taking. If the marauders had more experience with the *Skow*'s class, or lack thereof," he added as his head emerged, hair dishevelled, "the tables might've been turned, but not likely. Still, we needed to figure out what to do with our new acquisition. We couldn't sell it for it might've led to questions, and more pirates, or worse, an ID intervention."

"Even so," Fisher added, rubbing the back of his neck and laughing, "it'd be like trying to sell a goat at a horse auction."

Baines inclined his chin. "So, we brought her here, to the Yard, after we jettisoned the corpsicles still aboard, repaired the wounds we'd done her, and cleaned out the interior."

The pilot tossed the last suit article on the pile he'd made.

"With all her systems successfully brought back online, the resurrected and rechristened *Skow II* came under her own power to this long-term parking spot. If anything, we now had a full backup for every part—in case something went wrong with the *Skow.*"

"But I never thought I'd be backing up the whole darn ship," Fisher added with regret. "What can you do? The *Skow*'s become a hunted bird."

Jiri Plough, Fisher's petite engineer ran a hand through her long cinnamon mane. "No half-measures from you, Cap—you're a Fish with teeth." she extolled. "A real card shark who never runs out of cards to play, no matter how many chips are down or how grim our table's set."

"Well, little lady," Fisher replied, flashing his patented coyote grin down at her. "That's how we stay in the game is all. That's how we stay in the game."

"Speaking of which, Cap, what's our next move?" Cholla asked.

"We can't fire the engines out there," Fisher said. "The Demons might be able to trace us when they double back, which they surely will. We're gonna have to coast—as silent and cold as possible for a few days."

"Tractor beam?" Baines asked as he crouched and gathered the pile he'd made.

"Tractor beam," Fisher confirmed.

Baines stood with his effects. "Where to?"

"I've got a plan, but you may not like it."

The first part of Fisher's plan had a certain eloquence to it, and an element of pragmatism, but considering the alternatives, it had the trappings of a viable strategy. The captain was a man who trusted his instinct and when he got the ball, he ran with it.

"Having so many ships on the prowl for us is a statement in itself," Fisher explained. "We got the hottest potato that ever came out of the oven, and everybody will want to stick their fork in it—including rich Funders. One of our three acquisitions alone would fetch the finest price once a potential merchant or guild finds out the kind of response we elicited from the Imperium. If we pitch it right, it'll speak volumes, and I think I know where we might start, but first things first."

The crew stepped forward, tightening their knot around their captain.

"Apart from the Junkyard's stable gravitational parameters, one other aspect which makes it so popular is its location," Fisher said. "It lies in a corridor, at the perfect juncture of three major shipping lanes. Traffic here is regular, so it's quite easy for an unremarkable ship like the *Skow,* or *Skow II,* to get lost in.

"Unfortunately, all the stealth upgrades adorning the flagship are still aboard the *Skow.* Had no time to pass any of her hide-and-go-seek goodies over here to the surrogate. While the *Skow*'s playing cat and mouse with the Overlords, we have to rely on a different kind of subterfuge."

All heads leaned in. Fisher paused as he shrugged his shoulders and wiggled out of his enviro-suit. He didn't bother unfastening the belt-lock as Baines had done, pulling the whole suit down onesie-style until it hung between his waist and knees like a half-peeled banana. "Luckily, these same shipping lanes are plied every month or so by the God Squad, out on one of their religious crusades to spread the Word. They travel in small convoys of ships."

"Everything's small compared to a Demon flotilla," Baines remarked.

"True enough," Fisher agreed. "So, the Holies connect their pious dots with all the heathen, yet-to-be-emancipated worlds, broadcasting their beliefs across subspace as they go, on every channel in every known language. Most of the time, I tune them out, but this time I think I might lend them an ear, or twelve, not counting the freezies and the gearbox."

"What exactly are you proposing?" queried Bliter, wariness souring his visage.

With a wry smile, Fisher described the rest of his plan, and just as he suspected they didn't like it.

But they didn't question the captain either, not after what he managed to pull. All of them understood they had to position themselves as far away from here as quickly and as quietly as possible. Working as a team, they executed Fisher's orders exactly as instructed. Between Jiri, Doc, Baines, and Bliter, that positioning had to be a coordinated effort of timing, mathematics, navigation, and pure gall.

Firing up the anti-grav pads beneath the *Skow II*'s underbelly, Baines retracted the landing struts and brought the ship into a stable hover in the middle of the cave. After that, it became a delicate matter of intermittently locking onto opposite cavern walls with the tractor beam, drawing the ship left, then right, and a little left again, ultimately nudging the ship into a gentle forward tack.

The process was painstakingly slow at first, but the further they pushed and prodded the *Skow II* towards the cave's mouth, the wider the enclosure became, and with it their speed and margin of error.

Patience and tenacity ruled Baines' hand on the yoke and before long the lava tube vomited its charge.

They were out, hovering nice and neat in open space but still within the moon's crater.

Doc figured out the math for the next part of their escape. With the help of all the litter floating above them, he targeted the scuttled ships or pieces of space junk that had a greater mass than the *Skow II* or could be stacked together to mimic greater mass. Baines laid in the course and Jiri applied the right amount of tractor beam strength to draw the ship out.

In this way, they traipsed around the Junkyard until they achieved enough momentum to send her sailing out. It took Bliter a bit of effort to tweak the attitude jets to attain the perfect heading, but soon the *Skow II* coasted freely away from the yard—with her engines still cold.

Fisher smiled as the last bits of outlying junk sallied past the bridge window. The *Skow II's* resurrection may have been subtle, but it sure was memorable. The reawakened sister ship continued to silently glide towards the correct shipping corridor where, hopefully, her crew would find and latch onto the unsuspecting missionaries.

To that effect, Fisher thought, this might be a good time to take up prayer.

17: God Squad
Fisher

"These, *darn* zealots!" an exasperated Fisher complained. "When you don't want them around, they sprout up like weeds, infesting all of known space. And then when you actually do need them, the *fu*-lyers are nowhere to be found."

After thirteen days of cold sailing, most of the foodstuffs the crew had transferred over from the *Skow* came close to depletion. Hearing all his crew's protests, Fisher responded with some aggravated derivative of *my goodness* and *fudge me sideways with a spoon.*

All parties breathed a collective sigh of relief when they finally received the holy countersignal they so anxiously awaited.

Fisher took a deep breath to steady himself. "Okay everybody, it's poker time." He switched on the com and peered into the screen as the monitor came alive. Prefaced by a series of quick chirps and beeps, a two-way audio channel opened. But so far, no video feed, at least not from the holy side.

"This is Roland Fisher, captain of the *Skow II*—out of Ursula Minor," he clarified. "We picked up your broadcast and with our rations critically low, your promise of food and shelter sounds really good. I have a small flock of potential converts. If by the divine grace of God, you'd grant us an audience to plead our case in person, we might join you for a short while, strive for absolution and—" *board, fuel, resupply, invisibility.* "Enlightenment."

The captain licked his lips nervously, glanced away, and caught Baines grinning at him. "If I didn't actually *know* you," the pilot whispered, "I'd take you seriously."

Fisher flared his nostrils and pressed a finger to his lips. Baines raised his hands and mouthed a silent 'oops.'

The static from the other end maddened Fisher, so he dug deeper as he returned his attention to the monitor. "I bear my soul—open to you. I'll seek repentance for all former trespasses." The note of earnestness and guilt in his pitch was unmistakable, and unmistakably practised. Hopefully, it would come across as authentic—the food part sure was.

Fisher's heartbeats kept time with the radio static for a few more anxious seconds, but finally, his hails were answered. "This is the *Crucifix* of Shepherd Fleet One," an authoritative voice responded through the viewscreen speakers. "What happened to the original *Skow*, Captain, or did you merely change the name of that heap to make you feel better?"

Fisher's mouth formed a frozen O as a face materialized on the monitor, regarding him with a mix of smug amusement and disdain. It was none other than the pontiff responsible for his behavioural inhibitor, Cardinal Wisdan.

"Converts? Bah!" The bald holy man let out a dry laugh. "Con-*victs*, I would sooner believe. But no matter," he said in a more pious tone. "We're always eager to accept new sheep among our flock, even the black ones." The Cardinal's smile broadened, showing that he considered Fisher one of the blackest.

The Demons, Fisher could handle …this fat man was the shrewdest monster. But no turning back now. Recovering from his initial shock, the captain swallowed past a clenched smile. "Father, what a pleasant surprise," he extolled in a voice bursting with feigned bonhomie. "So good to see you after, what? Must be nine years now. You changed me with your lesson. My prayers have washed away—"

"Your verbal diarrhoea?" The Cardinal cut him off with a dismissive wave, "Spare me, Captain Fisher."

Fisher clamped his mouth shut as Wisdan toyed with a small node protruding out of his right temple, the small antenna which irrefutably marked the pontiff a Tolkane. "What kind of trouble are you in? If you're desperate enough to play at being a convert, it must be serious."

"Well," Fisher admitted, "our foodstuffs and other supplies *are* critically low. As to why, we were in the middle of a courier run and got diverted by circumstances from unfriendly space into unfriendlier space." The captain left it at that.

The Cardinal bowed his head briefly. "I understand. When you hit rock bottom, you'll find that God is your rock at the bottom. Say no more. Although I don't agree with your line of work, or your mannerisms, Captain, I perceive you speak with an open heart now. You and your crew have my leave to join us. We will resupply your ship and shelter you in our midst. You haven't strayed from your penance, have you?" Wisdan asked, his eyebrow arching.

"No, absolutely not and ah, thanks," Fisher said, exhaling in relief.

"Don't thank me, thank God. It is our mandate to shed light wherever we find darkness, but it has always been at His behest. He is the One that guides my hand. I am but a tool."

You got that right. "Great, well um, thanks to both of you. Fisher out."

The captain cut the transmission and threw Baines a cursory nod. The pilot flipped the switch and the engines began cycling up, reawakening after their long slumber. Starting from dead-cold, they let out a long rhythmic drone that scaled higher in octaves as they powered up.

"Sounds like the dogs are anxious to be let off-leash," Baines remarked.

When a flashing green light indicated the engines' readiness, the pilot let the reins go, and the *Skow II* streaked across interstellar space on a short fifty-kilometre intercept course with piety's convoy. Baines steered her into the midst of what turned out to be a fair-sized flotilla, inserting the *Skow II* so she would remain as close to the very centre of the armada as possible. There, she matched course and speed with all of her new friends. They were now part of the big and happy hallowed family.

Fisher looked out the bridge window at the closest missionary ships, which now effectively surrounded his vessel. He chuckled, having a rather perverted thought about their missionary position, and instantly feeling guilty for it.

Considering the narrow fissure his crew barely slipped through, he realized how lucky they'd fared. For a while, he'd been a Fish out of water, but now, safely back in the pond, the captain felt an urge to pat himself on the back. If no one else stood on the bridge, he might have done just that.

Their time on the missionary run moved without incident, for a while anyway. Matters changed when the Cardinal had the captain and his crew over for dinner. The meal proved a veritable feast the like of which Fisher's crew had not seen in months. The aroma of the roasted meats and exotic spices alone made them salivate in anticipation until their palettes confirmed the bliss of the payoff. Every crew member gave thanks to the Almighty for such a boon—doubly so when the free wine hit the table.

That was until Brumbal, the loudest, most voluble, and by far largest member of Fisher's six-person crew had indulged in too many goblets of the stuff. He let slip that the remains of the ship they recovered belonged to a Tolkane cutter called the *Inner Peace*.

Fisher dropped his fork and his indigestion began.

"You have survivors?" the Cardinal coaxed after he managed to extrapolate enough information from the drunken buffoon to piece the rest of the story together. Brumbal was having a grand old time, rheumy eyes oblivious to the withering gaze his captain shot him.

If the oaf wasn't seated at the opposite end of the table, Fisher would've kicked him in the sack to shut him up. But being such a large man, and so hammered, Brumbal probably wouldn't have felt it regardless.

Out the airlock, Fisher seethed to himself. *He's going out the airlock without so much as a wave goodbye.*

"Oh yeah, we found two of 'em, Father, and the robot's functional. It already kinda said hello," Brumbal cantered on. "But as for the two Tolkane, they're both froze-solid. Never thought the *Skow* would ever be doin' search and rescue, which still might

142

wind up bein' strictly recovery. No guarantee they'll be viable if we thaw the bodies. We're keepin 'em on—*burp*—ice, for now, waitin' till we get to friendlier, or at least more familiar space."

The Cardinal shook his head adamantly. Turning blazing eyes to Fisher he declared, "I need to see them, Captain—at once."

Fisher forced himself to nod, even allowing a pained smile to crease his face. *Right out the airlock.*

The Cardinal's 'At once' was thankfully not meant literally. But once he determined to have a look, Wisdan delayed his inspection only so far as etiquette allowed. Fisher knew from his past experience with the tyrannical man that there would be no debate. He had been cloistered under the Cardinal's wing for three weeks already as it were, with no uncomfortable questions asked or demands made. Fisher also understood that the holy man had taken a serious, albeit remote chance of reprisal from the Imperium for what might be construed as harbouring fugitives.

The Cardinal let the *Skow II*'s crew depart on their shuttle after dinner with the promise that he would ferry over, alone, the following morning after they all had 'a good night's sleep.' *As if.*

Fisher contemplated breaking from the convoy and making a run for it, but maybe Wisdan had given him the leeway to test the captain and see if he would do exactly that. The man was astute—no doubt there, but in truth, Fisher didn't want to double-cross him. No, trust moved along a two-way street. He'd let the pontiff inspect the robot and the pair of corpsicles as promised.

With a bottle of booze clutched in one hand and a bottle of stomach-placate in the other, Fisher retired to his cabin on leaden feet. Once he settled his stomach with the placate, he'd need a few shots of grog to take the edge off. The alternative, he mused, was chucking Brumbal out the airlock and the captain felt too tired to do that—Brumbal was an ogre.

Fisher's gut whined past the placate, and past the booze, but eventually, exhaustion sidestepped both and finally made it shut up. It didn't go quietly, assuring the captain the next day would be worse.

18: Wisdan
Fisher

Fisher awoke with just enough of a hangover to acknowledge what bad bedfellows placate and booze had been. Or could it be the insistent *chirp, chirp, chirp* of the klaxon relayed to his cabin from the bridge, signalling that the Cardinal's shuttle was on direct approach? Probably both.

"Get up, Fish," he cajoled himself. Cancelling the alert, the captain swung his legs out and down onto the small carpet that shielded the worst of the cold metal floor. The ID would feel right at home on this ship.

Fisher dismissed the ironic thought as he donned his clothes and boots before making his way to the shuttle bay. When the door shushed open, he had to stifle his shock.

The Cardinal stood proudly before him. Hands on ample hips, clad not in his traditional robes but an EVA jumper. Heck, he looked like a captain himself, completely unabashed as he met Fisher's gawk with a chuckle. As promised, the holy man had come alone, going so far as to pilot the small craft himself. *Maybe not such a hard egg after all.*

"Good morning, Your Eminence," Fisher greeted, feigning cheerfulness. "Have you breakfasted yet or did you want to see the corpsicles first, in which case you may not want to eat at all? Sometimes these things can look quite nasty."

"I'm fine, thank you. I would prefer to examine them as soon as possible." The Cardinal pointed to the prostrate automaton, still asleep on its curved metallic bed. "Your robot?"

"One and the same," Fisher said with resignation. He scratched the side of his head. "You want to take a peek at that too?"

"Not at all," Wisdan said.

Fisher arced an eyebrow. "Okay then, Father, this way if you please." With a sweep of his arm, the captain indicated the direction, before leading the Cardinal out of the shuttle bay and

145

into the adjoining corridor.

In no time, they reached the small med-lab where Dr Cholla busied himself monitoring the stats of the two cryo-tubes. When Fisher and Wisdan entered, he stopped his work, turned, and offered them an uncertain smile that bespoke of a fan in the presence of someone famous.

With a tilt of his head, the Cardinal asked, "Are these the tubes here?"

Remembering himself, Cholla nodded, "Yes, Your Grace, the male is behind me in that one and the female lies over here."

"I see. May I take a closer look?"

"By all means," Cholla said agreeably.

The Cardinal walked over to the tube where the frozen female lay and peered inside. "No," he said decidedly and with unmasked disappointment. "This woman is not known to me."

One Coldy-locks down, one to go. The tension in Fisher's shoulders eased.

Wisdan walked over to the male's tube and did the same. This time, he lingered. Fisher's trepidation mounted as the Cardinal's eyebrows arched higher and higher. The captain remained quiet, trying not to flinch.

At length, the big man looked up, eyes glistening.

Fisher forgot to breathe.

"As I said, I do not know the woman." The Cardinal's voice choked. "But if she is with this man, then she is no less vital. One thing is clear as light: we must thaw them at once." The pontiff's last words sounded as final as a judge's gavel.

Knee-jerked, Fisher snapped out of his trance. "No—*way*. Out of the question."

Wisdan sighed as he stood and joined Fisher and Cholla. "I understand your apprehension, given the circumstances, and quite frankly I don't blame you. Nevertheless, it is something we must do. Trust me, Captain, this reaches far beyond you and me. Whatever we do today marks but a token judgement to the big picture. In the end, we can do only what we *can* do."

"Well, I'm for doing nothing. You forget, Father, I'm no apostate. Heck, I'm not even religious," Fisher appealed.

"You think I don't know that?" the Cardinal laughed. "But whether you acknowledge it or not, you do have faith of a kind, Fisher. With it, you know this is not simply a religious or political matter."

"I thought those were the only things fuelling your engines. Are you turning over a new leaf?" the captain asked, bitterness roping his question.

Wisdan surrendered a smile. "Indeed, we are all leaves caught in the breeze, but where we land depends upon our decisions. They determine the earth on which we will consequentially come to rest." His grin straightened. "I could command you to thaw them, but rather I ask you to simply trust me on this."

Fisher shook his head and folded his arms. "I can't sanction this. These guys pose a potential threat to my crew and ship. Who knows what they were doing, stuck in an escape pod surrounded by a bunch of dead bad guys, above a Stricken in quarantined space no less? As far as I'm concerned, they're bad news, Father."

Wisdan held his gaze. "They are more of a threat to you in their current state than if you thawed them. The Imperium will eventually discover the truth about what happened and your involvement in moving these events along. When they do, you don't need me to tell you what will happen."

"Indulge me," the captain retorted, dropping his arms to his sides.

"Neither your ship and crew nor this whole armada, which currently shelters you, will matter one iota in the grand scheme of things. We are but a single sheaf in a vast tome. There are great and terrible things afoot, Captain, elusive things worming their way into existence, not merely causal but *caustic,* irrevocably so, if they succeed in roosting."

Fisher chewed his lip and shifted from foot to foot. The sudden urge to pee seized him, but his focus never wavered from the resolute Cardinal.

"For more than three weeks, I never questioned exactly what you were doing above that particular Stricken," said Wisdan. "I did not pry. It was not my province, Fisher, but now that Brumbal has sought fit to include me in your secret, I realize our purposes are indeed confluent. We must learn as much as we can, while we still can. And that means using everything—and everyone at our disposal."

Fisher's vacant stare ping-ponged to avoid Wisdan's steadfast regard. But begrudgingly, he wavered to the pontiff's side.

"Captain, when you decided to pick up the robot and this pair, you acted on gut instinct, right?" Wisdan pressed. "When you sought the Shepherd Fleet, you followed the same intuition?" Fisher's silence answered the man. "Well, now that you have come this far, what does your percipience tell you to do?"

"You're a ba—*grumpy* old man, y' know?" Fisher blurted.

Wisdan chuckled. "I see your behavioural inhibitor is working fine. That is good. I promise that your instincts are functioning just as well."

"Yeah, my instinct for stupidity maybe," Fisher muttered.

"Think of them—especially him, as a boon—a 458-year-old gift, to help you unravel the mystery surrounding your robot, if we are successful that is," the Cardinal added in a more sombre tone.

"What are you talking about? You're a priest. How the," Fisher struggled a bit, "heck could you possibly know exactly how old this corpsicle is?" He stabbed a finger at the male's cryo-tube. "*And,* what he was doing in that quarantined zone?"

"Oh, that is simple," Wisdan replied. "I know because I sent him there."

19: Connections
Fisher

While Doc made the preliminary preparations for the fugitives' resuscitation, the Cardinal agreed to have an early lunch with Fisher and the rest of his crew. Cholla came into the mess just as they finished their meal, only to report it would still take some time before the defrosting could begin.

"I understand," Wisdan said. He turned to Fisher. "In the meantime, Captain..."

Fisher nodded. Cardy wanted some private words. 'Private' meant a short walk to the captain's cabin, followed by a shorter walk to his liquor cabinet. Though no amount of alcohol would fully assuage his distrust of the situation or the man about to explain his pious connections to it. Words were just so much vacuum.

But if Wisdan wasn't on the level, Fisher felt confident he'd sense it. In the kind of business he more often than not immersed, intuition had always served him best—his forte and most bankable grace.

When both men had stowed safely behind the locked door and faced one another across a table, stiff drink in hand, the Cardinal elaborated, "As you are well aware, age no longer presents an issue to humanoids, provided they control the rate of propagation. Hominal bodies, whether Tolkane, Allianthan or any of the myriad sister species with whom we share this distinction, continue to function without expiry. So long as we are not met with some physical trauma, or exposed to some fatal contagion or mutagen," the pontiff added.

"I myself am 940 years old and I knew one of your two passengers long before you took your first breath. He became one of my most venerable apostates. For that matter, we all ascended from meagre beginnings, yet even they took root from some earlier impetus. And that is where I believe we should begin."

Fisher sipped his drink and gave Wisdan a quick chin nudge.

"Research done on the now-extinct Planet Earth saw significant breakthroughs in increasing life expectancy after the successful enhancement of what are called gene telomeres. I don't fully grasp the science behind it but the tech involved is sound. Both you and I are the product of this gift, which survived their holocausts—both of them."

The Cardinal hesitated and scrutinized the captain. *He's trying to gauge my reaction on the subject.* Fisher offered none. *Keep the eyes dry and give him my undivided attention.*

"Shortly before the first heinous attack, which destroyed the Humans' planet, a token contingent of their population escaped aboard a series of massive arks. The survivors brought this immortality science and many other advancements with them on their long exodus across the black of space. It's what made their emigration possible."

Wisdan stopped a second time and studied the captain. And studied. The sound of hidden machinery hummed softly in the background.

Fisher sat up. "Right, longevity—made their exodus feasible—I'm listening, Father."

"Much better," the Cardinal said. "Now, by some miracle, they avoided the Imperium. Their arks, battered after centuries of unabated travel through the interstellar expanse, limped into a surrogate system. Incredibly still intact, the ships came to rest on an M-class planet compatible with the Humans' biological needs. Their ships' engines cooled for the very last time, ending their spectacular careers. That world of course was Alliantha, my colonial home, and your ancestral home too, I believe."

Fisher shrugged and dropped his eyes to his drink. "It was never my home. Only my hell."

"I understand, but before your time, Alliantha flourished as a very congenial planet, sparsely populated by several congruous humanoid species: indigenous Allianthans and Tolkane colonists like myself. It took a while for the Humans to overcome their initial apprehension but eventually, curiosity overcame fear.

150

Communication paved the way to cooperation, learning, and ultimately an integration of the three species.

"The technology the Humans offered seemed simplistic but so radically different from our own that the combination of the two opened entirely new avenues for the advancement of our merged sciences and societies. With some genetic manipulation, the animal foetuses and plant seeds that they brought also adapted to and flourished in their new home. The Humans themselves rounded out the synergistic effect of the menagerie, intermingling into the social strata with your ancestors.

"For many years this harmonious and mutually beneficial relationship developed and enhanced until they produced the Tolkani daughter species—namely yours."

Fisher stifled a yawn and looked away.

The Cardinal's antenna spiked. He cleared his throat and continued a little louder, "As-I-indicated, *they* advanced *us* with their freely offered tech, but also through language and culture. Who we are today stems from those pivotal influences, including our habits and the words we speak, but their true gift proved less tangible and more profound. A new approach to thought itself, a way of looking at the larger picture beyond the dismal mindset of living in thrall, under the yoke of the Imperium.

"Admittedly, I am talking about philosophy and religion now. Although many different manifestations of each surfaced, they all held universal truths. In sharing them with us, the Humans brought us a sense of hope."

Wisdan levelled his gaze at the captain. "Now I know you may have strayed a little far from that path, but it doesn't require superior intellect to realize that that's the real reason behind longevity—a hope of spiritual fulfilment and renewal—a drive to coalesce all the minds and energies that make up the Universe. In so doing, we can truly unify it, make it accessible and *universal*… one collective consciousness to present to Heaven. This entire armada is but a token force towards that goal, that gift."

"That 'gift' sounds a little too philosophical to me," Fisher said, unable to mask his sarcasm. "Your beatitudes ring a little too transcendental and serendipitous. You want to merge with the Demons, you go right ahead. Last time I checked, all of us sorry warm-bloods are barely surviving, spinning round and round." He let out a wry chuckle. "We're stuck in an interstellar toilet, with perpetual crap falling on our heads while that sadist Exarch pushes the plunger, seeing which of us goes down first. Life's torture— survival of the fittest."

"And what doesn't kill you…" Wisdan countered.

"Makes you stronger," Fisher exhaled.

The Cardinal closed and opened his eyelids in affirmation. "You're proof of that. Same with the Humans. Though a remnant of their former race, still carrying the burden of their holocaust fresh in their hearts, it did not jade or taint them. It galvanized them. It's what truly made them, well, Human."

"If you say so," Fisher said noncommittally.

"I do. Apart from an inherent resolve to survive, they also bore a deep-seated need to share life, and none more than their leader. He epitomized that sentiment. To all and any listeners, he was the true exponent and visionary who—" the Cardinal stopped midsentence.

Fisher started. Without a word, he hiked a thumb over his shoulder at the door behind him.

Wisdan knitted his brows for a moment but twice as quick relaxed them, his frown easing. "Ah, no, the one of whom I speak is not your passenger. But we are all connected in this tale, including him. So many connections…"

The two men stared at one another for a time. No—Wisdan was looking past him, lost in his solicitudes no doubt, venturing out across some faraway plane.

Abashed at finding himself so invested in what the holy man had to say, Fisher harrumphed, "Okay, what's the story with your visionary guy?"

Wisdan's eyelids fluttered and he refocused. "Sorry, I digress—the burden of storing so much forbidden knowledge in this archaic brain of mine." *If your revelations are so forbidden, why share them with me?*

"Let me begin again," the Cardinal said. "The Human tech, manipulating the gene telomeres became the very cornerstone of our immortality. It allowed life on Alliantha to flourish in confluence. Human, Allianthan, Tolkane, and of course your hybrid race of Tolkani. The planet was verdant then, a lush and fertile world."

Wisdan steepled his thick fingers and examined their tips. "You see, Fisher, as a natural system, it worked because it had no design flaws. The true wonders and complexities of what makes life possible are scarcely understood, even by the greatest scientists. Thinking in these terms, the Human leader had effactually ushered in Alliantha's Golden Age."

A shadow crept over Wisdan's face. "Still, one hiccup occurred, innate to a few among his fold, a radical group of dissidents. Anarchists at a time when all Humans needed cohesion. They stole a—"

"Yeah," Fisher interrupted, a knot forming in his stomach. "I heard about them—the ones who got away."

"Yes, you do know about them." Wisdan gave him a half-smile. By his tone, he seemed genuinely impressed.

"Only what they told me at the squatter camp," the captain confessed, meeting Wisdan's gaze. "But I never really believed, well most of it."

"Oh, I was there, so I can assure you it is all true. That scar never fully healed. If you know the tale then you remember the irony of their escape from the rest of their race's doom."

Feeling suddenly abject, Fisher acknowledged him by raising his eyebrows and chin,

"Otherwise, the Human influence on Alliantha marked their leader's magnum opus. Also, his penultimate achievement."

Fisher leaned in and gave the pontiff a probing look. "What do you mean?"

"After that incident, their chief concerted his efforts on

153

salvaging and eventually rewriting his whole game plan, this time factoring in all other potential eventualities of co-existence. All except one."

"The Demons," Fisher guessed.

Again, Wisdan's eyes closed and opened. "They are a single-minded and relentless lot. And nothing is invulnerable to ID depredations. When they showed up, everything changed. You know the rest—that's when your own story begins—almost."

Wisdan regarded Fisher with appraisal, which made the captain shift uncomfortably in his chair. "Pardon?"

The Cardinal blew out his cheeks. "Apart from their many gifts, the Humans left us a certain legacy, which points to our destiny like a compass or beacon. It offers the right direction, one that will free us of the Imperium—with a way to do exactly that."

The captain's mouth went dry. "Are you serious? No tech comes close to challenging the Overlords. Nothing." *Then, what about the destroyed ID Ships you found, genius?* "It's been tried before, always with the same result. Vorancia was the last and the only one to achieve partial success. We all know how he fared."

"Yes, I know, but indulge me. What do *you* know of Briden Vorancia's dire tale?"

Fisher traced a finger around the rim of his glass as he weighed the pontiff's request. "He became the President of the LUW—League of United Worlds," the captain said in a tired voice, "*the* number one in his quadrant until the Demons came along."

"Yes," the Cardinal sighed, "Vorancia rose to prominence—a strong and revered leader, a good ethical man who believed in the greater good. And the last known person to stand against the Imperium's demands that he relinquish all control over his worlds. Instead of grovelling on his knees when the annexation warning came, he busied himself and his best minds to devise the ultimate defence grid against the Demons."

Fisher rolled his eyes and drummed his fingers on his glass as the pontiff went on, seemingly oblivious to the captain's growing impatience.

"The Garaxians tried, but they could not crack Vorancia's grid; they could not jump their ships past it. Their plasma and solar dynamo weapons proved equally ineffectual. Any attacks merely strengthened Vorancia's shields—and his cause. By repulsing the ID, he began to inspire not only the worlds under his protectorate but those beyond."

Wisdan lay his hands flat on the table and shifted forward. "An uneasy waiting game ensued. As driven as the Imperium was to eliminate discord in what they justified as 'their rightful merger with the infinite,' they elected to wait. Patiently, they watched. And they learned."

Fisher brusquely splayed his hands and fixed the Cardinal with an exasperated look. "Am I going to tell this tale, or are you?"

Wisdan raised his palms in surrender and chuckled. "You'd think that after close to a millennium preaching, I'd be warier whenever I fell into sermon mode. Apologies. Go on, Captain, please."

Fisher snorted. "They did learn—Vorancia's tragic flaw, which undid his prolific work. Despite all of his precautions, he had a penchant for satisfying a baser, more primal urge." Using his glass, he gestured to the Cardinal. "Some, like you, follow God, some follow sex and then there are those few who hold sex *as* a god. That's the kind of church where Vorancia worshipped."

"What do you know of his assassination?" Wisdan pressed.

"Happened during a week-long fringe world conference where he planned to share some of the latest upgrades to his already formidable defence tech."

Wisdan nodded. "In an effort to rally those worlds to his cause—include them in his literal and figurative sphere of influence."

Fisher inclined his chin. "Sounds about right. One of the delegates from Centauris X turned out to be the hottest, most alluring woman to grace the senses of the opposite sex. The blonde goddess seduced Prez over the first few days of those talks. And Vorancia unwittingly let it happen. What he didn't know was that

155

Stephen Fenech

she'd been genetically engineered to match his concept of the perfect female. Robust and willing, her enhanced body's pheromone levels rocketed off the charts. Once he breathed that poison, he couldn't resist her."

Fisher forked his fingers through his dishevelled hair. "But Briden Vorancia was no fool. You can't attain that level of office or defy the Imperium otherwise. Even after his companion's background story checked out, he had her body completely scanned for any weapons or explosives she might sneak into the bedchamber. Before he removed his body armour, he even tied her to the bed, not out of any S&M indulgence, but as a final provision for his safety in case she attempted to kill him with her bare hands or legs."

"Sounds like true romance," Wisdan commented as he sipped his grog.

"True enough," Fisher agreed, cracking a smile. "Far as he knew, Vorancia rendered her safe. What threat could a naked and subdued woman possibly pose?" He let out a quick snort-giggle. "A freaking kamikaze's, that's what kind. Some geneticist had a field day with this volatile 'woman,' concocting her to produce certain combustive chemicals naturally. They reacted together when released in the right sequence. The trigger—sex stimuli."

Fisher let out a long breath. "As Vorancia got busy fornicating with the femme fatale, at his most vulnerable, she grew aroused. Went helter-skelter orgasm. And *exploded,* taking him with her, so yeah, she was hot all right," the captain finished with a sardonic laugh.

Wisdan shook his head slowly. "The Imperium had effectively lopped off the head of the threat in a single master stroke."

"But they didn't stop there," Fisher reminded him as he poured another measure for both of them. "While the protectorate fell into chaos over the assassination, a whole battalion of sleepers, derived from the local populace, awoke and bypassed the relays across the entire defence grid. The infiltrators had been strategically placed in the systems before the Demons' surgical

156

strike. Without Vorancia's command protocols to override the commandeering, the grid came down."

A crawling sensation crept up Fisher's throat and made the veins in his neck throb. "The Demons stormed the sector in a tour de force of biblical proportions. They swept across the League's systems and seized control of every planet, moon, and space station therein."

"Except one," Wisdan prompted, gesturing with his glass.

"Right, the Florin System, where Vorancia's home planet orbited."

Wisdan shivered noticeably when Fisher mentioned the name. "The Imperium annexed every planet in the Florin System," the pontiff reflected. "By the most devastating weapon in the Imperium's arsenal."

"Yeah, the Whiplash—the stellar bomb," said Fisher. He tilted his head to one side and scratched the stubble on his chin. "That would be the worst. Gravitons detonated within the sun's core, not volatile enough to make the star go supernova or turn it into a gamma burster, but adequate for its corona to unleash a deadly long-duration CME flare."

The Cardinal took a long pull of his drink. "It wiped out all organic life on the four M-class planets within the habitable zone of its heliosphere. After the initial blast, the sun's nuclear activity diminished to a third of its previous yield of light and energy, starving those satellites of their lifeblood. Forever colder and harsher after that, the planets could no longer support even the hardiest, most adaptable species."

"Exactly right." Fisher's facial scar chose that moment to itch. He lifted his free hand and rubbed it between his thumb and index finger before continuing. "The bane pushed all of Florin's planets beyond the possibility of any terraforming, rendering them dark worlds—dark tombstones—Demon trophies."

Wisdan grimaced, pursing his lips until they trembled. "The Demons' Exarch visited such a reprehensible verdict upon Vorancia's home system, annexed it Stricken en masse, to make an

157

irrefutable example of Garaxian might. As the Imperium's figurehead, he does not concern himself with fallout or the decimation of innocents, including his own troops, provided he accomplishes the Imperium's goal."

Fisher hammered his glass down on the table. "To that wicked cur, the end justifies the means."

"If the Demons are indeed a literal derivative of hellspawn, born out of ancient legend, then you could best liken their Exarch to Hell's most diabolical potentate: Satan himself."

"There's a good comparison," Fisher said in a humourless tone. He poured another shot and retrieved the vessel. "So, tell me what I don't know."

"What you don't know," the Cardinal said, not missing a beat, "is that once the Exarch had complete autonomy over the former protectorate, the Imperium dismantled the defence grid tech used to oppose them, assimilated it, and made it part of their own arsenal."

"Heard that part too, actually," said Fisher to the small glass cradled in his hand. "Once they completely neutralized the threat, the Garaxians advertised their actions across every channel on the Box." He lifted his gaze to his companion. "That's how I caught wind of what went down."

Wisdan inclined his head before looking off into the mid-distance. "They took great pains to reveal exactly how they accomplished the assassination—to sow more fear and distrust among the masses."

"Well, Father, it worked. Everybody and their mothers know the Demons give no quarter unless it ultimately serves their manifesto."

The Cardinal swallowed. "None would ever attempt to oppose them. The roots of any collaboration had been effectively snipped. With Vorancia's death, they extinguished any hope of contest." He paused and observed Fisher for a moment. "Or so we were led to believe."

Fisher narrowed his eyes. "I'm guessing you broached the

subject because you think this business with Vorancia is related to us, here and now—this tech?"

Wisdan began to nod but then shook his head. "Not—exactly. It's something old that has been applied incorrectly or more to the point *incompletely*. Vorancia was on the right track, but it evidenced a case of too little, too late."

"Well?" Fisher tightened his grip on his glass. "What is it?"

"That, I cannot tell you."

Can't, or won't? "Okay, now I'm at a loss. I thought you said you knew."

"Yes, yes, I know what I said," the Cardinal blustered. "I know it exists. I know enough of the broad strokes concerning the concept behind the tech. And you're right, it's based on Vorancia's grid, but my knowledge is scant when it comes to the *how,* the *why*, and unfortunately exactly what it is. But—" the pontiff's voice petered again. "Your passenger knows. He is the key to this investigation, one of its cynosures actually, like that robot you carry."

Fisher scrunched up his face but Wisdan stopped him short. "Before you get cramps, let me explain."

"Please, and thank you," said Fisher.

"I didn't inspect your robot earlier because I know enough of its tale to assure you, I want no part of it. But with that same token, it connects to all of us—all of this."

"What *can* you tell me about Mr Gearbox?" Fisher asked as he tipped back his drink. Its burn calmed his nerves.

"Only that it is intrinsically linked to the Human Visionary I dealt with back on Alliantha. It is far older than anyone has guessed, primeval in fact. The Human leader knew that robot in your hold intimately, but even he could not guess its faceless origin. And he never fully trusted it."

Fisher dropped his glass on the table, his doubt of the Cardinal resurfacing. Was the fat man equivocating? "How do you know it's the same one?"

"He described it to me in great detail during our many

159

dialogues, often making quips about the yellow decal crudely painted across its torso."

"So, the smiley-face is the robot's trademark after all," Fisher laughed. "But why your reluctance to interact with it?" *Or to claim it?*

Wisdan's face darkened. "Are you sure you're prepared for this?"

The captain met his gaze. "Hit me."

"That robot is undoubtedly the most valuable asset in the entire Universe as we know it."

Fisher licked his chops and rubbed his hands together.

Wisdan made a warding gesture with uplifted palms. "Although priceless, you won't be able to sell it to any Funder or guild—if that thought crossed your mind. It may be an invaluable crux of causality, but ironically that also makes it the most dangerous appropriation you've ever acquired."

Fisher's shoulders sagged and his smile dithered.

"Entire planets including Earth were destroyed, *because* of it," Wisdan explained. "Even if you begged me to take it off your hands, I would not. And if you choose to destroy the robot or to merely discard it, you will only assure the Demons of their eternal tyranny, and still pay for your actions with your life."

The room felt suddenly too small, the walls closing in. Sweat trickled down the small of Fisher's back and a momentary panic set in. Claustrophobia—the chink in his armour. He took a deep breath and concentrated on the pontiff to steady himself.

"The robot is a game piece, a contradiction, and alas, your burden to bear," Wisdan said. "But I will help you in any way I can. Have faith, Captain. Other aid will come to you, in mysterious ways. Do not give in to despair—that is merely an impostor. Rather, think in terms of causality. Give credence to that prismatic force above all else: that you were *meant* to move this game piece."

Wisdan's words confounded Fisher but they also suppressed the captain's doubt and vanquished his phobia. He knew in his heart what Cardy told him about the robot was the divine truth.

Even so, it didn't make him feel any less sour.

"So, Father, I just stowed a living bomb aboard my boat. And if I divest myself of it, the Universe takes the fall. Great." Fisher glanced away for a moment before a tangent thought struck him. "You said the Gearbox is intrinsically linked to all of us. That must include the male corpsicle too. How is he connected?"

Wisdan put his hands on his knees and inhaled. "As I said, I knew your passenger long before your time. His name is Yaemin Resa. Captain of the late *Inner Peace* and a humble tech salvager when I first met him above Tolkane."

The Cardinal's antenna wiggled a bit, before wavering to stillness. "I was overseeing the construction of a new orbital church there when he showed up aboard the *Inner Peace*, offering decent tech at a reasonable price for the cathedral's living pod cluster."

Wisdan's eyes softened. "I liked him immediately, a self-confident man of substance with a serious intrepid mind. Completely in tune with the larger picture and the search for truth in the altruistic sense. He attached meaning and self-purpose to this ideal—so it was natural that he came into my flock."

Fisher allowed himself a brief grin.

"Although he continued his work as a tech salvager, he frequented my armada between jobs, sometimes for months on end. Resa became like a son to me, my protégé. Under my tutelage, he flourished like a star pupil, and whenever I learned the *Inner Peace* would join us for a stint, I was delighted, looking forward to the many philosophical conversations we would have."

"Sounds like a cozy arrangement," Fisher remarked.

The Cardinal ignored the quip. "Not only did Resa find hidden facets to the given credo of religion, he helped me see my faith through a new prism. We vaulted intellectually from each other's insight and I found myself apt to trust him implicitly, even in matters for which I harboured some doubt. He, in turn, trusted me with his innermost sentiments, and eventually with information that could be very dangerous, if the Imperium lit him up."

161

"I take it this intel your Resa caught wind of links to the robot, stuck like a fly to all the web strands we discussed." Fisher guessed, nodding as he pondered. "It's what ultimately blew him off your radar—that's where you lost him. And found the spider that wove everything together."

Wisdan smiled with his eyes. "Astute to a fault, my son. Yes, the matter involved a third party, a highly resourceful and well-financed Funder connected with Vorancia before his assassination."

The Cardinal let out a long breath, which made his gut balloon. It deflated as he drew enough air for his next disclosure. "He recruited Resa, retaining his services as a tech salvager. A high-risk operation that left Resa understandably troubled about the job since it required the *Inner Peace* to journey to the Human home planet—rendered sterile and quarantined millennia before you stumbled upon it."

Wisdan kneaded the back of his thick neck. "But Resa sensed something even more elusive than the impetus that prompted the ID's liquidation of that planet. He had been well-versed in the history and teachings of the Humans regarding their plight. Resa knew for instance that their tech stemmed from a long-extinct race called the *Dovan*."

Fisher flinched inwardly at Wisdan's mention of that name but kept that detail to himself for now.

"This invaluable Dovani tech held the solution to thwart the Demons for good. Yes, I'm talking about final salvation for us all. What form it will consequentially take is anyone's guess, but the Funder who hired Captain Resa evinced that its *seed* would be found on the Stricken, waiting to be uncovered."

"The robot."

"Yes," Wisdan said. "But neither of us guessed this at the time. For all of Resa's deliberation and the handsome incentives and advances offered, the captain questioned the motives of the Funder himself, whom he never met face to face except through an avatar or an associate, a rather shady character if I recall correctly.

"The Funder handed Resa a stringent caveat to disavow any knowledge of the Human and Dovan races, keeping any knowledge from his crew, which I'm sure he honoured when they set out."

"But he made an exception in your case," Fisher pointed out.

Wisdan dipped his chin solemnly. "Resa couldn't put a finger on what simultaneously ailed him about doing the job and drove him to its heart like a river to the sea. He struggled with this paradox for several days, about to tell the Funder's rep he'd pass on the job, when he decided to seek my advice on the matter first."

"And?" Fisher prompted.

"As soon as I learned the full extent of what passed between him and the Funder, I made a vital connection to the Human Leader back on Alliantha. I knew that, despite the shady dealings, events were coming to a head, tantamount to a butterfly effect."

Wisdan stopped and chewed his lower lip as if weighing his next words carefully. "I told Resa part of what I gleaned of the Visionary's game plan. And to that effect, for better or for worse he must go to unravel the truth within the truth."

The Cardinal ran a hand over his bald head. "Leave it to Resa to find something out of place from the get-go. If any one person in the Universe truly encapsulated the essence of lateral thinking, of *Wu Wei* for that matter, it was Resa." He took a sip from his glass before continuing. "My apostate told me quite plainly that something we'd not considered was afoot, and the only way to find out what it might be was by taking the job."

Wisdan's eyes brightened with plain deference. "I embraced his ability to, not only mirror my thoughts and convictions but to present something I had not considered. In hindsight, I think he didn't need any convincing—that, having already decided, only sought my blessing. Resa followed my suggested course of action utterly. I have regretted that decision for more than two centuries... until now."

Fisher cocked his chin. "So, who was this third party? Who was this *Spider*?"

"I don't know that either, except that during my centuries-long investigations into Resa's disappearance, I've come to learn, fairly recently in fact, that the ambiguous figure headed the same Centauris X delegation that had conceived Vorancia's suicidal assassin. Though the crime happened long after Resa's time, if we can revive him, maybe he can tell us that as well."

Fisher cringed inwardly. His scar complained again, demanding another scrub. *I need less, not more pieces to the puzzle!* During the Cardinal's diatribe, a silent cold war waged within the captain's mind. It's not like he and Wisdan were best buddies, but why had the pontiff shared all this dodgy info with him? What were *his* motives? Cardy held a position of power over him but what prevented him from just extricating the bodies and being done with it?

Maybe, Wisdan merely wanted to unburden himself after holding onto such hazardous secrets for two centuries, or maybe he planned to capitalize on them, use the *Skow II's* crew to do his dirty work in the near future. With nothing else but his auricular sense to guide him, Fisher found himself agreeing with the pontiff—and hating himself for it.

He began to ponder the deeper implications of Wisdan's revelations when the sound of the com interrupted him. Fisher pressed the answer button.

"Hey, Captain? Cholla here. Green lights across the board. Thawing has commenced."

20: Impetus
Resa

When the neural pathways fired up the cognitive processes in Resa's mind, his immediate impulse was to scream, convinced he was about to die.

But before he completely lost control, a projected thought, not his own, cut through his panic. As it reached his cerebrum, it took the form of a word association, which left a tingle in his synapse, a primal spark that assured him his consciousness would remain—if he nurtured the ember, with willpower.

He did. And the ember brightened. Riding a wave of euphoria through his mind, it quieted his alarm like a sedative.

The word was *safe*.

He clung to it as it filled the cinema of his subconscious, believing with all his wont that this primal message had been sent for a reason. To think otherwise—a ruse to let his guard down—would only reignite his suppressed terror.

Slowly, senses long-suspended in hibernation began to reactivate. He felt his pulse, his heartbeat, respiration, cold, sound, voices. He could smell too—some form of… antiseptic. His eyes didn't function, but he knew he still had them simply because they throbbed.

His mind geared up until a sudden epiphany embraced him—he was being thawed. The pain in his retinas marked a good thing, indicating rebooting nerves. As they recharged, the nerves sent messages of complaint to the pain receptors in his brain. He also knew his blindness would prove temporary.

The voices grew louder. When he first detected them, they sounded muted as though coming from down a long tunnel. Now, his ears registered greater distinction and more insistence.

Someone spoke to him. "Yaemin, can you hear me? It's Cardinal Wisdan." A note of supplication intoned that voice. The timbre waned, succeeded by steady measures of unbridled joy. The

165

name meant a great deal. Resa formed a smile in his mind. Or maybe he manifested the real thing, for the Cardinal's voice rose in tenor, sounding triumphant. Resa remembered. Beyond hope, his mentor—proof positive that miracles did happen.

It took some time for the captain to respond, his true recuperation beginning with a barely perceptible raise of his index finger. From one moment to the next, however, a modicum of strength returned. His coordination and reflexes increased to that of a fully conscious mind. The pain in his optic nerves lessened, replaced with the first static-charged scintilla of vision. It remained to usher in the details of what appeared to be the ceiling of some sort of hospital ICU—no, a ship's medical bay.

It would take weeks before he regained his ability to project, but that didn't matter. As his vision cleared further, he contented to let his body convalesce as it would, guided back from the null of frozen limbo by that steadfast shepherd of a word. *Safe.*

"She didn't make it—I'm sorry." That came from the short fat one who named himself Cholla. The words didn't register at first, but when they hit home, so did the sledgehammer. *Shyce?* A flood of dark despair followed, wildly metastasizing through Resa like a viral storm. Eyes darting, he began hyperventilating as though the air had been sucked out of the room.

The flustered doctor raised trembling hands as he stammered, "She was terminal before she went into cryo. But her illness kept in stasis the entire time in hibernation. We only detected it in stage three of the revival process. By stage five her heart stopped. She died in the same euphoric safe state you experienced, guided by the same watchword. She felt no pain. Just slipped away," he hastened to add.

"With a lie!" Resa shot back.

No amount of condolence or reassurance from the distressed

little man would placate Resa in this matter. Shyce had warned him it was too big and he promised her they'd make it. Still extremely weak from his recent resuscitation, the devastating news crushed him. She came into the escape pod. She was okay. Resa sank into a dead zone, trying to play back those final moments before the Demons destroyed the *Inner Peace*.

No wait, that's not exactly how it happened...

"There, there, rest easy, my son," Wisdan soothed. "You've endured more than your share of pain and grief." He put a bear-sized hand on Resa's shoulder. "We'll talk tomorrow."

Resa stiffened at the touch. "No," he croaked tersely. Abashed at his sharpness, he quickly amended, "Thank you, but no. I've slept enough, Father. I need to know everything now—for Shyce."

Wisdan hesitated, regarding the prone man with a level gaze. Resa met it unflinching. The Cardinal's eyes sagged and his antenna curled in. "Very well."

21: Captains
Fisher

Arms crossed by the sidelines, Fisher found Wisdan and Resa's sacred tête-à-tête most impressive. After helping Resa sit up, Wisdan brought his apostate up to speed on a great many affairs, beginning with his unassuaged heartache at believing him lost for good. The holy man succinctly recounted more than 200 years of galactic history in the span of a few minutes.

But the real marvel rooted in how craftily the Cardinal worded his recap when it came to his own comings and goings. Beyond any doubt, the big man censored his words, allowing for some hidden communication with Resa.

Wisdan beamed. "I had to pinch myself when I saw your face inside that cryo-tube—to make sure I wasn't dreaming, or chasing ghosts."

Almost imperceptibly Resa shivered. His guru didn't seem to catch it, but Fisher did.

"It's all uncanny really," vaunted Wisdan, "a bona fide miracle from on high."

For some unfathomable reason, the Cardinal didn't mention the robot, but Fisher wouldn't mention it either, at least not immediately. When the Cardinal finished explaining the *Skow* and *Skow II*'s abridged parts in their affairs, an awkward silence ensued.

Fisher broke it. "So, what do you remember? What happened on the Stricken?"

Resa coughed. "We were ambushed—a setup from the word *go*. We weren't *supposed* to be successful. Just bait, used to spring a potential trap. And spring it, we did," he added bitterly.

"I'm so sorry," Wisdan said, his voice brimming with guilt.

"Father, it's not your fault," said Resa. "I knew what I got myself into. I'm livid at myself for not being more careful."

"Do you think your Funder knew any of this before he sent you?" Fisher asked.

"Good question. Let's just say the odds never favoured us." Resa described the disaster on the sterile planet, which ended with the destruction of his ship and the loss of his entire crew. "We made for the debris field, thinking we'd get some shelter to mask our immediate jump coordinates, and maybe by some divine fluke outrun the Demons. But they anticipated the move—a squadron of interceptors awaited us. That's when things turned strange."

Fisher drew up to Resa's gurney. "Define strange."

"I remember getting cornered, tractors from all ships locked on and pinning us stationary. Even if we could escape the cordon, they were more than ready to interdict. The ID tried to hail us, but if I'm not mistaken, the com-link cut off and stayed off before we could answer."

Head lowered, Cholla carefully handed Resa a small glass filled with a blue-green liquid. "It's only an electrolyte booster," he said in a small voice. "With every vitamin and mineral your body needs right now."

"Thank you, Doctor, and forgive my earlier outburst," Resa said as he accepted the medicine. "You didn't deserve that. I'm sure you did everything possible." He tipped the liquid back and handed Cholla the empty glass before resuming his tale. "Without my ever ordering it, we somehow managed to fire on them first, which would be suicide under normal circumstances, but this was anything but normal. The Imperium ships didn't expect *any* kind of retaliation, so it caught them off-guard. Still, they could have taken us out at any time. My guess is that our cargo was so precious to them, they didn't want to risk harming it.

"Two interceptors were destroyed outright, which broke our energy cage. Once free of their tractors, well, it seemed the *Inner Peace* suddenly developed a mind of her own. The engines kicked in full throttle and she rocketed deeper into the debris field as if the ship herself decided to make a run for it.

"With no stabilizers to dampen our momentum in the sudden evasive, it slammed us against the bulkhead and knocked us unconscious. When I came to, that *thing* we hauled up from the surface was operational and acting of its own volition."

Most of Fisher's crew had since taken positions against the wall by the med-lab entrance. At Resa's revelation, they all exchanged incredulous looks. Or had fear made their eyes burgeon, knowing Resa's thing now squatted aboard their ship?

"By the ship's erratic buffeting, the ID still chased us," Resa said. "We sideswiped a few smaller rocks in the field—I could tell by the pounding. The ship changed the fragments' trajectories to cover her rear. Confirmed as much when I found a monitor. The *Inner Peace* forced the interceptors to slow and adjust course."

"The robot piloted your craft," Fisher surmised. "Probably using some form of WiDi interface."

"I know it made me nauseous, so yes, that's a fair assumption, having no one else available to pilot her. Shyce was there with me. I didn't see any of the other crew members, except Brenor. He was dead, neck snapped at an ugly angle, most likely from an uncontrolled impact when the ship went ballistic on the evasive tack. I can only guess that a similar fate befell the others.

"As soon as the robot saw Shyce and me still alive, it grabbed us both, shoved us through the escape pod gateway, and sealed the access tube. I figured the robot separated us to execute more drastic manoeuvres in the field without risking our lives. Either way seemed like suicide, but I reasoned two targets might confuse the assault and buy us time. Acting on gut instinct, I ushered Shyce into the pod, secured our tubes, and launched. The Demons ignored us completely."

Cholla looked down at his feet when Resa mentioned the dead woman's name. He retreated to the entrance and stood amidst the other crew members.

"As the *Inner Peace* shot away, drawing the interceptors with it, things became even more surreal," Resa regaled. "Using the pod's small tractor, we locked onto the closest substantial asteroid and made for it. Once nested and secured with a grappling piton, we had a good ten minutes before the automatic cryo protocol kicked in. From the pod's bubble window, we observed the action outside through a kind of emerald haze. The ignatia, I think, emanated from us.

"The *Inner Peace* put a fair but in no way safe distance between her and us before coming to an emergency stop. And exploding. Even through the aura, the blast singed my sight. The resulting shock wave sent debris hurling at us, but when it reached us, nothing happened. As though someone switched us off from reality."

Fisher turned to Wisdan, expecting the pontiff to rebuke Resa's preposterous tale. But the Cardinal kept his eyes forward, locked on his apostate and cast in solid stone.

"When my irises adjusted from the flaring ghost image," Resa said, "I confirmed all the ships had been completely obliterated. We were alone—but not for long."

Fisher felt his eyebrows climb to his hairline.

"Another Garaxian squadron jumped in," Resa explained. "This one helmed by a dreadnought flanked by a few heavy cruisers. The entire fleet broke formation, fanning out to sweep the field. At the same time, our cryo-tubes started cycling down our internal temperatures, imperceptibly at first, but then with mounting imperative. My body grew numb and my mind felt etherized, but I distinctly recall not one but three ships hover close and then veer off. They drifted near enough to see us with their naked eyes and yet they did nothing."

Brightening, Cholla looked up and his mouth opened, but then his features lost their verve, and he remained silent. Fisher knew Doc took his inability to save Resa's woman hard, guilt outweighing his scientific curiosity. Poor sod.

Resa coughed. "Another terrific detonation followed, more intense than the first, but with the same result. The entire second wave of Imperium ships was destroyed."

Fisher bit his lower lip, the scene of devastation above the Stricken fresh in his mind. *At least that much fits.*

"And we endured, still unharmed." Resa shifted on his bed. "I forced myself to remain conscious as long as possible." He fell quiet, drawing Fisher and Wisdan in. His mouth worked as if trying to frame his next words. "Now, I can't be certain, but I think one more ship showed up after the second explosion. This one didn't look ID, and it was alone. It just parked directly above us and floated. Then it faded as I froze..." Resa looked down at the gurney and fell reticent.

Had Cholla spiked that cure-all with something more? Or was Resa trying to digest the legitimacy—more like the lunacy—of his own bizarre fiction?

Fisher harrumphed. "Well, that's a load of bulsh—a real doozy," his inhibitor corrected quickly.

Wisdan spun and needled the captain with razor-sharp eyes. "Not another syllable." When Fisher offered none, the pontiff grunted and turned his attention back to Resa. "Is it possible you imagined the last part, perhaps the result of the cryo process?"

"Well, anything's possible, Father, but no, I don't think so."

"Do you have any more to add, my son?" the Cardinal asked.

"That robot obviously saved us at the expense of its own destruction, but why? It could have easily escaped, yet it chose to lure our pursuers away from us before going kamikaze."

"A puzzle indeed," Wisdan agreed. "One of many to be certain."

"What is certain," Resa said with sudden ire, "is that the big question mark looms even higher. The trouble is not past, it has deepened." Blazing eyes seized Fisher. "Captain, by retrieving me you've kicked a hornet's nest so hard and good it will never settle down again—a nest that had been dormant for more than two hundred years."

Fisher's jaw dropped, too stunned to reply.

"Don't disillusion yourself with any notion of profiting from this," Resa derided, "or that it will soon be over. Any chance of subtlety is gone. We've lost whatever advantage the robot achieved on our behalf. The Universe as we know it will never be balanced until the big causal question is answered."

Fisher tightened. "You're fuh-nin welcome!" He squished up

173

his face at his own jumbled retort. "If up to me, I'd shove your as-inine self right back in that cryo-condom and leave you frozen right where I found you."

Resa took a deep breath and placed the palm of his hand against his forehead. When he spoke, his voice sounded laboured by his condition. "Don't be an asshole. If it were that simple to undo the damage you've caused, I'd agree. I am insignif—"

"You got that right," Fisher cut in, terse as a whip. "You *would* be less of a pain as a corpsicle."

"Captain Fisher!" Wisdan roared. "Behave. You too, Resa. We're all in this together, remember? Now let's keep a civil tongue about it."

"I am insignificant," Resa continued. "As is your crew and ship, and this whole armada, and all our gatcham races combined for that matter in the grand scheme of things. By keeping us in stasis the situation stayed in perfect stalemate. You have unwittingly shuffled the pieces out of their deadlock, for what? Profit? Glory? If I could undo the harm you caused by forfeiting my resuscitation, I would do so, gladly."

"Your gratitude overwhelms me," Fisher carped.

"Did you ever ask yourself what has gotten the Imperium so spooked to merit such an obsession with one single robot?" Resa pressed. "Has them still on high alert after the robot destroyed itself?"

"As a matter of fact, I did."

"And?"

"I'm still working on it," Fisher admitted. "But I'll have an answer. I always do."

"Then let me help you with it." Resa's sudden change in tone sounded so disarming, every other face in the room went blank. "The solution is simple really, barring the fact that I no longer have what I went down there to retrieve. Let me complete the job—as if I had, according to my original plan."

Wisdan gripped his chin as if cornering a thought. "I see. Work the problem backwards. Hand your Funder an empty crate."

"Exactly," Resa said. "We might find out what this is actually about. I am the only one here with a direct link to the Funder, the one person who instigated the whole op to the Stricken's surface. I would need a ship of course—this one should do fine since the captain's already on the run from the Imperium."

Fisher folded his arms brusquely. His incoherent baulk was a study in umbrage as he grappled for a fitting rejoinder—one that would make sense.

Wisdan's glower silenced him.

"We can take this ship," Resa went on, pausing briefly to glance around the room, "whatever its type, and break away from Father's flotilla before something untoward happens to his holy fleet. Head for the same designated rendezvous point I planned to make all those years ago."

Resa stopped, his antenna doing push-ups as it reactivated its tiny muscles. Before Fisher could laugh, the Tolkane regarded him again. "I have some connections, and with them added to your own knowledge base, Captain Fisher, we'll cull our resources, trace the links together and see what turns up. It's our best chance to still unravel the mess, after this setback. It's our only chance to get pointed in the right direction."

"So, you think you'll just commandeer my ship like that?" Fisher spat. "Well, Mr Apostate, that head-worm of yours must be cross-wired, cause you're forgetting the part about this being *my* ship."

Silence.

Fisher snorted and lifted a finger. "Let's just make one thing clear—"

"I'm only a passenger. You are still the captain, and will remain fully in charge," Resa calmly finished for him. "It was never in question. However, now that fate has sought to intertwine our purposes, you must sense as well as I how elusive this gambit has become."

Fisher's gaze swept his crew's blanched or sour faces—all seemed to convey some variation of, 'What have you gotten us into now?' The captain asked himself the same question.

"Apart, we can only do so much," Resa said, drawing Fisher in again. "But if we pool our assets, Captain, we multiply our efficacy and our success factor. It's unfortunate that the one key element to this puzzle: the robot we lifted off the Stricken, destroyed itself in the fight."

"Actually," Fisher said, feeling strangely magnanimous towards Resa on this one point. "It didn't."

Resa started and made slits of his eyes. "Are you toying with me, Captain?"

"Not at all. Ask the Ref."

Resa spun on Wisdan.

"It's true, my son," the Cardinal said, bowing his head slightly.

The apostle's doubt should have been sated, but to Fisher's shock, even his crew's supportive head bobs and smiles only amplified Tough-nut's incredulity and scepticism.

"But I saw it aboard the *Inner Peace*," Resa protested. "Scant moments before the ship completely incinerated!"

"Your robot is here," Fisher reasserted.

Resa's brows sprang higher. "Here—*how*?"

"We found him floating in the debris field, clinging to a hull scrap from your former vessel, which you might recognize. We scooped him up at pretty much the same place where we picked up your sorry butt." Fisher explained the rest of the details, unsure whether to feel chagrin, pride, or fear at his disclosure.

To Fisher's relief, Resa allowed a wan but genuine smile to soften his features—his first since his resurrection. "Then, we do stand a chance after all."

"If you say so," Fisher muttered. "I'm not sure I want to stand for anything."

"Even so, I must insist that we break away from the armada, at once," Resa said.

Fisher exhaled. *'At once'—definitely one of Wisdan's.*

"Father," Resa pressed, "with every moment we delay, nested

within the fleet, the more we endanger all the innocent lives of your flock."

"What about my flock?" Fisher objected, a smirk playing on his lips, "Heck, what about their handsome shepherd?"

"Fisher," Wisdan quaffed, "I may be a 'card-in-all,' but considering what you've done and what you have in your possession, you and yours are hardly innocent."

The Cardinal's smile diminished as he turned back to Resa. "I understand, and you are right of course." He hesitated. "But I can't help but feel I'm repeating the same mistake, sending you off on such a dangerous errand, so soon."

Resa reached out and touched his mentor's forearm. "Father, in the first place that was never a mistake, it only seems that way, and secondly, this is my choice. That robot has cost me dearly." Resa's voice cracked a little as he withdrew his hand. "But I believe in my heart that the payoff will be worth it."

Wisdan let out a breath. "Then I won't try to dissuade you, but please, stay as long as you can. I have no wish to sacrifice my fold as oblation, but we will shelter you in any way we can. Anything you need is yours for the asking ere you depart, my son."

"Apart from giving Shyce and my crew a proper funeral service to pay my last respects, what I need most I must ask of the good Captain, but that can wait. There are more immediate exigencies. I'll need access to a Box, wired with some real stellar-cartographic strength," Resa said. "And before any of that, I could sorely use some form of stim, artificial if it must be, that you can supply."

"We got both," Fisher said. "The right Box and the right stim—good old-fashioned coffee and, thanks to Jiri, probably the best in the Universe."

"Anything else?" Wisdan asked, placing a hand on Resa's shoulder.

Resa pondered a moment before managing a sheepish smile. "I would, if it's no great bother, have a proper meal, after the service of course, but before I'm resigned to this ship's rations. My

177

stomach feels like it's digesting itself, and as I recall you always kept a master chef in your employ." Wisdan and Resa exchanged the briefest of looks, but Fisher caught it.

"Splendid," the Cardinal said as he rubbed his palms together. "I'll make all the funeral arrangements. The chapel aboard the *Crucifix* is more than adequate. We can shuttle over to my ship with the deceased immediately. Captain Fisher, you and your crew are more than welcome to attend the service."

Fisher shook his head. "Unfortunately, I can't spare any of my team, if we're going to ship out so soon. I want to make sure the *Skow II* is frosty after her slumber when poker reconvenes. Besides, I warrant they'd feel a tad uncomfortable with that congregation, me most of all—wanton ways and such."

Baines stifled a snigger.

Fisher ignored him. "Still, I offer you my condolences, Resa. You two go ahead. Just ping us if there's anything you need from our end or when you need a lift back."

"On that note, Resa," Wisdan said, "we needn't linger here for you to begin your investigation. You can use my private tech suite aboard the *Crucifix* to gather what information you might need. It is equipped with a Box boasting the very latest gear, very intuitive with an interfacing neural net to assist you. Things have come a long way since we last spoke."

"I'm sure they have," Resa said.

There it reared again. Fisher's lip quivered at the Tolkanes' inflections. To an untrained ear, Resa's requests would appear on the level, but Fisher had honed a fluency with intonation and voice stress patterns, and what he grasped beneath their exchange he didn't like. *Things have come a long way since we last spoke.*

The funeral request was understandable, but he knew Resa didn't give a rat's bunghole about food—food for thought more like. What Golden Boy really said: *I need some words with you in private without this rabble listening in.*

"Time has been rendered superfluous to my mission parameters," Resa said. "So, the contacts I hold should still be valid, or at least the offices those contacts represented."

"You refer to your Funder?" Wisdan asked.

"He is one of many, but yes, his affiliations warrant further investigation, provided we can do so under a constant cloak of subterfuge. That will be key to all our actions, henceforth."

"Hey," Fisher said. "Subterfuge is my middle name."

Everyone in the room shared a grin before Resa leaned forward, drawing Fisher and Wisdan close enough so that only they could hear. "I ask that you keep this between the three of us," he whispered stringently. "There are greater forces at work here than we can begin to comprehend."

"Okay." Fisher frowned. "What do you mean?"

"For one, no projectile launched into the second, larger wave of Imperium ships. The power needed to generate that kind of mass effect from such a great distance is, I believe, part of the truth we seek. Let's leave it at that for now."

Then loudly Resa announced, "I'll away with the Cardinal to begin my search proper. Once I've gathered enough resources to proceed, I suggest we regather here to discuss a precise exit strategy—the three of us, and of course, any crew members Captain Fisher deems fit to include."

Just then, Jiri showed up with a tray laden with steaming mugs of coffee. She offered one to Resa. The rich aroma of the fresh brew spiced with chicory filled the room. "First order of business," she said brightly, before adding in a matter-of-fact tone, "Things were a little dull in engineering. I heard my name, so I thought I'd make myself useful."

"It's about *time*, Jiri," Fisher prodded.

"Always is, Cap, always is," she chided back.

"Thank you, Jiri," Resa said. His creased expression softened after his first sip. "No really thank you, and to you, Fisher—my new captain."

When Resa lifted his mug in a shallow toast, Jiri laughed, tilting her head towards Fisher. "Nothing new about this one. He's an old school, old fart, through and through."

"Yeah, and that's why you love me," Fisher chortled. He took a long draw from the steaming mug. "Like I said, Resa, best stim in the Universe. Jiri gets my vote every time."

After they emptied their coffee mugs, Jiri retrieved a clean jumpsuit and boots for Resa. New apparel donned, the Tolkane shook hands with Fisher before he and Wisdan departed with the deceased woman aboard the Cardinal's shuttle.

That night, while recent doubts hopscotched across Fisher's mind, he played back the latest turn of events. Despite the bizarre convolution of purposes and the complicated string of events that brought them together in what seemed like an apropos, if not preordained juncture, Fisher did warm to his newest passenger. But so did his suspicions about the man. And it wouldn't take a sage to point out that the feeling was mutual.

Fisher wanted to believe he had nothing to lose by joining forces with the puritan, if not for Resa's equivocations. Instinct had always guided the captain, kept him alive. He knew enough of plots and intrigue to hold his tongue while Resa's stilted dialogue with the Cardinal took place, lest he make the truth even more elusive than it frightfully appeared. Fisher needed answers as much as Resa, and if he didn't get them soon, the boon of his relationship with instinct might come to a screeching halt.

For certain, with Resa thawed, Fisher would have to be more on his guard, watching the dodgy Tolkane—with his ears. And that meant just on the outside, here and now.

There *was* a plot within the plot, percolating underground, and slanting the surface. Fisher felt its tilt during Resa's admissions, but couldn't peg it until now, abed in his cabin staring up at the ceiling. Here, it took firm root. Fisher sent his own gnarled roots down until they found water.

After all that Resa went through, down on the Stricken, why didn't the elusive Tolkane automatically gravitate towards the robot? Exactly as the Cardinal had done, he all but ignored the frigin thing when they strode past it on their way out, as if the robot had some sort of contagious, incurable disease. Well, to that extent, maybe they'd be right.

But otherwise, for all his explanation about everything leading up to his plight on the ghost world, Resa dodged clarifying the standoff he'd berated Fisher about. He only described one side of the paradox: The Imperium. He never divulged what lay on the other side of that equal sign, or for that matter what the equal sign represented. Fisher guessed the robot—cause it sure as hell wasn't the wannabe martyr.

As to the Demons' opposition, without question, it wasn't anyone the captain knew or heard about. Vorancia posed the last, and the Imperium quashed that insurrection as only they could quash it. *Only the Demons*. The challenge marked a historical one to be sure, but short-lived, neutralized, and never repeated in all the years since. The edict completely ingrained itself in Fisher's mind since the gears of his own brain began to churn, even before Resa got marooned above the Stricken. Nobody opposes the Imperium, *nobody*.

All the races under Garaxian rule existed as innocuous pawns in the scheme of things, so definitely none of them. The Imperium won *that* game. Any species allowed to go on had been deemed already conquered. So, what got the Demons so freaked out?

Despite what Wisdan had said, Fisher couldn't bring himself to believe one lousy robot reaped such infamy—easily taken out by a single ID missile. Heck, even a well-placed shock-rifle blast might permanently short-circuit Mr Gearbox. But then again, the automaton had survived the destruction of the *Inner Peace*.

The Cardinal's warning resonated through Fisher's mind: *entire planets including Earth were destroyed, because of it*. Yet, according to Resa, the ID didn't want to harm it…What secrets did the robot possess? What could it possibly know? With a sinking feeling, Fisher sensed the truth would uncover something even deeper, something beyond harrowing.

Also, Resa spoke of his Funder as a single enmity, one person. The Cardinal mentioned that Resa's patron had been part of the same delegation from which Vorancia's black widow assassin emerged.

In this regard, of the Imperium, he did not speak. So, who the frick was this implied opponent? Despite the two hundred years of elapsed time, might it possibly be the same faceless Funder who hired and financed the *Skow* to be his courier ship? Even so, Fisher's patron bit it aboard the *Maelstrom* when the Demons destroyed her. Something connected their stories, but what? And how did all the flies and spiders, living or dead fit into this web?

Fisher's frustration fulminated as he failed to frame thoughts sharp enough to vent it. He tried to curse aloud, but his behavioural inhibitor instantly snuffed it, which only irritated him more.

Rather than putting puzzle pieces together, his efforts unhinged them. Furthermore, the puzzle grew in size and complexity, burying him under even more disconnected pieces.

And just when these vexing mysteries tired him out enough to fall asleep, one more grabbed hold. Resa had plainly said that 'what he most needed' would be asked of Fisher himself, and that it could wait. Had Wisdan's pupil inferred that it *must* wait? If so, wait for what?

Fisher had meant to ask him about it when that shrewd and artful Cardy interceded, cunningly steering the conversation on a different track. The fat man took 'crafty bugger,' to a whole new level, a furtive pirate in his own right. The captain chuckled in spite of himself. He'd just have to file it away in his puzzle box and hit Resa for an answer after they parted ways with the God Squad.

Fisher resigned that if it could wait, as his new passenger indicated, then he could wait too. Eventually, Fisher would get his answer. He always did. Considering his limited resources, he concluded, how bad could it be?

22: Locking Horns
Fisher

"Are you out of your eff-n-mind?" Fisher howled, blood squeezing into his facial scar.

Resa set his jaw in stone. "We can't wait any longer for the robot to choose when to turn himself on. The only way we're going to find out why that damn machine is so important is by reactivating him ourselves now. Force him to contend with us."

"What, so he can commandeer my ship and turn my crew into stew when he decides another evasive manoeuvre is in order? No way! Up until now, that robot's been behaving, unlike you." Fisher threw up his hands. "As if I didn't already have my share of detractors. You tinker with that thing all you'll do is peeve him off—rile him back into berserk mode."

"Like you are now?" Resa pointedly observed.

Fisher had been haranguing Resa for several weeks about the other man's unstated request, only to be dismissed with a cursory 'nothing for now.' He dug in his heels and demanded an answer, got it.

And exploded.

"Look," Resa pressed. "I know it's a risk assessment but that robot is the quintessential piece, the keystone to this whole malformed construct. I knew it as soon as I laid eyes on it. That's why I took it off that godforsaken planet."

"Well, you didn't get it very far, and besides, if not for me it would still be lost and you'd still be a corpsicle. I'm just exercising my salvage rights."

Resa's face tightened. "Ever since the *Skow II* left the skirts of the Shepherd Fleet, you've been warring with me, Captain. That's two solid months of pain now, not just for me but your whole damn crew."

"Maybe that's because I'm getting sick of all those proximity alarms reminding me to hightail it out of every frickin sector you've suggested, sallying out just before a Demon squadron catches up. Maybe, having to move twice as fast, and think twice as hard as our enemies is wearing my patience to the bone, not to mention leaving my crew's nerves frayed. How can I not hold you accountable?"

"With the Imperium on our heels, we had to re-establish my crucial ties on Tolkane as soon as possible."

"Sure, so we barge in there and let everyone know," a steadfast Fisher shot back. "Didn't the fat man tell you the story of Vorancia during your little powwow? The Demons would have sleepers set up all over your homeworld. We have to be more evasive, keeping our ears low to the ground. The *Skow II* should have taken the roundabout way, hitting some of *my* more trustworthy contacts in the Barduman System. They would've been able to verify the legitimacy of your links before Your Sainthood went marching in to reconnect them. We could've avoided all those traps completely and still be flying under the radar."

"Your *plan* would have taken too long," Resa countered, "considering the heightened Demon surveillance—your fault to begin with after your blunder of the century. You tripped the Garaxians' wire, hoisted the red flag. Start asking questions to third parties and extra ears enter the loop. And that would have accomplished the same thing: disaster."

Unable to crack Resa's unnerving composure, Fisher quipped, "Wisdan would be proud of such an officious little pri–pr—pr—puritan!"

"Yes," Resa agreed, nodding his head brusquely. "Proud indeed that I still have the capacity to put up with such an asshole."

"If not for you, life aboard my boat would never have become this tense. You're the one sowing dislike and distrust like a farmer on speed, risking all our lives in a hazardous game of cat and mouse."

Resa maintained his calm as Fisher vented. For two months he had kept his promise to function solely as a passenger, respecting Fisher's authority with the day-to-day running of the ship. But when the Tolkane's 'might I propose' s and 'perhaps we could' s,' regarding their strategies and logistics grew more and more frequent, Fisher began to resent him.

Smiling, Fisher would respond to such proposals with, 'That's a fine idea, Resa' and 'I'll have to think about it,' and leave it at that.

According to Bliter, this drove Resa out the hull, but outwardly he kept lucid and said nothing to Fisher, preferring to retreat, retrench, and eventually take matters into his own hands.

That sometimes meant sidestepping the captain and asking the crew members directly for the things he needed. That, to Fisher, circumvented his authority and drove him out the hull and into the thruster tube, especially when the rest of the crew started backing Resa up with: 'I think he's right, Captain' and 'Hey, I never thought of that, Resa.'

So irksome festered into nasty and nasty gave birth to intolerable, or just tolerable enough without it coming to blows. Fisher's behavioural inhibitors continued to suppress his profanity, but he compensated by levelling slights against the holier-than-thou Resa.

Fisher developed a knack for pushing Resa's buttons, but the Tolkane would play pacifist and simply breathe to expunge on those more heated occasions. Resa determined 'not to stoop to Fisher's debased level,' stating as much during their numerous rows.

The crew got used to the regularity of the captains' verbal fencing. All too quickly, they learned the futility of trying to contain the pair's rancorous bickering for it only served to drag it out even longer. Instead, they ran for cover and waited until the shelling stopped. Once both men had vented, the crew could enjoy a few hours of peace, until the next bout.

But now, they reached a crossroads where neither would budge.

They'd barely arrived in the Shekani Sector when Fisher ordered Baines to cut the engines and bring the *Skow II* to a full stop. While they floated about aimlessly in the vague nebulaic zone, the dispute between Fisher and Resa had deteriorated to the breaking point.

"Enough of what brought us to this impasse, Fisher. That cargo is just as much mine as it is yours and I insist we bring the robot back online."

"Yeah, but I'm *the captain*, remember?"

Resa glared at Fisher. "Don't you dare play that card in this matter. Rebooting that automaton transcends anything concerning ship duties. You gave Wisdan your word that we'd work together on this. Your wants are nimbused by the greater need. We all have a shared stake in this, and last time I checked that includes you."

"Cards? Stakes? Yeah, we'll dice to settle it."

"I don't gamble," Resa said.

"Yes, you do," Fisher snapped. "You took a g-dm gamble going down to the Stricken, with quite a poor hand I might add. You left the *Inner Peace* in Inner—*pieces*. Maybe, gamble with your karma on this too. Except this time use that forehead whisker and plead advice from on High. Maybe, your gods'll kick some sense into that revenant butt of yours. So, just-possibly-maybe, you'll stop speaking from it!"

Resa compressed his lips into a tight line. "Maybe, just because I'm a religious man doesn't mean I won't punch you in your blasphemous face."

"*Maybe*," Baines cut in, "you won't have to do either—if you two can break away from your pissing match to listen."

They both spun and stared at the pilot.

Baines pointed to his console. "I think the Gearbox has decided for himself." He spoke softly, but his tone implied a shout. "Robot's fully awake. He's hailing us—wants us to join him."

The effect of Baines' revelation was instantaneous. All the tension in the room purged like a deflating balloon, forcing the combatants to adjust to the sudden and radical paradigm shift. Whatever alien design governed it, the robot's reawakening superseded both plaintiffs, effectively muting their white-hot argument.

Fisher recovered his wits and moved perfunctorily over to the console. "Tap it in," he croaked, his throat raw as he forced down his terseness. "Open the channel."

With a brisk nod, Baines turned back to his console.

"Hello, Captain Fisher, Captain Resa. Please join me in the ship's cargo hold. I've been waiting for a very long time to have

186

this meeting, in light of my anticipated Juncture. The time has come to fully reveal myself and my intent to you. And for you to learn your roles therein."

Fisher exchanged a worried look with Resa. "What do we do now?"

"I think we should do as it requests," Resa said. "We're all on the same team, Captain Fisher." He tilted his head towards the monitor. "Including that robot. Might as well be on the same page as well."

"Thanks for the reminder but it sure didn't sound that way. Mr Gearbox said something about us having parts in *his* intent."

Resa remained silent and stared.

Fisher knew why, since becoming acquainted with the Tolkane's mannerisms: Resa only awaited Fisher's 'captain's verdict'—one he would respect.

After a moment, Fisher sighed. "Okay, we go in, armed. Just you, me, and Cholla. I'm not risking anybody I don't have to. I want the door sealed behind us after we enter the hold. Baines, you and Bliter man the console. Monitor us."

"I recommend you all wear environment suits," Bliter said. "That way if the robot becomes hostile, I can blow the hatch and recover you later."

Fisher shook his head. "I don't think that'll be necessary."

"With all due respect, Captain, a bit of caution is warranted," the navigator pressed.

"Look, between both my ships, the robot's been with us for months. I hardly think it means us any harm now, and besides isn't it obvious he's wirelessly linked to some if not all our systems, including any airlock overrides, including communications? He knows everything we've just said. Remember what Resa told us about his own ship? Robo's hail was just a show of... courtesy."

"A gesture to put us on equal ground," Resa added.

"Yeah, exactly," Fisher said before realizing with whom he just agreed. Grimacing inwardly, he squared his jaw. "We go in."

23: Beacons
Fisher

Mr Gearbox looked more functional than Fisher remembered. Resa too had had but a glimpse of the robot's potential, and that while immersed in his etherized state. This first real contact seemed all so unnerving, especially when Bliter sealed them inside, effectively cutting them off from the rest of the ship.

"Play nice," Fisher said under his breath as he advanced on the robot.

It floated before the advancing party a foot above the deck like some bizarre metallic scarab doing a pirouette on its hind legs—if that's what they were—too many gadget-laden appendages to tell. They all fanned out in every direction from its oval form like a porcupine's quills.

The robot had a ghoulish countenance, if not for the big yellow smiley-face crudely painted on its black torso, in sharp contrast to the rest of its shell. That icon, greeting them now, helped put Fisher at ease. It seemed so idiotic he began to chuckle.

Resa turned and fixed the captain with an incredulous stare. "Really? Now?"

Fisher laughed all the harder. He couldn't help it, about to treat with the most prized object in the galaxy—a universal cynosure, second only to the god particle itself. Mr Gearbox had a proven track record of destructive capability, to nullify any contention as easily as a wildfire negated dry bracken. And Fisher found it all completely hilarious.

The robot slowly panned his upper torso so his only eye fixed on Fisher. "You are a brazen character, Captain Fisher," it greeted. "And a percipient one too. You do right and well to dispel your peers' anxiety. Their fear of me is unwarranted, but you must remain wary of those who seek me. For I hold the key to your salvation—and that of your Universe."

"Oh," Fisher said in mock relief. "That's what all the fuss is about? You got a name, Robo?"

189

"My name is, or rather the name given to me is Beacon. You may call me that."

"Okay, Beacon, why the wake-up call?"

"Solidarity. You are heading into a trap," Beacon said. "And though it behoves me to tell you, whatever we decide here, you will not escape it. I seek to usher you in and hopefully through."

Fisher's smile vanished. "You saying you *want* us to get caught in this snare?"

"Not precisely," Beacon corrected. "It is a trap which must be sprung if we are to unveil the greater trap beyond. The timeliness of our actions in this matter is most crucial. It shall invariably lead to a future consequence I call the Great Juncture."

"Can't say I like the sound of that, whatever *that* is," Fisher said.

"I speak of the culmination of events that must unfold in their due course—and they will. It is an infinitely long prediction model, but also a mathematical certainty."

"I don't like riddles, Beacon," said Resa with a touch of asperity. "Speak plain."

"Apologies. It is not my intent to befuddle you with my choice of words. Let me explain everything you need to know."

"*Need* to know? That's a crafty way of admitting you'll be doing some filtering," Resa pointed out. "But even filtered information is better than none at all. Carry on."

"I've been monitoring your progress ever since you joined Cardinal Wisdan's armada," Beacon said. "And am aware of everything about your intentions. Your direction is sound, but without my immediate intervention, your method will only lead to irreversible folly and ruin."

"Oh, so you know about our plan. Spying on us, eh?" a bemused Fisher asked.

"Well, yes, spying if you will, but I like to think of it as reconnoitring your progress without interference. Unfortunately, this recent hesitation will misalign our collective purposes. The time to second guess one another is over. We must tear away the veil of obfuscation and organize ourselves with poise and audacity—before the Juncture reaches its zenith. When it does, we must prepare to act decisively and in concert, if there is to be a future."

"What are you suggesting?" Resa asked. "What do you even mean?"

"We follow your plan," Beacon answered. Resa's node straightened and his mouth curved—into a grin.

"Great," Fisher said, suddenly dejected.

"But with one difference, which I will explain in a moment," Beacon clarified. "As I said, a trap awaits you regardless of your strategy Captain Resa or yours, Captain Fisher. I'm sure that you both appreciate the gravity of the situation from your experiences thus far, but understand this. The Imperium has been pursuing me long before either of you came into existence, for thousands of years, across several galaxies.

"Numerous races were sacrificed and made extinct for the sake of my safe delivery to the Juncture. There have been countless periods of waiting, with my being in stasis. I am not without my own defensive capabilities but have relied heavily on the strengths of various species I've encountered to develop the tech to combat the oppressors. It has always proven a case of too little, too late."

Beacon's domed orb tilted up and his upper torso panned left for a protracted moment before returning to the three men. "Until now. The last race I interfaced with—the Humans of Earth, facilitated the breakthrough in the technology I needed to finally crack the cycle and carry out my mission.

"Unfortunately, someone sabotaged and betrayed us to the Imperium before I could launch my counteroffensive. My counterpart and I deemed it best to waylay the Demons by remaining on Earth while as many Humans as possible evacuated the planet. Since the Garaxians had targeted me, they calibrated their tech to seek my energy signatures.

"The mass exodus of arks under the command of another trusted colleague left the system, trying to evade the hammer

191

stroke in a bid for the race's survival. They got away before the plasma hit and consumed their planet, rendering it Stricken. Those left behind could not escape the doomsday bomb in time and perished."

Fisher shivered, recalling his first glimpse of the ghost world that brought them all together. Resa dry-swallowed.

"The Demons knew exactly where I wound up but for some reason did not extract me. They maintained a constant vigil, having me essentially secure in a prison. I sensed my wardens monitoring me from distant polar stations, waiting to see who else would show up. That went on for centuries. Eventually, I had to conserve my power, for when it would be needed again. I switched my primary circuits into hibernation mode, phasing power cells down to near-zero expenditure. A new stalemate had begun.

"In this way, I preserved much of my energy for what I gleaned would be another long wait. A relatively short time afterwards, a minute level-one proximity alarm sounded in my external sensor grid, signalling a potential reactivation protocol, but it never reached level two. That would have fired up my direct neural processors for self-actuation and awareness of my environment, one step below full functionality and operational parameters. I concluded that someone tried to extract me from my plasma tomb on the Stricken, but failed to do so or for some reason aborted the attempt."

"That would have been me," Resa supplied.

"No," Beacon corrected. "Long before you, Captain Resa. I know this for a certainty."

"So, you didn't cut that tube back to the building yourself? The tunnel through the hardened plasma?"

"No. I'm sorry."

"That's okay, Beacon," Fisher soothed with a sardonic lilt. "It's just another mystery to add to the ugly pile Resa buried me under."

Ignoring the slur, Resa kept his attention centred on the robot. "Beacon, what *did* happen back in that debris field above the

Stricken? I have a vague recollection, but considering my state of mind, I'm not entirely sure what I saw. You rescued us, didn't you?"

"Yes, you inadvertently reactivated me when you took me off Earth. My emergency activation protocols kicked in. I spidered."

"You—what?" Fisher and Resa asked in unison.

"I sent out all interface and sensor signals to ascertain my exact predicament. In essence, I seized control of your ship. The situation devolved beyond grim, though more for you than me. They baited you with me, and you took it. Still, your actions convinced me to risk saving you. I accessed all ship's logs and called up your work records, affiliations, and communiqués. At the same time, I put eyes out on three levels: local, system, and sect, to monitor the Imperium's tactical approach. I ran the numbers to 2.6 million variations for our best chance of survival. My choice seems to have evinced the correct one."

"How long did you take to do all that?" an amazed Cholla asked.

"3.7 seconds," came the flat response.

"Show off," Fisher chided.

"As stated, I had to assume immediate control to prevent my recapture, and that of Captain Resa. I deduced your significance within the scheme of my long-played affairs and knew you had to survive. Your arrival has added something of a wildcard to the endgame the Imperium forces us to play."

Fisher laughed and tilted his head towards Resa. "Welcome to the poker table after all, Mr Holy."

"I tried to save your other crew members," Beacon went on in a morose tone, "but after we escaped the initial cordon, the Demon interceptors let out such a barrage, they took out your shields in the first volley. Half your hull breached with the second. Most of the crew perished this way either from the impact of the ordnance or the vacuum of space, but some I regret to say took too many G's from my evasive manoeuvres and met with physical trauma, crushed against bulkheads. We fled. The Demons followed."

Resa nodded solemnly, glancing at the hull fragment of his late ship. It still splayed in the corner of the cargo bay floor behind the robot.

"The Demons didn't want to destroy the *Inner Peace* outright," said Beacon, "which they could have done easily enough at any time. They needed to entrap and disable her only. If the ID had extracted me, they would have siphoned your brains for information before killing you. I used this foreknowledge to gain a tactical advantage. After successfully evading pursuers for so long, the pursued does grow wise to their methods."

Fisher smiled at that.

"Marrying your spacecraft's defences with my formidable tech, I remote-piloted the ship on an unorthodox course through the accretion disk of Earth's former moon, putting as much distance between the *Inner Peace* and the Demon vanguard. I knew your ship wouldn't survive my gambit, so I purposed to get you and Officer Shyce—the only other survivor—off the vessel and into what I call a *Shroud*."

Resa blinked. "Was that the ignatia I saw surrounding our pod?"

"Yes. That done, I took the *Inner Peace* to what I deemed to be a safe distance and brought her to an emergency stop. I made the interceptors believe we had burned out our power cells—we almost did actually. The Imperium ships closed in, holding stations with tractors locked to keep the *Inner Peace* in thrall. That's when I ignited the vessel's engine cores.

"The discharge found the path of least resistance looping back through those same energy beams connecting every Demon ship in the vicinity, causing a chain reaction. I turned their snare back on them. They had no chance."

"I remember that," Resa said. "But then moments after that explosion a second larger Imperium fleet showed up and held station over our pods. I thought we were dead, but they didn't do anything. It was like they couldn't see us."

"That is how a Shroud works," Beacon explained. "The

energy shield derives its power from a latent form of dark energy, not unlike the Demons' plasma, except not as volatile. I can generate it to encompass small objects or bits of tech to render them invisible to any scan, including visual. I phased you out of this reality for a time. As the shield weakens you return to the proper phase. Within the bubble you still can perceive everything in your former reality, but not so for any outsider looking in. That is how I saved you and tried to save your pilot. It is also how I endured."

"Okay, that's a lot to digest," Resa said. "I'll take your word on it, but there's more—" He licked his lips. "Now at that point, events became blurry, and perhaps I may have imagined it, but after you, something obliterated that second fleet too."

"I wouldn't be surprised," the robot admitted. "If there's one thing that I've learned about the Demons, it is this: they do not tolerate discord, so failure to them is anathema. Their ships are all linked to each other like a colony of ants. Information and instructions lead back to their Exarch who sits upon a central locus of the Imperium like the hub of an immense wheel.

"Through their superior tech, the Exarch holds command override protocols over every single ship in his fleet. He can simply tell any given vessel to destroy itself through a hard-wired subroutine integrated into every vessel. Their society is a forensic one, devoid of all emotion except one. Fear.

"The Exarch doesn't need to command loyalty. He already has it because every Ice Demon lives with the knowledge that somewhere another Garaxian has a finger poised on a button, which can cause his death. The second fleet's destruction was simply the exaction of penance for their commander's failure."

"I under—" Resa did a doubletake. He raised a finger. "But then, moments before unconsciousness took me, I'm fairly sure I caught a glimpse of one more visitor before my lights went out completely. A single ship this third time around, but I didn't recognize it. Could you shed some light on this?"

"Interesting," Beacon pondered, his single orb sloping at a

forty-five-degree angle up, a ninety-degree angle down, then tracking back level to Resa. "I'll give it some thought. For now, perhaps we can add the mystery to Captain Fisher's ugly pile."

"Couldn't have said it better myself, Bee," said Fisher. "Really."

The robot's seeing-dome panned slowly between the three men, the light hum of servos its only sound. "I assure you that we'll get to the bottom of this but for the sake of solidarity and efficacy, I will need some assistance."

"Dr Cholla and my team stand ready to assist you," Fisher said.

"Unfortunately, your cadre cannot give me the kind of support I need. Someone else *must* join us."

Fisher started. "Nobody else is joining this dysfunctional family of ours. It's bad enough without adding another body to the mix."

"I'm afraid you're very mistaken about that," Beacon countered.

"I am? Which part?"

"All parts."

"Really?" Fisher drew up before the robot, tightening his grip on his sidearm.

"Yes," the robot replied. "And I must prove it to you before we go any further."

Two hatches in Beacon's torso sprang open. Out of them a pair of metallic arms surged forward and seized Fisher by the torso, spinning him around so that he faced his crew. A third appendage tipped with a syringe snaked up behind the captain, arching over his right shoulder.

It paused a second. Then dove down with surgical precision into the flesh at the base of Fisher's neck. The captain yelped.

"I suggest you all back away," Beacon warned. "I know how this must look but it is necessary. Dr Cholla, you will escort me to your med-lab. I do not wish to harm your captain, but do not force my hand. I assure you that all will be set aright. I can say no more

196

until I have completed this task."

Beacon moved forward, impelling his hostage in front of him. Before he reached the doors, they flew open and the crew rushed in, armed with some angry-looking guns. The barrage of heated expletives, struggling to escape Fisher's mouth, came out as a jumbled slur of single consonants. Was it the effect of the inhibitors kicking in or whatever the darn robot jabbed him with? Fisher couldn't tell and he didn't care. He fulminated uselessly in the middle of an ugly situation about to get a lot uglier.

Beacon stopped.

The crew aimed.

"Fools," Resa flared. "Don't touch him." His shout pierced the claptrap, stunning them all to silence. No one breathed. "Stand *down,* all of you!" he demanded. "Captain Fisher will be fine. Quickly, Dr Cholla, do as Beacon commands. Take them to the med-lab." When the crew didn't move, Resa cursed under his breath.

Cholla finally diffused the situation. "Guys, I think he's right. Let's all cool our jets. Give the robot and Resa, the benefit of the doubt—he's been right so far," the doctor added as cheerfully as possible.

Fisher's heart trip-hammered. Unable to speak, paralysed by fear, drugs, or both, he could only nod emphatically at Doc's plea.

The crew still hesitated a moment longer, but Cholla's assurances finally mollified them. Slowly, begrudgingly, they dropped their weapons and stood aside, letting the robot pass with his hostage. Cholla took the lead.

A grim march from the cargo hold to the med bay followed, with the doctor leading the procession, shadowed by Beacon holding Fisher fast, and the crew trailing several paces behind. Cholla seemed optimistic, and Fisher found it contagious. Nevertheless, the captain gave sincere thanks to Wisdan's deity that it was a short trip.

When they reached the door to the med-lab, Cholla fingered his access code on a control pad beside the entryway. The door slid open with a firing of servos and a sigh of pneumatics. Beacon drew up beside the entryway and slowly rotated towards the doctor. The metallic arms supporting Fisher's sagging form extended as if making a religious offering.

"Here, take your captain," Beacon said. "He will recover shortly." With that, the robot gently deposited Fisher into Cholla's waiting arms.

Beacon's upper trunk wheeled towards the rest of the crew as he backed up through the threshold. "Right now, you cannot understand my motives and feel betrayed, but I assure you that I bear no ill intent. You may feel obliged to thwart me, but you cannot impede my efforts without injuring yourselves or the ship. So please, for your own safety, do not try to hinder me. I have delicate work to do over the next several hours and must divert most of your ship's resources to the task at hand. Be patient and don't attempt anything foolish. You will understand everything soon enough. Trust your robot."

With that, Beacon sealed himself in the lab. Once the door had locked, the crew rushed in to help Cholla, struggling with Fisher's dead weight.

"Fish, you okay?" Baines yelled. "Fucker went and stabbed us in the back—in your case, literally. We can cut the power to whatever he's doing or loopback a surge when he plugs in to fry his neural net. That'll give him his just desserts. A robot with no power is just a hunk of scrap."

"Scrap," Resa reprimanded, "is what this ship will be if we try and tinker, Baines. Do not dare interfere."

Beacon's voice came over the loudspeaker just then. "Crew of the *Skow II*, I strongly recommend that you all retreat to the cargo hold for the time being. In five minutes, the rest of the ship will be incapable of life support. I suggest you comply immediately."

Baines glared at the Tolkane. "You want to say that again, Resa?"

24: Confluence
Fisher

Fisher rubbed the tension from his temple, then the itch from his scar, not believing his ears. "Leave him?"

"Yes, leave him," Resa said. "Beacon did the same with the *Inner Peace,* commandeering it for the sake of survival."

"Yeah well, we all know how great that turned out." Fisher walked over to the curved piece of the *Inner Peace*'s hull, still sitting on the cargo bay floor and bearing the late ship's insignia. He wound back and gave it a good hard kick. It let out a dull metallic thud.

"Faith and fate, Captain," Resa said behind him. "They go hand in hand. It is the divine that sets us up in the right position like game pieces on the board before stepping back. It falls to us to make the moves and take the match. I'd rather be a game piece on the winning side. Let the robot do what he says."

"Wonderful, I'm now a prisoner on my own ship," Fisher grumbled as he turned to face him. "It's been four freaking hours. Nothing's happening."

"I would take that as a good sign," Bliter said, drawing Fisher's notice. "And it's not like we have much of a choice. Rest of the ship is well below the line. Even if we could do something, we just can't get anywhere to be effective without compromising our safety."

"Even better, Bliter," Fisher scoffed. "Tell me something I don't know. Anybody got a deck of cards?"

Sullen, Fisher paced back and forth in silence between the crew. They all stared at their feet as he passed. Hours more dragged on before the captain finally joined them in their informal seating arrangement.

"Cheer up, Cap," Jiri said in a positive tone. "This wasn't your fault, and nobody on the crew holds you responsible. Besides, we're not dead yet, bored to death maybe."

Fisher gave her a bleak smile. "Thanks. But I ain't about to

199

initiate trust-falls or lead you all in a sing-song."

"No way," gasped Jiri in feigned shock. "That *would* kill us." Everyone smiled at that.

"Well, we got enough rations in here for a few days of lockdown. Guess we should start thinking about sleeping arrangements."

Before they addressed that next order of business, the com-link speakers buzzed to life, startling them all to their feet. "This is Beacon, thanking you for your continued patience. I am pleased to report that the ship's auxiliary power is currently being restored. All other compartments will have full life support in seven minutes. Med-lab will remain off-limits until tomorrow morning, but you will have complete control over the rest of your ship. Once again, I thank you for your patience and your leap of faith."

Click!

Relief flooded through Fisher. Resa's shoulders and eyebrows slackened. He looked pleased too. Like a light being switched back on, the cargo hold erupted with excited conversations, everyone milling about, trying to talk at once.

"You need to stay calm and quiet inside," Beacon told Resa and Fisher outside the med-lab door. "When we enter, please observe only. Do not interact with her in any way. That you may do tomorrow. She is still very vulnerable to external stimuli. It's not that dissimilar to the first stages of your reanimation, Captain Resa, except for one added component. Any jarring auditory interference can send her into shock."

The robot's domed orb tracked in until it settled on Fisher. "I'll apologize now for my intervention and my surreptitious behaviour. I needed her presence post-haste and could not allow further dalliance on the subject with what Pilot Baines described as your 'pissing match.' I'm also sorry for the small injury I caused you, Captain Fisher. I needed living tissue to replicate and you held the closest DNA match."

"You could have just asked," Fisher said morosely, his hand automatically reaching for the pinhead scab on his nape. Resa merely shrugged.

"I must say, Captain Fisher, you are full of surprises," Beacon said.

Fisher frowned, having no idea what to make of the remark. Probably best he didn't.

"Now, if you'll both follow me. Remember only to speak in whispers."

Beacon led them into the heart of the medical bay where a small ramp sank onto a circular grated-metal platform. Fisher looked around and nodded in satisfaction. The *Skow II*'s med-bay rivalled the upgraded facility aboard the *Skow*. Who'd have thought that pirates would keep such an advanced and well-stocked med bay? In any case, it sure served Beacon well.

Fisher shifted his gaze to the mysterious robot's pet project. In the centre of the small O.R. alcove, a gurney supported a cylindric incubation tube, its semi-circular glass maw splayed open. A pair of surgical waldoes hung limply from the ceiling grid close by and a stainless medical cart filled with stacks of small monitors and consoles stood adjacent. Several wires and tubes connected to a female humanoid body, dressed in a baby-blue patient smock partially covered by a thin white sheet.

The woman lay atop the stretcher inside the opened tube. The steady rise and fall of her chest confirmed that whoever she was, she was alive.

"This," Beacon said in a barely audible tone, "is my counterpart, Anne Morrison, or rather her rescued and restored mind, housed in a bio-engineered living vessel of your Tolkani anatomy. Like me, she has come a long way to make it to this point. In her, hope is rekindled... for us all."

The robot's voice carried a note of emotion, but it may have been the effect of Robo's needle jab or Fisher's mental exhaustion.

Stephen Fenech

25: Revenant
Fisher

The fifty-something woman sitting up on the medical bed in front of Fisher and Resa had aged well. Better than well. She was a very attractive female with high cheekbones, bladed features, and a shapely physique. Her lively blue eyes regarded Fisher now with a deep perceptiveness that surpassed his own.

Without exchanging a single word, he sensed a heroine's strength and experience in the woman before him. As though parsing his observation, his latest guest smiled a benevolent smile that made her face glow.

"Hello Captain Fisher, Captain Resa," Anne greeted in an avuncular tone. "So, you are the two men responsible for my rescue. Beacon has filled me in on several encouraging details of our situation. I'm also pleased and grateful for my successful resurrection." She put a hand in front of her face and inspected it. "Even if he had to stick me back in this same old shell."

Fisher frowned. "Sorry?"

"Doesn't every woman want to look and feel younger?" she asked with a laugh.

"Now that you mention it, why didn't you get a younger body? —not that you look bad now."

"As Beacon explained it, the reason has to do with compatibility. When I translated from my biological form into a digital reality, I had physically reached this precise age. The two have to be matched perfectly with my physiology at the time. During the reciprocal process, any deviation from the exact pairing would cause incongruence. All the background programs running my mind and body would seize, rendering me stillborn."

Anne paused and looked down to examine both arms. She raised her legs, bare from the knees down. "I seem to have lost all my freckles."

Her smirk faded and she cast an earnest look at Fisher. "But I'm more than content. It's not just the satisfaction in prolonging my life, but in seeing the potential fruition of my life's work. You know there aren't many races that can say they got a second kick at the can once they found themselves in the Imperium's crosshairs. In fact, there are none."

"Good point," said Fisher.

"With the risks you took, you made this possible, Captain Fisher, whether you understood the full implication of the path you followed or not. *You* made *me* possible. I guess I could consider you my brother, genetically speaking of course."

"In that case, hello, Sis," Fisher laughed.

Anne's grin joined his but as her focus shifted to Resa, it straightened. "We may represent three separate generations, three separate races, but we unite now to carry out the same purpose."

"That being?" Resa asked.

"I'm talking about the emancipation and continuation of the Universe." She finished with a strident nod. "We'll succeed."

The woman's confidence bordered on such temerity, Fisher found it inspiring. He glanced in Resa's direction. By the Tolkane's firm jaw, he seemed equally moved. Perhaps on that note, His Holiness found some common ground with Fisher at last.

"So, you know our story, Dr Morrison. What's yours?" queried Fisher. "Why are you so important and where the—fu, f, f—!!"

"—fuck, did I come from?" she finished for him.

"Um, yeah."

"I was born quite a long time ago on Earth, as it was formerly known before the Demons turned it into a wasteland. As I understand, I'm your ancestor, and you're my scion, my legacy." Anne tilted her head towards Resa. "A daughter species of our combined genetic lines—Tolkani, the hybrid congenital to a Human/Tolkane union."

She briefly outlined the events of her life that led her to Beacon and the technological revolutions and revelations that followed.

"When we learned that the attack was imminent, we had to ramp up our plans," Anne said. "Knowing the tech we developed wouldn't be ready before the strike, we took what we had so far, housed it in a packet and placed it in the capable hands of my most esteemed colleague, Dr Baron Fieldbank. Baron took the first of our three versioned packets with him when he left Earth for good, He led the most massive exodus of ships our world had ever known.

"Starliners, retrofitted to serve as generation ships, embarked out of system with as many people as they could accommodate. The arks searched for a possible haven to continue our way of life—and our work in case we failed. Beacon gave him some indication of which sector would offer the Human race its best chance of success."

Dr Cholla, who'd been busy with a diagnostic tablet at the far side of the lab, stopped his tabulations and joined them.

Anne gave him a warm smile before continuing. "As for myself, I knew the Imperium's attack would target Beacon. His energy signature made him the ID's painted target on the planet. I chose to remain behind and continue our research until the last possible moment. In so doing, Beacon and I gave the evacuating Humans a chance to get away, to hide their escape. We knew we couldn't run, for wherever Beacon went, an attack would follow.

"And the extinct race that sent the robot our way tragically demonstrated that even if Beacon did split, it would make no difference. The surge had already been released. Our planet would still be doomed. We had to ensure that the Imperium believed it had completely neutralized the threat we allegedly posed."

Fisher exchanged a knowing look with Resa.

"As for version-two of the packet," Anne went on. "Baron and I alone picked a secure location, far removed from Earth and Baron's fleet—somewhere either party would know and eventually go if the other failed outright. That's where we sent this second packet and agreed to direct our own packets, if and when we completed them. Again, Beacon tenured some good advice about how to proceed with this three-fold plan but decided that we should not tell him, lest the Demons compromise his systems and discover the location. So, we left him in the dark."

A chirp and brief whine sounded from across the room, drawing Fisher's notice.

"Still am," Beacon admitted as he floated forward. The

memory of a plunging syringe fresh on the captain's mind, he instinctively took a step back, not fancying a second inoculation from Mr Gearbox.

As the robot drew to a halt before Anne, she inclined her head and turned to Fisher. "After Baron left, we launched an unmanned probe containing this second packet with what we'd developed thus far. The small vessel managed to win free and disappear out of system before the Demons killed my planet."

She squeezed her eyes shut for a moment and sighed. "They're a forensic, calculating bunch."

"You'll get no argument from me there," Fisher said.

Anne's eyebrows gathered in. "After that secret launch, between the countermeasures and the weapons my team devised, we made our breakthrough with the third and last packet—on the computer model's tech specs at least," she amended. "But we couldn't communicate our discovery to Baron, who had long since departed aboard the arks. We had to maintain radio blackout, so as to not jeopardize their safety. And trust that Baron would achieve the same success with his version."

Fisher stepped closer and shivered. "Can't imagine hanging back, watching that sh-*shih*-stuff coming at me. What happened?"

Anne gripped the side of the mattress and hunched forward. "In earnest, Captain, I thought I would die with my planet." She brightened and took a deep breath. "But then, as I versioned the most recent updates into the third packet and made my peace with God and destiny, a mere nine days before the plasma hit, Beacon told me he found a way to save me."

Anne nudged her chin at Mr Gearbox and beamed. "He came to me that night while I looked up at the star-studded desert sky, as the monstrous plasma bomb filled it like the Auroras—beautiful really." She squared her shoulders. "But salvation outshone it."

Cholla lowered the tablet to his side. "I must admit I've never heard of such an organic/binary transformation. How did Beacon accomplish this feat?"

Anne fanned a hand through her hair. "By extracting my brain patterns and with them my thoughts and memories through their biochemical signatures, Beacon converted them into base-state energy, then into binary code. In real-time, he housed them as a fully integrated electronic version. My essence co-existed as a separate entity within his positronic matrix."

Cholla's breath caught and his body grew still, except for his smirk, which stretched from ear to ear.

"My corporeal body died of course," Anne explained. "Once my mind vacated the premises. But my consciousness and genetic identity lived on. Although I would exist on a very diminished subconscious level, I still retained the faculty of my brain functions and could even communicate with my host.

"Beacon had the original vessel that splashed down with him placed a stone's throw outside our HQ in Phoenix. Being comprised of the same plasma coming to annihilate us, rendered the pod immune to the effects of the scourge. He wanted the vessel in plain view for later extraction.

"When Judgement Day came, he retreated inside the alien craft and sealed himself in, with me safely stowed aboard his brain. There was still a good chance we wouldn't survive the attack, but I agreed all the same. What choice did I have?"

"None," said Fisher. "Your alternative—a final date with oblivion."

Anne's chin bobbed in affirmation. "Besides, it gave us a historical opportunity to finally break the Imperium's cycle of conquest. I very much wanted to protect the sanctity of life for all the unborn, a chance at a life free from ID tyranny—for all races. The Imperium's strength will only increase with time and any potentially effective weapon against it has an expiry date."

The thought of Vorancia made Fisher's joints tighten.

"As I said, three packets existed," Anne continued. "The older version we sent out by itself. The packet we sent away with Baron. And the packet Beacon and I kept working on. Unfortunately, our packet—the completed one—was destroyed in the initial attack, and the one aboard the probe was, relatively speaking, a dinosaur. But Baron's should still be viable. And if I know my colleague, still out there. If so, we would only need to recover the packet, and if not fully completed, tweak it to bring it up to the same level as the one we finished developing."

Anne paused her explanation and appraised Fisher. "Beacon mentioned that you were couriering a packet as well."

"Yup," Fisher said, rubbing the sides of his trousers briskly. "That was sure darn strange. Our Funder's rep, a real eerie cookie like Resa—I mean, Resa's contact. Mine laced the gig with a few prerequisites, but his one sin qua non was our course. He didn't allow us to deviate from that. We picked up the packet and got handed our jump coordinates—prearranged to the metre. And a downpayment—which was still a lot of upfront cash. The Funder threw in a bunch of internal upgrades to sweeten the *Skow*. But after we found what was left of Resa's ship, including his sorry butt, we got stuck, in the deepest pile of sh-sh-shrapnel imaginable."

Fisher scrunched up his face, feeling as though he accidentally relieved himself. Anne furrowed her eyebrows but remained quiet. Grateful for her silence, the captain blew out his cheeks and picked up his tale again, "We were supposed to hook up with another Tolkane cutter to make the drop and collect the bulk of the credits the Funder still owed us for the job—a gas giant where he waited to take delivery aboard the *Maelstrom*."

Resa flinched as though stung.

Fisher wrinkled his nose. "What's with you?"

"Nothing," Resa said with a dismissive wave. "Just a slight spasm from my reawakening node. Go on, Captain."

"Right," Fisher said, making a mental note. He refocused on Anne. "So, as stated, the ship was supposed to lie in wait but things didn't go exactly to plan. The Imperium found the *Maelstrom* first." His eyes darted to Resa but the Tolkane's scrutiny now tethered Anne.

Fisher shook his head. "They left it in one big mess. We crept in under full stealth—that's what saved us. Turned out to be an ID interceptor. The Demons knew we were coming and set us a trap, a big one. We ran for it."

The captain filled his lungs and scratched the stubble on his cheek. "Figured the ID were hunting the packet but when I took a peek, I only found historical records or some such," he said with an offhand flourish.

Anne leaned in. "Explain *some such*."

"Oh, I don't know, archaic really. I opened it and couldn't make heads or tails of the data stream, coded in a language I've never seen before—maybe some archaeologists' crap, command protocols and the like."

Anne started, her eyes enlarging.

"As for the device," Fisher said, "I gave it some juice and tried it, but it didn't respond—benign. Perhaps the gadget was an antique and the Funder merely wanted it for posterity."

"Is that all you found?" Anne asked, her voice pitching higher. She shifted off her bed.

Fisher began to nod but stopped short. "No, wait, I noticed a really odd thing. The label on the casing had been written in English syllabics. I recognized them as the Human tongue. Wisdan mentioned some extinct race even before you guys went bust, and though I wasn't a hundred percent certain, I thought the two might be related. The label on the packet read D-O-V-A-N. Doe-van—at least that's how Cardy pronounced it. Anyway, after Brumbal's blunder, I thought I'd keep that piece of info under wraps."

Anne went white. "Where did you get it? Who's this bloody Funder? What exact route did you take?" She fired her questions one after another in rapid succession, fear igniting her shrill words.

When Fisher told her, Anne sprang off the bed, startling everyone as the bed careened back on its casters to slam against the wall. "I have to see it, at once!" *Not again.*

But Anne's command brooked no argument—her alarm, infectious.

26: Confidence
Fisher

"What is it?" Fisher asked over Anne's shoulder, worry flooding his tone.

Still dressed in her blue patient smock, Anne dismantled the packet with deft hands. She didn't hesitate. Her manner suggested she couldn't afford to. Her robot-like movements paused only when she asked Cholla for a specific tool.

With laser focus, Anne looked and acted as though diffusing a bomb, especially with Cholla leaning over her other shoulder holding a small arsenal of scanning devices.

Fisher chewed his lip. "It's not new tech, that's for certain. See here?" He pointed through the sea of arms into the guts of the packet. "Standard encryption, microcircuits, light-diode pathways, sub-standard processors."

"No, Captain Fisher," Anne said as she worked. "It's not new tech." She unceremoniously dislodged part of the console. It grated loudly and hung suspended by a few loose wires. Anne let the component dangle over the side of the metallic box. "It's all ancient in fact. This is my dinosaur... except for this—" She pointed to another part, which had been hidden by the section she removed. "—homing beacon, integrated into the heart of the circuit board."

Silence fell like a pall.

"The rest of course is an early prototype of my own research based on the Dovan advancements. In effect, this is my tech, the second of the three packets." Fisher found himself chewing both lips. He tasted blood.

As soon as Anne disassembled the device into seven components of various sizes, she reached into the centre of the pile and lifted the small piece she had identified.

Anne presented the part to Fisher. "This has been your bane since you picked up your payload."

"Shouldn't we just destroy it?" the captain asked, trying to sound hopeful.

"No, these moles are linked. Destroy one and it signals the cavalry. Really only one thing we can do with it. Take out the trash."

Anne led a small procession to the closest airlock.

"I scored a stash of lifter-bots from the Cardinal," Jiri offered. "I can program them to help speed it on its way. Give whoever is tracking it the illusion that we're still moving, at least for a while."

"Good thinking." Anne smiled down at Jiri's cheery face, making the petite girl beam.

When all had been readied, the outer hatch opened and the vacuum swallowed the device with its escort of orbiting bots. Jiri sent an instruction through her com-pad and the three objects shot away so fast they were gone an instant later.

"I wonder if something similar didn't happen to you too, Captain Resa," Anne speculated.

Resa sighed. "Your guess is as good as mine, but I wouldn't be surprised."

"Actually," Fisher said, his grin sliding towards Resa as he did, "things didn't get wonky with us until after we de-corpsicle-ized Mr Freeze here. You can chalk that one up to this overstuffed oaf here." Fisher gruffly jabbed a finger into Brumbal's pot belly, making the big man laugh. "And of course, Resa's guru, your holiest-of-holy leviathans."

Resa drew back and shot him a look of umbrage. "Captain, don't be more of an asshole than you must, and watch your mouth about the Cardinal."

"Forgive me. I forget how I must behave in the presence of such a divine paragon."

"At least Fish didn't swear, nor could he," Baines chided, clearly attempting to diffuse the tension.

Fisher turned to Anne his tone growing serious. "Is there anything salvageable from what's left of *this* packet?"

"There wasn't much to begin with," Anne lamented. "This packet represented an early prototype, a preliminary model we extracted from Dovani design. All of our research—decades worth—happened back on Earth. We lost it in the strike."

Fisher's shoulders slumped. He was about to voice his regret when Anne brightened, enough to light his way. "But with Beacon's help, I'll see what I can do—once I get dressed," she added with a chuckle. With that she left, heading back to the infirmary.

Anne disappeared down the corridor with Beacon floating right behind her. Jiri searched her captain's eyes, glued to the departing pair. "Guess it's a good thing Beacon brought Anne around, eh Cap? Cap?" she chimed louder.

Fisher turned and faced her.

"You look like a Fish out of water," she observed.

"Feel like one too," he admitted.

"Don't worry, Cap. Anne's already proven worth the effort of bringing her back," soothed Jiri. "I think she'll turn the tide in our favour when the real shitstorm hits."

"Only time will tell," Fisher said. "It's all about time."

"Always is," Jiri agreed.

"Till then, we have to ante up and see where it goes. Where *we* go, and how we'll wind up."

Fisher warily swept the faces gathered around the mess table. After dinner that night, the *Skow II's* crew watched Anne Morrison, with fascination. Understandably, they could not move past the bizarre arrival of their newest crew member. Neither could he.

Anne seemed to sense this and although she sounded tired, she remained attentive. "You asked me earlier, Captain, why I'm so significant. I'm important because I have the lexicon you require, the knowledge to find the only viable effective weapon to neutralize the Demon interdiction and, with Beacon's help, make it work. Once deployed, the weapon will repel the Imperium for good. As the only living person aboard this ship who knows where we must go to begin our search, I'm crucial."

"Okay, I get it, I do," Fisher said. "When and if we find it, you know how to retrieve and deploy it." He leaned in and peered at Anne. "But doesn't that strike you as a bit of an uphill battle? We've been tracked up until now, and that's just the surveillance sh-tuff we've learned about. Who knows what else is going to get thrown our way? And the Demons have a lot of throwing power."

Anne studied Fisher. Her chin bobbed ever so slightly, but her eyes beelined into him. They prompted the captain to reach his own conclusion.

"I guess any change can be painful," said Fisher. "But sometimes it's necessary, and nothing worth doing is ever easy."

The corners of Anne's mouth curved into a smile.

Resa broke the moment. "I'm curious about your suspended animation. Could you describe it to me?"

Anne pondered for a moment before replying. "It wasn't suspended at all. Continuous but slow, plodding on like one long hazy dream. I remained semi-conscious on a vague level, but it felt more fantasy than reality. I knew I was still alive, but the levels of consciousness kept changing. I would slip in and out from one reality to the next. The mental image of Beacon helped me keep it together whenever the fear took hold, and it often did."

Fisher shifted his gaze to the ebony robot hovering over Anne's shoulder. He tried to picture how an image of that could possibly assuage fear. And failed. Barring the yellow smiley-face, if he dreamt of that, he'd wake up screaming, with fudged underpants.

"It scared me shitless," Anne confessed, as though sensing Fisher's thoughts. "Knowing I'd become nothing more than a bunch of digital blips and bleeps."

"You were reduced to the binary code of a computer A.I. program without the A, of course?" Cholla marvelled.

"A self-aware program, right," Anne confirmed. "Considering how long I was out, I needed constant assurances from Beacon to stave off my pending madness. In that much, he truly lit my way, right through the Valley of Darkness. You might say he helped my new iteration stay in touch with my inner Zen."

A sad knowing smile crossed Resa's face. "I can relate. Mine was one big frozen zero. I touched no awareness, nothing, and no one."

"What do you remember?" Anne asked. "Prior to being frozen, I mean? Can you tell me anything about what you saw? Might give us a few more clues."

Resa recounted his tale as he had done with the others, finishing with his account of the second fleet's destruction. When Anne nodded, he stopped.

"As Beacon undoubtedly told you, the Demons themselves

214

destroyed that second wave," she said.

"So, that's it?" Resa asked in stolid disbelief. "They went and destroyed ships from their own fleet?"

"It's not like their ranks need replenishing," Fisher reminded him.

"Yes," Anne said. "It was penance for failure. Death is the only penance they know. Even if it's unnecessary overkill, they'll do it to make their point. They have no compunction about destroying their own just as readily as their enemies. I wouldn't be surprised if the ID also destroyed whatever capital ship sent in that second wave. Likely the whole freaking battle group."

"I knew the Imperium to be cold," Resa said in astonishment. "Even in my time, but a command ship and its entire battle group seems senseless."

A bitter smile creased Anne's face. "I've seen them do it before and if there's one certainty about the Demons, one you can bank on, it's this: they always have a finger on the button."

"That's a comfort," Fisher mumbled.

"Well, an inherent disproportionate sense of paranoia, megalomania, and intolerance will do that to you, but," Anne pondered, "perhaps therein lay their greatest weakness."

"I wouldn't put *weak* and *Demons* in the same sentence," Fisher said. "That button's ability seems pretty invulnerable to me." He examined Anne more closely. "It does beg a question though. How the heck could you know all this anyway—that homer device notwithstanding? Even compared to Mr Freeze here, you're prehistoric."

"Beacon," Anne said without hesitation. "He is primarily a learning/teaching machine. Apart from our time together on Earth, he and I were digital roommates for more than 3000 years. He gleaned everything about your tech within seconds of his reawakening in this era. Before he brought me back, he bolstered my own expertise, my digital IQ concerning pretty much everything digital. I basically stood on the shoulders of a giant."

Her eyes flitted to the automaton. "As for non-digital matters, my trusty robot told me more than a few tales of his past, in similar situations. His story's likely the longest wild goose chase in the history of, well history."

215

"And the chase isn't over," Beacon reminded her.

"True," Anne agreed.

"Wonderful." Fisher sagged back and picked idly at his empty plate with his fork.

Anne gave the captain a sympathetic look before turning her attention to the others. "As to exactly how the ID facilitate their kill protocols, I honestly don't know. But it does seem to ensure stringent loyalty under the strictest code of obedience. Maybe that's why their imperialism succeeded as they swept across the stars."

Fisher let out a low whistle before something occurred to him. He straightened in his chair. "Wait a sec. The ID are more thorough than this. If the Imperium had us locked on with that homer the entire time, they should've been able to nab us back in the Junkyard. Why didn't they close in, then?"

The question hung in the air unanswered.

"Dr Morrison?" Resa cut in. "There's more."

"More?" Anne narrowed her eyes. Though not directed at him, Fisher felt the weight of her scrutiny.

"Yes," Resa said. "After something eradicated the second fleet, I'm fairly sure, quite certain actually, that one more ship entered the debris field, right behind the second wave. That last vessel was not an Imperium ship."

Fisher's throat went dry when the colour drained from Anne's face again. "What is it?"

Anne bit her lower lip. "You would do well to remember this, Captain." Her voice sounded hollow like muted pain. "Inexorable as their dynasty might be, the Demons aren't the only ones we have to worry about."

Fisher did a doubletake. *stalemate… deadlock…* "What?"

"They're not the only nemesis trying to invade and subvert the Universe to their dark purpose. There is another—with greater malevolence and limitless power to match them."

27: Dark Sector
Fisher

The Dark Sector faced Fisher like an infinite black wall, devoid not only of light, but any sign of life: no visible stars, no celestial bodies, and no other ships. With the *Skow II* holding station, about to pass through it, his hands trembled on the controls. A bead of sweat trickled down the small of his back.

Had there been another ship in there, any form of communication would be in blackout. It was going to be a passage through the ultimate penumbra, where any glow emitted by his tiny vessel would be abnegated as soon as she produced it.

The draining effect already prevailed in many of the ship's other instruments, panels giving strange readings, tricked by the anomalous gravitational and magnetic distortions, which would soon beleaguer the *Skow II*'s passage. A similar taxing had apparently sucked the life out of Fisher's drawn and pale-faced crew.

The captain looked across at Baines, seated beside him in the co-pilot's chair at the front of the bridge.

Baines nodded. "Ready when you are."

Fisher lifted his gaze to Anne, standing between them. "Best I understand it, the reason it's so dark in there is that the monsters have no more matter to gobble up. While back, they sent in a few probes, remote-piloted by robots. Together, the team of gearboxes charted a course clear to the other side and back—so it can be done."

"But?" Anne prompted as she rubbed her temple.

"But they were robots, so they could handle G's that'd turn us into paste. Their plotting specs are likely outdated. It's the Universe after all, and things are always changing—though, maybe not so much in there."

Eyes still fixed on Anne, Fisher extended a hand at the inky veil filling every horizon outside the forward window. "Regardless, we're about to travel through the most hazardous vector in known space. That's why we're alone out here."

His glance took in Dr Cholla, standing a little further back. "Still, Cholla's the brain on its real poison. He can speak your

217

language a far cry better than me, right Doc?"

"Um, I'll try Captain," the doctor said as he stepped forward. "In essence, the Dark Sector forms a minefield of singularities, Anne. A single supermassive black hole, or several lined up for that matter, would be much easier to handle in comparison."

He adjusted his spectacles. "But this region is made up of multiple stellar-mass black holes, punctuated with an array of primordial singularities. Normally, the gravity wells should all be marked by accretion disks, which would offer us some light, but something in this sector caused an abnormal shift in dark energy, enough to blow it all out."

"Dark energy has been turning the astrophysical tide on dark matter, for some time now," Anne put in. "Many Ph-Ds hypothesized that it'll eventually erode the scaffolding, win the cosmic tug of war—in a few trillion years or so."

"True," Cholla allowed. "But here, the dark energy and the gravity wells it pens seem to have locked in a standstill." He leaned forward and traced his finger along one of Baines' monitors. The image showed an organic series of curved but parallel green lines, like a topographic map of a mountain range. Except these lines undulated, merging in places and widening in others. "We'll have to tread along their respective Schwarzschild radii, balancing the vicissitudes of ungodly gravitational tidal forces while the singularities orbit one another—and hopefully navigate between them."

Cholla straightened and tilted his head towards Fisher and Baines. "These guys will have their hands full just keeping the ship from getting ripped apart by the concentrated protons screaming along the event horizons. But the same infinite energy has one trade-off."

"Centrifugal power," Anne guessed.

Cholla's smile widened. "We'll use it as a gravity assist while steering clear of the worst of the temporal storms caused by frame-dragging."

"You might say, we'll be changing dance partners quite a bit," Baines added with a grin. "And the ship's dance steps will be like threading a needle during a bucking earthquake in a forest of tornadoes, while all the clocks go schizophrenic."

Anne braced her hands on her hips and stared down at the pilot. "Wow, Baines, that makes me feel so much better. As if my time and reality shift isn't fucked up enough already."

"The counterbalancing spacetime wells offer us another boon," said Cholla. "Their centrifuges and frame-dragging work hand in hand, much like a woven tapestry, but with threads of velocity. As Baines alluded, 'threading' them will expedite our journey, using both in conjunction like an accelerator to slingshot us through. With Beacon's help, our voyage in and out of the void should not last more than…"

Cholla raised a finger and traced an asymmetrical pattern in the air. Fisher smiled at Doc's usual way of doing math equations in his head.

"Eight hours," Cholla finished as he met Anne's eyes. "But admittedly, every second of it we'll be dancing on an invisible razor's edge."

Fisher took a deep breath. "Well Doc, looks like we got a full shift ahead of us."

Gluing himself to the helm controls once again, Fisher flipped open the com and cleared his throat. "Okay kiddos, the gravity of the situation demands we drop all dalliance and focus on the beeline. This is the craziest patch of woods we're about to enter so strap down your willies and sit tight. Be ready for anything, including Resa's hysterical praying." The ship-wide broadcast erupted in garbled static while Fisher laughed at his own slight.

A moment later, he let his smile drop and became all business. Fisher held his air as the first burn kicked in. And the *Skow II* began her precarious immersion into the blackened corridors of the circuitous maze.

While Fisher manned the main controls, Baines rode shotgun, monitoring the wax and wane of myriad distortion fields and spatial epicentres. He and Fisher worked in tandem, essential to get the *Skow II* safely through, coasting along the fringe of multiple and in some instances overlapping event horizons.

Baines' stern countenance mirrored Fisher's. They functioned together, symbiotically, synergistically, like a pair of lifter-bots. No room for their usual banter. And zero margin for error.

The crew knew it too, but unlike Baines and Fisher, so

219

engaged to be afraid, the others could only watch and wait while their ship took them through the sector's Stygian core.

The Dark Sector affected everything from light to gravity to time, but to the people experiencing it, the Dark weighed heavily on their souls. Time crawled. Became strange…

When Resa surfaced from his meditations, he found Fisher's crew performing their tasks perfunctorily. They kept conversation to a minimum minds drifting, somewhere at a Lagrange point between vulnerability and stalwartness.

Through his reawakened projection ability, he sensed the crew's thoughts as they retreated within themselves, dividing their time into set periods to suppress the endless monotony. Some prayed. Even Anne sat with her eyes closed, meditating in serene contemplation. He could almost hear her peaceful thoughts and glean her mindset, which centred on faith and hope. Remarkable woman, like…

Only Beacon seemed unaffected by their passage through the Dark Sector. Always busy, the robot sailed between the crew, who remained crouched on their chairs like silent islands. From one workstation to the next, Beacon interfaced, tabulated, and shifted to the next. All heads turned to watch him work.

Beacon's actions exhibited deliberateness—clever, showing the crew by example the best way to deal with their apprehension.

Whatever his true purpose, the robot definitely had a positive impact on them all. He kept them resolute and fixed on hope. They never gave in to despair and eventually emerged from their mental cocoons to gather and support each other. Resa smiled inwardly to himself. They would stay the course.

Fisher might be an asshole, but he sure picked his crew well.

28: Red Giant
Fisher

Fisher squinted as he took damp blistered hands off the yoke. "We're out." The wash of red light penetrating every window and bathing the bridge confirmed as much.

Relinquishing full control to Baines, the captain exhaled and rotated his chair to face the crew. Shoulders sagging, eyes brightening, their relief was palpable. As they turned away and cleared the bridge with buoyant strides, Fisher felt a sense of absolution or at least benediction, but way too exhausted to acknowledge it aloud. Too exhausted to move.

"Out of the worst of it anyway," Baines clarified in a bushed voice. He raised a finger out the forward window, then pointed it down at his monitor. Fisher followed the pilot's languid gestures. A massive red giant star loomed dead ahead, its aura saturating the expanse and Baines' expression with flaming light. It also filled the pilot's viewscreen with ungodly stats.

"Right about that," Fisher acknowledged. "That thing weighs in like VY Canis Majoris, only meaner—even without the kind of x-class flares it can generate. Just keep us clear of Red and drinks'll be on me—once we nail a safe course, and with any luck, a parking orbit around some local rock. My brain's running on phantom power."

"Already done," Baines said. "Course correction's laid in and—we're good. See?"

Fisher nodded as the pilot tilted his head towards his screen. Sure enough, distant pinpoints of light twinkled on their adjusted heading, barely visible through the giant's overwhelming swathe.

With thrusters on full, the *Skow II* streaked along a path perpendicular to the massive solar winds the star emitted. Heading towards the closest cluster, she emerged from the red aura into the friendlier obscurity of interstellar space. The ship too was a pinpoint, dotting a course through cold dark vacuum, though not nearly as shadowed as what they just passed through.

"Actually," Baines amended. "There's no real clusters ahead. Just a few quiet stars and rogue planets, but at least all the black holes are behind us—and a good A-men to that."

"Amen to a lot of things, including Red," Fisher said more seriously. "I knew Resa's contacts would turn out bogus. If Morrison and Beacon hadn't humoured the saint, letting him steer us there, I'd have told Thaw-butt to go take a flying fh–!–*hike*."

"You don't need to convince me," Baines agreed. "Even with the homer gone, we still had to outrun and outsmart the ID way too many times for my liking."

"Good thing we have Beacon," Anne said as she strode back onto the bridge. He's kept us on our toes and a few steps ahead of the bastards."

"True," Fisher said over his shoulder. "Except that one-too-many steps ahead forced us to fly blind through the Dark Sector. Even from where I come from, that's playing with fire."

"Like courting the Imperium," Anne said.

Fisher put his hands behind his head and leaned back in his chair. "I still can't believe we leapfrogged, unscathed."

"I had every confidence in you two flyboys, as did Beacon. You both proved handy in a few tight spots long before the Dark Sector. Pulled us through a ton of fucking shit."

Fisher cast a pained look at Baines. "It's not fair."

"What's not fair?" Anne asked.

"Nothing," Fisher said as he dropped his hands and leaned forward.

Baines sniggered over his shoulder at Anne. "Just Cap's behavioural inhibitor, courtesy of Resa's guru."

Anne knitted her brows and frowned at the pilot.

"It's an implant, surgically inserted into Fisher's cortex with integrated biometrics," Baines elaborated. "Prevents Fish from using any profanity when vexed by something or someone—a present from Your Eminence, Cardinal Wisdan. Problem is, our good captain likes to swear."

"Really?" Anne said, an amused smile playing over her lips.

"Oh yeah, he has a real proclivity for it. He's an artist—or was," Baines chirped.

"One thing's certain," Fisher cut in, happy to change the subject. "Any chance of subtlety is history. When it comes to subterfuge, we've moved far past the point of no return. There's no going back to the way things used to be—as in quiet-like."

"Yes, but would you want to go back?" asked Anne. "Being feigned partisans of that way? Change is good, especially in this. Like you said, we have the hottest potato and the Imperium scared silly at the same time. Something's percolating, which has the potential to bring about a fundamental shift in the hierarchy of the Universe. Something that might make life worth living."

"Yeah, but it can also shorten it pretty quick," Fisher pointed out. He levelled his gaze at Anne. "I hope you're right."

"Resa's probing did reveal quite a lot actually," Anne said.

"That delegation from Centauris X is dead," Fisher finished for her.

Anne dipped her chin. "All dead, confirmed hits, murdered, with one unaccounted for."

"His Funder, yeah, he told me—more loose ends. Ever since I took that stupid courier gig my whole life seems threaded with loose ends."

"But do the math," said Anne. "There's more. Someone is covering their tracks, not just from the Demons, but from us as well. Even Resa's contacts at the shipyard back on Ursula Minor were lit up by that radar. That's a little too fishy to be a simple coincidence. Anyone who had any knowledge about the *Inner Peace* is either dead or missing."

"Except for us, and the Cardinal, Fisher noted. "And the Card's a little too immersed with his chapel on retrorockets and his flock of interplanetary sheep."

Anne's eyes narrowed. "How well do you know him?"

Fisher harrumphed. "Cardy? Are you inferring? Heck no. Staunch and annoying maybe but he's no methodical killer?" He shook his head, about to laugh off the notion but it died on his lips.

Resa never actually met the Funder, only an associate of his, and it'd been on the Cardinal's advice that he took the job. No, it couldn't be him. But then again, Resa did have that little private audience with the man.

"All we know for sure," Anne said, her conviction plain, "is that there's a new game in town, we're on the centre of the board, and we don't know the damn gamer."

Her dubious tone weighted down on Fisher like a freight train. But he let it chug past, too preoccupied plying the meandering tracks of his own unpleasant thoughts.

29: Sunrise
Fisher

"So, what are we looking for?"

Anne's response came automatically. "Just maintain this heading."

But that's exactly what Fisher had been doing, for more than a week now, nothing more, nothing less. The engines ran on full thrust, his patience ran on pure steam.

Still, he trusted this woman, this reincarnated Human, brought back from a dead planet in an all-but-forgotten epoch. He trusted her because she gave him the kind of response he'd have given anyone who distracted him when doggedly focused as she was now.

That appeared odd through one prism, perfectly normal through another, and pretty much defined his whole relationship with her. Fisher found he liked and respected Anne's fierce candour. It made her authentic. He suddenly wondered how she felt about him.

"Jumps and even skips are out of the question here," Anne said. "I have an approximation, but remember, what we seek is supposed to be hidden. Otherwise, any passing ship might stumble upon it. We have to be methodical and systematic. Rushing it will only debauch our efforts. The *Skow II* might easily hop over the right destination threshold and just keep on going."

Stuck at the helm, Fisher would breathe easier, if only he knew what that destination was.

As though trying to reconnoitre his thoughts, Anne studied him intently for a moment. Then filled her lungs and voiced his case for him. "If I had gleaned the precise location where Baron made the drop, we could be done with this crazy business." Frustration fretted the edge of her voice but she quickly recovered. "It's out here Fisher—I know it."

"How?"

"Because it's where Baron and I agreed we'd bring it."

"It's gonna be a long ride, Anne." Fisher sighed. "This guy—

225

Baron—you really trusted him?"

"Let's just say I trusted him more than I ever trusted myself. His probity was righteous and august."

"But maybe his secret got out and his packet stolen, his covert mission ambushed. I don't know, something beyond his control. We are talking about the Demons here. It's possible there's nothing out here, Anne."

"True, but what alternative do we have?" Anne's grimace mirrored the captain's vexation, but then like a sunbeam peaking past a drifting cloud she brightened. "We just have to think outside the box, Fisher. Change the lure at the end of your fishing rod. Baron knew the stakes all too well. He also knew chaos."

Fisher drew back and wrinkled his nose "Pardon?"

"Entropic chaos," Anne explained. "Ranging damage enhancement sets to predict the outcome in invention systems. Baron knew it intimately. Back on Earth, he was a world authority and proponent of the scientific field. He foresaw the parameters of this dystopia and how to best navigate it. Baron made it component to our survival. Bearing that in mind, he would have found a way."

"Okay, if you say so," Fisher replied, unconvinced. "Just remember, way or no, things didn't go so well on Alliantha."

Anne opened her mouth but checked herself. Her face lost expression and her manner grew distant. She silently mouthed the planet's name, as though conversing with a ghost, *Alliantha*.

"So, what was life like on Earth?" Fisher asked, trying to lighten the conversation. "Before you met Beacon and got mixed up in this mess? How did you fall into your current role?"

Lids aflutter, Anne's eyes found Fisher's. After a moment, she blew out her cheeks.

Anne recounted her childhood, education, and the first few days with her ancestor's logbook—how it opened up a window into the past, a vision of an exciting life on the high seas. She had to explain many unfamiliar terms and concepts to Fisher, but he took great pleasure in her vivid description of such a simple tech-less life.

"It was Percy's story, but it became mine as well. Much of the personal sentiments written on those pages reflected my own. I delighted in following his story, often taking the heavy tome to bed with me. I'd read until late, under what's called candlelight to help create the atmosphere of the era.

"Shortly after beginning one of my late-night reading sessions, I saw something which quite frankly didn't compute. All the notes in the log that preceded this particular entry—378 pages worth, had been laid down concisely and thoughtfully, penned through experience no doubt. But the entry which began on page 379 revealed a man consumed by doubt, faced with matters beyond his comprehension. Seemed as though that entry had been written by another person entirely."

"What happened to the captain?" Fisher asked, his curiosity piqued. "Did he make it to Alliantha?"

Anne shook her head and gave him a half-smile. "Humans were not always immortal, Fisher. He died. But before then, apart from recounting his role in the second half of the Seven Years War, the rest of the captain's tale dealt mostly with his trying to make sense of the conundrum. His subsequent entries became less concerned with the event he had witnessed and more with his affairs back home. He led a full life, finishing out his service to His Majesty, King George III—his ah... Exarch," Anne clarified. "He then took a post at the British Naval Academy in his native country, England, and married the woman of his dreams."

Fisher swivelled the pilot's seat to give Anne his full attention. "And?"

She shrugged. "And together they had five children: three boys and two girls. I'm descended from the second son. From what I gathered, Percy's marriage was a happy one, centring on love. His last entry spoke of satisfaction and joy at living to see the birth of his first grandson. He never mentioned the occurrence in these last entries, but I'm willing to bet it was one of his last conscious thoughts, before setting sail over that last horizon."

Elbow on the chair's armrest, Fisher propped his chin on a closed hand. "And 300 years later, you took up his torch."

Anne nodded. "I had to, even though it wasn't my dilemma to begin with. Call it intuition, I believed what the captain witnessed did happen, and it was my duty to see his question answered, one

227

way or another. It haunted me. Convinced me that I inherited his logbook for a reason. The anonymous sender's letter concluded as much—said I was the right person, *meant* to have it."

Fisher started, suddenly remembering Wisdan's prophetic words about causality and the captain being *meant* to escort the robot. Were they all meant to be here?

"You see, before any of this started, I was pretty content, living comfortably with my salary. I worked bloody hard to achieve it after all but…" Anne's voice trailed off as she considered her next words.

"But you felt there was something more, beyond your teaching vocation," the captain guessed as he sat up again.

"Right," Anne said, appreciation lifting her voice. "Like some sacrosanct purpose where my training and experience should be applied. More and more often, I found my mind drifting to Captain Morrison's quandary, thinking that might provide my answer, if not for one resounding dilemma: the serious lack of coin—um credits."

Fisher laughed. "Can certainly relate to that. As to your higher purpose, Wisdan hinted something similar about me."

"I don't doubt that one bit," Anne said. She looked out the window. "In my case, I obsessed with the investigation but not in any fanatical way. I nurtured it through methodical research, pondering modicums of info that trickled in while trying to connect them with strands of conjecture. But the entry that began on page 379 became my Holy Grail. That led me to Beacon. To Baron."

Anne's gaze returned to Fisher. "And now it's led me to you. Tell me, what do you remember of your early childhood on Alliantha?"

Blood rushed to Fisher's cheeks and he felt his smile vanish. "Trust me, that's a long, much-less-idyllic story than yours."

"As you said, it's going to be a long ride."

Fisher tapered his eyes. "Why do you want to know?"

"I'm your forebear, and Baron Fieldbank, whom this Cardinal Wisdan described as a great man, was my most esteemed colleague—while Earth was still Earth, a living and breathing habitable M-class. I want to know more about how our Plan-B worked out. It might even shed some light on what we're trying to do here. Do you need any more reason than that?"

Silence.

"So, tell me," Anne pressed.

Fisher exhaled. "Not much to say." His guarded tone became absent. "Never knew my parents. My first memories began at the orphanage on Alliantha in a squatter camp, just before the second holocaust. Sure, we had all the amenities of the Human tech, but not the skillsets to make it go. I was there when the Demons invaded the camps and rounded up all the Humans, stealing some of my closest friends away from the fold."

Fisher picked at his facial scar as he dredged up the memory. "Alliantha had always been subjugated to the Imperium's oppression, but the ID considered it nothing more than a planetary hovel, us inhabitants, a bunch of inferior louts. So, they left us alone."

Lips quivering, Fisher swallowed. "But when they learned of the Human exodus there, they went ape on the whole planet. We all suffered after that. Resources vanquished, executions of those with the closest ties to the Humans, but for the most part, us 'daughters' fared better than your peeps."

Fisher's voice took on a dark timbre. "I still have nightmares about it, watching the Demons herd them into a compound where the ID tortured and summarily incinerated them. The Alliantha Wisdan speaks so munificently about—" he shook his head. "Never seen it. Just a stark beaten rock, one step up from subsistence and dog-eat-dog survival of the fittest."

He raked a hand through his hair and let out a wry laugh. "But at least it's not Stricken… not yet anyway."

Sudden emotion pulled Anne's mouth down. She hung her head and sniffed. "Their only crime was a will to survive."

"Yeah well, that was enough for the Imperium. They eradicated your race and left us to languish with the scraps of the planet. They even razed the orphanage, so, I was truly alone."

Anne's eyes lifted. "How did you survive?"

"Violence," Fisher returned acerbically. "I may not have been born into violence. But I was sure raised on it, raised in the capital of violence, to *be* violent."

Fisher felt a feral tightness come over him and he blurred with anger, but then his shoulders sagged. "You take away a kid's hope for the future and he grows up real frickin quick. I kept to the shadows. Learned to think *street*. And I was good at observing. Played my cards right and survived. Game learned, I made some headway and things became a little easier. Don't get me wrong: there were days fate dealt me a real bad hand, unsure if I'd see its next light, but I clung on like one stubborn S-O-B."

Fisher paused and dropped his voice low. "This one night, I got ambushed, rolled, and banged up something critical. The punks left me for dead in an alley. Some crazy lady drew up—just a stranger mind you—thought she meant to finish me off. Pilfer my corpse. I was in such pain, I almost welcomed it."

"What happened?" Anne blinked. "Did she... hurt you more?"

Fisher looked up at the ceiling. "No." His voice grew hoarse. "She helped me more—more than any person had a right to be helped." Anne leaned in as his eyelids slowly opened.

The captain met her penetrating stare. "She put me in an air-taxi, told the cabbie to take me to a hospital, and fastened a com-pad to my wrist. Two days later, when I recovered, I checked the com-pad's D-base. The screen showed more than forty thousand credits topped up in my name, verified with my DNA signature. And an apartment waiting for me at a modest condo complex, completely paid up, for the next ten years. A header on the pad's touchscreen read: UPHILL BATTLES."

Anne's breath caught. "How can you say that isn't as idyllic? Fisher that's—that's—fucking beautiful."

Fisher snorted back a pang of emotion and laughed dryly. "Craziest thing is I never saw her face—being dark, and I was too bloodied up. Never learned who turned my tide."

"Well, she apparently knew you," Anne remarked.

"I guess," Fisher said noncommittally. His eyes lingered on Anne for a few moments. "Makes me wonder though." He turned and looked out the bridge window, catching his reflection in the glass. "After that night, I got good at seeing through people. Maybe it's a glimmer of Resa's projection—nothing fluent mind you, but enough to help me gauge the really shady ones. With time, I carved my own little niche out of hell, but with the better part of forty thousand credits to my name, my racket launched into a fairly lucrative one. It led to a series of contraband ops aboard a few on-world merchantmen. Through that, the doors finally started to open."

The captain's tone softened as he regarded Anne again. "When I could afford to procure my first ship, the *Skow,* life turned over a new leaf for me. I left the Alliantha System. First time in my life I actually considered myself happy. I never stopped hating the Demons for what they did, but truth was, they let me operate my little enterprise with about as much interest as a bull would a fly. Salvage and cargo transport ultimately led to my single shady stint in the courier business, which unfortunately landed me in this clutter."

"But, messy or clean, I bet everything makes more sense for you out here," Anne volunteered.

"Yeah exactly," Fisher said in an appreciative tone. "It's freedom: the buzz of knowing I'm in control of my destiny. It's always been more peaceful up here for me. The Dark is open. I hate—fear, closed spaces," the captain confessed. "But more than that, it's impartial. Doesn't care who I am or how frigin warm my blood is."

Fisher paused and faced the window once more. "A wise man once told me, 'Those who glide above the wind surpass the most turbulent storm'—I don't know," the captain said, surprised and embarrassed at his many admissions, some of which he'd never divulged to anyone before.

A faint smile curved the corners of Anne's mouth. She reached over and touched his arm. "It's okay, Fisher, I understand. Such wisdom defines us both."

30: Sun Raze

Anne

After three weeks visiting a handful of neighbouring systems, with nothing but expired crystalline pulsars, frozen dead moons, and luminescent stardust clouds, it was still no joy.

But as the *Skow II* arrived in an unremarkable binary system comprised of an asteroid belt cloistered between two equally diminished brown dwarfs, Anne had a sudden epiphany and raced up to the bridge.

Even as the ship braked to a graceful stop, Fisher and Baines wheeled their g-seats at the sound of her running boots. Anne drew a fierce breath as she sidled up between them. "Baines, retrace our steps to where we first emerged from the Dark Sector. Mimic the exact apogee and perigee before your first course correction. From there, I want you to plot a new course."

"Where to?" the pilot asked, hands already reaching for the controls.

"Directly towards the red giant."

Baines and Fisher gaped at one another, open-mouthed. And Anne knew why. The gateway's daunting doorman and the sector's dominating body was only slightly less vicarious than the Dark Sector creeping over it.

Baines broke the uncomfortable silence. "Are you kidding?"

Anne set her jaw and held his disbelieving eyes.

Fisher crossed his arms and tilted his head to match her facial stance. "Why?"

"A hunch. I want the *Skow II* to continue, with no course correction until the gravity of the star reaches out. Even then, we keep moving right to the point-of-minimum-safety if we have to." Though Anne felt sure it wouldn't come to that.

"You mean the point of no return." Baines slowly rotated his chair to face his captain. "Fish?"

Anne held her breath. Fisher's lip quivered but he didn't baulk.

233

With a low whistle, Baines forked a hand through his hair and turned back to his controls. "Guess Cap's not the only one open to extreme measures."

The sound of air scrubbers ventilating the bridge and the odd ping of sensor relays answered the pilot.

His movements wooden, Baines punched in the coordinates from the ship's navigation log and fed them into helm control.

The rising drone of the *Skow II*'s FTL respooling filled the bridge. Satisfied, Anne turned around and exited Fisher's wheelhouse. Moments later, the ship winked out of the system—the first in a series of relatively short hops that took her back to the tenuous waypoint.

As soon as the *Skow II* flashed into the right coordinates, she headed on a direct trajectory towards the Red Giant, using conventional thrusters.

It was a lone unnamed godstar, bright enough and big enough to eclipse its smaller stellar cousins, nimbusing or occulting them while its solar winds completely washed all of space in overpowering radiance. It represented the antithesis of the Dark Sector, which flanked and juxtaposed the celestial juggernaut.

"The sun's emitting ion cyclotron waves," Cholla reported. "And peculiar radio waves on a frequency that blinds not only our visual spectrum but all others as well. It will create havoc with bandwidths, sensors, and reception."

"Great," muttered Fisher, already anxious at Anne's proposition, doubly so when the first nudge of thrust settled him into his g-seat. He'd learned to trust Anne's unorthodox, sometimes bizarre program. Anyone else—Resa for instance, and he'd have told him to go 'F' himself. By adhering to Anne's directions, periodically tweaked by the robot, ship and crew had survived. But now, that trust wore thinner with every kilometre the vessel drew closer to the giant star.

A few hours later, Fisher checked the gravity stress on the

hull, and his anxiety ratcheted up a notch. A cold sweat percolated down his back as the numbers steadily climbed, taking them from green to cautionary yellow.

"Are we still okay?" Anne queried.

"We're still within acceptable tolerance," Fisher replied over his shoulder. "But there's no saying if and when a bow shock or an acceleration anomaly might occur. That's uncommon for certain, but we're in uncharted territory and who knows what the Big Bang conjured up in this sector. A sudden gravitational whiplash of that magnitude, exacerbated by the star's radical velocity curve would cause the hull to buckle and fold like a tin can. Baines wouldn't have enough time to say boo, let alone reverse thrusters to hold station."

Moments before entering the red zone, the *Skow II*'s main computer insisted it was a fool's errand, and that it take over. Fisher silenced the alarm but not its import.

"I always keep my ship on manual override," the captain explained. "Don't like relinquishing control to a machine if I can help it. That way, if I die it'd be nobody's fault but mine." He paused, eyes processing the climbing numbers. "I think I'm about to change my position on that."

Baines let out a hollow laugh. "Cap's right, Anne. Anybody with a spaceship and half a brain knows red giants command special respect. A ship venturing this close to a mass like that is like a child smoking a cigarette while playing with an open box of unmarked explosives."

As if in agreement, the hull began to buckle, its metal groaning. Before the *Skow II* protested louder Anne chimed in, "Damn it all, you're both right. This is insanity. And I'm its bloody architect. Hold station here, Mr Pilot—while we still can."

Fisher coughed. "Okay, Ms Scientist, what do we do now?"

"We scan," Anne returned with a ghost of terseness. "We *science*."

The captain's tone sharpened. "Isn't that what we've been doing?"

"Yeah," Anne conceded, no less incisive, "but not from a stationary position. It may garner different results."

Fisher bit his lip and stared. Anne averted his probing. And they both sank into gloomy silence. Meanwhile, Baines brought the *Skow II* to a rocky stop. The captain could almost hear his poor vessel breathe an exasperated sigh of relief.

Even though mere kilometres separated them from the fateful red zone, the ship's computers kept compensating for the overwhelming gravity. The *Skow II* remained relatively safe while the crew scanned and scanned again, across every frequency and spectrum. But always with the same negative result.

By the following morning, an overwrought Anne wandered onto the bridge, uninterested, face vacant, movements lacklustre. Her crestfallen look and demeanour tore at Fisher. He climbed out of his chair and joined her.

She met his study. "I was sure we would've seen something by now. Thought I knew Baron better than this."

"Don't be too hard on yourself, Anne," Fisher said as he gave her shoulder a gentle squeeze. "I kind of saw the logic of it. Matter of fact, when I searched for a place to stow the *Skow II*, I shut off all assets and coasted in quiet. Just let her drift beside the roaring metropolis of junk an-" Fisher abruptly cut himself off.

"And—what?" Anne asked, facing him. All other eyes tracked in.

Fisher wheeled towards the window, where his reflection, burnished red from starlight stared back encouraging him. *On to something... Almost there. C'mon, Fish, think.* Then it hit him. "Wait a minute."

He spun on Baines. "Cut all the sensors. Cut all systems. Cut everything that isn't crucial in either keeping us here or keeping us alive."

"What are you thinking?" Anne's voice pitched higher.

If the electric glimmer in her eyes gave any indication, his excitement had caught her off-guard, sweeping her up on a resurgent wave.

Fisher didn't want to disappoint her, not now. With some effort, he slowed his breathing. "I think it's time we just had a good old-fashioned look out the window—polarizing filters only," he cautioned. "No scopes, no digital suppression, no enhancement or interference of any kind."

When they adjusted the window's polarizing filter to knee down the glare of the star's photosphere and keep it within a safe viewing range, all they saw was the same omnipresent red haze.

Fisher's shoulders sagged. He'd picked up Anne's crest only to fumble and drop it a minute later. He stared out the front window.

"Sorry Fish," Anne said to his back. "It was a good idea."

All tightness, Fisher's wrinkles etched into gorges. "Turn the ship around, Baines, and take us the frick outta here. Fire up the sensors while you're at it." He faced Anne again. "Maybe we can retreat a bit. Try it again from, well, not so close."

Baines started the manoeuvre and the *Skow II* nudged into a 180-degree centre-axis pivot. The view out the window panned right, but just before the ship reached halfway, adopting a 'beam to' position, a glint of something caught Fisher's notice, its edges shimmering like a mirage.

The captain gasped. "Whoa, *whooooa*!" Once again, all heads shot to him. "Hello," he said in a more familiar tone, feeling his coyote's smile fill his face. "Looks like I ain't done fishing yet. Baines, continue the manoeuvre, but don't-go-*anywhere*. And belay my sensor order." He turned to Anne. "Come with me."

Unable to contain his elation, Fisher fled the bridge with Anne in fast pursuit.

"Where are we going?" she yelled after him.

"To the stern," he yelled over his shoulder.

"What's there?"

"Another window!"

A good thirty strides ahead of Anne by the time she arrived at the rear portal, Fisher had his back to the glass, chest rising and falling steadily, thumb hiked over his shoulder. His grin stretched to his ears as she joined him.

"Bingo," Fisher proclaimed.

Anne swallowed uncertainly and squinted out the window. Her breath caught. Then her face lit up.

Fisher chuckled. "Found it too, did you?" He turned so they could share the view. Anne wrapped an arm about his shoulders.

Stephen Fenech

The dark mass, previously lost in the roaring noise and blinding ignatia generated by the monster sun behind it, was now clear as day. For the most part, it resembled a black sphere framed by the star's light flaring behind it, bleeding past the dark orb's horizon like a multilateral sunrise.

"Our own thruster heat blinded us," Fisher said, threading his arm gently around Anne's waist.

"Of course." She leaned into him and inhaled. "It created a parallax distortion."

"I didn't notice it till we turned tail," Fisher said. "For a flash, I might've seen it spike on the e-band peripheral sooner, if we weren't so busy shooting ourselves in our darn feet. Despite the gravitational lensing that star causes, it never blinded us. We blinded ourselves the whole time."

"Baron, you," Anne giggled.

"Your colleague was one impossibly smart S-O-B."

"And so are you, Captain Fisher," Anne beamed as she drew away. "For finding it."

Her praise amplified his esteem. "Thanks," he said, and meant it.

Fisher looked back out the window and blinked. "So long as we use reverse thrusters—on negative impulse only, we'll have a clear line of sight all the way in, fall gently into the shadow of that rock. There's just enough bleed from the star that it should moderate the temperature on the planetoid's dark side. Once shielded, the gravity relief will allow us to crank the sensors and search for your precious packet, no worries."

"One thing though," said Anne, her crow's feet converging. "How can this planet even exist out here, so close to that furnace? The mass force it must generate to maintain such a slow, almost non-existent orbit, and repel the gravity of that star seems, well impossible."

"Not, if you consider the mass itself," Cholla supplied behind them. They both turned. The podgy doctor stepped forward, tapping a stylus against a tablet he held in his other hand. At his back, hovered Beacon.

"Or the amount of dark energy in the void looming beyond,"

238

Cholla added, pointing the stylus out the window like a wand. "This entire system may be the result of what ejected from that blight."

"But the planet is a pebble by comparison, not even equal to Earth's late moon," Anne protested. "Yet its proximity to the star reflects the mass of a gas giant.

"Super dense matter, like crystalized osmium, would do it," Cholla said.

Anne frowned. "Going from a metal to a crystal, like coal to a diamond?" Her tone clearly stated she was not swayed.

Cholla only smiled. "Think, neutron star—without the star. If it is crystalline in nature, Anne, perhaps that had a hand in eluding our sweeps. It would refract any spectrum curves. And if it's charged by radio waves of the magnitude coming from that hell beyond, invisible. If you're trying to hide anything, anywhere, that *would* be the place to do it. It's all about astroseismology, specifically helioseismology."

Blank stares surrounded Cholla. He put his effects down on a nearby console, took off his glasses and rubbed his number elevens with his free hand. "Stars sing to us as their infernos rage internally, passing myriad radio waves, microwaves and such, towards their core before bouncing them back."

He reseated his glasses and drew up closer. "But their song depends greatly on the density of their core and the fuel they expend in the process. If you learn the tune exactly, and by *tune,* I mean vibrations—3D oscillations, harmonics, quadruple modes amplitude, radial modes, and markers, you become fluent in not only the notes of the song but the anti-notes as well. That would be the space or breaks in the discord of chaos."

Fisher continued to stare. But Anne nodded.

The doctor took a deep breath. "Dr Morrison, I believe your colleague should be considered a maestro in such decryption. He must have placed what we seek in the lee of the planetoid to shield its presence with the red giant's solar wake."

Cholla geared up to full-throttle didactic mode and nobody stopped him so he cantered on. "As for the creation of the hiding place itself, just consider what lies next to it—all the fire and

239

pressure needed to produce it. My guess: a rogue planet, maybe a gas giant as you indicated, but with an osmium core, impacted with and was instantly consumed by the star. It was transformed in one way, but immutable in another. In essence, something didn't mesh with the nuclear fusion and the sun ejected it as an undesirable."

Cholla panted. Fisher laughed. And Anne's head darted between the two of them.

"Dr Cholla's hypothesis is sound," Beacon declared over the doctor's shoulder. "And his deduction, correct."

"Loves a mystery, this one," Fisher quipped, wagging a finger at the doctor.

"Are you saying the star *barfed*?" Anne exclaimed, eyebrows springing high.

"Um, put bluntly, yes," Cholla said.

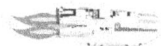

The *Skow II* coasted in reverse, backing in smooth and deliberate on impulse power. But when the gravity of the dwarf planet reached out and exerted its own considerable draw force, it pulled them in closer and closer. Once completely engulfed by the shielded haven of its influence, Baines compensated by turning the ship's forward thrusters on.

The pilot chuckled. "This'll be a walk in the park, Fish, after what we just 'pulled' with the star."

"Yeah, but don't get too confident, it might be smaller, but that's just the way it looks. The gravity at the surface of that little tyke can crush us just as quick if we get lazy."

"But what about the packet?" Baines asked. "Wouldn't that be crushed down there too?"

"For sure—if it was down there," Fisher said. "This Baron guy really had the smarts about hiding this thing. He would've figured out the math of the op, before parking such precious cargo. It's safe. I'd bet my cabin on it."

"Lagrange Point?" the pilot asked.

Fisher bowed his chin. "Lagrange Point."

The point in space which assured a gravitational stalemate between the red giant and the crystalline planet, or barycentre, was precisely where they found the packet, tethered to a fixed-position buoy. A shadow within a shadow. Baron truly gave them the perfect hiding place, they all agreed.

It took a few moments to locate the buoy once they knew where and how to look. It required even less time to remove the packet's link to the buoy and retrieve it with a small fleet of lifter-bots and the ship's grappling claw. Soon after, the packet, slightly larger than a double-thick briefcase, floated in the cargo hold, kept aloft by the orbiting bots.

"Crafty bugger—that Baron," Fisher marvelled. "Would've liked to meet him."

"He would've felt the same about you," Anne said. "Jiri told me how you retrieved the *Skow II* from your ah, long-term parking garage."

"She did, did she?" Fisher smiled.

Baines laughed. "Yeah, they could swap hide-and-go-seek stories."

"And this is the biggest one yet," Fisher said. "The quintessential motherlode. Now, we got two of the hottest potatoes in the potato game."

"Except, this one's also an endgame," Resa reminded them. "And it's far from over."

The laughter stopped.

241

Stephen Fenech

31: I-Quandary
Fisher

Beacon immediately brought the packet into the tech lab and unzipped it. The device had a small solar amplifier on one side to keep its circuitry from being damaged by the cold. The rest of its surface was flat grey metal, hinged with super viton seals around its edges.

"I'm confused about something, Beacon," Fisher said as the robot worked. "Back on Earth, why didn't you just keep all that info about the packet locked in your innards?"

Beacon's upper hemisphere curved towards Fisher. "Same reason, Captain: compromise. The Imperium was after me. If they managed to shut me down, they would've gained access, rendering all our efforts for naught. I had to delete any relevant files and place my trust in Baron."

The robot turned back to the packet. "Now, let me see how far that trust takes us. Dr Cholla, I could use your assistance with unlocking the packet."

Cholla's eyes lit up. "Absolutely."

"As for the rest of you, I ask that nonessential personnel save any further questions and keep your distance. No offence but at this stage, you would only delay the process."

"Beacon's right," said Anne. "I'll liaise, checking in periodically to apprise you all of any developments. In the meantime, let's leave these two brilliant minds to work in peace. We have to discuss our next strategy—no need to wait for the packet to reveal its secrets."

"A bit premature to make any plans, don't you think?" Bliter complained. "We'll have to know how we can use it first."

"No harm in preparing," Anne returned. With that, she dragged them away to the mess. Their deliberations kept them quite busy and quite short with one other—they all seemed to hold different opinions on the matter.

By the time Beacon called them back to the lab to reveal his initial findings, the only accord the crew reached, which couldn't really be called such, was that they had to get the lay of the coast before setting out. Ideal, except the consensus on *that* point was that it would be impossible.

Bliter eventually offered them a suggestion that garnered the greatest acceptance. "Since we're flying blind and trying to stay under the radar anyway, I think the next natural step would be to try for Vorancia's homeworld. Florin IV might be a whiplashed Stricken, but that also makes it uninhabited, so we can traipse around at leisure."

Fisher looked at the navigator in surprise. "Bliter, that's a really good idea. Vorancia did have a working prototype of this technology after all. Besides, Resa has some experience with salvage ops on a Stricken."

"Right," Bliter said. "We might uncover some leads about using the finished product, whenever Beacon figures it out that is. Even if we glean a potential *what not to do* when and if we get a chance to deploy the tech."

Resa frowned, the lines on his forehead creasing into fissures. The tip of his small antenna traced a full circle. "Yes… we might get some traction there but didn't the Imperium decipher Vorancia's version? They would have rendered it useless by now or, *gachami*, learned how to exploit it against such efforts."

Cheeks flushed, Bliter spun on the Tolkane. "It's a risk assessment," he snapped. "But a chance we gotta take. We'll find no more answers out here."

Anne stepped between them and raised her palms. "We'll just have to wait and see exactly what Beacon uncovers. Then go from there."

Meanwhile, the *Skow II* continued her escape trajectory, effectively distancing herself from the hazard of the red giant and hurling back towards the hazard of the Dark Sector.

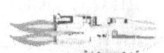

"Something's not right." Fisher did not mask the worry in his voice.

"What's not right?" Anne asked.

He slowly rotated his g-seat away from the bridge console to face her. "When we crossed the corridor through the Dark Sector on the way in, the ship's computer automatically mapped out the flight path, including all the course corrections due to stress factors, tidal shifts, time dilations, gravitational anomalies— basically any events we had to steer past for the entire journey across. It logs them for future reference, leaving the most current and therefore accurate record of digital markers to follow back."

Anne's brows furrowed. "Okay?"

"Normally for a return journey, it's a simple operation with the math already done. I enter the markers inversely from bottom to top for the new flight plan. All the navigation metadata from the log's specs: position, velocity, direction, and such, gets plugged into helm automatically. Then I just let the ship take us back through."

"But?"

"But when I ran the numbers, they don't synch. Helm is giving me an error message."

"Are you saying the computer data is flawed or corrupted? Do we have to plot a brand-new course back?"

"No, and yes," the captain said.

Anne folded her arms. "Explain."

"We'll definitely have to plot a new course, but this mess wasn't due to any data corruption. The log has an instantaneous double-backup. If an aberration occurred, there'd be a disparity between one or two of the three data streams. They're identical. And apart from the redundancies, sensors all over the ship confirm what the three streams all agree upon—is bogus."

Anne narrowed her eyes. "What *are* they agreeing upon?"

Fisher stretched his arm towards the tactical display on a secondary monitor. "The closest anomalies beyond the threshold have been affected, skewed by something and, judging by the

245

numbers we got on the way in, it's no natural occurrence. The singularities and dark energy conundrums marked their territory long ago."

"Unless," Cholla piped in, "you subscribe to the thesis that causality itself is affected in spacetime quantum ratios, passing so close to singularities, especially when they're spinning."

Blank faces answered him.

"English, Doc," Fisher said.

"Actually," Anne ventured, "I think I understand what the doctor is driving at. With even one of the incredible masses back there causing a curvature in spacetime, there's the theory that events preceding a linear journey through such an anomalous dimensional matrix, like what we experienced in the Dark Sector, are altered. Shifted to tandem reality, force-skewed by divergent radical quanta from the chronological continuum. If you multiply that equation by the sheer number of conflicting singularities, who can tell what route we actually took."

Fisher scowled. "Anne, you're not helping."

She raised a hand in defence. "Sorry, Captain. What I mean is that the black holes stretched and bent our route and the events of our journey so thin that time and events moved backwards, or sideways."

"Precisely." Cholla's smile broadened. He seemed grateful.

"I say, somebody, somehow, fu—zzed us," Fisher said, slowly wagging a finger at the console. "The ship's central computer convinces me that the problem's not systemic. The new numbers it reads out of there have skyrocketed off the chart. For us, mortally so. Could very well be that the Imperium detonated some kind of weapon behind us after we crossed. But I'm not about to enter to find out."

"How the fuck did this happen?" Bliter seethed, projecting his glower at Beacon. The robot's domed orb panned to take him in, but he remained silent.

Fisher exhaled. "Regardless of how it happened, Bliter, something inside there has been triggered, altering the gravimetric and temporal balances, on an apocalyptic scale. Sorry, Anne, the corridor we came through—no longer exists."

Beacon continued to watch.

Anne paled. "Are we… trapped?"

"No," Fisher shook his head firmly. "We're delayed is all, but substantially. The Dark Sector is just that: a sector. It's defined by the anomalies within. So long as we see stars, we're good, but we are going to have to steer clear, veer around the expanse. That'll add considerable time to the journey cause it's uncharted, but even that's negligible."

"So, what's the issue here?" Anne asked, tilting her head to one side. "Because I can tell by your tone there's more."

"It's even more of a backroads route to take than going through the Dark Sector—well, the one we came through before it shattered. Not sure what we'll find. We can do a series of short skips, but jumping without knowing what we're jumping into, well I wouldn't recommend it."

Anne nodded. "I see your point." She ran her fingers through her hair. "We might get lost for starters, or dead for seconds, if we jump into something the ship can't handle like a sun or gas giant."

"Exactly Right," said Fisher. "And we always run the risk of jumping into Demon turf. Like I said it's really uncharted and therefore dicey territory."

"Well, I don't like it," Anne admitted. "But it seems we don't have much of a choice. I'll let you run your numbers, Captain. You know your ship best, but give me some details."

Fisher inclined his head and turned back to his console. He called up a short-range scan on its main viewscreen. With his finger, he gestured to the black mass, which occupied half the monitor's generated star chart. "We'll stay just outside the Dark Sector's fringe and hug it along its outer horizon wall, adjusting course as we go. Then follow its arc until we get a good line of sight with familiar space. I'll keep the *Skow II*'s navigation computer on a constant looping scan, comparing our star charts to the stars we pass. When it gets a match, it'll alert me. Then we can jump long and make our way to Vorancia's system at speed."

"Vorancia's grave, you mean," Baines amended, his dull tone indicating he didn't like the prospect.

Anne ignored the pilot's remark and turned to Beacon. "Thoughts?"

"Captain Fisher is right," the robot replied in a reticent tone. "The Dark Sector no longer offers us an option. Given the circumstances, it sounds like a good plan."

With a brisk dip of her chin, Anne faced Fisher. "Do it."

32: Juxtaposition
Anne

Over the rim of her coffee cup, Anne's eyes swept the bridge. The *Skow II* had followed a series of short skips based on the optical acuity of her short-range sensors. If the gambol target came within range of the ship's visual spectrum, they skipped to it. They didn't dare chance anything beyond.

As such, the view ahead of the *Skow II* became a constant sight: stars swathed in a magenta and blue celestial aura to the left of the craft and the domain wall of an impenetrable black void to the right. The time—drawn out as it was, the routine—every crew member working diligently at their station to facilitate the ship's progress, the course—following the uncharted arc of what felt like a perpetual juxtaposition: everything moved like clockwork.

Until the sensors suddenly went crazy, sending klaxons into pandemonium, with a proximity alarm getting high-tally on Baines' console.

Fisher leapt to his feet. "What the—*now*?" Fumbling for a fitting curse, he let out a vexed rush of air and clenched his hands.

"Small fleet of ships," Baines reported. "Flying straight for us, but—"

"But what?"

"At really slow velocities," the pilot answered.

"The Demons?" asked Anne, sidling up beside Fisher.

"No, it's something else," Baines said. "Quite a few, couple dozen, but they're small. All transports—possibly freighters or pinnaces of some kind, but like nothing I've ever seen. Wait… two of them are Tolkane ships."

"Scan them for weapons." Fisher's tone matched the tight lines of his facial severity. "Do they pose any threat?"

"Nothing immediate. They seem innocuous, no weapons, far as I can tell. No signatures other than—" Baines paused. "—standard nuclear fusion drives."

"Are you kidding me?"

"No Fish, the Tolkane ships might have FTL but they're

249

archaic too, even by your standards."

Fisher ignored the remark. "Can we pass them by without a fight? I don't want any undue fuss."

"Yeah but..." Baines' reply hung in the air a second time. His eyes glued to the monitor as he waited to confirm something. After a long moment, he cocked his head up. "Fish, they're hailing us—with email."

"Who are they?" Anne asked, her suspicions fluttering red flags.

Fisher silently read the text on Baines' screen while idly tracing a finger up and down the length of his scar. At length, he bent down and typed in a response on the pilot's keyboard.

"Hmm, Tolkane ships..." He lifted his eyes and studied a smaller separate monitor above the first for a long moment. "and—yup, I-dent transponders match what the registry on the Box is saying. Wow, after all this time..."

"Talk to me, Fisher," Anne said.

Fisher met her gaze. "Heard about these guys in the squatter camp. Strange, Cardy brought them up recently too. I dismissed the tale as so much bullsh-ock. But Wisdan was adamant. Guess the holy tank was right. We referred to them as 'the ones who got away.'"

Anne let out a tired breath. "Just tell me for Christ's sake."

"You're not going to believe this, Anne, but they're Human, like you."

Anne bolted upright, spilling a measure of her coffee over her hand. "What?"

"They were part of the exodus from Earth."

"How the hell did they get out *here*?"

Fisher lifted his shoulders. "Good question. What I know of the story is that these guys devolved into a churlish lot, anti-religious racist freaks peddling doom and gloom—your society's underbelly."

Anne gasped. "No. The Apocs?"

Fisher arched an eyebrow. "I know that name—it's what we call punk agitators still causing all sorts of headaches in and about Alliantha, Korian III, and Ursula Minor, but they're Tolkani like me."

"Could this crowd be part of that same rabble, Fish?" Brumbal asked from the entryway.

Fisher shrugged again at the big man before giving Anne his full attention. "If I recall the tale correctly, they caused an incident—quite nasty. Then, the rats just upped and scurried out of the system, setting out on their own." He pointed to the Box. "In that ship."

"Are you saying they escaped the second holocaust?"

"Long before it," said Fisher, running a hand through his hair. "They split shortly after the Humans first arrived."

Anne pressed her eyes into thin gaps. "What do they want now?"

"Only an information trade."

"What *kind* of information?" Her wariness ratcheted up another notch.

"Seems they lost their only engineer to an accident, and have no idea how to repair their flagship's engine containment fields. They asked if we had a spare robot aboard to go take a look. I said no of course, but we *could* spare Jiri for a turn. She's better than a robot after all, in several ways."

"Thanks, Cap," Jiri said, returning his smile.

A heaviness weighted Anne's gut, pushing it down to her knees and her lips formed a tight line. "You're not seriously considering docking with them?"

"We don't have to," Fisher said. "Jiri can send a small diagnostic platform from ship to ship towed by a pair of lifter-bots. She can address whatever issues they have entirely by remote, and let them fix their fields themselves."

Anne chewed her lip. "Fisher, this is a bad idea. The Apocs were nothing but trouble, even in my time. I think they're after more than information." She looked down at her mug and the coffee that had soaked and scalded her hand. So shocked at the revelation, she hadn't even registered the burning pain until that moment.

As she placed the cup down, Anne's thoughts turned to Beacon, still in the lab with Cholla. She used the bottom of her shirt to wipe the dark liquid from the back of her hand and raised her eyes to Fisher again. "Get an explanation about their escape first—one that makes a lick of sense. But I already know if the Apocs are involved it's going to stink."

"You're right. They're murderers and terrorists, but look at their ships and where they *came from*. Besides, it wouldn't be the first time I had to deal with dredges and pirates."

"Okay, point taken," Anne said. "What do we get in return? It must be something really good unless—hey, you're not finally seeing Wisdan's light, are you?"

"So, you've learned the whole story now," Fisher chortled casting a wry grin at Baines, "Funny you should mention Cardy, cause he shared your sentiment about these guys."

Anne blinked, pitching her voice higher. "And you're still considering it?"

"They say they've charted this far sector, all the way back to our own familiar haunts. Jiri could download their charts, which would speed things up substantially on our end. No more relying on visual acuity, no more guesswork, no more slow-mo."

"Well, I can't argue with that," Anne admitted. She knew the Imperium or something even more unfriendly was hot on their trail, and getting closer. The sabotage of the Dark Sector confirmed it. The Apocs definitely presented the lesser of the three evils in this game, and if the *Skow II* could jump again...

Anne cast a wary glance out the bridge window as the first Apoc ships appeared. "Still, it might be a trap," she made herself say.

Fisher gave her a lopsided smile, which plainly said he'd already thought of that. Anne hated to admit it, but he'd won her over.

"Look," Fisher cajoled. "We've been playing it safe ever since we thawed Resa, doubly so since we resurrected you, Sister. What's the worst thing that can happen with this bunch?"

Anne stared.

33: Down Load
Fisher

"We are the Apocalyptic Sedition. Prepare to be boarded," the gritty face on the screen commanded.

"You're funny," Fisher shot back.

"Captain," Baines said beside him. "They're firing on us."

"*Firing?* I thought you said they had no weapons."

The hull grumbled under the impact, but no klaxon rang.

"Direct hit," Baines announced.

"Any damage?"

"No."

"So?"

"So, apparently, they do have them," Baines said with rare ire.

"Care to elaborate?"

"They have weapons, if you can call them that, but they are completely ineffectual, harmless to the *Skow II*—as demonstrated," the pilot said.

Fisher frowned. "Then, why bother?"

Baines raised his shoulders. "Maybe they're trying to get our attention, like a toddler throwing a tantrum at not getting its way, or maybe…"

"They're trying to distract us," Fisher finished for him. "Jiri, you downloaded all their charts, right?"

"Aye-aye, Cap."

"Good work. Baines, get us the f-heck out of here. I think we parleyed enough with these hicks."

"Captain, I… *can't.*"

Fisher turned rigid at the news. "What in Cries' name now?"

"There's a digital gridlock over the entire ship. Most systems are offline."

Resa stormed into their midst. "Coming from them?"

"Negative," Baines said. "There's another ship, just arrived, jumped in right behind us."

"Quick!" Fisher shouted. "Run the specs on the newbie."

"Twice our size, plasma drive, it's an ID scout—no wait... plasma torpedo bays, phase-cannons, multifacet tractors, rail guns—serious fangs. They converted it into a goddam battlewagon. It's got us on fast lockdown."

Face sallow and drawn, Baines looked up at his captain. "Sorry Fish, but we ain't goin' anywhere."

Baines' pronouncement ignited a verbal war. Across the tenuous no-fly zone finally established between Fisher and Resa, fresh accusations reneged their shaky armistice. Bliter stood on the sidelines adding his own fusillades. Anne and Baines exchanged hurried glances while the rest of the crew stared at their feet and stewed.

Fisher and Resa faced off, fists balled and quivering. Their collective rage fulminated. Before it led to mortal combat, the pilot jumped out of his seat and forced himself between them.

Like a referee intervening at a boxing match, Baines pulled them apart. "Look!" he shouted, eyes blazing at each in turn. "It's an ID ship all right, but no ID. There's freaking Apocs flying that bird." The pilot's news quelled them all to silence. Even the non-combative crew members looked up.

"You sure?" Fisher asked, unconvinced.

"Yeah, I'm sure. The only thing we still have control of is the sensors. Apart from the ambient temperature inside its shell, there's all kinds of telltale heat signatures moving up and down that ship. The Demons run cold: no engine fire and no body heat. I'm seeing multiple heat sources of exactly 37°C coming from the bridge of the scout."

"Is that even possible?" Anne asked. "How the hell did they get their hands on ID tech, and an ID boat?"

"*That,* Dr Morrison, is a good question," Baines admitted.

Regaining command of his anger, Fisher turned to his engineer, his voice hoarse from his row. "Jiri, what the heck happened over there?"

"Can't tell for certain, Fish. My platform wasn't in that clunker-tub too long. As soon as I had the link-up with their engine,

I knew their issue was cockeyed. Containment seemed nominal and their engine, fine, well for a piece-of-shit antique that is," the engineer amended.

"Any anomalies?"

"Nope, nothing I could detect. But like I said I wasn't in there that long."

"Long enough," Resa pointed out. "But you only followed orders, Jiri. Your *captain* on the other hand is responsible for this mess. Had we skipped past these heretics as common sense screamed at him to do, none of this would have happened."

Baines let out a low whistle and cowed his head low, clearly bracing for his captain's carpet bomb run.

"What?" Fisher snarled pure vitriol at Resa, "Listen, you self-righteous holier-than-thou god-pawn, Anne said 'don't dock.' I *didn't—frglhn*—dock!"

"You never docked physically," Resa countered, his fallout no less trenchant. "But did so digitally, obviously opening up a backdoor for them to seize the *Skow II*'s computers. Once again, your reck—"

"Shut it, Freeze," Fisher spat. "And while you're at it, why don't you just plain freeze?"

"No, Captain," Bliter said. "Let Resa speak. He might have something to fix this clusterfuck—a situation you put us in."

Fisher withered the navigator with his glower, but it was Baines who spoke up. "Bliter, might want to retract that insubordinate poison—while you still got a pulse."

"It's my fault," Jiri said, raising her hands in surrender, her small voice carrying over the tumult. "I saw the Apocs as inferior when I looked at their tech and got sloppy. Sorry Cap, I take full responsibility."

Fisher smiled wryly. "I love you little girl, but it's true, I thought I could handle them. I'm the one who got sloppy."

"Where the fuck was the damn robot during all this?" Bliter seethed.

"Beacon's been with Cholla," Anne floated over a heavy sigh.

255

"Working practically 24/7 on the packet." Her eyes became slits. "You already know that."

Bliter ranted on as if he didn't hear her. "It's supposed to be the one wise to the Demons' ploys. Hasn't it seen them all by now?"

Though Fisher hated to admit it, Bliter had a point. "Why don't you go fetch him?"

The crewman snorted. "Happy to—if you and Resa are done with your little fuck-in."

"Just shut *up* already," Jiri said in a tired voice. "And stop being such a dick, dragging this out."

Bliter's face cringed but before he could do just that, Anne harrumphed, "Now that we're all stuck here, Fisher, for everyone's sake, please, tell us as much as you can about the Apocs. Any insight into their past might help us in dealing with them now. Before they throw us any new surprises."

"Tale's done, Anne," the captain griped. "Nothing to add."

"Try me."

"Like I said before, all this business happened way ahead of my time. They committed a crime and escaped, long before the brunt of the second holocaust wiped out your race."

Fisher stopped and rubbed his scar. He considered leaving it at that but Anne's jutting chin and unblinking stare made him go on. With a half-hearted shrug, he continued. "Right from the get-go, the Apocs segregated themselves from everyone on Alliantha, including their own. Became hostile to the Alianthans, doubly so to the Tolkane, but most of all to the daughter species, namely us Tolkani. The Apocs feared what the new race meant, likening us to genetic pollution."

"Pollution?" Anne's features tightened.

"The rest of the Humans treated them with disdain, but pretty much like having a brother you hate, you want to kill him, but you never will, cause he's your brother. The Humans needed everyone to rebuild their race, which sadly included the nasty ones."

"So, what about this crime you mentioned?" Anne prompted.

"Way I heard it, bunch of Apoc hardliners hijacked that Tolkane ship out there—murdered her crew. They used her to fire heavy ordnance on a crowded church. Decimated the building, killing hundreds attending service and more in the surrounding square. It constituted the first racial attack on our planet. The authorities went after them of course but they never found the dissidents. The Apocs were never brought to justice Just disappeared."

"Until now," Anne said. "Okay, so they commandeered this Tolkane ship—a single ship, and now they acquired all these other shitboxes and one ID scout. How does that happen?"

"Heard a few more rumours while doing runs on the merchantmen," said Fisher. "Off-world stories trickled in about other ships getting similarly skyjacked, but the crimes could never be pinned on these rats specifically. Space is, well big, and filled with a wide range of pirates."

"Don't I know it," Baines put in. "When you meet a pirate in the Dark, Anne, it's usually for the first *and* last time—only one of you gets to fly away."

"True that." Fisher thrust his chin at Baines before turning back to Anne. "But if you're asking for my best guess, I figure it's what the brigands know. If they had no qualms about forcing their way aboard one ship and wasting her crew, I think they didn't baulk about repeating their offence to collect this fleet of clunkers."

"Yeah," Baines said. "Question is, are they about to repeat that offence?"

"Time will tell." Anne let out a breath. Her eyebrows pulled together before diving down into a V. "But what made them want to vacate not just the Alliantha System, but all of known space to stumble upon these cold barrens?"

Fisher lifted his regard to the ceiling as he pondered. "Maybe they somehow caught wind of Baron's little plan—with the packet and all—and decided to go after it on their own."

"I never credited the Apocs with that much intuition,

257

forethought, or intelligence for that matter."

"Yeah," Fisher said. "Maybe *they* don't deserve the credit, but with all due respect, Anne, who's got whom by the short and curlies?"

"Point taken."

"So," the captain speculated, "they somehow acquired the intel about Baron's packet and with their misguided sense of purpose and propriety, went after it."

Anne scoffed. "Don't tell me they encountered an Imperium scout and pirated their way aboard *that*. Hell, even if all the Demons aboard were dead, they couldn't have seized it, let alone taken command. Environmental controls alone would have hectored them to no end."

"It's obviously not the Apocs turning these gears," Resa surmised. "I think there's more to this little scenario than what we see on the surface."

"Always is," Fisher agreed, rubbing his temple. "And I have a really sick feeling I'm going to hate it."

34: Down Luck
Fisher

The hatchet face on the video screen bore human features where they should be but that's where the semblance ended. Where not disfigured, they creased and contorted to form a mask of hate. Above a cracked rictus of a mouth, a bent nose protruded, pushed left of centre by some vicious fight, probably to the death, Fisher guessed. Disproportionate serpent eyes glared at him with a perverse brand of maliciousness as if considering how best to disseminate him.

"Name's Slynn. I'm captain of this fleet and your jailer. We got a fix on all of your crew," the Apoc said, pouring contempt into every word. "Get to your cargo hold at once, including your robot. Make sure it brings the packet there. Won't bode well for the rest of you fucks otherwise. I got biometrics to ensure you do exactly as I command—and plasma flashes if you don't."

How could they know? That singular question coursed through Fisher's racing mind.

Baines covered his mouth and whispered, "Fish, we really gonna lay down arms for these pricks?"

"Just do it," Fisher whispered back.

"Listen, I gleaned something else from Jiri's little sortie. Scooped some of Cardy's lifter—"

Fisher pressed Baines with a stern look, which silenced the pilot.

"Captain Slynn speaks truly about having plasma flashes," declared Beacon in a voice for all to hear, including the varmint on the screen. "I parse their energy signatures. The discharge from such weaponry can easily penetrate our hull at the subatomic level, bursting once it contacts air. It would harm neither me nor the packet, but would quickly incinerate anything organic. We must comply."

"Robot's got the right idea," Mr Malevolence called from the viewscreen. In a pointed voice that dared them to think otherwise, the Apoc warned, "We're monitoring your every step, Captain, so don't fuck it up. Your crew's lives depend on it."

"We will comply," the robot repeated.

The video screen went blank. Free of restraint, the crew exploded with pensive unrest, hands raised, fingers pointing—or stabbing, faces clenched or blanched.

His seeing dome still locked on the now darkened screen, Beacon's voice rose above their verbal chaos. "We will COMPLY—with our own edicts."

Deliberations abruptly ceased.

"If you're going to speak on our behalf," Bliter thundered into the silence, "demonstrate the goddam tech to us before those cocksuckers get their hands on it. Who's to say they won't paste us once they get what they're after, which is only you and your packet? The rest of us are expendable."

Beacon rotated his torso so that his smiling caricature faced the crew. "I will do what I can once we get to the cargo hold."

Seeing the limited effect of the robot's words on the hesitant faces of his crew, Fisher added, "Trust your robot."

"Exactly," Beacon agreed. "Don't let fear live in your minds rent-free, for not all is as it seems. This is not a defeat, merely a setback—a necessary one." Then he added, "This is where our nexus truly begins."

Fisher knew Beacon's appeal would only further perplex his crew but it provided a good distraction to keep panic at bay. He needed every one of them to be frostier than the Apocs …frostier than the Demons.

"The questions will be answered in the causal storm, which now gathers," the automaton went on. "It is all a mathematical certainty."

When Beacon finished, all faces zeroed in on his smiley-face as though hypnotized by some ridiculous-looking demigod.

"Shall we?" the prophetic robot prompted.

The crew snapped out of their trance and started moving.

When they had all congregated in the cargo hold, Fisher

opened another video channel to the ID scout. "We're all here Slynn, *you creep*," he added under his breath.

"Yeah, all accounted for—good. That the packet your robot's holding?"

"Correct," Beacon confirmed.

"Stay where you are and don't move. We'll be right over and—"

"Captain Slynn?" Beacon addressed.

"What?" the Apoc said irritably.

Beacon held up the metallic briefcase in front of him as though presenting an offering... or a sacrifice.

Slynn blinked.

Fisher started.

Beacon acted.

A panel snapped open in the middle of Beacon's torso, revealing a ramrod. It sprang out, punching through the packet in a flowering torrent of circuit fragments and silicon dust. Electrical shorts and blue static discharged from the pulverized tech packet. The robot's arms released what they still held and the bits fell to the floor.

Before anyone could react, a fourth diminutive arm emerged from the robot's backside and snaked over his shoulder like a scorpion's stinger. A nozzle at its tip dipped down and sprayed the remnants of the packet's circuitry with a red, highly viscous liquid. The exposed electronic boards and processors dissolved and smoked, fusing into the metal grating of the cargo hold's deck.

Fisher bunched up his nose as an acrid burning smell permeated the entire space.

On the viewscreen, Slynn's eyes blazed into tempests. He sent enraged expletives firing in every direction like shrapnel. "Fool!" he hissed. "Your goddam crew's gonna die for that. And I'm starting with you. The Over—"

A searing hyphen of green laser light stung the small console below the monitor, bursting the metal box in a torrent of amber sparks. Slynn's nefarious face fizzled and vanished within the monitor's frame as the feed went offline.

Fisher spun to see Beacon extending a fifth arm tipped with an angry-looking plasma gun pointed at the defunct board. From the weapon's muzzle, a thin column of white smoke rose towards the ceiling.

"Guess that concludes today's broadcast," Baines said. Fisher followed the pilot's voice and found him staring at his own reflection on the darkened screen. He let out a timorous laugh. "Off the air until further notice." The pilot released a breath and turned to Fisher, a resigned look etching his features. "They're gonna fry us now, you know, with those flashes."

"Trust your ro——" Beacon's voice cut off. His abrupt silence drew the crew's focus. They stepped closer to the robot.

Without warning, a series of internal alarms and mechanical paroxysms seized Beacon. His appendages fanned out in every direction, extending and retracting randomly.

Fisher recoiled, barely avoiding the swinging adjuncts as he twisted and collided with Cholla, right behind him. The impact knocked the startled doctor's glasses from his face.

"Slynn is——tink—errrrrrrrrrr—ing. Beeeeeeeee—ing shhhhhut—downnnn.n.n.n.n.n.n.............." Beacon managed with surprising calm. His voice steadily dropped octaves as all of his lights dimmed or winked out.

With an imperious thud, the robot crashed to the floor, teetered a moment, and lolled awkwardly to one side, in as close to a horizontal position as his splayed and extended gantries would allow.

Mouths agape, the crew froze.

"No!" Jiri cried.

Fisher gulped in solid disbelief.

Anne stepped forward and raised her hands in a calming gesture. "Nobody panic. Our robot's not dead. He's incapacitated, but still in there. I can *feel* his presence." She sought Fisher's eyes. "Captain, remember what Beacon told you about pushing you through an inevitable trap? I think this is it."

Fisher started, then nodded fervently. "Anne's right. Beacon warned me about this. Resa and Cholla were there too. Makes sense now. Just stay frosty guys and we'll get through this."

"Just have to trust our robot," Cholla offered in a reasonable voice as he crouched to pick up his glasses.

"Trust?" Bliter shouldered his way past the others, bumping Cholla as he made to stand. The collision sent the hapless doctor sprawling forward on all fours. Still safely clutching his spectacles, Cholla let out a grunt.

Bliter's rage surpassed the Apoc's as he squared off and confronted Anne. His face resembled a shrivelled beet, veins straining against the skin of his neck. "Your *robot* just fucked us— that heap of dysfunctional shit with parts."

"No, Bliter," Anne replied in a flat tone. "Beacon just saved us."

"Saved?" The incensed navigator was beside himself. "After what we risked getting that bloody packet? It could've at least shared the tech with us first, your cross-wired *toaster*."

"Calm yourself Bliter," Resa cautioned.

"Fuck you. I don't want to die like this!" Bliter punctuated his wrath by slamming a fist against Beacon's inert torso. The impact made a dull metallic thud. Other than the hollow noise, the robot did not budge or react in any way.

"Bliter," Fisher said in a low monotone, "take—your-own— advice. You'll live longer." The captain kept his manner and expression calm and dispassionate, but the feral tremor tingling in his eyes proved enough to silence the navigator. It silenced everyone.

Fisher knew why. It was their first glimpse into the core of his severity—a facet he'd never unveiled to any of them. His *street* release.

The only crew member who'd come close to seeing that valve fully open was Baines. And only once. When they'd been locked in mortal combat with the pirates who tried to steal the *Skow*.

An echo of that time sounded now. But as Bliter lost his nerve, finding a new interest in the floor, the tension sapped. The rest of the crew exhaled, and let their shoulders sag, their relief, tangible.

As for the strain cording Fisher's own fury, it too simmered, or rather gave way to something new and—overwhelming. Something he had never suffered in his hardest years. Vision drooping as if pulled down by invisible weights, Fisher gazed dully at his crew. The tragedy mirrored in their empty stares reflected his heartbreak. Crushing guilt drained his resolve in an undertow of defeat.

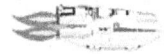

The blue translucent collars placed around the necks of the *Skow II*'s crew were painless; the implication of what they signified was not. The Apocs had fitted the hybrid devices with metal plates fused into their surface where an array of tiny blinking lights did laps around the entire ring. *Not just ornamental bling*, Fisher surmised.

Although Beacon had destroyed the packet, permanently removing the valuable playing piece from the board, Slynn did not follow through on his death threat with the others. If anything, relations with the *Skow II*'s captors improved.

Still outwardly hostile, Slynn's squad seemed desultory as well. They'd lost their conviction when Beacon changed the rules of the game. The Apocs would now fear the Imperium as much as Fisher's crew, perhaps more.

Fisher knew the Demons were reprehensible, capable of horrific things in the name of their manifesto. Their reprisal for the Apocs' blunder would not be pretty and, he was willing to bet both of his ships, the Demons had given the Apocs a foul taste of it already. Their dread seemed all too palpable.

Fisher kept quiet when the curs boarded the *Skow II*, weapons trained and collars waiting. The boarding party did their jobs unceremoniously but without the vindication or wanton violence for which they'd achieved their notoriety. He guessed the ID had given the rogue dregs explicit instructions not to damage the crew.

Beacon must've been counting on it when he took his earlier liberties. The robot had an intimate knowledge of Demon behaviour from his millenniums-long evasions no doubt. But where would it lead them now? And to what end?

The question stuck in the captain's mind as the Apocs fitted his people with the half-glass, half-metallic devices and escorted them one by one off his boat. When Fisher's turn came, the Apocs steered him into a small shuttle and off the *Skow II* for the short ride over to the awaiting ID scout.

Feeling the cold press of the collar against his neck, Fisher's head felt too heavy for his weakened shoulders. For the first time in his life, he had been completely outwitted by an enemy, and now it would cost him—cost them all, more than any among his devout cadre was willing to pay.

***

Except one.

Stephen Fenech

35: Slynn

The interior of the scout looked almost identical to the outside. Anne recognized the same walls of latent plasma, the *Glass* as she remembered it, suffused with inconceivable energy, icy cold, forensic, soulless.

But there had been modifications as well to accommodate the warm-bloods. Most of the panels spoke of Imperium design, but also old tech interfaces even she could recall.

The ship itself was a hybrid, and had to be. Otherwise, they'd all be dead. The ambient temperature was but one retrofit. Anne expected to find several more alterations for the resident Humans.

But no considerations, human or otherwise quelled the effect of Slynn's frigid orbs. Anne did her best to ignore him as he scrutinized her from behind the transparent vestibule door. She kept her gaze averted, taking a scientist's genuine interest in the ship's functions while making careful observations that might aid the captives. Her eyes fell upon...

***

The sound of servos firing and the glass door shushing open brought Fisher out of his contemplations. Slynn strode past, all but ignoring him. The Apoc beelined for Anne until his face loomed inches from her own. His crooked sneer cut like a knife.

"With the collars, you got no chance in hell of escape. Wander anywhere you're not supposed to, we won't hunt you down and punish you. Your head will simply blow the fuck off your shoulders. The devices are designed to explode if you pass the virtual perimeter we've designated. As captain of this fleet I—"

"It's admiral," Anne interrupted. "If you command more than one ship, you're an admiral."

Slynn gaped for a moment before giving her a look of pure frost. His malevolence pronounced itself even sharper up close but Anne didn't flinch. "What do you plan to do with us?"

"Plan? We're planning nothing, and I prefer *captain,* bitch. The sound of *admiral* makes me want to puke. Reeks of the system—your bullshit system. We just have to hold you till the Overlords arrive."

"Okay, *Captain,*" Anne retorted. "So, you sold your soul to them. Are you fucking crazy?"

The Apoc shrugged. "We made a deal in exchange for our lives."

"What kind of deal?"

"I learned real quick how to survive, playing for the winning side. Couldn't sacrifice the essence of humanity, breeding with animals, diluting our gene pool with alien DNA. Who knows what diseases they'd introduce, those fucking Tolkane with their deformities? Remember AIDS?"

Suddenly possessed, Slynn reached out, seized Resa by his collar, and yanked him forward a step. The Apoc stabbed an accusing finger at the Tolkane's small antenna and taunted, "See this—it's a goddam abomination. It ain't natural!"

"And the Demons are?" Anne flared back.

The Apoc let out a sardonic laugh as he released Resa. "Well, it's not like I'm planning on fucking one of them."

"Maybe not," Anne gave back "But they're definitely fucking with you."

"Nothing we can do about that." Slynn paused and suppressed his vehemence under a thin veil of sincere curiosity. "How are you still around anyway? After we left on the exodus, thought you went up in the blaze when the plasma hit?"

"One of life's little ironies, you might say. But what's your story? That's the really interesting riddle here."

The Apoc indicated Resa with another jab to the Tolkane's chest. "This one probably already told you—his version anyway. We tried to save our race from the Tolkane infestation. But high and mighty *Fieldbank,*" Slynn spat the name like a curse, "preached the exact opposite. Me and my gang could only endure it for so long before we took matters into our own hands. None of this would've happened had we succeeded in offing that fuck back at his university on Earth."

Anne's eyebrows vaulted. "That was you? It *was* an assassination attempt? Baron told me he got caught in the blast of a randomly placed terrorist bomb."

Slynn snorted. "Yeah, that's what the media said. But no, I went after that imperious cunt. Cops caught wind of our scheme, my people got skittish, and sloppy. Our plan got foiled at the last minute. We still triggered the damn thing, but their fuck-up forced us to randomize. Too unpredictable—that wily son of a bitch. All we did was give him a souvenir."

"The attack blinded Baron," Anne explained to the others.

"All the good it did us. With your robot's help, he got replacements real soon. And we never got the chance again, not directly." Slynn let out a fulsome chuckle. "Instead, we let the Overlords do what they do best."

"I thought you were purists, in the vilest sense of the word, justifying the harm you inflicted in the name of your messed-up morality. What? The Demons don't fit into that backwards philosophy? They represent the epitome of what you loathe and then you go and throw in with them?"

Anne paused and took Slynn's measure. "Or could it be that when your surgical hits began turning out a few critical spoils, they gave you some pull? Then your so-called idealism devolved into greed and piracy."

By the slight widening of Slynn's eyes, Fisher knew Anne had hit the mark. Though the myopic villain would never admit it, his silence affirmed Anne's deduction.

She slowly shook her head. "A sorry-ass bunch of hypocritical anarchists, turned pirates, reduced to thralls. Now, you're nothing more than the Demons' bitches." Anne's tone sharpened. "And what exactly were you letting the Overlords do?"

Slynn's grin snaked into something savage. "Seeing you're all collared, no harm in a little brag. We found no future under the Baron's dictatorship. Knew we had to leave. Just didn't know how.

269

Then the solution fell into our laps not long after the arks hit final atmo on Alliantha.

"A fellow subversive and true believer, gave us some valuable intel about what the tyrant had brewing—with the packet. How it would only piss off the ID. Proved it to us. Showed how to force the change we craved. He helped us get the shit we needed and set us on our course."

Slynn threaded his calloused fingers together and cracked his knuckles loudly. His leer cornered Anne. "We hit the Tolkane scum with everything we had, made short work of them with our new weapons, took their ship, and went on our little crusade."

"Crusade?" Anne prompted.

"Mini-nukes. Razed a church and wasted a square's worth of the plague—dare steal our religion? That flaming pillar surging to the sky sure looked sweet—our statement, a show of the new world order and our parting gift. Then we got the fuck away from that stinking cesspool planet."

Anne's eyes stormed into twin cyclones but she bit her tongue and exhaled. "Okay, what did you do after you left Alliantha? How did you amass your little fleet?"

Fisher smiled inwardly. Anne did a great job at keeping the miscreant talking, playing to his maligned ego. The *Skow II*'s captain just stood there and watched the A-hole—with his ears, while maintaining his abject look of defeat, which wasn't entirely an act.

Slynn's facial features clenched in different directions, an apparent struggle between avarice and contempt. "We did what we do best, sister: anarchy. Admittedly, our first hijack on the sewer planet went a bit rocky, but after that, it got easy. We outsmarted the suckers, same way we outfoxed you, and continued to grow in bodies and hardware."

The Apoc's face suddenly darkened. "Until the Demons found us."

Fisher felt sure, despite all of Slynn's smug bravado, the Apoc shivered at the recollection.

"Once they realized we were Human, they planned to kill us. But then had a change of heart and spared—well, half of us," Slynn amended.

The left corner of Fisher's mouth curved up. *I knew it.*

"The Demons singled me out," said Slynn. "Interrogated me alone, stabbing all sorts of probes into me. A goddam mental purgatory I never thought possible. But in the end, I walked away. They wanted to know where we were going, why, and where we came from—more than happy to tell them that last bit. Gave them the truth, which saved my ass and curried some favour."

"Then—" Slynn paused, gulped, and checked himself. When he did speak again, the timbre of his voice slowed and dithered in volume. They divided us into two groups. Ripped half my crew to shreds while the other half watched. I was one of the lucky ones."

The Apoc lowered his head and stared at the glass expanse of floor. "They housed my fleet in one of their big-ass capital ships and escorted us FTL to this sector. Gave us this scout to boot and trained us on how to operate it. Said they wouldn't kill the rest of us—if we remained here and kept surveillance for them over the turf."

Slynn looked up. "They forbade our own ferreting, assured us the packet would be found—by the robot. Just had to keep the ID's sensors keyed on his signature. You're precious Beacon led us to capture you twats." The Apoc's smirk returned. "And now, it's done."

Pain and anger wrestled for expression on Anne's face. She fought to keep her voice under control. "You betrayed your own species—to them. Do you even realize what you've done? You've destroyed the very thing you wanted to preserve: humanity!"

"You didn't see what they did to my crew."

"*After* you told them," Anne admonished. "Every Human on Alliantha is dead. Dead, because of you, because of your weakness."

Slynn's orbs burned with conviction. "They were dead already. I just sped things up. Almost poetic—save the race by

271

destroying it."

"You disgust me." Anne's reply came flat, unemotional.

"Fuck you," the Apoc seethed. "You'll learn your place soon enough, if they allow you to live, like they did us."

"You call what you're doing living? They set you up, like pawns. It's how they roll—it's how they fuck. It's always been like that with them. You may be part of this trap, but hello, the trap is sprung. When they have what they want, you no longer serve a purpose."

Anne threw her hands up and leaned in. "You think they'll just let you go with a smile and a wave goodbye? They hate us. The Demons learned the packet was out here but even they couldn't locate it. Now, with the packet gone, you'll come up no dice when they arrive. Think about what that means. You hand us over to the bastards, the final game pieces, it'll be checkmate for everyone *not* Demon. Get it?"

Anne had not feigned the yearning in her voice but Fisher knew her words were lost on the cretin. Slynn just gawked back at her as if struck dumb.

"Quit now," Anne beseeched. She backed away from the Apoc. "Let us go. You can still save yourselves."

"We *are* saving ourselves, Morrison, handing them what they want."

"But you aren't," Anne rallied. "The packet's toast, history."

"But the robot ain't. It obviously downloaded the packet's tech into its banks first. Why do you think we left it aboard that former bucket of yours? I got an armed guard on its ass 24/7 and ID protocols, forcing it to power-down, and stay down."

"You did what?" Anne's face turned ashen.

But Fisher gleaned her inwardly storing this valuable titbit of information.

Slynn's face, on the other hand, flexed wrinkles into a taut mask of triumph.

"How did you, they know?" Anne asked.

The Apoc let out a mirthless laugh. "Nice try."

Just keep him talking Anne. Despite his arrogance, this prick feared to tell her something—a truth he didn't trust himself to divulge. Fisher noticed the slight inflection: Slynn hid something darker.

Anne immediately changed tact. "Okay, I get it. You obviously knew about the packet but how did your fellow dissident? What happened to him? Was he one of us—human too?"

"Yeah, he was human." Slynn paused and swallowed.

Again. Something twitched in the Apoc's eyes, an involuntary tremor. Whoever he was, Slynn's co-conspirator did not align with Baron—a given, but neither did he scheme with the Demons. *With limitless power to match...*

Before Anne could press the Apoc further, Slynn turned to Fisher. "Thanks for returning my rightful property. It's the very least you can do after wasting the entire crew I sent after your ship. And besides, you won't be needing it any longer."

Stephen Fenech

36: Circuitry

Anne

Once Slynn's crew left their captives alone, the heated debate reignited, but this time Anne quickly interceded. "Quiet, all of you. Let's keep level heads and figure this out together."

"The only way we'll keep our heads is if we don't move past the perimeter, wherever the hell that is," Bliter said pointedly.

"You're forgetting something," said Anne.

"What?"

"Beacon is outside the perimeter, still aboard the *Skow II.*"

"Yeah, but you heard that prick. It's shut down, with *I-D* protocols. It can't help us."

"Haven't you moved past that same old distinction?" Anne asked. "Think of a robot strictly as a machine and that's precisely what you get." She suddenly remembered how Baron used to think of Beacon in that same way, but as the crisis loomed, Beacon became more humanized to her late colleague. Her thoughts strayed to Fisher.

"*He,* told us to trust him, Bliter and that's exactly what we're going to do." Anne took a deep breath. "In the meantime, focus on what we can do rather than on what we can't. We might be able to help ourselves, even if Beacon remains incapacitated."

Anne turned to the others. "Now, let's think this through. We have bombs attached to our necks. Dr Cholla, do you recognize some of the tech here, even a small part to unravel the manacles or press to some advantage?"

Cholla pondered for a moment, tracing a finger along the curved shackle around his neck. "Well, the Apocs have been out here for a long time, decades alone. Remember what Slynn said, 'they won't hunt us down'? He's betting on our compliance with such mortal restraints. This leads me to believe our captors don't monitor them all the time. I surmise it's tech they don't know how

275

to decipher or control. The ID just showed them how to activate it. The Apocs' sights are on the top prize, namely Beacon. They see him as much more of a threat than us—even in his current state. Might be why they separated us. We're contained. He is not. That'll give us some latitude." He paused when Anne lifted a hand to her collar.

She offered him a genuine smile. "Go on, Doctor. Please."

Cholla gave her a brief nod before turning to the others. "I suggest we work the problem backwards. Look for the perimeter itself first. I noticed when they escorted us to this part of the ship, the circling lights either sped up or slowed down. I believe the lights will become a steady beam if we stand close to the boundary. Then, we can test the wall for a weakness and see how it correlates to the triggers in these devices. Check the response-versus-proximity factor."

The doctor looked over his shoulder, and then past the crew, as though making mental notes on random spots of the glass bulkheads. "Once established, I feel quite sure the perimeter will specify certain details about the layout of the ID scout itself, like a partial blueprint. After a barrier inspection, I'll take a closer look at the units themselves. That will undoubtedly give us some indication of how best to proceed."

"Good call, Doc," Fisher laughed, giving Cholla's shoulder a gruff squeeze. "Now I know why I hired you."

"Just taking Dr Morrison's advice, Cap," the doctor said, stealing a meek glance at Bliter. The navigator continued to brood but didn't attempt a rejoinder.

Anne's eyes glistened, as impressed as Fisher with Cholla's substantial contribution. She thanked the doctor and faced the crew. "Okay, first things first. Resa, above being an emissary of providence, you're also an experienced salvager. And from what I hear, a proficient one. Could you lend us your expertise in that field as well here?"

Resa cleared his throat. "For what it's worth, yes, of course."

As if seized by a painful epiphany, Bliter harrumphed. "I can help Resa with that much."

Raising his brows, Fisher said in an almost avuncular tone, "Great Bliter, welcome back to the team."

Huddling together, the crew began to hash out a plan.

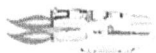

Anne awoke with a start. This latest dream, if that's what it could be called, had finally and thankfully convinced her that she wasn't going crazy.

Apart from the dread of not knowing when the Imperium would turn up, the mats they'd been given to sleep on weren't exactly conducive to slumber. Sheer exhaustion over the last three days took care of that.

When she finally did lose consciousness, what ensued in the cinema of her brain provoked anything but rest. It wasn't a dream, but a subliminal broadcasted message. Almost imperceptible at first, then filling her mind with clarity before dopplering back to nothingness.

It grew louder with each successive episode, louder, clearer, more concise and implicit. The message projected into Anne's mind came from Beacon.

She fought it for a time, believing it nothing more than a synaptic glitch conjured by her overwrought mind racing against time—like she was forced to do during Earth's final days. But when she opened her cognizance to Resa's brand of *Wu Wei,* and stopped resisting the flood, Anne understood.

In the three days prior, the captives had pooled their mental resources, working the problem systematically, with diligence, conviction, sometimes abrasiveness, but always united and resolute on steering their dire situation away from the impending cliff.

Cholla and Resa had worked well in conjunction. Through limited trial and error, they soon had a good indication of the ship's interior and how much of it could be accessed before the devices around their necks would do what they threatened.

Cholla had figured the perimeter wasn't a perimeter at all, formed by some seen or unseen barrier. The boundary was a programmed subroutine hardwired into the explosive devices. The collars didn't communicate with a secondary bay station at all. They talked to each other and self-actuated.

If the prisoner crossed the threshold the bombs would go off, but more disturbing, they also keyed on the host's body temperature. If removed, the collars would sense the drop and also detonate That aspect of the tech, Cholla surmised, was definitely Imperium, as Demons had no body temperature above zero-C.

The ID heated the confined space of course. Otherwise, their pawns would have all frozen to death. Since the Apocs too had warm blood, it made sense that the rest of the ship had been retrofitted in the same way.

But the *Skow II*'s crew had no illusions about their chances. Their path would be laden with a lot of fluid hurdles and unknowns, which had to be properly scoped before they could risk any escape attempt. Any one of a hundred variables, if executed just shy of perfect, could carry a death sentence. Ironically, time marked the real wildcard in this arena.

Much to the crew's surprise, Bliter came up with the first sparks of an escape plan and how to execute it. The navigator reined in their collective revelations and talents, shepherding them towards their best course. At the same time, Beacon's first subconscious transmission got through.

And now, after her latest subliminal dialogue with her robot, Anne had her answer. But definitive plan or not, it assuredly would not be pretty. For better or worse, their countdown to *a* doom had begun.

37: Misdiagnosis
Slynn

Slynn tried hard to repress his fidgeting, with no success. He couldn't let the rest of his crew see. Too wound up already, they'd take it as a sign of weakness. After decades on the drift, waiting and patrolling dead space for the Garaxian fucks, his moment to shine was at hand.

Tooth and nail, he'd fought way too long and tough to secure his place as leader of the Apocs—his position for life. And being immortal made it all the sweeter.

But he knew he was fucked-up.

Abandoned by his mom, raped by his stepdad and beaten to within an inch of death by his older half-brother had merely set the stage. Misdiagnosed with mental instabilities in high school, he became addicted to those calming drugs and the kind of people who could supply them. That led to gang warfare on the inner streets of Baltimore, which seeded the movement he alone had spurred.

The Apocalyptic Sedition was his baby, his Antichrist. Everything that led up to its inception were all setbacks, but also battle scars, fuel for the prolific anarchy he'd wrought ever since, and would continue to throw back at society, as thanks for making him the man he festered into today.

Precisely why he had to watch his back so carefully. Others got tired of his rule, attempted to wrest control of the fleet from him. He made all of them take a stroll out the airlock.

Being a hammer, made everyone else a nail, but his crew's loyalty teetered like rusted pegs stuck in rotten wood—clinched poorly by fight or flight. The only code they lived by. He'd be a fool to think otherwise.

No, the payoff peeked out just around the corner and nobody would question his authority again. He might have been a minor player up until now, but he had bet on the winning side, the only side. No time to feel skittish, now that he got confirmation from the Overlords that they were on their way.

But he was.

For the hundredth time that day, Slynn moved his hand along the barrel of his shock-rifle, still trained on the switched-off robot. "You're what all the goddam fuss is about?" he snorted. "A dysfunctional gearbox." He punctuated his remark by jabbing the end of his gun inches from the trinket's yellow decal. No reaction.

Seemed a touch of painful irony that he'd spent most of his years on Earth trying to destroy this fucking machine, and now that it sat in plain sight, he couldn't so much as scratch it. The Demons wanted it back intact, and if he took any liberties, they'd end him. Slynn knew what the fucks were capable of. Maybe they wanted to rip the robot apart themselves—so, just as good.

The captain let out an effusive laugh but it quickly lost its force. He spun on the other men, savage eyes sweeping the faces that flanked him. "Where's our fucking relief? Should've been here by now."

"You can go, Boss," his second-in-command, Maste offered. "Janiz and the others'll show up any second." He gestured to the inert robot. "He hasn't budged since the protocols kicked in. With the additional restraining module we attached, the four of us can make sure he stays quiet."

Slynn fixed Maste with a corrosive glare. "It, you cur, the robot's an *it,* and I say five, five, *Five*! At all times, regardless! Understand?"

Maste glowered but his retort died on his lips and he only dipped his chin.

Slynn scrutinized him for a moment longer. Satisfied, he said in a slightly less volatile tone, "Good, you don't want to test those waters. Bark at me, I bark louder. Match me there, I bite to kill. Got a pit bull's jaws, and nobody fuh—ah! —*cocckkkk*—sucker!"

The sound of cascading explosions blasted through Slynn's IFB earpiece, cutting the Apoc's diatribe off. The intense squeal caused a circuit overload that blew the receptor.

Slynn tore off his headset, his free hand rushing instinctively to his wounded ear. He stood there blinking in stunned silence before realization took hold. His earpiece had been audio-proxied to the scout's barricade. "Those dumb—*asses*. Jesus, they must've tried their luck against the first perimeter. Never told them about the second one. Even if they did get past the first, they'd still be trapped." Shaking his head in disbelief, the captain went on with quiet vindication. "Stupid, stupid fucks, shoulda believed me."

"Collar or not, the second barrier guarantees an instant fry for anybody fool enough to cross it," Maste explained to the other guards. He faced his captain. "Good call keeping the robot separate."

Slynn gave him a perfunctory nod. "The Overlords will be right-pissed about Morrison and her ilk, but we did our due diligence. One of the Demons' own will take the rap for that blunder—serve their Exarch's fucking penance. With any luck, it'll be the same maggot that wasted half our crew, so a good goddam riddance."

Slynn donned a spare headset and stabbed its cable-pin into the closest base console. A discombobulated symphony of chatter and red alert klaxons sounded, some of which he didn't recognize. The Apoc's chest tightened. Maybe his initial appraisal hadn't been the correct one. One thing for sure, trouble was unfolding aboard his Demon flagship.

"Report!" he yelled into the mic. "Somebody!"

"Burdoni here, Cap. Panel's gone nuts. Multiple detonations between the first and second perimeter. Outer boundary's still intact. If there's any survivors, they'll be trapped inside the second defence line."

"Do we got eyes down there?"

"Negative. Surveillance cameras went offline with the first explosion," said Burdoni.

"Then fucking get some down there!" Slynn demanded. "Double-time it."

"Copy that."

"Wait! Burdoni, you go. Bring the whole team. Tell'em to stay on our side of number-two perimeter, even if you don't see the prisoners. If they're still alive make sure they can't cross it. I'm shuttling over."

"Will do. On my way."

When Burdoni clicked off, Slynn lingered a moment in nervous contemplation before locking gazes with Maste. "Get on the blower and keep an open channel to every ship in the fleet. Tell 'em to keep their keys open on *your* com-link. I want them to come in close and stay on high alert. All guns hot—the *real* guns the Demons gave us, ready to fire on the ID Scout. Nobody budges till I shuttle back over here and give the all-clear. Understood?"

"Understood," Maste said astride a fervent nod.

Slynn brusquely pointed at the other guards. "You three stay here with Maste. If the toaster so much as twitches, blast the fucker!" *Screw the Demons.*

With that, the Apoc leader raced out of the hold and into the shuttle bay proper. With every bound, Slynn felt his control of the situation ebb further and further away.

38: Boxing Pandora
Burdoni

For such a corpulent man, nearly as wide as he was tall, Burdoni could still sprint. He heaved his weight down the corridors of the alien ship as fast as his immense trunk would carry him—pausing only long enough to open a ship-wide channel and relay his captain's orders to the crew aboard the scout.

Although aghast that the captives went and offed themselves, tripping the explosives, he could also understand why. Burdoni knew only too well how mentally excruciating it was to live without hope. He almost envied them.

By the time the large Apoc arrived at the outer barrier, he was panting, chest heaving as he sucked air in great gulps. Burdoni stopped and scanned the fringe of the barrier, exactly as Slynn had instructed. Much to his relief, it looked unaffected, its telltale buzzing loud and steady. But he frowned at the cameras—still intact. If they didn't go boom with the prisoners' heads, might it be that their CCDs got fried by the flare?

Still winded from his exertion, Burdoni made an effort to report into the wire-com hovering over his ruddy cheek. "Second perimeter's g—green, Cap," he managed. "I'll hold point, till you get here."

"Good," Slynn's voice answered over the com. "What do you see?"

Burdoni lifted his wire and slowly shifted his eyes up and down, left and right. He couldn't believe he'd made it down here first. What happened to his shipmates? And where were the prisoners' bodies? The blast radius would've been minimal to be sure, but he should still see some sign of visible damage between the second perimeter and the virtual barrier twenty metres further in.

"Had to cross the first boundary to set them off…" his voice tapered to silence as his cognitive wheels switched a higher gear. Without bringing the mic back down, Burdoni said to the air,

"Should see a damn gore-fest of spaghetti bits right now."

Equally puzzled and cagy, the Apoc raked his fingers through his thick black moustache, the only hair on his shiny white head, still beaded with sweat. He arced a brow. "Unless, the devices malfunctioned inside the first perimeter or they figured out a way to—"

Thwack!

Something jarred Burdoni's head from behind. When the glass floor rushed up to meet him, he realized the sound came from his splitting skull. "dis—arm," he mumbled as his lights faded to black.

***

Fisher stepped over Burdoni's inert form and studied his piggish face. *Sorry, Big Guy*. He reached for the Apoc's com-link, switched off the microphone and deactivated the second perimeter. As it shushed to silence the captain stood to weigh options.

He chewed the inside of his cheek, eyes dropping to the heap at his feet. "Gonna need your help, every ounce of—"

A flash glinted across Fisher's peripheral. He ducked as a free-flying cudgel sailed over his head. Slanting sideways, he wind-milled on one foot.

Dropped.

And met the bulky carriage rushing towards him. Somewhere behind the captain, the iron hammer crashed against glass.

Swinging his other leg like a bat, Fisher kicked his assailant's feet from under him. The attacker stumbled and went down with a loud beastly grunt.

An Apoc without a gun—one can only be so lucky. Then Fisher took the giant's full measure and thought otherwise.

Fisher dove for Burdoni's gun, but his foe proved surprisingly quick. Still prostrate, his arm surged up and seized the captain's ankle mid-flight, forcing him to pancake hard against the glass floor. Fisher landed with a spine-jolting crunch, wincing against the searing pain that shot up and down his body.

The barrel-chested monster climbed to his feet and wrenched

Fisher back so savagely he felt his organs change places. With an ogre-sized hand forming a manacle around the captain's ankle, the giant dragged him backwards on his stomach—to where the misfired cudgel awaited. Ogre hefted the brutish weapon in his free hand.

"Don't use gun," Ogre cooed. "Girly weapon, that. Crush head with hammer. I like make blood!"

Great, simpleton and serial killer. Rather than resist, Fisher flipped onto his back, ignoring the stabs of pain the sudden move caused. He arched his back as high as it would go. *Give the free leg enough leverage.*

In a lightning move, Fisher scissored both legs, bearing all his weight down on the captive leg while the other rocketed straight up.

The move forced the giant to hunch forward. Fisher's boot hit the Apoc's chin with such force, his jaw snapped off. And hung by strands of sinew.

Ogre howled in pain, roaring over the sound of masticating bone. He lost purchase on Fisher's ankle and dropped the cudgel, hands flying to his ruined face.

Fisher cartwheeled back, fumbled for Burdoni's gun, aimed, and fired two quick shots into the man's chest. The spray of blood that erupted from the Apoc's back painted the wall behind him in a red abstract of viscera.

The captain had no time to admire his body count. The sound of running boots by the outer entrance sent him diving for cover behind Burdoni's thick body.

And not a moment too soon. Shock-rifle bullets whistled everywhere, many peppering Fisher's ample human shield. They caused the dead man to convulse like a dancing puppet.

Fisher's situation ratcheted to critical, but tempered to such odds from his trials in squatter camp hell, he snapped to. Without thinking, he slipped the barrel of the shock-rifle between Burdoni's arm and torso, set it to explosive and blasted his new foes to kingdom come. The floor shuddered once and fell still. The ringing in Fisher's ears silenced everything like a shroud of white noise.

After a moment, he stole a peek over Burdoni's riddled

corpse. Through the dissipating smoke cloud, rendered luminescent by the dormant plasma in the walls, he saw the blast's effect on the other Apocs. The bulkhead they chose for cover had boxed them in, intensifying the detonation's efficacy like a pressure cooker that just went bust. It instantly diced and vomited them from the kill box in every direction.

Alone again and by some miracle still alive, Fisher scampered to his feet and lowered his eyes to Burdoni's vacant stare. "Thanks, Big Guy." The captain scarcely heard his own voice through his ringing ears. He stole a glance at the other corpses, and let a wry smile cross his face. The outcome the fat man had counted on with Fisher's crew had been created by his own.

But Fisher's grin quickly faded when he sniffed the acrid air again. Through the sulphuric stench of the recent explosion, a definitive note of barbeque arose to overpower the other smells. He wheeled around. And immediately noticed something on the floor behind him.

In the exact centre of the room, a thin trail of blue light traced a linear path back and forth across the miasma of Apoc body parts, cauterizing them as it passed from one wall to the opposite. As his hearing returned, the captain made out the familiar buzzing of a reactivated barrier.

Fisher groaned. One of the buggers had had enough foresight to take out Burdoni's com-pad. That's what they'd been aiming for all along before reactivating the shield with their own. The captain got off his lucky shot in time, but it now effectively trapped him inside the barrier. Again.

Fisher surveyed Burdoni's mass a third time and let out a heavy sigh. "Bloody is as bloody does, but why is nothing *ever*—bloody—easy?"

With that, the captain crouched and strained to lift the big man.

39: Stars or Bars
Slynn

When Slynn entered the bay where the second perimeter had been, he grew livid. The barrier was down and Burdoni stood—within it! He leaned against a rail, back to the captain. At least the explosives or the fat man's gun had done the job. Cretin blood and guts plastered every glass wall and bit of floor.

Bunching his nose up at the pervasive stench of smoke and cooked flesh, Slynn paused to take it all in. Body parts filled the recess below the railing, where Burdoni still trained his shock-rifle.

But just because the big man had enough sense to cover the only way out, didn't quell Slynn's bile. Not one bit. "What part of my orders did you not understand, you tub-of-shit?" When Burdoni didn't answer him, Slynn saw red. "You fucking deaf as well?"

The Apoc ran up to the blood-drenched railing and clapped the big man hard on the back. When he did, two things happened: Burdoni pitched gracelessly forward over the railing to the recess one metre below, and Slynn heard the *zh-zh-zhireeeEEEEEEE* sound of the second perimeter getting reactivated behind him.

Eyes bulging, Slynn spun to find Captain Fisher, covered head to toe in blood, a maniacal grin snaking across his face. In one hand, Fisher waved a com-pad, still attached to a dismembered forearm. Safely outside the perimeter, the *Skow II*'s captain looked like a wily mouse that narrowly escaped the cat.

"Are we really gonna play this game, Fisher?" Slynn let out a derisive tsk. "My crew's on their way, I'm the one with the gun and it's packing a whole lotta hurt with your name on it." Slynn raised his control pad and punched in his shield-deactivation code.

Nothing happened.

Disbelieving, the Apoc tried it again.

Nothing.

Slynn raised his rifle and fired. When the projectile hit the perimeter grid it vaporized. His frustration blackened and he fired again. And again. His rage fulminated further with every impotent result. When he tried his headset, static answered him. Rabid orbs found Fisher. Only then did he notice the collar had vacated the captain's neck.

***

"Bit of a role reversal, wouldn't you say?" Fisher called from the other side of the barrier. "Make no mistake, Slynn, you're alone on this ID boat." His gaze swept the enclosure. "Except for what's left of this lot."

With the dismembered arm, Fisher gestured to Slynn's headset. "You won't be able to get any messages out to the rest of your tubs while you're in there. And you can't deactivate the bars of the holding cell. They've been retuned and encrypted. You did know that was possible since you set up these defences? Or maybe, your knowledge in these matters is woefully inadequate and you haven't an eff-n clue what you're dealing with."

Slynn's sneer bored holes into Fisher. The utter contempt etched on the Apoc's face fixed him with pure corrosion.

Fisher met it square and impassive. "The Demons like to keep it that way. It's one of the things they do best. But 'you-know-them.' And more than anything, Slynn, that's why I pity you."

Slynn didn't respond to the revelation, but his eyes burned hellish torrents like the fires of the Apocalypse. Silent in defiance, silent in defeat, the pirate would remain that way no matter what Fisher said—nothing left to say.

Beaten, the Apoc would go to his death in that same emotionless manner.

Fisher removed the com-pad from the forearm and let the bloody member fall to the floor. Without another word, he turned and walked away, leaving the vulpine captain to his doom.

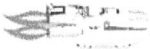

Fisher wound through the ID scout, treading carefully over several more Apoc corpses. They accounted for what remained of the brigands—the ones his team had taken out. Too bad they had to fight fire with fire.

He peered out a window. To his relief, the other Apoc ships held station, still on hostile alert, but for the moment they seemed oblivious to his crew's escape.

"Fisher?" Anne's voice came over the headset he'd lifted off one of the fallen renegades earlier. He had set to the special frequency Cholla had instructed the *Skow II*'s crew to assign them.

"I'm here," Fisher replied. "How'd we fare above?"

"Collars did their job. The console holding the *Skow II* is history. Cholla has the command protocols."

"Good. Rat's in his cage," said Fisher. "I'll meet you guys in the shuttle bay. There's something I want to take a quick look at first. Then I'm on my way."

"Hurry," Anne urged.

Stephen Fenech

40: Tit for Tat
Maste

The team of four guards Slynn left aboard the *Skow II* wagered on how many sorry asses the captain would find minus their heads.

"Judging by the multiple explosions," Maste pointed out, "I'd bet on the higher sum. If only the blasts were more spread apart, we could've done a proper headcount." His compeers sniggered at his pun but their enthusiasm seemed insipid and stretched.

Maste deflated his lungs and inspected his rifle. "Too much damn overlap though—like they rushed the perimeter together. Or might be that—"

Ah-weeeh-oooh-weeeh-oooh-weeeh-oooh-weeeh-oooh

The oscillating drone of a proximity alarm sounded, indicating an arriving shuttle. Maste and his squad immediately hushed to silence and sobriety.

"Positions—quick," Maste ordered. They all fell in.

Any crewman with a sense of self-preservation knew to let Slynn broach the subject first. If matters went bad, he'd take out his anger on whoever asked. For that same reason, they kept their eyes and guns trained on the robot.

Maste waited and listened for the chorus of sounds that heralded a docking shuttle. His anticipation mounted with the *cling-clank* of coupling gantries unlocking to retrieve the ship's landing carriage. The small vessel's impulse drive revved down followed by a series of pneumatic exhalations and turning gears. More clangs sounded as the grappling pads took hold of the craft and locked it down in its berth.

Thirty seconds later, solenoids clicked and servos fired when the shuttle bay access door swished open behind them. Maste held his breath. Footsteps—more than one set, but no voices.

Maste frowned. "Captain?" he asked over his shoulder. "Did you bring our—"

"Relief?" asked a voice *not* Slynn's. "Bet your sorry butts we did."

Three of the four Apocs wheeled, rifles ready, fingers on triggers. But before they could line up a shot, the escapees let out a barrage of shock-rifle bullets, perforating the robot's guards like

Swiss cheese.

Except Maste. He dove forward at the first sound of Fisher's voice, tucked and rolled behind the android. Crouched with his back pressed against the robot's angled torso, he roared, "Any closer, Fisher, I'll fry every last one of you and blast a new toilet hole in this mechanical motherfucker!"

"Whoever you are!" Fisher yelled back. "You're outnum—"

Maste hoisted his shock-rifle above his head and fired a heavy burst, spraying bullets indiscriminately behind him.

***

Fisher's crew jumped for cover. But Brumbal could not evade the torrent in time. Slow on his feet in the best of situations, the bulk of the Apoc's barrage caught him square in the chest. The big man's ribcage erupted in a maelstrom of red. He was dead before he hit the metal floor.

One of the bullets passed clean through Brumbal and caught Anne in the thigh. The impact drove her down in a forced pirouette.

Fisher dropped his rifle. Seizing Anne under her shoulders, he surfed her to relative safety behind the curved piece of scrap from Resa's former ship. She looked hurt bad but in no immediate danger.

"Forget it, man!" Fisher howled. "It's over!"

***

Heart trilling, Maste reloaded. "Only thing over is your fucking breakout!" he yelled across his shoulder. Remembering Slynn's orders, he turned his keys on to the rest of the waiting fleet. "This is Maste. Code Red—they've escaped. They're back on their—"

Shrrrippp!

Sudden shock stole Maste's voice from him. His head slumped forward. Swelling orbs fastened on the conical tip of an electrical arcing tool protruding through his solar plexus. He could only stare in abject dubiety as his sizzling blood blossomed around its metallic point.

Ro—bot? The unvoiced question echoed in fainter cycles as the Apoc's awareness slowly ebbed. And he knew no more.

41: Fire with Fire
Fisher

Even as he careered towards the bridge, Fisher braced for the shelling. On Slynn's orders, the Apoc fleet would be ready. When Maste alerted them, they'd break their cordon around the ID scout and encircle the *Skow II*. Although their weapons were obsolete, unlike the incapacitated ID bird, they could still do serious harm to his ship with her shields down.

All these thoughts raced through his mind as he threw himself into the captain's chair and raked the console, flipping switches with a sweep of his hand. Sure enough, once in attack formation, the Apocs targeted their guns. And fired.

Fisher blanched as he felt and gauged each hit the *Skow II* took. He'd expected as much with her inertia dampeners still offline. But not *that* much. The weapons the Apocs fired on his poor vessel were far from obsolete. Though riding shotgun with the dire revelation, the captain could *feel* the louts had no experience firing them. They misfired the weapons.

He sorely wanted to fire back, but even that would have to wait. Shields took precedence here above all else, including the engines—the pounding against the hull reminded him of that fact all too well.

As the constant strobe of blasts outside the window played havoc with Fisher's irises, he executed several command protocol shortcuts. Deft hands punched buttons with lightning alacrity. Fingers hammering the controls, he activated several simultaneously. No time for finesse with this hands-down, hands-on final exam. If he didn't pass this test, it would be final.

Fisher pressed the last switch. Its indicator light blinked yellow before changing to solid green, indicating high tally. Still seated, he launched his chair with his feet towards the tactical display monitor. The chair's castors sang as if sensing his urgency.

To Fisher's relief, the red progress bar indicating the *Skow II*'s shield strength raced to its finish line. The Apocs' bombardment dampened.

Satisfied with the old girl's cycled-up armour, Fisher juiced and respooled her engines. Then, her weapons.

Out of his peripheral, Baines limped in to join him, dragging a leaden leg behind him.

Fisher blinked. "You too?" *I already lost one.*
"Ricochet, struck me a glancing blow," said Baines, wincing as he did." But sure hurts something fierce."

"Can you fly us out of here or you want me to take the helm?"

"I can fly but I might need some 'help.'"

Fisher knew the kind of help Baines required: the synthetic variety. By no means a drug addict but his pilot did have a penchant for a certain recreational fuel called JPP, or *Just Press Play*. Baines would and could self-administer from time to time through his arm pad. Now was one of those times.

"Permission to self-administer," Baines asked as he plopped down before the helm.

"Okay, make the fat lady dance for me." Fisher turned away from the pilot to examine the engine FTL console. A sudden realization staggered him. "Baines, wait!"

"Too late!"

A chill swept through Fisher. "The Apocs hit our main engines before the shields came fully up. We got thrusters only, like them. They just levelled the playing field." Into the com, he shouted, "Jiri, wherever you are, engine room *stat*! Bring Beacon!"

To Fisher's horror, Baines transcended into his own world, a world free of pain but also fear and caution. The pilot bellowed his euphoria. The *Skow II* lurched forward.

And *rammed* the closest Apoc ship so hard under her bow that the shields gave in momentarily and everyone, except the berserk pilot, went flying off their feet.

But the stunt bashed the Apoc ship like a bowling pin, sending it pitchpoling, bow over stern, careening back to collide against two more of their vessels. Together all three ships slew into a fourth, providing a momentary window for a possible escape vector.

Fisher's attempt to swear went nuclear, but his behavioural inhibitors kicked into overdrive and the megaton F-bomb came out as slushy gibberish.

Until he calmed down enough to utter the remnant of the mushroom cloud, "Gh--ahhhhhh-dd—mm--outta here yes, but in, fuhlhsnnnn—*ooone* piece, youuuu crazy fhhhhhhhh-fungi!"

"Sorry, Cap-ooh," Baines murmured through his ether "My bad."

Fisher blazed at the pilot, worried at the ceiling, blazed at the pilot some more, and finally exhaled in heated exasperation. "Whoever created behavioural inhibitors—should die!"

The *Skow II* broke away from their captors' fleet but couldn't make any headway. The Apoc ships matched their speed easily with conventional thrusters. They had since stopped trying to use the Imperium's weapons and reverted to what weapons they did know how to fire. Using multiple field attacks, their vessels unleashed a hyphened web of laser flak and incendiary munitions across the *Skow II*'s bow in a panicked effort to slow her down.

The Demon imperative hung over the Apocs' heads like a pall and judging by the sheer fierceness of their attacks, they understood the stakes. With the odds no longer stacked in their favour, this demonstrated an act of desperation: their last chance to right something that had gone so terribly wrong.

And a good F—U to that!

Meanwhile, Baines laughed at the controls as he navigated each obstacle. "It's a prison break!" He bobbed his head from side to side like a happy toddler. "This is ridic—ulous, *miraculous,* but ree—*dic*—ulous. We're getting through, Cap-oh. We'll be okay."

"Yeah, I can see that," a white-knuckled Fisher replied tersely. "But are *you* okay?"

"*I feel funny—like honey. Flowin' like runny honey through the crannies and the cunny*," Baines sang quietly to himself. "*Ain't fixin' holes with money. Fillin'em on sunny honey, Bunny*." With that, the pilot threw his head back and let out a raucous laugh.

Fisher rolled his eyes to the ceiling before attacking the com once more. "Jiri, how you *doing* down there?" The Apoc ships were gaining on them, coming up alongside. "This *is* ridiculous." Fisher found himself forced to agree with his doped-up pilot.

"Cap?" Jiri's face filled the screen. She paused, throwing a glance over her shoulder to verify something. "Running a bypass, but we're going to need to divert power from the shields to continue spooling up the engines."

"Great!" Fisher griped as Baines danced contentedly in his seat. "How much of a dose did you take?"

"Small one, Fishy!"

"How small?"

"Itsy-bitsy topped with a little ditzy" Baines chuckled. But then his smile straightened. "Don't worry, Fish, I can handle it now. Pain's gone—so is the fear—that's the key. Just gotta figure out what's being thrown at us—flow round it, like Resa's Wooooo *weeeeeeeeee*!"

As if on cue, Resa appeared at Fisher's side. He too gawked at the insane flyer.

"Easy for you to say," Fisher tittered uneasily. "You're high!"

"Yeah, but I'm coming down. I feel the throb in my leg again. And it's making me, mad!"

"Mad is good," Fisher said in a hurried voice. Baines' anger indicated his private trip came close to its end. A thin smile crossed the captain's lips. "Now that you're mad, Baines, what can you do about the Apocs who angered you?"

"Get madder. It's a madhouse." Baines set his jaw and narrowed his rheumy eyes. "Weapons have come back online. Ahhhhhh-ll right! Payback bitches! Time to blast the fuckers!"

Fisher braced himself. His pilot had never sounded more vehement than he did just then.

"All bets are off, Fish. I'm flyin' back! Take that Demon twat out."

"No." Fisher planted his feet, his stance matching his adamant tone.

Baines' shoulders slumped. "After this knockabout, least part of it—communications array maybe?"

Fisher leaned forward and gripped Baines' shoulders. "Whatever you do, Flyboy, don't—touch it."

Baines tilted his head up and met Fisher's ironclad scrutiny. "But they'll use it to signal the ID."

"They wouldn't dare. Trust me, Baines, their only option now is to run—not that they'd get very far. Anything to interrupt the Imperium's protocol like destroying that scout outright or even severing its communication array would prove disastrous—for us. They'll have a constant link back to the Imperium. If we sever that connection, the Demons will know for sure we got away and might intercept us. Cripple these guys only. Let the Demons have the A-Punks."

"Okay," Baines relented. "Then it's high time I do what I do best."

With a certain relish, Baines ran his index finger down a jury-rigged key bus populated by unlit buttons. He brought them all on high tally as his digit brushed the entire bus. Red and yellow lights sparked to life, deepening the furrows of the pilot's tight concentration. The panel's radiance also cast an orange glow against Resa's uncertain face.

"Here come the fireworks," Baines announced.

The *Skow II* let out a strange barrage from her aft and side guns, which sent subtle incendiary submunitions, the size of lifter-bots, hurling towards the flanking and trailing ships—some close enough to dance if not kiss. The munitions intercepted the small fleet like a cloud of chafe and detonated. The effect was instantaneous. The effect was… nothing.

The ships continued their pursuit.

Fisher and Resa stared at the pilot.

"Wait for it," Baines instructed with slow deliberate calm.

None of the Apoc ships were destroyed, but just as the closest vessels came abreast of the *Skow II,* they dropped back again, as though trimming thrust. Or losing it.

A moment later, their deceleration began in earnest and a few seconds after that, they coasted far behind the *Skow II*. To a dumbstruck Fisher, it looked like they gave up pursuit. Until the Apoc ships started pitching and yawing, a couple colliding with one another—a fleet of dead sticks.

Baines danced in his element, well past the anger stage of his chemical voyage. "Your turn!" he exclaimed, a lopsided smile curving his mouth. "But you won't be going anywhere—ever." The pilot broke into a snicker.

Heart ablaze with vindication, Fisher joined Baines in his moment of victory. *For Brumbal, for Alliantha.*

"I've never seen anything like that," Resa admitted, his reserved voice policing his amazement.

"Me neither," Fisher agreed, wavering between wonder and alarm. "What was that weapon?"

"Special cocktail of my own," Baines said over his shoulder. "Static-cluster bombs married with antimatter infusers and keyed to heat signatures. I um, retrofitted a fleet of Cardy's lifter-bots to go kamikaze. My minions seek out a ship's engines, lodge themselves in the vessel's intake/outtake manifolds, corrode fuel lines, and fry any circuit pathways and servos—permanently. The precious bomb-bots then drag the target's momentum and force it to bleed all of its propellent." Baines grinned ear to ear. "No pow, just a quiet knockdown punch."

"And you planned to tell me about this, when?" Fisher asked in mock exasperation.

"Like I tell you everything I do." Baines' mischievous look became contagious.

"Stoner or not, he's my man," Fisher clapped his pilot on the back.

"Can it do the same to a modern ship, like the ID scout we left back there?" Resa asked.

Baines cast Resa a wink. "Good question. I could use some of that ID tech intact. Punks stranded out this far, it'd be an easy pop-back. Throw the rat out the airlock, and claim that bird as recompense for the *Skow*. Imagine, our own Imperium scout to zip around in." The pilot made an exaggerated steering gesture with an imaginary oversized wheel.

"You're kidding, right?" Fisher said. "That ship's tainted with ID protocol. In other words, it's a flying bomb. Sorry, Baines, that's one piece of chattel we're passing on. Your secret stoner weapons worked on these heaps, and that's good enough for me."

Baines shrugged. "It's the thought that counts."

Resa gave the pilot a half-smile. Fisher turned and looked out the window. "As things stand, the scout's only temporarily dysfunctional with Slynn trapped aboard. By the time the Apocs shuttle back over to that ship and get her working again, we'll be long gone. The Demons will get them when they arrive."

"They may not wait that long," Resa pointed out. "I suggest we do something unexpected and not simply run post haste. If the Imperium links in and there's no response, they'll know the Apocs lost the trophy and they'll be toast."

"The kind buttered with a whole lot of Demon plasma," Fisher said.

Resa nodded. "The problem is their lost prize and its current custodians are still too close to the toaster."

Fisher caught Resa's drift. "A command protocol to create a mass effect in that scout's engines would have a blast radius that could still kill the *Skow II* at this distance. You got a point, Resa," the captain agreed, going so far as to offer the Tolkane a pained smile.

Resa returned it, his node coiling up. "Anne's told us countless times, 'the Demons always have their finger on the button.'"

Stephen Fenech

42: Moles and Fishing Poles
Fisher

Once Baines relinquished the energy of the shields, Jiri transferred power to the main engines. The *Skow II* successfully executed a short skip of roughly 600 000 kilometres—far enough to take them out of the immediate vicinity of the Apocs' defunct flotilla and their soon-to-be arriving host.

Experience told Fisher that his crew would have enough time to get their bearing and think out their next move properly before any hostiles arrived. He sure knew Jiri could use the time to get all systems running according to their proper spec and design. Besides, they all needed the reprieve, especially after losing Brumbal.

The captain still questioned how they managed to pull it off. Anne had left him in the dark for most of the op, giving him just enough intel to keep him onboard as it were. But no more.

As soon as the *Skow II* had settled into a stealth drift, sensors primed and trained for any bad company, Fisher marched down to the infirmary to get some solid answers.

He found Anne sitting up on one of the beds with her injured leg extended down its length. Cholla bent over it, wrapping a poultice while Beacon hovered nearby. They all looked up as Fisher approached.

The captain must have looked as wound-up as he felt, for Cholla quickly announced, "Well, I'm done here. I think Jiri might need some help with the recalibration diagnostics. Captain." The doctor gave Fisher a curt chin bob as he hurried out.

Anne lifted her hands in surrender before Fisher could vent. "I know, I know, I owe you a full explanation," she said.

"It better be good," Fisher griped. "Brumbal bit it back there for this fu-rigin escapade of yours. I've never lost a crew member, Anne, never!"

Anne swallowed. "I know. I'm sorry, Fisher."

"How did you know about the fire?" he flashed.

"Partly through Cholla and Bliter, and Beacon helped a lot. Now, before you get that look, let me explain. As you've parsed, fire was the key. We needed a source of heat to match our own body temperatures. To remove the collars without setting them off, we had to trick the devices into thinking they still had us."

"Yeah," Fisher retorted. "But even so, they were locked. I recall trying mine several times and all it did was pi-*pee* me off. One minute there's nothing for it and the next, it's like removing a jewellery necklace. So?"

"We had to unfasten the *virtual* lock, which happened to be clinched to the other side of the first perimeter ...or was it the second? That part was Beacon's doing.

"Bliter stepped up after that with fire-coils to get us properly started. The stuffing from our sleeping mats provided the fuel. As Cholla had correctly guessed that the Apocs formed a skeleton crew. As such, they didn't monitor the cameras beyond the second perimeter as diligently as they should've."

"I know all this," Fisher complained. "But how did you piece that together? And it still doesn't explain how Beacon could've helped. He wasn't there and, oh yeah, the rats shut him down."

"I wasn't shut down," Beacon gently defended. "I only appeared that way, to mollify the Apocs."

Beside himself, Fisher derided, "Look. There are three types of people in the Universe: those who make things happen, those who watch things happen, and those sorry as—*anines* who come and ask what the f—ront just happened. Why are you shelving me into the third bracket? You're both playing me for a lackey or a puppet when you know I'm neither."

"Please, Captain," Anne soothed. "That's the last thing we want to do. And I swear to prove it to you. But first, what happened at your end?"

"What do you think happened? I did as you asked. After you split with the whole posse, I waited by the second perimeter in case any Apocs arrived. Have to admit that part was clever. When my first customer arrived and saw no bodies it never occurred to him that somebody might be lying low in the vicinity.

"After taking out the breathing planet, a psychotic ogre, and a handful of Slynn's trigger-happy grunts, I found myself trapped a second time. Had to improvise, set myself on morgue duty to make it look like all the Apoc body parts belonged to us."

Fisher bent down to rub his tight calves, then his ribcage, still tender after his piledrive to the floor. "I chucked half-fried arms and legs between the two perimeters." As he spoke, he mimicked the movements he described. "And then, just as I lobbed the last stinking part against the wall the second perimeter miraculously goes and deactivates itself."

Anne stifled a giggle at his animated gesticulations. Fisher let it pass, realizing how humorous the image must have looked to an onlooker.

"Propping up Mr Two Tonnes almost crippled me! But he played his part well. Our friend, Slynn bought it, racing straight into the trap. One serpent head lopped—at least that part of the plan worked out."

Anne's lips quivered and she held in her sides in a blatant effort to remain serious as Fisher went on.

"Figured Beacon had eyes on me with the cameras when the perimeter deactivated the second time around. So, it seemed a safe bet he could change and encrypt the command protocols governing it. Confirmed as much when I picked up a com-pad from one of the dead Apocs."

"How did you authenticate it?" Anne asked, her frown indicating the robot left her out of that particular loop.

Fisher shrugged. "Well, the display panel showed a perimeter-activation prompt, and beneath it, flashing letters read:

TRUST YOUR ROBOT

Despite Fisher's ire, Anne smiled.

"That at least saved me another fight, which I was definitely not prepared to take on." Fisher turned to Beacon. "By the way, how did you know exactly when and how to do everything else aboard the ship when you weren't even on it?"

"I linked in," Beacon said in a matter-of-fact tone. "As far as the Apocs believed, if the lights ain't on, nobody's home."

Fisher let out a hardy laugh at the robot's use of slang. It helped quell the captain's anger. "Okay, you did that spider thing you do," he began, still not convinced. "But how did you know how the Apocs would react, and where, and when? It's like you had a blueprint not just of the scout, but their behavioural tendencies, and time itself for that matter."

"I lifted it all from the command protocols of the Imperium's data stream moving between the two ships ever since they hijacked us. And while they guarded me, I gleaned from the sound waves of their voices, the causal inflections and syntax. The Apocs were completely oblivious to the fact that I heard everything they said. They said quite a lot.

"As for control, I mimicked the ID protocol, which superseded that of the Apocs, to get you back to the *Skow II*. Otherwise, even with full control of our captors' limited tech, the ID protocols would have sealed off your escape. The second perimeter presented one of those proprieties. That's why our foes had no fear of your escape."

"Why didn't you just off those punks when they first captured us? Heck, you could have done it with that handy-dandy arsenal, ever ready to bust out of that metallic trunk of yours. You made short work of that camera after your grandstand with the packet as I recall. And I can't forget your little welding job with Humpty Dumpty down in the cargo hold."

"The risk was too great. The Apocs might have alerted the Imperium. For that matter, I could have made your ship go cold, but that might have harmed you and jeopardized the success of your escape."

"Yeah," said Fisher in a sour tone. "Tell that to Brumbal."

"As I told you," Anne reminded him, "It wasn't all Beacon. I communicated with him, explaining any logistical conflicts with the plan's execution. He told me how best to proceed. And that, the Imperium would arrive soon. We had to act, or our efforts would've proven for naught."

Fisher narrowed his eyes. He'd been waiting for this. "Nice, but how did you communicate with him in the first place?"

"Projection," Anne replied without hesitation. "It's something I apparently picked up when Beacon used your DNA to reanimate me."

"You mean like Resa with his antenna?"

"Yes," Beacon confirmed.

Fisher blinked. "I think you're mistaken." With one hand, he pushed back his hair, still matted with Apoc blood, from his forehead. "See any nodes? Resa's the one you're talking about."

"You have it too, Captain Fisher," Beacon said. "Remember, I used a blueprint of your genetic matrix, not Resa's, to make the chrysalis housing Anne's mind."

Fisher searched their faces for bull-crap but they remained squeaky clean. Butterflies fluttered in his stomach.

"What do you know of your childhood?" Anne asked, cutting through the awkward silence.

"You asked me that already," Fisher said, not trying to hide his bitterness about the topic.

"Yeah, but before that?"

"Not much. Nothing."

"Understood," Beacon acknowledged. "Nevertheless, you do remember that I resurrected Anne from your DNA. Captain Fisher, you were born with the Tolkane trait of projection, from a pure Tolkane parent, though granted, you've never learned to use it."

Fisher tucked in his upper lip but did not challenge the automaton as he went on. "I saw the benefit of passing on that trait, along with your dominant genes to Anne. Thought it might come in handy. The worst thing that would've happened was that she'd never learn to utilize the gift—but I knew better."

Anne smiled at that.

"You got me there," Fisher admitted before something else occurred to him. "How is it that *you* can project, Mr Machine?"

"My initial manufacture took place a very long time ago and

my entire existence has been a work in progress. I've seen countless races and have had eons to study how sentient beings function. Remember, Captain, whether you look at my parts or the components of your own flesh and blood, underlining all matter is energy—our common denominator. I learned projection by attenuating my sensors and emitters to the right frequency."

Fisher exhaled slowly and threaded his fingers together. His knuckles cracked dully. "So, that's the *how*. What about the *what*?"

"I instructed Anne to follow Bliter's plan concerning the fire," Beacon said. His hemispherical seeing-dome panned to her.

Anne tilted her temple towards the robot as she took his cue. "Once we had the collars off, it wouldn't be long until the temperature drop would make them detonate," she explained. "As Cholla surmised they would go off by proximity to the first perimeter, but that they took their reading from each other. The trick was to keep them warm, and together, before transporting them en masse past the actual perimeter defence.

"The ID configured the devices to accommodate one, perhaps two people trying to escape the corridor, not everyone at once. Having them stacked together kept their detonators from going off when we breached the first perimeter. Rather than use the collars to knock out the laser wall of the second perimeter, we had Beacon do that for us. He deactivated it for a few seconds and ran an ID maintenance subroutine so it wouldn't trigger any alarms."

"You know the rest," Anne said. "More important than any of the obstacles we faced was the console that had a stranglehold on the *Skow II*'s systems. We had to move against that first and take out that linchpin—the one vice linked to our ship that couldn't be subverted. It had to be physically destroyed."

"I thought all Demon tech was linked," Fisher said.

"Almost all," Anne corrected. "That device presented something new. Once activated and targeted it could not be corrupted. Literally its own boss, the instrument worked independently of the Apocs and the ID scout. Not even the Imperium protocols could talk to it. Beacon tried as well, and

306

failed. It's proof-positive the Demons themselves have upped their game."

Anne paused and threw an expectant glance at Beacon, but the robot didn't have anything to add.

Her eyes found Fisher again. "Still, it wasn't infallible. Beacon figured it out, which was good because if that box remained up and running, any other part of our plan would've been trumped. To that end, we needed as many as we could spare to deal with all the Apocs between us and it."

"Yeah, I saw the mess you guys left," Fisher said.

"That's why everyone fanned out and left you alone, to fend for yourself, as only you can."

"Story of my life," Fisher allowed, pinching the bridge of his nose.

"I had every confidence in you, Fisher," Anne offered.

The captain bowed his head slightly. He felt like a fish thrown back into the sea. "Okay, that makes sense now. Thank you, but from now on keep me in the loop. Or, have I caused you to mistrust what I say? Or what I'm doing?"

Anne pressed her lips together and exchanged another eager look with Beacon's painted-on smiley face. Fisher found it ridiculous since the robot had no face—until it dawned that it was that projection crap they just finished talking about.

After a moment, she nodded and turned back to Fisher. "No, not you. But someone."

"Someone? Aboard my ship?"

"Yes."

Fisher's blood ran cold.

"That's why so much of the information we shared with you has been filtered or overtly deflected," Anne said. "This wildcard has plagued us since, well, I cannot say for certain. It's nothing that you said or did, but we couldn't afford to divulge some of the key information in another's presence."

"Who is it?" Fisher demanded.

"I can't tell you."

The captain's tone sharpened. "Can't, or won't?"

"Trust me, Fisher, I wish that I could, but even Beacon is not certain. Even if we did know for sure it might jeopardize the outcome."

"Outcome? How can it affect the future, other than ridding us of a menace?"

"Time will show us," Anne said. "But if we force the wildcard's hand ahead of the Juncture, our disaster curve would only spike. We must be patient. Trust me and trust—"

"Yeah, I know, trust my darn robot." Fisher suppressed his indignation as the inhibitor suppressed his profanity. "Problem is, he ain't my robot."

"Thank you," Beacon said.

"For what?"

"For acknowledging that I am more than the sum of my parts, that no one owns me, and that I am sentient."

"Well of course you're sentient." Fisher tsked. "Any idiot can see that, even if you look like a pair of beetles, joined at the head. Your makers definitely had a sense of humour. Anyway, Beacon, you're welcome."

"It's as Captain Fisher says, Beacon," Anne put in. "No one owns you. But I think the Imperium would be quick to disagree."

"They're not the only ones," the robot added.

Fisher took a deep breath and rubbed the back of his neck. "So, what do we do about this new development?"

"Do?" Beacon asked, his seeing-dome tracking Fisher's face. "We can do nothing. We must carry on and wait for the other pieces to move across the board."

"We've taken a leap of faith with you just now," Anne said. "Divulging even this much information carries a risk."

"Great." Fisher slumped into an available chair. "I'm honoured." Languid eyes drifted to Anne's bandage. "How's the leg?"

"Oh, fine," she laughed. "Cholla did a good job staunching the wound. It's my head that's developing a will of its own."

"What do you mean?"

"To be honest, I noticed it the first time Beacon revived me. Thought it some kind of incongruity between my digital cerebrum and the chrysalis Beacon grew from your harvested DNA. Nothing painful mind you, but it is—rather odd."

Fisher sat up in his chair. "Explain."

"Well, in the corner of my field of vision, I see a double image."

"Like your vision defocusing?" the captain asked.

"No, but that's a good guess. It's like having a split signal from two sources on the Box, or an extra security visor feed but in an organic frame. I'm seeing two programs at once like a picture in picture."

"Okay?" Fisher prompted.

Anne chewed her lip. "Anyway, seems I got something similar imprinted in the lower left of my field of vision, seated in my peripheral mostly, with just a hint visible when I look forward." Anne panned her eyes to the left. "But like this, I can view it as definitely as I see and speak to you."

"That's bizarre—are you high?" Fisher thought of Baines.

"I wish."

"Could it be a memory scar or the result of a concussion?"

"No, I don't think so. It feels real but there's no other stigma attached."

"Okay, what do you see?" Fisher asked.

"It's hazy, like a cross-focused light through a shroud. It's blurred, but not moving in any case. That's my closest assessment of what *it* is. I'm finding it a little disconcerting, but other than that there's no other stimuli." Anne turned to Beacon. "Can you explain it?"

Beacon shrugged off the matter. "A mental relapse, possibly an echo of your former consciousness before you fully integrated into the chrysalis. It will pass in time, Anne, I promise."

"I know, I know," Anne laughed. "Trust my robot."

"While you're at it, trust your captain too," Fisher added as he alighted from the chair. "At least once he's had a proper shower. Look at all this Apoc blood. My god, I must look like a walking corpse."

Anne bunched up her nose. "And you stink like one too," she chortled.

Fisher agreed, joining in her mirth. He made claws of his hands and struck convincing zombie poses, shifting his jaw to one side and letting his mouth gape wide. He must have looked completely ridiculous as he changed poses and prodded Anne because she laughed all the harder. He carried on for her amusement.

But when the moment passed, he gave her a hard look. "All kidding aside, Anne, I know there's more. It's high time you both fill me in on the details—free of sieves. And frankly, I want to know everything."

Anne stopped laughing.

43: Catalyst
Fisher

The translucent body bag containing the ashen corpse of Brumbal slid gracefully out of the airlock chute. As he watched it go in stoic silence, Fisher ran a finger down the length of his scar. So strange seeing his crewman in such a placid state, remembering how animated and at times overbearing Brumbal had been in life. But for any annoyances, he could be counted on: a steadfast crew member who always meant well.

Fisher shivered then, recalling his joke about pushing Brumbal out the airlock after the big guy's drunken folly with Cardinal Wisdan. It led to the thawing of that vexing holier-than-thou Resa. Something Fisher had rued ever since.

As the bag crystallized outside the ship, floating carefree, away into interstellar space, Fisher said more to himself than any in attendance, "Farewell Brumbal. Hope your next life proves better than this one ever did."

The sound of sobbing behind him made the captain turn. He walked over to a teary-eyed Jiri and placed his hands gently around her shoulders. She sucked back her grief through her nasal passages once, twice, before meeting his reassuring gaze.

"Strength, girl," Fisher soothed, "for Brumbal."

"He was the strong one," Jiri sniffed. "And the brave one. He took out the first couple of Apocs with his bare hands so we could get their guns."

Fisher swallowed but kept his voice firm. "We all did our part—and that includes you. Wherever Brumbal's gone, he knows this too, probably raising a glass of wine to you as we speak."

Her eyes glistened as she managed a thin smile. "Aye-aye, Cap." Pain filtered her grasp at strength. "All systems are in the green. We're good to go, whenever you give the order."

He gently lifted her chin with one hand and gave her a warm smile. "I *order* you to take a break. It's okay. Bliter can cover you."

"Thanks, Cap, but no. Better busy than miserable. The more I

311

can focus the less I'll dwell."

Fisher searched her face a little longer before acquiescing. "Okay, but if you change your mind, I won't dock your pay."

Jiri let out a wan laugh. "Like you pay me anyway." She gave him a fierce hug.

"That's my girl," he said, laughing. "That's my girl."

Jiri disengaged herself from Fisher's embrace and left the room. After a moment, Anne turned to the captain. "So, where do we run to now?"

"That's a good question. Might as well start with the charts we scooped up off the Apocs," Fisher said.

"Are you serious?" Bliter baulked in disbelief. "Those charts will be complete and utter shite. They're forged. They have to be."

"No, I don't think so," Fisher maintained. "They can't manufacture charts like these, Bliter. Their ship's computer hard-burned them directly. It's read-only after that. Jiri played it smart. When she saw their engine problem had been a ruse, rather than cry wolf, she dug into what we needed, and even what we didn't, and *then* bailed. She had access to the schematics of all the other Apoc ships, and that's how Baines knew exactly how to program the lifter-bots." Fisher glanced in his pilot's direction. "Sorry Baines."

"Sure Fish, steal my thunder," Baines chuckled. He arched a brow and raised a finger. "You know I did try to tell you my bomb-bot secret just before they boarded us." He paused and bit his lip as he pondered. "Then again, with the fast lockdown, it would've only pissed off the Apocs even more." Baines yawned and stretched his arms above his head. "You're right though. Jiri's one clever birdy."

"The problem is not that the charts are false or falsified," Beacon supplied as he floated into the airlock vestibule. "But in the fact that the Imperium will anticipate such a move."

Baines lifted his shoulders and exhaled. "So, we'll keep jumping the whole time." His pupils flitted to Fisher. "Even they can't patrol every possible jump point, especially if we vary our trajectory and change each span at random."

"Yes," Beacon conceded. "But there is something more."

Fisher quivered at the robot's deliberate tone. "More? I thought you downloaded the entire contents of the packet."

"You are correct. I possess the packet's contents. And have unravelled the full schematic for the weapon as laid out by Baron Fieldbank—also currently stored in my banks. I have deciphered and assembled a means of deploying it as well."

"But?"

"But I still need the catalyst to trigger it," Beacon replied.

"Catalyst? *What* catalyst?" Fisher felt the blood drain from his face.

"More importantly, where exactly do we find it?" Resa asked in a voice that indicated he'd already guessed the answer.

Beacon's seeing-dome took in Resa before dialling back to Fisher. "The crystalline planet where we found the packet was no coincidence. Baron Fieldbank chose that location for a very specific calculated reason."

Everyone stopped breathing.

"The substance we need as a catalyst, to trigger the contents of the packet, lies back there *on* the surface of that planetoid. And that is where we must return."

Stephen Fenech

44: Affluence
Fisher

Before long, the foreboding red giant's intense penumbra imbued the *Skow II* with auburn starlight, basking the ship's hull in a fiery cast that penetrated every window.

Fisher didn't like its garish colour. Although limited to the windows and the projected square of light on the floor beneath each pane, it still gave the corridors of his ship the dark pallor of some sinister church. Polarizing the glass of the windows subdued the glare, but made the light appear a deeper crimson, like blood.

The air seemed to move about the bridge like a liquid: profuse with anticipation, with apprehension, and with aversion. Captain and crew knew they tinkered with a well-established geas but none more than Fisher.

Instead of bringing them closer, the first few jumps the vessel made took her further away from the crystalline planet. Fisher argued that such a strategy minimalized any chance of pursuit. It was still untried space for them but as he suspected, the Apocs' charts proved on the level.

The *Skow II* doubled back to the sector along an arbitrary string of skips that left it on the far side of the giant star, opposite the crystalline planet. Then, cloaked by the same flaring swathe that kept the planetoid hidden, the ship followed an ellipse safely outside the world's orbital path around the sun.

When the *Skow II* intercepted the enigmatic tyke, Baines announced, "Here and clear. Sensors confirm we're all by our lonesome."

Fisher nodded as the sphere shimmered back into view. "Jumping back into hell is probably our safest course of action considering how we left those Apoc dregs. The Demons must know by now what went down. They'll have learned that we got the Apoc charts. So, with any luck, they'll think we're using them to make a run for it."

"Probably track us along our last trajectory," Baines

postulated. "My guess would be somewhere along the convergence between familiar space and this unknown expanse."

"You're forgetting something," Fisher pointed out. "It's not unknown to them. We are talking about the Imperium after all. They might anticipate even this insane U-turn."

"Still, wouldn't they assume we're making a run for the known quadrants?" Baines' question sounded more like a plea for validation. It hung in the air unanswered.

Resa cleared his throat. "A lot of assumptions there too, Baines. That seems to be the captain's modus operandi."

Fisher bristled at the unexpected barrage. "What the flux do you mean now, Resa?"

Baines pinched the bridge of his nose and exhaled. "Here we go again."

But then, much to everyone's surprise, Resa spun on his heels and strode off the bridge without another word, leaving Fisher fuming at his back. Still exasperated, the captain wheeled on Beacon. "Tell me you'll have everything you need to complete this weapon soon—before I kill somebody?"

"That's the plan," the robot said.

Fisher flopped down in his captain's chair. "I just hope it's all worth it, Beacon."

The robot's dome tracked in. "It will be worth it, Captain. It will."

Fisher sighed. "Well, clock's ticking. Let's get what we came here for and get gone."

Following a replayed telemetry, the *Skow II* reestablished an identical geostationary position above the inscrutable C-class planetoid, exactly as it had done the first time around.

Despite all the setbacks, the debauched plans, and the trying struggles with that pious-to-a-painful-point Resa, Fisher felt some partial relief. For the first time since being forced to team up, his cadre worked completely and unequivocally in concert.

"So, now that we're here, how do we get the stuff without getting crushed by the gravity of that mighty morph down there?" Fisher threw the question out for anyone's target practice.

"Leave that to me," Beacon said. "With my ability to diminish or amplify the dynamo of my core, I can create reverse supermass like anti-grav pads, though on a planetary scale. The field will negate the planetoid's enormous gravity. But alas, I must go extravehicular to do so."

"Why is that?" Fisher asked.

"The planetoid will exert substantially less pull on my physical structure. So, I can get much closer than the *Skow II*, enduring the small world's tidal forces that would doom your ship because of its Roche limit. Sadly, I cannot remain aboard to do this. The mass effect would cause a hull breach as your ship is literally sucked down to the world's surface around me."

"I'll take your word on that one," Fisher said.

Beacon's upper hemisphere panned a one-eighty, giving the captain the back of his head. "I took the liberty of retrofitting three of your low-yield nuclear torpedoes and programmed a firing sequence that will produce the required effect."

The robot's head returned to Fisher. "The three nukes will be fired in succession towards the planet's surface. They will detonate one on top of the other as they reach terminal velocity, a moment before impact. Staggered eleven seconds apart, the ordnance should be enough to excavate a sufficient amount of the substance, before the bombs themselves can be crushed or their reactions fused."

Cholla nodded. "Like mini-suns."

"Correct," Beacon said. "The synergized blasts will fling fragments of the crystalline substratum into space, where I'll be waiting with my net to capture as much of them as I can—before the particles get sucked directly into the red giant. I will then tow my catch back to the ship."

"But what about the EMP from the blast?" Cholla asked, a

frown drawing his mouth down and his eyebrows up. "Wouldn't it fry your circuits if you get that close?"

"Tell him, Anne," Beacon said.

"It won't, Doctor," she confirmed. "I witnessed something similar back on Earth when Beacon and I first um… met. Beacon's impervious to anything of that nature."

"Exactly how much of the catalyst do you need, Beacon?" Resa asked.

"As much as possible," the robot said.

Fisher ran a hand through his dishevelled hair. "And how much is that, exactly?"

"At this point, I cannot give an exact quota for certain. I am attaching a peripheral micro-lab with me to sample the grade of the particles when I am out there. Only then will I know how much is required to have the proper efficacy."

"We should get started," Anne said.

"Trust your robot, Captain," Beacon pressed. "My systems and carriage were designed for jobs like this. I will not fail."

Once Beacon left the *Skow II*, Fisher noticed a familiar listlessness settle over his crew. He couldn't blame them after being imprisoned aboard the Apoc ship only to get put back into a similar dynamic so soon.

Fisher lost sight of Beacon within moments of the robot's departure, but Baines managed to track his every move on the scanner—for a while anyway. All the static chatter made communication impossible, so Fisher had to time the procedure as accurately as possible before giving the signal to fire the mini-nukes. The macro had been pre-built into the weapons array, so Bliter only had to hit a single button.

Seemed simple enough, provided the armaments didn't malfunction or take out Beacon on his descent towards the surface. The robot refused Jiri's offer to equip him with a tether, stating that it would only hamper his manoeuvring capabilities.

So, Beacon was truly alone out there but that's how the robot rolled most of the time, for eons actually, lots of waiting in a cryo-like state, similar to Resa's hibernation.

An involuntary jitter saddled Fisher's thoughts when they strayed to the Tolkane. Not for the first time, Fisher recalled the secretive meeting the virtuous revenant had had with Wisdan. Why not hang a sign? Fisher knew Resa still prevaricated about somethings, but thinking about the Tolkane's motives felt like picking at a scab. Although it irritated and worried him, if he pried too deep, too soon, it would bleed all over again.

Thanks to Beacon, Fisher incurred another scab to pick at. When he asked the robot why he didn't fire on the Apocs from the first moment, Mr Gearbox dodged the question. What the f-athom was he waiting for?

Unless... no, Fisher couldn't accept the implications of that possibility—a notion too terrifying to court and contemplate.

Anne caused another scrape. When Fisher asked her for the unfiltered truth, she merely offered some mumbo jumbo about causality and tangents, putting an elusive creampuff on the situation with her words. And words, the captain reiterated to himself, sucked at the brain like vacuum.

His head felt suddenly heavy. Although he wasn't moving, physically, the cast of faces in his mind gave him the impression that matters were spiralling out of control, that he'd been put in a dead heat, racing headlong towards his own death.

But, Fisher resolved, once Beacon returned with the catalyst, they'd finally have their master card over the Imperium. No more vacuum to haunt him. He'd either get an answer that satisfied his intuition... or he'd jump ship and let the Garaxian toilet flush him down. Until then, he had to endure the longest wait since this whole fiasco began, if not, his entire squalid life.

"Time's up, Bliter," Fisher commanded. "Punch it."

The weapons array lit up like a Christmas tree as the *Skow II* carried out its firing sequence. The first of the three torpedoes launched. From his view out the bridge window, Fisher never saw the torpedo itself. Only its tail fire, as a laser-thin arc of yellow light connected ship to world. It raced fast enough under its own thrust, but with the pull of the planet's enormous gravity, even the computers' scanners had a hard time tracking its flight.

Eleven seconds later, just as the thin wire of light faded, the next torpedo relit the ghosting line anew. And eleven seconds after that, the third. The whole process took a mere twenty-two seconds, but it seemed much longer than that. The trio of nuclear torpedoes had streaked away from the ship, screaming on identical trajectories to the planet's surface.

Everyone held their collective breath as they watched, and waited.

As far as Fisher could tell nothing happened. "How much of a lag before the—"

"Something faint," Baines quietly reported, eyes locked on the monitor. "Just a brief murmur of a reaction. Hmmm. Okay, yeah scanner's definitely picking it up now—a plume."

"Particles? Enough to escape? Did they break atmo?" All this rifled out from Bliter, leaning forward like a quivering tree about to fall.

Baines looked up from his monitor and shot the navigator a brusque look. "That would be three, *I don't know*'s, Bliter."

Cholla coughed. "I imagine the particles won't have a problem with any of that," he offered, his calm visage matching the diplomacy of his voice. "If the dwarf planet does have an atmosphere, it would be either squeezed in so close to the surface—mere metres—or so thin that it wouldn't be a hindrance either way. The plume shows something has pushed away from the surface. As to gravity, remember the red giant. Even from this distance, that sun emanates the more formidable of the two gravitational influences. If the particles succeed in attaining a certain escape velocity, the star's mass will nullify the planetoid's draw on the absconding particles."

"Like a tug of war," Fisher said.

Cholla tilted his head forward. "Precisely."

"And Beacon's caught in the middle of it," Anne reminded them, a timorous spectre brooding her drawn expression.

"Trust your robot," said Fisher, trying to sound optimistic. "I'm sure Beacon has everything under control—provided he dodged our three bullets."

Resa folded his arms. "Really Captain? At a time like this, can't you see Anne's concern? Don't vilify the situation by being such an asshole."

Fisher gritted his teeth. "Shut up, Resa before I take that whiskered head nipple of yours and shove it up your butt. It's obvious that's where you're projecting from."

Despite Fisher's hostility behind the image, Anne laughed at the slight. "Both of you, quiet. Beacon programmed those launches himself, within a nanosecond's accuracy. He'll be fine."

"We'll know soon enough," Fisher said. "Given the time when he left to the time we fired the nukes, plus whatever he needs to grab the particles, I'd say he'll be down there a while yet, unless something happens untoward. Baines doesn't have a fix on Robo yet, but he'll be able to track him soon enough."

"Roland—?" Baines called. The nervous note in the pilot's voice was unmistakable.

Fisher went numb. *He never calls me by my first name.* "What?" he gulped.

The pilot craned his neck slowly to face his captain. "Something's happening, un—toward."

Fisher leapt to his feet. "Where? Beacon?"

"No," Baines answered gravely. "Not Beacon... everywhere."

"What the f-heck. Explain!"

"I've got something on the scope—multiple bogeys. It's the Demons, I think," Baines said.

"But of course," Fisher said bitterly. He rolled his neck. "Will we have enough breadth?"

"We can't go in and retrieve Beacon," Cholla pointed out. "Even at this distance, the ship can barely hold her own. If we move any closer to that planet, it will suck us down or disintegrate us." The doctor inhaled. "I'm afraid we have to wait for him to come back to us."

"Perfect," Fisher spat. He swept his gaze around the command deck. Fresh lines of worry creased his crew's faces, no doubt mirroring his own. "Spool up the FTL, Baines. If we don't move now, we'll be hemmed in. Standby to punch in an escape vector on my command. How far are they?"

"That's the thing," Baines said plaintively. "I can't get a proper reading on radar or lidar. The signals are coming from all points at once. They're garbled, and going viral. Like I said, everywhere."

"That's—impossible," Fisher snapped. "The frickin' thing's busted. Jiri!"

"Cap?"

"Rig a portable and take it off widespread zoom. Narrow the beam and plot 50 K focal targets. While we're at it, best do things the old-fashioned way and keep our eyes out the window."

"That—won't be necessary," Anne announced in a voice that stopped Fisher in his tracks.

He frowned. "Which? The portable, or the window?"

"Both," she said, pointing a meek finger towards the porthole beside her.

Fisher limped to the window, noting with mounting alarm the ambient flashes of white light strobing through the glass to land across Anne's stricken features.

Peering out the glass, Fisher's breath caught in his throat as it plunged into his stomach.

"Fuck—me," he said.

45: Exarch
Fisher

As the same white flares ignited through every window, turning the bridge into a dazzling but morbid discotheque, Fisher realized something with a wry sense of irony: Baines' scanner hadn't malfunctioned after all.

Presently, the lambent blinking stopped. All eyes widened, staring fixedly in supplication from out of every available window. They all took in the dauntingly vast and growing armada, which crowded every conceivable bit of space. The closest wave of ID interceptors, slopes, and cutters parked tight enough to form a net around the *Skow II*, but beyond those heavy cruisers, destroyers, and dreadnoughts blocked the rest of open space itself.

As if that wasn't enough to wreak havoc with Fisher's nerves, Baines confirmed that within sensor range of his scopes, more than a hundred capital ships, *capital ships,* each larger than a standard dwarf planet, all held station, forming a perfect spherical halo around Fisher's insignificant blip of a spacecraft. The Demons, whose omnigalactic reputation for overkill was paralleled only by the cold calculative way in which they executed such measures, had finally surpassed themselves. This amassment wasn't just overkill, it was over-overkill.

The *Skow II* floated like a yolk effectively encased inside the shell of a giant mechanical egg, about to be yoked. Hemmed in, his worst fear realized, Fisher... laughed. Small wonder Wisdan's behavioural inhibitor finally, thankfully failed. The captain knew they'd been cutting it close for a while now and expected they'd bump heads with the Imperium eventually. But nothing could have prepared him for the scale of this tactical response.

Despite their audacity and his warped sense of flattery at being smack dab in the middle of the Garaxian Central Armada, Fisher skipped terror and accepted his fate in all this. A strange calm washed over him—his precursor to insanity? Yet, even facing these odds, he still retained the ability to navigate priorities, think things through, and take charge.

323

"Do we have eyes on Beacon yet?" Fisher said to the air.

No answer. Everyone just stared, so entranced by the overwhelming vista that his voice was lost on them. To the captain, their silence felt like a body bag.

Unacceptable. He needed them to buckle down to task. Free of restraint, he demanded, "What's the goddam status? Where's our fucking robot?" Everybody jumped. *Ah, now that's more like it.* Giving the Demons a silent note of thanks, Fisher stretched his vulgar legs until they found some traction.

Baines spun in his chair, ready to snap himself. "Look out the window, Fish. Beacon's fifty metres off our port bow."

He must have appeared as bewildered as he felt for Baines pointed. "Out there."

Fisher's relief at the sight of the robot's familiar beetle shape quickly floundered. The automaton no longer had his net, which could only mean...

"Beacon didn't get what he went down there for. He didn't retrieve the particles." Fisher spoke in a matter-of-fact tone, but when he turned back to the desensitized crew no one even registered that he said anything at all. Except Bliter, who paled and clutched his gut, looking as though he might throw up. The captain took a deep breath and repeated, "He doesn't have the catalyst. We're screwed."

Gazing back outside the window, Fisher noticed something even more troubling than Beacon's failure. The robot made no move to converge with the *Skow II*. He hadn't budged an inch in any direction since Baines pointed him out. Just floated there, happy to remain stationary between them and the Imperium like the last remaining chess piece placed in the centre of a stellar board. If Fisher didn't know any better, seemed the robot was grandstanding both parties.

Beacon didn't move. The *Skow II* definitely didn't move. And the Demons hadn't let out so much as a shiver. The entire armada sat still, parked but more than ready and capable of snuffing out Fisher's tiny heap in an instant.

But they didn't.

"What the hell could they be waiting for?" Fisher murmured.

It was a game of chess all right between his crew and theirs. But who would make the first move?

The lone chess piece took that liberty. Beacon rotated on an axis so that he faced the *Skow II*. Despite the red giant's brilliance filtering past the gaps afforded by the armada, and the robot being fifty metres away, Fisher could still discern the yellow smiley-face painted on Beacon's upper torso.

A beeping sound surfaced out of the quiet din, punctuating the communications array. Without looking, Fisher knew it came from Beacon.

"Open the channel," Fisher instructed. "And Baines, for the sake of posterity—"

"Right," Baines acknowledged with a nod. "Channel's open."

"Crew and captain aboard the *Skow II*," Beacon hailed in a cryptically formal voice, "this is Robot T-261 of Garaxian Core Fleet Seven. On behalf of His Munificence, Exarch 5303 of the Garaxian Imperium... I officially accept your surrender."

"My—*what*?" Fisher's brows sprang so high, he was sure they had catapulted off his forehead. He shared a look of complete devastation with Anne.

"Apologies for my deception, Captain Fisher," the robot continued, "but it was vital for the sake of causality and the imperative merger towards equilibrium within the Universal Crib. That is why I did not fire upon the Apoc factionists when they first took your crew prisoner."

Your crew? Fisher's spine turned into an icy pole.

"I had to be certain that the renegades placed their pivotal call to our Garaxian Overlords," Beacon explained. "Make sure the Imperium was on its way. I am sorry but I have inexorably prewritten your doom in my circuitry."

Shitfuckpissdamn! Beside himself, Fisher lurched forward over the console. "I don't get it, Beacon. First, you save us from the Apocs who planned to deliver us to the Demons, and now you decide to throw us under the bus anyway? For what? The credit?"

"You misjudge me, Captain," the robot answered in what sounded like a hurt tone.

Fisher forked ten fingers through his hair before tersely

dropping his hands to his sides. "Oh wait, did I miss something, Beacon, or should I just call you Robot T–the-fuck–261 now? We're drowning and instead of throwing us a lifesaver, you throw us a hand grenade!"

"What I do must be done, including this circumvention," Beacon replied evenly. "It's for the greater good. More players than you know roam within this arena—and the wider theatre."

Anne's hand found Fisher's arm but he pushed it away. "All I *know* is that after all that crap about trusting our robot you go and hoodwink us. Played us for fools with nothing but brutal chicanery, when we placed our fullest trust in you. You just betrayed your goddam friends."

"In the name of all the races under the Overlords' command—not only yours, Captain Fisher—I submitted your surrender to save you."

"Wow, good job. Guess this catalyst and packet business was just so much underhanded horseshit."

"We had to come back here to deliver the packet to the Imperium, personally and complete. Trust me, Captain, this is the lesser of two evils. I must give my masters what they demanded in its entirety, for your sake as well. Otherwise, your ship and crew would invariably be destroyed."

"You didn't baulk at entire planets being destroyed," Fisher shot back over the com.

"I am a harbinger, true, but not wholly in the way you grasp and consign. I serve as but a proxy forced to leave several planets, several races behind long before the Dovan, in order to save them. I sacrificed more beyond count to save life itself. In truth, the ID have tinkered with my protocols. I had no choice in—" Beacon's voice cut off midsentence, leaving a perplexed Fisher trading frowns with Anne and Baines.

When Beacon resumed, his voice adopted an even more authoritarian tone. "Captain Fisher, Exarch 5303 has come here to oversee our transaction from aboard his command ship, the heavy cruiser, *Infernalis*. The Exarch wishes to address you directly."

A flash of vertigo seized Fisher. *The* Exarch, of the entire sodding Empire—here?

Suppressing his dread, the captain faced Anne and griped through globs of pure bile. "This is getting better all the time. Guess I should feel flattered to merit such a prolific executioner."

Anne met his flagging gaze. "Faith," she whispered, "in causality."

"Cap-ten Fiss-ser," an ethereal voice chimed in through the com. The voice sounded outlandish, reptilian, female—sort of. "You are guilty of being in possession of stolen Imperium property and abetting a Garaxian target, a trespass which carries an automatic death sentence for you and your crew. There is no escape as you have undoubtedly surmised."

No shit.

"I ask you most solemnly, are you a penitent man?"

Legs wobbling, shrinking down even further, Fisher said in a monotone, "That depends—if it's justified."

The Exarch seemed to receive the captain's response with equanimity. "I would normally make an example of your end befitting your trespass, for the education of others."

Fisher shuddered, remembering Vorancia. At the very least this bastard would turn Alliantha into a Stricken.

"But due to certain mitigating circumstances, in part thanks to the diligence of T-261, I will stay the knife, provided you serve your penance another way. In the spirit of fostering good faith, I may regard your illegal trek to the Juncture as simply escorting my robot, a task that befits your undercaste race within the strictures and codes of the Supreme Garaxian Imperium."

"O—kay," Fisher said, knitting his brows.

"Long have I awaited this moment," the Exarch said. "Long has the entire Imperium, including most of my 5302 predecessors exalted to this station before—"

"Ah, Exarch?" Fisher cut in, interrupting the demigod's diatribe. The Imperium's supreme figurehead, the most powerful being in the entire Universe was effectively shushed. Baines could only gawp at Fisher, his face vacillating between sheer admiration and abject terror at his captain's audacity. More like, his lunacy.

Fisher didn't fully appreciate his pilot's reaction, too intent on the iconic robot floating just fifty metres outside the window.

"Beacon's yours then," the captain said. "He's downloaded the contents of the packet you need, so why don't you just take the robot and go on your merry?"

"Bea-cone?" A pause over the com. "Oh, you refer to Robot T-261. It is and always has been a mere tool to serve our ends. The packet it carries is a weapon, a countermeasure not against us, but against the target I seek, which I'm afraid, is still aboard your ship." *Target?*

"I'm… at a loss," Fisher said.

"We captured Robot T-261 when it was sent to the Human homeworld, now Stricken, as a probe to roust out our target, our *fugitive*."

"It's pronounced Bea-*cun* by the way," Fisher corrected. Baines' face went white. "I thought the Dovan sent him to Earth."

"Initially, they did," the Exarch said. "But we intercepted the robot. The Dovan received Bea-cun, as you call it, from an earlier race, the Strithum, and they from the Vandar, and so on backwards from epoch to previous epoch. A long troublesome pattern evolved that forced us to terminate races in pursuit of our fugitive, precisely 432 spanning 7.2 million galactic years before the Dovan ever found Bea-cun. We adjusted and realigned its protocols and controls.

"Under the pretence of developing the packet, we allowed myriad races, including Dovan and Human, to 'tinker' as they saw fit, while Bea-cun gathered more intelligence on the fugitive."

Another pause. Fisher breathed, swallowed, breathed.

"Two-Six-One has explained to me the meaning of the name bestowed upon it," the Exarch continued. "A fitting name, but not in the context you intended. It does not imply the bea-cun of Earth's saviour and messiah, but its nemesis, herald of the world's destruction."

Anne went rigid at the mention of Earth, but her face betrayed no other reaction.

"The Dovan inadvertently led us to Earth. If that planet had not been sent the robot, perhaps it would not have become involved. We might have never noticed such an inferior backwater world."

The Exarch sighed, "But, where Bea-cun goes, the fugitive follows. Where the fugitive goes, Bea-cun pursues. Their relationship has grown symbiotic. And *we* must chase both, ready to execute the masterstroke against our adversary, for in galactic terms they are never far apart. To avoid loose ends concerning the weapon, any race that has had contact in some major way with either is eliminated."

Fisher surveyed the faces on the bridge, trying to gauge the crew's reactions. He noticed Resa doing the same. When their eyes met, the Tolkane looked away.

"But after annexing Earth, Stricken, we tried a new strategy. Humans thought and acted differently than any of their predecessors. Rather than pass on their doom to the next race, they held onto Bea-cun. This puzzled us at first but later festered our credo with troubling ramifications. Their mindsets presented something new, which might pose a possible threat to the Imperium itself. The fugitive summoned peril enough.

"Still, we received Bea-cun's signal from Earth and the plasma bomb had already been sent. As with the other races, we had to stifle the Humans for their primal association, whether they grasped their aid to the fugitive or not."

While the Exarch spoke, Fisher concentrated on Beacon, trying to make sense of his motives, as if he might somehow glean the robot's true directive beneath his duplicitous layers by staring him down. All the captain achieved for his efforts was watery eyes.

When Fisher turned away and remeasured the faces surrounding him, he still came up blank: they seemed equally deadpan. *One of them sure had a fucking objective.*

"We came to Earth," the Exarch went on. "Saw that Bea-cun remained there intact but the packet went missing. Our target had gone to ground, following the long-established pattern. This time, however, we set up surveillance stations across the planet and the entire system. And waited, using Bea-cun as bait. Our target eventually did as we expected and tried to extract Bea-cun from the dead planet's surface. It failed and we closed in but when we tried to capture the fugitive, it slipped through our fingers and won free."

329

Resa. Eyes flitting to the Tolkane, Fisher balled his fists and cursed under his breath. "Why do you want this rogue so bad?"

"The fugitive bears its own unique weaponry. If unleashed against us, it could spell doom for the Imperium—ultimately for the countless races that live under our protectorate, including yours. It poses the greatest threat to existence ever conceived. That also underlines the reason it has an invested interest in Bea-cun."

A quivering touch on Fisher's sleeve drew his regard to Jiri's glistening eyes. His heart went out to her. Even now, on the cusp of a certain end, her lips pressed tight in a look of determination, as though to reassure him. He smiled down at her, squeezed her small hand and planted a light kiss on her cinnamon crown.

"Our target tampered with the robot," the Exarch said, breaking the tender moment. "To taint our protocols, which the first few races enhanced. When we first uncovered this secret, Bea-cun was en route between race twenty—Zenpharae, and race twenty-one—unpronounceable in your tongue. But only after he arrived on Earth did the weapon reach effective fruition. The threat posed by our menace has since escalated. Now, at this Juncture, it has grown imminent."

"Hence the armada," Fisher ventured.

"Correct." The Exarch sounded impressed. "The anomalies in this system, so close to the red giant will prevent the fugitive from evading us. The ships also form a requisite component of our snare. The fugitive is an elusive, ephemeral one as time has illustrated, but there will be no escape for it this time. We have kept tabs on your progress, intervened at times, and tied up loose ends at others, waiting until the moment to strike found symmetry. We have come at last to the Juncture's coup de grâce."

Cold beads of sweat trickled down Fisher's back, but he forced himself to ask anyway. "What loose ends?"

"Several actually," the Exarch answered. "The fugitive took care of that defiant knave, Vorancia, acting of its own volition. Admittedly, I saw the logic in it. Since Vorancia's defence grid had targeted us, we naturally claimed responsibility for his deterrent's removal—and his elimination. We didn't have a direct hand in his assassination but given the comprehensive benefit, took the next natural step and destroyed Vorancia's system. All the galaxies-wide fear Vorancia's penalty garnered gave us eons of harmony and profit with the races in his former protectorate.

"Still, we couldn't very well let the fugitive run amok for it too gathered strength, against us. From the moment the packet resurfaced on Korian III we had to take more stringent measures, erasing all workings with unflinching resolve and extreme prejudice. We started with Ursula Minor where your previous ship made prime dock for its retrofit. We destroyed every ship in the religious convoy that harboured you for a time, after boarding the *Crucifix* and executing the one called Wisdan."

Resa reeled at the news and just managed to suppress a verbal howl but Anne caught the Tolkane's full projection and physically shuddered under its impact.

And somehow, Fisher sensed both reactions in his mind. He too felt an instant tightening in his throat. *The Cardinal's dead. You murdered a selfless priest, you rotten fuck.*

"Casualties of war," the Exarch explained as if bored with the matter. "The Apoc contingent who surprised us with the news of the Human resurgence and infestation on Alliantha, presented the most recent component that needed curtailing. They too became part of our new baiting strategy until of course, they exhausted their usefulness. Considering Humans in any form or number too tenacious to suffer, I decreed their race an enemy of the Imperium. Like the colonists on Alliantha, I had the rogue sycophants eliminated."

The Exarch cantered on, forensically talking of mass extermination as though nothing more than cleaning a kitchen counter.

"Bastard," Anne hissed.

Fisher brusquely waved a hand to silence her. He wanted to scream himself but held his vehemence in check. "One more thing. Why do you give Beacon the designation, Robot T-261?"

"For the same reason that we number all aspects of our society. Mathematics provides the only truly universal vocabulary—for our language and the common tongue of the Universal Crib. Robot T-261 is no exception—the 261'st, still-active copy of the original probe, but the robot's mind embedded in the construct is the same cynosure.

"Most of the other copies remain. Some are mere shells in stasis aboard our capital ships, ready in case we require spare parts, some serve as decoy drones placed to lure the fugitive or his associates and some have been destroyed by those same parties. Bea-cun marks the real hub. Through it, everything in the Universal Crib—future and futurity itself, hinges. So, I ask you once again, Cap-ten Fiss-ser, are you a penitent man?"

Fisher squared his jaw and braced his hands on his hips. "I won't grovel, if that's what you're gunning for, flinging allegations at me and my kind. Besides, I wouldn't know how to help you even if I wanted to. We're just a bunch of toilet-bound undercastes after all."

Fisher paused and licked his lips as he refocused his ire. "But what I do know, Mr Exarch, is that you wouldn't just volunteer your little history lesson, and all your morbid secrets therein, out of a need to make small talk. You've been scanning my tin can ever since you arrived. And the *only* reason we're still alive is that you can't seem to find whatever the hell you're looking for."

Silence.

Fisher trembled under the immense pressure of the dangerous gambit he found himself playing. But with the cards dealt, he could not back down now. Facing death, he wouldn't do it on his knees. He would remain unflappable. "So, why don't you do our precious 'Crib' a favour, and take a flying ubiquitous fuh—"

"Master?" Beacon's stringent voice broke through Fisher's rant.

The captain grunted. *Bout time Mr Malfunction weighed in.*

"If the fugitive is still hiding aboard the *Skow II*," the robot broadcasted, "it has likely veiled itself in a verse-semiphase. But even so, cannot win free. And must remain quantumly anchored to this point in spacetime. If it pleases, let me bring you the technology you covet to quell the danger posed by the renegade. I vouch for its authenticity and efficacy. The sooner you have it, the sooner you may turn it against the fugitive and break the standstill, extinguish the source of the Imperium's hazard forever and anon.

The *Skow II* will remain held, but must not be harmed, lest you repeat the energy-taint folly of Race-193 and Race-316. Will you comply?"

A longer, more vacuous pause ensued. At last, the Exarch spoke. "Robot T-261 speaks sooth. The sword it wields is indeed double-edged. We will comply."

"Captain Fisher and his crew will also submit," Beacon answered before the captain could refute. "He knows that you hold his ship in thrall with tractors, digital lockdown, and tertiary measures and will not make any attempt of flight, thus keeping our pinpoint vector on the fugitive accurate."

Fisher opened his mouth to protest when Anne cut him short with a vigorous shake of her head.

Beacon addressed the crew then, dropping all formality for something more familiar. "Captain, your crew will remain safe, I promise. And Fisher, please do not endeavour anything rash… especially now."

"Wouldn't think of it."

"Now then, I must say, goodbye." Beacon's transmission ended with disturbing abruptness. Anne glanced around nervously and hugged herself.

"That sure had a note of finality to it," Fisher remarked.

All eyes aboard the *Skow II* watched with uncertainty as a small battalion of Demon combat drones, flying in V-formations approached and descended upon Beacon. The drones looked like slightly larger versions of Beacon himself, except for their being festooned with wing-foils and loaded with guns and missiles, lots of them. Bedecked with such an impressive array of ordnance, just a couple of the robotic fighters would've been enough to take out the *Skow II* without so much as a burp.

Beacon rotated to face the drones as they drew up and slowed. They formed a van around their charge, the undeniable MVP of the entire ugly endgame to this eternal cold war between titans.

The mechanical procession glided away from the *Skow II*. There seemed no glory in Beacon's escort to the Exarch's ship. No measure of welcome. It looked like a funeral procession with mechanized pallbearers ushering a coffin.

As the robotic squadron disappeared behind the closest interceptors, Fisher's attention broke from the window and slowly searched the silenced bridge.

Everyone's face told a different story. Jiri and Baines stared back with bright eyes, eager for their next orders, Cholla's eyebrows worked in several directions as he pondered deep in scientific thought.

The corners of Resa's mouth pulled down in a devastated grimace, his face had drained of colour, devolved into a ghost of his former self. And Anne—she appeared comfortably numbed by an epiphany that sent her faraway into some distant, deferent paradigm.

The Exarch's voice disturbed the silence. "As Robot T-261 has indicated, we hold your ship in our grasp, with many multiple restraints. If you have integrated any concealed malice into the robot's circuits, we will know before we attempt to download the packet's data. Then, we will strip the flesh from your bodies, one micron at a time."

46: Infernalis
5303

Aboard the *Infernalis*, Exarch 5303 finished his transmission and switched off the com. He lifted a pallid hand to his face and studied it as he pondered. Robot T-261 was correct. The armada *had* caught the fugitive within the perfect halo trap. But even this could be construed as a deadlock. Such a snare would never fully contain the alien target without the tech to restrain it permanently: a combination of tool and weapon, with the means to effectively deploy the weapon. The Garaxian supreme leader would not follow the fate of his predecessors for their failure to eliminate the outlier's threat.

All of those before him had struggled so long and hard to attain the prize only to serve voluntary penance for their impotence. With the invincible fist of the Imperium standing poised to do his bidding, Exarch 5303 had built a true dominion upon the foundation of his progenitors' knowledge, succeeding where they had faltered. Yet even now, nestled safely behind the first rank of the Empire's fiercest predator ships, all their guns and munitions trained on the enemy, the Exarch's confidence wavered.

Exarch 5303 turned away and glided through the corridors of his glass-shrouded ship, atop a glass palanquin, which responded to his thoughts, past the ranks of his Highguard, who marked his staunchest most virile warriors. He moved with definitive purpose towards a concave window at the forward fortress block of his strongest ship.

From here, the Exarch watched with dispassionate scrutiny as the squadron of combat drones ushered Robot T-261 away from the *Skow II*, still visible through a narrow slot formed by the flanks of intermediate ships. The drones escorted the mechanical slave back to the *Infernalis*. The Juncture had reached one tick of the clock before its zenith. There would be no mistakes.

Across the galaxies, every undercaste race had revered the Imperium's illustrious figurehead in their own way. Some as a god, others as the devil but after this triumph, the Garaxians themselves will believe their Exarch to be both.

Exarch 5303 had stomached enough dereliction of duty in his relatively short time as ruler. And had to exact countless verdicts of penance to uphold the sacrosanct mandate. It all led to this moment. Penance had always been the cornerstone of the dynasty that the code served—as the pitifully antagonistic, mixed-breed crew aboard Captain Fisher's ship was about to find out.

But first things came first.

From his viewscreen, Exarch 5303 watched as Robot T-261 entered the *Infernalis* through a plasma curtain. The barrier dragged like stretching plastic as the automaton penetrated the small portcullis.

The squadron of combat drones held station only long enough to ensure their charge pushed completely through the screening annex. Then, in a burst of thrusters, they streaked away to resume their fleet patrols.

Another escort, comprised mostly of probes and security bots met Robot T-261. Members of the Exarch's Highguard also stood in attendance, ready with weapons drawn beyond the mechanized first rank.

After Robot T-261 passed its initial security assessment, the Highguard led it through the winding glass corridor painted in a translucent pastel blue glow.

Every probe present in the massive auxiliary block tested and retested Robot T-261 a thousand times. They utilized every protocol in each analysis to ensure that T-261 had not been tampered with. The robot thralls performed thoroughly, assiduously, and dutifully as their governing dictates demanded. They demanded a lot.

In real-time, the whole procedure took less than an hour combined, but to 5303, stuck in limbo, the diagnostic proved painfully long and laborious.

The mechanical slaves delivered T-261 into the reception area, married to the central bridge of the *Infernalis*. The Exarch could have easily executed any order from his command block but he needed to see the robot—the fulcrum holding the future in place—with his own eyes.

"You have demonstrated commendable skill and merit on such a long, penitent journey," the Exarch observed as he drew up to the robot. "Thus far, I consider your actions laudable. You have served the Imperium well."

"Master," Robot T-261 replied.

"But this, Cap-ten Fiss-ser, disturbs the natural order. He disturbs me. Although our scans revealed that he is no Human, the captain bears too many of their hazardous traits and tendencies. And as recently discovered, he is—connected."

"Fisher is merely a pawn, a means to an end," the robot said. "I suggest you eliminate him and be done."

The Exarch widened his reptilian orbs. "Patience, T-261, the Entity remains our prime concern. You did not discern which of Fiss-ser's crew it had infiltrated?"

"No, Master," T-261 confessed.

"Why then did you not simply kill all aboard and destroy the ship?"

"The fugitive monitored me. Had I instigated a full eradication, like igniting the engines, or even killing one crew member and been wrong, the fugitive would have phased into true form and escaped—as it has done many times before in similar situations. With the energy vice that Core Fleet Seven creates, that is no longer the case."

Exarch 5303 swallowed and contemplated. As though to emphasize the robot's point, its seeing-dome panned to the left, reflecting several armada ships through the glass behind 5303. A new possibility took root.

"You may confirm these instances through Imperium archives," T-261 added. "Then, this Juncture, the ideal space to nurture the physical demands of the Entity's restraint, would not have been possible. Remember also that this marks the correct Juncture in *time* as well. And your last remaining chance of success."

The Exarch narrowed his eyes into slits. "And why is that, T-261?"

"The Entity has grown stronger than I anticipated and the fugitive housing it grows restless. But now that I have aligned all the conditions and constraints of the Juncture, it is afraid. The Entity knows it cannot escape from within the confines of the Halo, both physical and quantum-mechanical."

The Exarch walked around his robot, completing a full circle. "This tech—the packet you deliver—builds on what Vorancia had developed?"

"Yes, Supreme Leader," T-261 confirmed. "I have completed and readied it for deployment. At the moment, the fugitive remains trapped but the cage is by no means permanent. If the armada should break its current formation even slightly, the Entity can slip free of our tethers and you will never have the opportunity to capture it again. Furthermore, it may learn the tech's fundamental properties, find a flaw and press it to its advantage."

"You speak of the blade's other edge. What of it? Have you gleaned anything new? Do you still deem the fugitive's dire threat against the Imperium real?"

"I'm afraid it is real, Master, a clear and present danger to the entire Imperium."

The Exarch folded his arms. "Explain."

"When I routed the ship through the Dark Sector, the fugitive manipulated the spacetime anomalies generated by the singularities' overlapping tidal wakes. It discharged dark energy *as* we passed. By the time we reached the far side, the expanse deteriorated into a more volatile energetic form, utterly different from when we entered. I have correlated data streams to substantiate the discrepancy, which you may also examine."

"How will it accomplish its ploy?" the Exarch asked, feeling a weight flatten his chest.

T-261 trained its bulbous robotic orb on the Exarch and locked. Amidst the whirs of internal servos firing, the automaton answered, "The fugitive will send its destructive signal using an amplified form of antitelephone. But I know not its exact delivery method, only that by its very nature, the Entity can accomplish it."

"And if it meets with success?"

"The energy unleashed from the singularities' collisions will

338

rend the fabric of spacetime, having a cascading effect, not unlike the first antimatter to matter transcendence, what Humans called the Big Bang. Chronology will aberrate. Time as we know it will come to a stop.

The Exarch's nasal cavities quivered. "What then?"

"Time will collapse, drawn backwards towards a reversed temporal pole by what can be best described as a tachyonic cyclone. All races including the Garaxian Empire would, at the very least, be sent back to their infancy if not their very inception. If that were the extent of the time shift, the fugitive, or any other race with considerable tech in that era and a similar lean towards conquest—the Amalgam for instance—could then easily extinguish the Imperium, putting an end to your long-standing epoch before it begins."

The Exarch inhaled fiercely. He dug his sharp nails into his palms to stifle the sudden urge to strike the robot for the mere mention of the Amalgam. That archrival race of tall aliens from Messier 64—the Evil Eye Galaxy, had been responsible for close to two trillion Garaxian deaths before their formidable empire was finally neutralized in a protracted and bloody campaign led by Exarch 1677.

Exarch 5303 forced himself to look away, pretending to take an interest in the cast of service automatons and Highguard in the immediate vicinity. Stomaching his ire, he returned his attention to T-261 and asked with deceptive calm, "What about at most?"

"The effect will soar exponentially and synergistically—to the point where causality itself is irrevocably violated," T-261 said without hesitation. "Unable to cope with such strain on the physical laws that govern it, the spacetime continuum will be destroyed, obliviating not only this surrogate realm, this *Universe* but all quantum realms within the Crib."

The Exarch studied T-261 long and hard as he calculated the validity of the robot's implications. The Imperium's highest potentate hesitated, his confidence dithering as he came to a decision he did not relish.

"Begin the download at once," the Exarch commanded. "We must seize this chance and exploit it utterly. I want to see models

339

and an execution plan on our peripherals. We cannot afford to waste any time."

The Exarch dropped his gaze to the robot's torso and with new derision scrutinized the yellow symbol emblazoning its black shell. "Have a service-bot rid you of that. Since it no longer forms part of your guise, you need not allow the degrading emblem to mar your torso any further. It reflects poorly on the high office you hold within my coven."

"Yes, Master, at once."

47: Juncture
5303

Robot T-261 plugged into the central banks of the *Infernalis,* monitored by several security bots and analysis automatons, all religiously guarded by fully-armed Highguard. The Exarch had since returned to his command block aboard the heavy cruiser, wanting to be alone. He had already seen enough, needing only to inspect the robot up close. Now, 5303 craved the opposite.

The android would fall into the purview of the Exarch's more-than-capable assemblage. They would faithfully ensure T-261 reported back as soon as it had something to share. But the robot had left the Exarch feeling uneasy.

Everyone in the game had so much to lose and the robot alone held the fate of the Imperium in its hand. T-261 truly was a beacon, the light of which the Exarch both loathed and desperately required to maintain his focus in what had become a highest-stakes intergalactic endgame.

On the pretext of that same resounding fact, he remembered the robot's warning. And immediately began accessing the Garaxian command network to examine the position of each ship in his vast armada. The Exarch demanded updates from his massive capital ships, all close enough to exert the full force of their arsenals with a single command from 5303. *I do wield the strongest hand.*

Then a sense of remorse, if that's what it might be called for a creature devoid of emotion, crept up on the Exarch. From the moment of his exaltation, it had always been that way: a simple equation of power built upon power in endless growth. The only challenge he ever faced came from Vorancia, and the Exarch had been robbed of that victory by the Entity. But now, 5303 could absorb that success by destroying the Entity. Exarch 5303 would exceed exaltation. Today, he would experience his apotheosis.

The Exarch began inspecting the security protocols that governed the ID core worlds when an incoming communication signal stopped him short.

"Downloads are complete, Your Munificence," T-261 reported. "You may examine them on your console. Weapon parameters are available in 3D hologram projection. Generate, if it pleases."

The Exarch was late to disengage the interface. The core worlds could wait. The Imperium's ultimate nemesis could not.

The projection's rendering of the weapon's deployment seemed flawless but would require a substantial discharge from their plasma energy shell. That demanded more power than the *Infernalis* or any of the dreadnoughts might supply.

That kind of energy could only be produced by capital ships. They would have to come in closer and tap through virtual conduit relayed into the nearest dreadnoughts. And that required too much time. The alternative was to break formation and allow a capital ship to enter the foray and directly release its torrent. But once they dropped their unified tractor beams, currently fixed so intently on the *Skow II,* the energy vice would fail and the Entity could win free through the power gap.

Unless...

With the energy vice Core Fleet Seven currently manifests, that no longer holds true. The Exarch allowed a thin rictus to trace his corpse-like lips. If he destroyed Cap-ten Fiss-ser's ship first, the blast would leave the fugitive's essence disarticulated, weakened—and still trapped.

As matters stood, the energy held the fugitive pinned. The loss of its corporeal form would render it more vulnerable and pliant. Naked. Then, they wouldn't need the capital ship's energy output at all to accomplish the same task. The *Skow II* no longer mattered. The Entity remained ensnared in corporeal form or not. The explosion would disorientate the fugitive for a time and make its capture all the easier—and the sweeter when it realized it had lost.

"Have the capital ships approach as tightly as possible. I want the gap narrowed," the Exarch commanded over the com. Not one iota could be left to chance. "Make ready the weapon for immediate deployment."

Staring over the console, the Exarch mused quietly to the frigid air before him. "Missiles. I would think a hundred should do it, and why not? It may be overkill to merely weaken the fugitive, but as for that impetuous Fiss-ser, those last seconds when he sees his fate flying towards him will provide his absolution. He will reflect upon the lacking nature of his insubordinate ways, beg to have the kill order rescinded. And as the Tolkani merges with the natural state, he will feel—*gladness*—knowing that his penance has been duly served."

The sound of Robot T-261's voice cut through the Exarch's dark contemplations. "May I remind you, Master, that we must await the capital ships to establish their virtual conduit—to facilitate and seal an adequate energy transference?"

The Exarch leaned into the display, dominating it. "T-261, I *command* you to begin the interface and make ready to activate the weapon as per the simulations. Before we launch the weapon, we must destroy your transport ship by conventional means—a routine precaution of course. Have our interceptors clear a path between us and our target. From the *Infernalis'* tubes, I want you, T-261, to launch one hundred missiles at the *Skow II*, immediately." Through his viewscreen, the Exarch regarded Robot T-261 with cold pallid eyes, espying as he did that the robot's torso no longer bore the yellow decal.

"Yes, Master. The primary weapon is cycling up, patched to Halo for a drop. All ships encircling the *Skow II* have received their variable co-efficient markers to initiate the procedure."

The Exarch watched with growing impatience as T-261 paused to absorb its new instruction set. Then the robot slid agilely from one console to another console, and another, dragging several peripherals to various workstations to perform different tasks. The sound of punching buttons in rapid succession ensued. From his own console, 5303 confirmed that the robot had indeed followed his orders to the letter.

"Intermediate ships have banked to offer the *Infernalis* a clean line of sight with the *Skow II*. One hundred missiles are locked and loaded," T-261 declared. "Programming launch sequence. All tubes are open and ready for deployment. Ten-second programmed countdown awaiting your command."

The sneer returned to 5303's lips. "Fire."

10, 9,

The Exarch left the viewscreen station, gliding briskly to the outer window. This would be a moment played over and over in his superior mind until eternity faltered.

8, 7,

The air on the bridge of the Exarch's cruiser suddenly and inexplicably expunged, replaced with vacuum. All security-bots and every other independent automaton deactivated, all the Demon crew flash-froze and floated weightless in silent serenity. And a lone robot, somehow magnetized with the glass floor, traced the buttons of three separate consoles with three sets of metallic fingers too quickly for any other eye to follow... had there been another eye to follow.

6, 5, 4,

A sudden loss of inertia wrenched the Exarch backwards. Threw him to the glass floor of his command block. Still on his hands and knees, heart racing, he cocked his head up. From the low angle, the scene from the window swam, interceptors dancing in erratic violence. No, they didn't move at all. 5303's whole world spiralled.

Through the pandemonium, the sharp ping of a com-link sounded, patched into the Exarch's rocking enclosure.

The familiar voice of Robot T-261 filled the compartment. "Incoming message from Fugitive. Message follows: Exarch, cannot accommodate you," the robot droned. "It is you who has lost the Juncture's endgame. To the victor goes everything. To the damned... well, you'll see soon enough. ...Message ends."

3, 2... 1.

Steadying his wits, the Exarch regained his feet, staggered across the teetering floor to the domed window, and braced himself. Face pressed to the glass, the Exarch could only gape, stricken by the impossible view. The *Infernalis*—his own ship backed away.

No, the heavy cruiser remained stationary. A new linear cavity appeared where his command block should still be nested, where it had been attached to the vessel scant seconds before.

Then the truth suddenly dawned on the Exarch: the robot had jettisoned the entire block and now the module drifted swiftly away from its mothership.

Before 5303 could cry for help or react in any way, the window lit up in a dazzling display of streaking lines of light. They all blasted out of the open torpedo tubes of the *Infernalis*. They all hurled directly towards his command block.

The Exarch held his icy breath as all one hundred missiles fanned out, flowering around his lifeboat, to stripe past the circular edge of the module's domed window.

All except one.

Penance ...is served, the Exarch thought as his command block exploded in a thousand hellish torrents, flaring out in every direction from the infernal vortex.

***

Thus ended the reign of Exarch 5303, and though he had not fathomed it as he met his final doom, 5303 would be the Garaxian Imperium's last Exarch. In that at least, he did achieve his coveted apotheosis.

***

From the bridge of the *Skow II,* Fisher did a doubletake as the tiny ejected object beyond the closest rank of interceptors detonated. It looked like a fiery spider sitting in the middle of a web of light, briefly fanning out from the event's destructive epicentre. With vindictive urgency, the entire salvo of missiles hurtled towards his own ship.

At their horrible approach, Fisher grew strangely detached. It would be a quick end, climactic no doubt, sadly unsung, but beautiful all the same.

Time slowed.

As the Exarch had done, Fisher held his breath and braced for the fatal disintegrating impact that would mark his end.

The tendrils of light zoomed straight towards the *Skow II* ...and past it.

Their tail-fire caged the ship with ninety-nine bars of light. Then a blinding bouquet of fire. The *Skow II*'s bridge rattled in the surge of their wake.

"They overshot us!" Fisher wheeled around to track them.

The missiles skittered out of formation changing to independent trajectories. The captain could only watch in disbelief as he ascertained their true targets.

What happened next was purest, ungodliest Armageddon.

48: After Math
Fisher

Explosions mushroomed everywhere, building one upon the other with increasing efficacy. The missiles had started the symphony of obliteration, taking out the closest interceptors with surgical hits to their engine drives and weapon arrays.

Wide-eyed, Fisher could only gawk as the munitions and submunitions ignited next. Like some malefic orchestra escalating towards a crescendo, they turned each ship into another bomb. The mayhem cascaded backwards through the armada like a gale-driven wildfire—a chain reaction scattering universal destruction, which only multiplied in severity as it affected the larger ships further out.

But the swathe of devastation moved forward as well, threatening to consume the *Skow II* and turn her into molten fractures.

In thrall to the infernal orgy, the crew froze. But not Fisher. Eyes blazing, the captain reacted with the reflex of a cheetah. He sprang past Baines and punched the console buttons to dial up the ship's shields to maximum—but to something else as well.

Even so, the lashing from the cataclysmic torrent bucked the *Skow II* mercilessly. The tiny ship caromed several times, but her shields held, with the first wave.

Not so with the second. The convulsive impact cracked too mighty a blow. And breached the hull.

"Fire up auxiliary power," Fisher roared. "Emergency armour! Compartmentalize or we're dead."

Baines' hands flew at the controls, fumbling to make it happen.

"Done," he shouted back.

The third wave wreaked havoc with the ship's pitch and yaw, but the hull held on to its scant integrity. "Turn her into the wave," Fisher commanded. "Match bearing. We can ride the rest of the aftershocks well enough."

"What the hell happened?" Anne cried.

Fisher let out a hysterical laugh. "We just survived being in the middle of a fucking bomb that went boom, that's what—a miracle in itself. Our airframe should never have been able to withstand that level of pressure shock. But it did."

When the immediate threat had passed, Fisher scanned the *Skow II's* internal sensors. The core shields and bulkhead doors held, but roughly a fifth of the ship had been opened to vacuum. Several fracture tears and one small gouge—that would take some serious welding and resealing—if only Brumbal were still here: he was the real maintenance expert. No prime dock ruptures at least.

"How many fix-or-die warnings tripped?" Jiri asked over his shoulder.

"I think all of them. Jiri, better get down below and suss out the worst ones. Get Bliter to give you a hand."

Fisher looked out the window to see the dying cinders of the Demons' armada. The Imperium's entire shiny fleet had been reduced to a staggering melange of debris, charred black and burning. And that was only the extent of what he could see. The magnitude of some of the explosions had been so great, nothing remained of the vessels but vapour.

"What about the capital ships?"

"Working on it, Fish," Baines answered. "Short and long-range sensors are fried."

Fisher nodded curtly. "Jiri, can we limp out of here? Even the Dark Sector is preferable to waiting for those behemoths to arrive."

"Bad news, Cap. Engines are toast too," she said.

Fisher grimaced. "So that's it then. We dodge the bullets from the little pricks just long enough to take it up the ass from their big brothers."

"That's funny," Baines said.

Fisher was not amused. "You must be high, again."

"You needn't worry about them, Captain," Bliter announced, striding onto the bridge.

"There you are. What do you mean?"

"The electronic fog caused by the irregular plasma discharges will have calmed by now—enough to see again." The navigator turned to Baines. "Check the scanner, if you please. Should be working again."

"Oh so polite," Baines chuckled as he lowered his head and searched his console. His smile quickly straightened. "Fuck me, Captain, he's right. They're gone, completely. Trace matter only, which fits. It's just stardust and ghost signatures, but no ID juggernauts."

"That's... *impossible*. Those monsters shouldn't have even felt the concussion let alone been destroyed by it."

"Reading's right, Fish. See for yourself."

The captain tightened his jaw. "How?"

"I have a hypothesis," Cholla said.

Fisher turned to the doctor. "Let's hear it."

"It's quite possible, Captain that the missiles fired were aimed at the closest targets merely as a distraction. I know the Demons do kill their own but certainly not at such a monumental showdown. And the—whatever the heck they scanned for—was never found. That whole notion of another fugitive as they claimed might have been part of an elaborate hoax—a hoax, I'm guessing, conjured by Beacon himself."

Fisher stared.

"As you say," Cholla went on, "those capital ships sat too far from us to get caught in the firestorm, so I think Beacon sent those missiles to provide a veil through which he executed a more elaborate plan of attack. Remember, he knew a lot about the Demon tech—far more I'd wager than he let us know. Perhaps the android found their security protocols and exploited them as he did back on the Apoc scout we were imprisoned on. Then, launched some kind of virus to, well to do what viruses do."

"Y'know, Doc, sometimes you scare me," Fisher said.

"It does fit the facts," said Anne. "The Demons are a paranoid lot. I've said it time and again: they always got their finger on the button."

"Right," Cholla declared with new verve. "I believe it was some kind of force-vice germ causing a self-actuating evisceration in communication with one of their infamous self-destruct protocols sent up to all the capital ships."

"Looks like Beacon stepped up after all—when it really counted," Anne said morosely.

"A-huh," Fisher agreed. "So, he's gone for real?"

"You saw the explosions," said Anne. "It's just debris out there."

"Yeah, but it was also just debris when I first found him. Hell, there's a piece of scrap from Resa's former ship still aboard this vessel." Fisher looked out the window, his mind drifting faraway to his other ship, his lost bird.

Baines' cough brought Fisher back to the bridge. The pilot's resigned smile and slow head bob indicated that he correctly parsed the target of his captain's regret.

Anne broke the moment. "Ever since I got the hang of projection back on the Apoc ship, I developed a kind of warm sensitivity to Beacon." She placed a hand over her heart. "Here— a good familiar vibe connected to him, even when he wasn't broadcasting. Well, that sense is gone. All I have now is radio silence."

"Is that the same feeling you had when those drones took Beacon away?" Fisher ventured. "Looked to me like you were having some sort of epiphany."

Anne smiled. "Yes, Beacon sent me that euphoric catchphrase of his."

"Trust your robot," Fisher guessed.

"Exactly."

Guilt rang against Fisher's chest, remembering his final recriminating dialogue with the robot. "Okay, so I pegged him wrong. Beacon sacrificed himself for our sake, taking out all the ID ships and hardware. Sorry Robo, wherever you are."

"Amen," Baines said to the air. "And cheers."

The captain breathed and faced the others. "For the moment

the *Skow II* might be this shitstorm's orphan but the fact remains, there's still a trillion-trillion more of those ugly fucks out there to contend with, and they're not going to be happy about this mess."

Fisher pinched the bridge of his nose, gaze drifting to Anne. "The next Exarch is going to step up twice as fast and will want to know who the hell could stage such a coup and get this far with it. That's one big-ass pendulum needed to sway the odds. Sorry, Anne but we haven't stopped anything. Just postponed it."

"That remains to be seen," Bliter said.

Fisher's eyebrows sought one another, nonplussed at the navigator's latest Bliterism. But before he could address the riddle, a more immediate question budged ahead. He faced Cholla. "Even if what you say is true with the virus, those fakeout missiles shouldn't have inflicted such utter destruction, on the interceptors maybe, but not the dreadnoughts. Any ideas about that one, Mr Professor?"

Cholla lifted his shoulders. "Sorry Cap, I wasn't privy to that part of Beacon's tech."

"That's a relief," Fisher chided.

"I was," Anne piped in. "Quite simple actually. Every ship surrounding us had its shields down to maintain the corral. Even so, the missiles facilitated a more effective and immediate delivery system for the catalyst. Whatever the technical parameters of the cause and effect we witnessed, I believe the Exarch forced Beacon's hand. Made him do something he didn't want to."

Fisher leaned in. "Go on."

"Before I say anything else, let's lay one thing to rest, Captain. Beacon didn't bullshit you about the need to return here. The crystalline planet was paramount. Its element completed the formula for the weapon. This catalytic substance locked in its surface affected the plasma, catastrophically. Beacon had some inkling about this even before we began enhancing the Dovani tech."

"Okay," Fisher said.

"But the real key to all of this is the Glass. It has been all along. We just didn't see it—no pun intended," Anne added with a brief chortle. "The Glass, unlike anything found on Earth, burned so hot when it first arrived that the seabed around its aura hadn't just transformed, it winked out of existence—or so I thought."

"Or so you thought," Fisher prompted with a smirk, sensing her answer at hand.

"What I know now after our incarceration aboard the Apoc's ship is that it hadn't been a reaction so hot, but a reaction so *cold,* below zero Kelvin or -273.15°C."

"The threshold of absolute zero, where all particle motion stops? Shouldn't that be impossible?" Cholla asked, scratching his head. "You can't have *negative* volume."

"Yes," Anne confirmed. "If you look at our physics— thermodynamics, volumes, temperatures occurring naturally in this verse."

"Wait," Fisher cut in. "You're saying those temperatures exist?"

"Yes. A system or structure on the cusp of absolute zero still possesses quantum-mechanical zero-point energy."

"The energy of its ground state," Cholla said.

"Right," Anne confirmed. "The kinetic energy of that baseline condition can't be removed. But, as those armaments just demonstrated, we can briefly tap into the physical properties of the Glass as it occurs *beyond* the strictures of our Universe. And that will give us an advantage."

"You're planning on exploiting this alien tech?" Fisher asked.

"Alien sciences to be precise," Anne corrected. "The tech will be ours."

Fisher shot her a sceptical look. "Hot or cold, it's still playing with fire, Anne."

"No doubt," she conceded. "Only modified plasma energy can exist at this temperature, but the properties of something that cold can also make it volatile, so that when it reacts with something equally capricious, namely the catalyst, if not properly contained, it can unleash explosive energy, affecting the matter around it as it seeks the path of least resistance back to equilibrium. The properties of the Glass share a kinship with the anomalous behaviour of water when changing temperatures."

"You mean expanding when it cools and vice versa when it gets hot," Fisher tendered.

Anne dipped her chin. "The same holds for the properties of the plasma. It exists in its truest base form *below* absolute zero. It constitutes an energy source from a seventh dimension, a plane beyond the Universe as we know it."

"I've heard theories about this kind of spatial transcending through the domain walls separating multi-dimensional verses," Cholla supplied. "But they were only theories."

Ignoring the doctor, Fisher faced Anne. "So, what you're telling me is that this *shit* doesn't belong here, but somehow is here?"

"Affirmative."

"How does that happen?"

"It was brought here."

"By whom? The Demons? The fugitive? Beacon?"

Anne threw her hands up. "I don't know, Fish. Beacon remained quite vague about it. What I do know now is the plasma's entropy. It's minimalized as temperatures descend to absolute zero."

Fisher shrugged. "Yeah, Physics 101."

Cholla's face lit up. "The thermal energy of matter vanishes."

"Right again, Doctor," said Anne. "But beyond, or more accurately below that point, the matter itself simply winks out of existence—as it attains negative volume—in our Universe. The quantum-mechanically-created thermodynamics of the plasma in true form exists for less than 1×10^{-24} seconds, or one yoctosecond in the confines of this Universe, before the plasma as we know it replaces it a nanosecond or two later. It exists as plasma energy in vacuum, until it contacts matter in any form. Then, it becomes dormant as it *warms,* changing into its solid state, which resembles melted glass, but the plasma within remains active—in latent form."

Fisher scrunched up his face, trying to wrap his head around concepts definitely above his woeful scientific knowledge. Anne shifted her gaze to Cholla, who nodded emphatically—of course. The captain would have to hit the star pupil for the kindergarten version later. If there was a later.

"The catalyst changes that rule," Anne went on. Fisher's ears perked up. "It's something anathema not only to the plasma but to any form of nuclear fusion. It nullifies the strong force. That's why the red giant barfed." Anne paused and took a peek outside the window. "I'm beginning to suspect that star is our finish line."

"That star will be our finish, period," Baines remarked, "if we don't haul ass and hightail it outta here."

"Anne, you did say this was a simple concept," Fisher reminded her. "When does your explanation get to that point?"

"Shouldn't all of those ships have vanished, winked out as you say?" Cholla asked.

"For the most part that's exactly what happened," Anne said. "The bulk of each ship was literally erased—flipped into negative volume—within the immediate vicinity of the flashpoints. The detritus we see is what remains. The material left on the fringe of the individual event horizons from each reaction. It constitutes parts of the hull too far from the reaction's epicentre to follow the rest of the matter down the drain to oblivion. Remember the reaction triggered instantaneously. The Demons probably didn't even know they were killed—that super quick."

"How do you know all this?" Fisher asked.

"Well, Beacon explained a lot to me, but even he didn't recognize the exact link with the crystalline planet."

Fisher considered this for a moment before a new thought dawned. "Then, how did your pal, Baron know?"

"That, Captain Fisher is a great question. And were he alive today, it would be the first question I'd ask him."

Anne exhaled, sweeping the faces waiting on her next words. "As for my own scant info, when the Apocs first brought us aboard the scout, I saw the correlation on their engine plasma monitors. There's more to the latent energy in the Glass that all the Imperium ships use, a property that allows containment of the volatile mix."

Anne kneaded the muscles at the base of her neck. "Christ, Fisher, they're made from it. Beacon launched virus triggers to reverse the polarity of the charge of that containment. And their engines cycled up to critical mass, exactly as Cholla surmised. Boom, in one fell swoop, the entire armada gets destroyed."

Baines' slow whistle drew everyone's notice. He ran a hand through his hair. "Best laid plans."

Anne gave the pilot a half-smile before regarding Fisher again. "As for the packet you carried, it was mainly a cypher key to unravel the Dovani tech. The packet that Baron left floating above that planetoid down there was the completed one. But both contained temperature codices explaining the formula and execution protocol to make it all happen. In conjunction with the catalyst, the packet formed the perfect weapon against the Demons, the one we just used to annihilate one of their armadas— same principle as the Big Bang."

"It was a big bang all right," Fisher said mildly. "So, what did Beacon do to make the tech work in concert with everything else? Anne?"

Through gleaming eyes, Anne met the captain's stare. "Beacon committed suicide in order to save us. He destroyed himself and the *Infernalis* so no one aboard the Exarch's flagship could rescind the command before it killed the fleet. Even though he severed the source of the transmission, it still delivered its final potent bane."

"Yeah, but how?" Fisher asked, rubbing his temple.

"Isn't it obvious?"

His hand dropped. "Not really. No."

"He must have gotten access to the Exarch's command protocols, and like I've said, they always kept their finger on the button. When you're that paranoid, someday you're going to make the mistake of pushing the wrong—damn—button."

Fisher let out a breath and inclined his head. "They pushed Beacon's wrong buttons."

Baines shrugged. "Makes sense, Fish."

"Now, I have a question for you, Captain," Anne said.

"Shoot."

"How did you know about the right shield modulation when the shit hit the scrubbers?"

"I didn't," Fisher admitted. "Might be intuition, but I think I just ran on autopilot. Had my own epiphany at that crucial moment—Wisdan, Demons, Glass, something I recalled from back on the Apoc ship. Anyway, it happened so fast, like being guided by providence, some subliminal connection."

"Perhaps a connection to Beacon," Anne postulated.

Fisher fixed her with a look.

"In any case, it might be the earliest signs of projection. Whether you believe what Beacon said or not, you're someone's prodigy. Maybe there's hope for you yet," Anne said with a wink, "fostering future generations of little fishes,"

"I rue the day," Baines lamented.

Fisher snorted past his grin. "Thanks for the vote of confidence, Stoner."

The pilot's smirk joined Fisher's.

When the moment passed, the captain arched an eyebrow. "Hey, Baines, that reminds me."

"Fish?"

"Posterity."

Baines smiled with his eyes. "Right."

"What are you two talking about?" Anne asked.

"Explain it to the lady, Flyboy."

"That's a 'Fish bubble,' Anne," said Baines. "One of Cap's coded instruction sets reduced to a single word. We use 'posterity' whenever we want all eyes and ears aboard the ship to remember. Record all AV, external and internal, in case we need to investigate later. When Beacon hesitated, Fisher got me to hit the record button."

He pointed to his console. "The Demons probably scanned us as soon as they jumped into our space, but we knew for certain when that ID creep gave Fish his long-winded speech. After I pushed the button, our own senses perked and kept tabs on, well, just about everything."

"We always knew we had the hottest potato, spooking the Demons like we did," Fisher added. "All those ships confirmed it, but with the Exarch himself showing up—may he rot in hell—that cinched it. They trapped us with so many ships for a reason. They weren't just enclosing our little rust bucket in their mighty weave. They trapped this fugitive, whom I'll wager is still aboard. Small wonder the ID took their sweet-ass time getting here. They literally jumped in from every direction at once before crowding around even tighter."

All faces sought to dock with the captain's now. He let them berth before explaining, "Mr Exarch spoke true: Beacon was never the prize. He was the bait." *The equal sign.*

"If we had a stowaway, I'd have known," Jiri said as she took a seat at her station. "So, bait—for what, Cap?"

Resa unfolded his arms. "Jiri's right, the Exarch scanned the ship and found nothing. It's just us here, Fisher."

"There is no fugitive," Bliter jeered. "You let that prick know we had nothing aboard the ship and he never contested it."

"Yeah Cap," Jiri added. "Maybe the Demons scanned for Baron's packet."

"Good guess, and I might even agree with you, except that before the Apocs met their overdue demise, I'm sure our friend, Slynn divulged, though unwillingly, the fact that Beacon destroyed the packet after he downloaded it. They would've known that anyway if Beacon conspired with the Imperium, even if he feigned all that. Something still stinks in here, Jiri, and for the sake of 'posterity' we're gonna find out."

"Fisher's right," Anne agreed. "They were looking for something else, something much more elusive than us, well, most of us," she added in a cryptic tone.

"But, like you said," Bliter griped, "Beacon used the tech to kill the Demons, destroying himself in the process, so it no longer matters."

"Apart from being stuck in yet another junkyard with some serious hurt done the ship," Baines reminded him. "Unless we get some form of propulsion going and fairly soon, that red giant out there will swallow us up without so much as a burp."

Fisher shot Cholla a familiar look. "How long we got, Doc, before that happens?"

Cholla adjusted his glasses as he considered the question. "We were protected in the lee of the planetoid's barycentre before our knockabout. But without the engines to nudge us back, we're technically out in the open and therefore vulnerable to the star's draw."

The doctor pressed his lips together and looked up for a moment. "As matters stand, it'll depend on a few things. But most especially on the gravitational tides between the star and the crystalline planet, which of course depends on the planet's solar orbit, how close it is to periapsis—its closest point, or perihelion to the sun."

Cholla lifted a hand and wagged his index finger like a lecturer getting to his crucial point. "That might speed things up, but if we are at its furthest point, its aphelion, we should be fine for a few days, a week tops. Then, regardless of orbit, the red giant will begin to exert its gravity. Imperceptibly at first, but the longer we stay out here, eventually push will come to shove. We'll fall headlong, and no amount of thrust can save us. We'll burn up."

Fisher drew his chin back. "So, we tackled the little pricks and their big ugly brothers. And now, Pops 'll jounce us anyway. Bit ironic wouldn't you say?" His question ended with a demented titter.

"What about the shuttlecraft?" Anne proposed.

"We could get out in the shuttle," Baines said, his scepticism plain. "But still wouldn't get very far in this neighbourhood."

"Can we use the tractor beam with this debris, as we did back in the Junkyard?" Cholla asked. "Maybe slingshot us a bit farther out while Jiri deals with the engines? Perhaps we can jury-rig them"

Baines shook his head. "No way, Doc. The tractor conduits got completely FUBARD in the maelstrom. It's the engines or nothing."

Fisher chewed his lip before turning to Jiri. "We all know what takes priority here. Even the ruptures can wait—Baines and I can handle them and besides they're all in auxiliary compartments. I need a firsthand diagnostic appraisal of the engines. You got your work cut out for you, little girl."

The captain turned and fixed Bliter with a stern look. "You can help her. While the rest of us wait for her report, we're gonna conduct our own investigation, Bliter—because it matters to me. The Exarch never found what he claimed to be hunting for, which still leaves something vacant on the other side of that equation. Understand?"

Bliter's eyes smouldered under the captain's scrutiny, but he kept his tongue.

The corner of Fisher's jaw knotted, but he let it pass as he curved his carriage square to Jiri. "Patch in the video feed here before you go."

Giving him a brief nod, Jiri fanned back her cinnamon hair and dropped her head to the console. She placed her hands on the keyboard. Almost immediately she looked up. "Sorry Cap, looks like the connection got fragged when we took the pounding. I'll need to get down to the mainframe and retrieve the files from the video banks directly."

"Great," Fisher said with a touch of asperity. "Any more good news?" The captain ran the palm of his hand along his facial scar as though trying to rub it off. After a moment, he blew out his cheeks. "Okay, do it. Then straight to the engines."

"Will do. I won't need Bliter—not right away." Jiri smiled as she stood and left the bridge.

"I have a theory of my own," Resa said, following Jiri out the door.

Fisher watched him go.

Stephen Fenech

49: Twilight

Fisher

Fisher reached over Baines' shoulder and pressed the button to activate the ship-wide com. "Everybody, muster on the bridge immediately, Jiri you too. Where are you?"

After a slight delay, she answered. "Still here beside the mainframe, Cap. Just accessed the files."

"Good, burn a disk off the hard drive. I want the camera and sensor recordings from every feed starting before the Demons broached the subject to after they went boom. I want to see them all."

"Copy that."

Fisher kneaded his belly absently. Something in his gut bothered him like a strained muscle, but he couldn't quite pin it to any one thought. As he tensed, he noticed Anne staring at him. Her eyebrows worked like confused caterpillars, but before she asked, the sound of footsteps drew his eyes.

Fisher cocked his head as Baines joined them on the bridge, followed by Cholla. The two men seemed to notice it as well for they cast similar frowns in his direction.

"You okay, Fish?" Baines asked.

"Fine," Fisher said. "Three more, then we can finally kn—"

"No—Resa!" Jiri cried over the com. It hadn't been switched off. A din of commotion. Her voice brimming with terror. Both infectious.

"*Nooooh!*" Jiri's blood-draining shriek filled the bridge.

Thunder cracked… Then static.

In the stunned silence, Fisher froze. Until realization took hold. A shock-blast?

Fisher bristled. Hissing between clenched teeth, he sprinted for the door, practically knocking Bliter over on his way out.

"You!" Fisher barked at the startled navigator as he tore past. "Rack-room. Bring guns!" he shouted over his shoulder.

Everyone bounded after the captain. The clamour of their

stomping feet resounded against the floor's metal grates, matching cadence with his pounding heart.

Fisher turned the corner into the engineering rack-room and skidded to a halt. Resa crouched over the sprawled form of Jiri. The captain knew the second he saw her that she was dead, killed by a shock-rifle bullet. The shot had been set to maximum spread, straight through the temple. Not a lot of blood where the projectile entered her skull and lodged, but its forward pressure wave left a horrific mess behind her head.

Floundering for expression Fisher blurted, "Stand back, you fuck."

Resa stood up slowly, but when his eyes met Fisher's, he blanched. "Wait one minute, Captain. This isn't how it looks. I found Jiri dead."

"Nice try, Asswipe." Fisher stabbed a trembling finger at the com-station beside Resa. "We all heard her over the com!" The captain burned like white fire, unable to shirk the torturous thought of his beloved Jiri murdered, the victim of a heinous act. She resembled an ashen stranger like one of the piled-up corpses of the second holocaust on Alliantha.

Running footsteps. Fisher spun at the sound. Bliter drew up with three shock-rifles, one slung over his back and the other two gripped in each hand. He passed one to Baines and thrust the other in Fisher's hands. "It's loaded."

Fisher took the safety off and trained the rifle directly at Resa's chest, ready to impale him with the barrel. "Now, you piece of shit, slowly back away against the wall."

Resa complied, putting his hands up in a placating gesture. His surety, his pretence of officious piety, all gone now. The Tolkane seemed only mechanically cognizant as though genuinely fazed by something he did not grasp, or simply another ploy? Prevaricating, knowing he was pinned and wriggling and fucking guilty as charged? Resa's face always made it hard to tell.

Fisher's own detachment mirrored that of Resa, as if they felt and thought the same thing... causality.

Something clicked, bringing Fisher out of his trance—Baines and Bliter unlatching the safeties of their rifles. When they raised them in line with his own, the captain thrust his jaw out in grim approval. And Resa stood before them, unmoving like a statue awaiting a vandal's cudgel.

Cholla's face creased in tight-lined confusion. His shoulders trembled as he took in the inexorable scene and the woe it promised. Only Anne's hard-pressed lips and set jaw revealed a firm doubt. Catching a glint of that look was the only thing that stayed Fisher's finger from where it quivered on his rifle's trigger.

The quandary became a cell, its air thick with doubt and suppressed violence.

Fisher breathed.

Resa breathed.

Anne spoke. "Captain, please, do I really need to spell it out for you? There's a fucking orgy of evidence. Before we judge Resa on what we think we heard, what we think we see, let's look at all the facts. Fisher?"

"I see fine," Fisher remonstrated. "She's fucking dead, Anne. Dead!"

"I know, but be rational. Think, motive."

Fisher hesitated, but his vision fuelled his ire, made it self-actuating, made him resist.

"Roland."

Anne's voice cut through the captain's dark ether, not so much by the fact that she addressed him by his first name, but by her lifting tone, which supported a great deal more. It punched through his roadblock of angst and he found he could at least begin to think matters through.

A few tense moments later, it decided him. "Baines, play back the video logger right here while we all wait. Let's see, what we see."

Baines lowered his weapon and moved over to the CPU mainframe, now stained crimson with the backsplash of Jiri's lifeblood. Propping the rifle against the console, he attacked the keyboard, fingers flying deftly as he tapped each keystroke. His face tilted up to the monitor to check his figures. He pressed his lips to a thread's width before launching another keystroke barrage. It went on for a few minutes.

Finally, Baines turned and faced his captain. He slowly shook his head. "All erased, Fish. It's gone."

"How convenient." Fisher couched the butt of his weapon under his shoulder and lined his eye with the sight, toward its Tolkane mark. "Okay Anne, now you got your motive."

"Have you even considered," Resa scorned in a voice of steel, "that maybe Jiri was the one doing the erasing?"

"Right," Fisher said, his tone dripping with sarcasm. "She erases the logger, then erases herself? Do I look like an asshole? You were the only one in this area close enough *to* kill her, to carry out your fucking crime. Everyone else was up on the bridge or thereabouts."

"Your line of thinking is flawed, Captain. What about the weapon I allegedly used to murder her? Shouldn't it be close by, if I shot her as you suggest?"

"He's got a point, Fisher," Anne said.

Fisher lowered his rifle and flung her a corrosive glare. "Don't you dare, Anne, not in this."

Anne threw up her hands. "Fisher!"

"No!" he flared.

But a moment later, Fisher hammered his boot on the metal floor. He wheeled on Cholla. "Doc, go see if you can find anything. Follow your nose. Think sulphur, ozone. Start in the vicinity, then fan out."

Cholla dry-swallowed, his number elevens working meticulously while his eyes darted between Fisher and Resa. He clearly doubted the Tolkane had done any harm to Jiri, but by his hesitation, Doc also didn't want to further rile his captain. Tempers had flared to a flashpoint.

Fisher snarled like a dragon about to breathe fire. Doc retreated a step—the middling, unprepared knight about to get torched.

At length, Cholla pursed his lips and jiggled his chin briskly. Mouth sagging into a grimace, he turned and hastened out of the room without another word.

Once Cholla left, Fisher trained his scowl on Resa. "So, how you gonna defend your alibi? Why would Jiri mention your name on the com a second before she swallows a bullet? Explain that one away, Mr *Fugitive*. If Cholla finds the weapon you won't have to worry about the Demons having their way with you. Make it easier on yourself. Stop the pointless charade and fess the fuck up."

Resa groaned. "I didn't kill Jiri, and I didn't erase the logger. I didn't even know you *had* any stupid footage."

"And I didn't take you for a murdering, son-of-a-bitchin' saboteur. Words are vacuum. Maybe you went and sold out the Cardinal—kept the Demons in the loop ever since we thawed your evil ass. What are you hiding now, Resa?"

"Nothing."

"Baines told me about a certain com-link we found: from the *Skow II* back to the dockyard on Ursula Minor, shortly after we thawed you. The same dockyard the Exarch destroyed. How can that be when the *Skow II* never docked there? I only brought the original *Skow* there. The secret homer Anne found points to you too."

Fisher swept the muzzle of his rifle towards the console. "But this surveillance recording wasn't something you anticipated. Not part of your grand plan, that we'd check such things after our conversation with the late Exarch. You had to devise something pretty quick for that one, eh?" *I have a theory of my own.*

"Open your eyes, man!" Resa thundered. "That packet was yours anyway. You had it in your possession while I was still in cryo. Maybe it was your Funder?"

"My Funder got killed, aboard the *Maelstrom,* so maybe it was your Funder," Fisher roared back.

"That's—quite possible, now that you mention it." Resa's change in tone surprised everyone. He seemed to find his calm again and centred on it, which Fisher found disconcerting. "He'd been part of the same envoy as Vorancia's suicide bomber. As for the *Mael*—"

Fisher barked in triumph. "So, you admit there's a tie. The assassin, the Funder, and you."

"Yes, but I didn't know my Funder, except for the recovery job he hired me to do, and I never met him face to face. Just an avatar or an associate. Speaking of which—"

"We don't know your Funder," Fisher cut him off a second time, "or any of his associates either, except you. You are his representative, so you're accountable, and as long as you're alive the threat you pose is the threat he posed."

Resa let out an exasperated grunt. "That's assuming he's behind this, but even so, I was never part of it. I'm no iconoclast and definitely no assassin. The job he recruited me for—in that, I was also betrayed, remember? Fisher, you're letting your emotions rule your mind."

"Fuck you." Fisher spat. His pupils dropped to Jiri. "You got no goddam idea—watching my crew get picked off one by one!"

Resa faltered for a second. He kept swallowing as if forcing down several waves of repressed anguish. At length, he met Fisher's dragon fire. "Yes, I do." His answer only made Fisher smoulder more.

Resa exhaled, tilted his head to the ground and rubbed his temple. "Look, Captain, I didn't murder Jiri or sabotage any part of this mission. I've helped it." He lifted his gaze and sought Fisher's face. "It was my idea to reactivate Beacon, which led to Anne's reincarnation, remember? I've been integral in helping it."

"To your own end," Fisher retorted. "Where's Beacon now? He was wise to you, but wouldn't let me follow his hunch because of his fixation on causality. No, Resa, you've harried this mission at every turn. I'm a real asshole if you expect me to believe that. You did do it. Admit it!"

Resa raised his hands in surrender. "Okay, Fisher. I admit it— I think you're a real asshole."

Fisher took the slight with volatile calm. "I doubted you right from the start, but *Wisdan* implored me to trust you. He's probably rolling in his grave over that one."

"You leave the Cardinal out of this."

Fisher went on as if he didn't hear Resa's reprimand. "Maybe you beguiled the Cardinal at some point. He hands you divinity, and you hand him duplicity. Maybe you used the fat man to gain access to our meanderings prior to your thaw. Or maybe he was your Funder and set us all up."

Resa stared while Fisher shook with conviction.

"Maybe he was the fugitive, the missing link and you, his rat, his go-to flunky lickspittle. Maybe *he* sent you to the Stricken, or maybe you sent *yourself* and you're the faceless-cock-sucking-Funder!"

"And maybe," Resa said in a defeated tone, "you're insane."

"The Exarch mentioned someone tried to pull Beacon off Anne's grave-world and failed. He meant you."

"No." The Tolkane punctuated his adamancy by stomping his foot against the grating. It let out a metallic clash. "When Shyce and I went down there, we found a tunnel already excavated. Someone had gone down there before us."

"Prove it."

Resa pressed upturned palms to his face. "You know I can't."

"Exactly, the fact of the matter is we can't ask Beacon, we can't ask the Exarch, and we can't ask Wisdan. We can only take your word, on what? Faith?" Fisher's lilt of contempt showed how much stock he took in that notion. His glance swept back towards Jiri's corpse again. The ghost of her last imploring words echoed in the captain's mind: *No—Resa...*

Blood running hot, Fisher opened his mouth to renew his litany when the com pinged loudly.

"Captain?" *Cholla—at last.*

"Yeah, go ahead, Doc."

"I've found the weapon."

"Where is it?"

A considerable amount of hesitation followed at the other end of the channel.

"Well?" Fisher demanded.

"It's... it's in Resa's quarters," Cholla confirmed. "Looks like it was fired recently. Barrel's still hot."

Hearing the news, Resa's knees wobbled and he pressed a hand flat against his chest. He looked heartsick. But then, his pallid features turned red as he rallied his anger. "*Gatcham*—I'm being set up."

Cholla's voice echoed over the com again. "Something else, Captain."

"Just get down here." Fisher cut the com-link and railed on Resa. "I've heard enough and seen as much. You're a bane, a real fucking monster. But no more. It's time to prosecute." He aimed at Resa's heart.

Resa's face tightened into his familiar I-refuse-to-be-flustered look. He regarded Fisher evenly, his head whisker standing at attention. "Listen to me, Captain, listen with more than your ears. You're good at that, remember?"

Resa had always been the nonlinear type, talking in riddles to build the mystery, but something cut through to Fisher now. The captain sensed his suspect sought some sort of tangency with him. And he responded as though undergoing a startling revelation, a stigma biting deep into his mind.

Fisher rolled his eyes back feeling the pull of a spell as it penetrated his cortex. His irises widened as sudden cognizance seized his mind. He touched his head, squirmed a little, then a lot, raised his rifle to the ceiling, directed the muzzle at the floor. Something invasive like an untried drug troubled his ability to reason. He faced the others.

By their open mouths, they clearly saw him trip to the point of real indecision, real pain, frustration. Rage. A silent war between obstinacy and supplication? He could not form an opinion one way or another, except—

"Don't you fucking dare!" Fisher rasped. He braced his legs

and stabbed the rifle forward again in a textbook display of choler and hostility.

"If you don't listen," Resa snapped. "We're *all* dead. Get it?"

"I'm not listening to you. I make my own decisions, got that?"

"Fine!" Resa shouted, taking a step forward. "If you won't listen then go ahead you stupid, truculent, half-breed bastard."

"don't…" Fisher's resolve crumbled under the brazen Tolkane's relentless lashing.

But Resa's face reddened into a mask of defiance. "I do what I must. But you?" He leaned forward and stabbed a quivering finger at Fisher. "You don't have the stomach or the balls to be captain when it comes down to it. Jiri's death is your fault and the guilt is eating you alive. That's what you're *thinking*, isn't it? You didn't pull the trigger, but you did kill her. So, why not one more, you dickless fuck?"

Undeterred, Resa took another, bolder step forward, bringing him within a metre of the business end of Fisher's rifle. "You'll wind up killing your whole crew. Then make no mistake, you won't be far behind. Only then, when you're all alone, your menace *finally* contained, about to die with no one left *to* blame, will you realize what a gods-up-the-yin-yang, mother-fucking ass-*HOLE* you are!"

Fisher opened his mouth to protest, closed it again. His eyes softened.

Then he pulled the trigger.

Stephen Fenech

50: Malefactor
Fisher

When the shock-rifle bullet passed through Resa's heart, the Tolkane collapsed, lolling neatly to one side in a foetal position. Resa appeared as reserved in death as he had been in life. Unlike the shot that'd caused Jiri's fatal wound, Fisher did not set his rifle to maximum. Apart from the small cauterized entry and exit wound in Resa's chest, he displayed no other sign that he died. He seemed so peaceful, he might've been asleep.

But he was deceased, as Fisher confirmed when he bent down beside the inert Tolkane and found no sign of breathing and no pulse. Resa placidly stared past the captain's crouched form, gazing up at heaven. He looked serene as though his karma had gained ultimate *Wu Wei* in Nirvana.

The sound of bounding steps drew the crew's heads to the entrance. But Fisher hadn't finished his examination. While their backs were turned, he patted down Resa's jacket. And found something very odd in one of its side pockets. He fished it out. Quietly depositing it in his own pocket, he rose to join the others as Cholla charged into view.

Doc possessed the mind of a genius, no doubt there, but physically a blunder—not obese but round about his midsection like an owl that had eaten one too many field mice. So, when he stopped short of the crew, spectacles askew, he immediately bent forward and braced his hands on his knees, too winded to speak.

"Cap let Resa have it," Baines informed him as Cholla tried to get his breathing under control. The doctor's features contorted into constricted lines of horror.

"Spit it out, Doc," Fisher said brusquely.

One hand still fixed on a knee, Cholla raised his other, palm out in a defensive plea for more time. Meanwhile, he continued to pant. "Looking for, weapon, ch-checked the systems, ship-wide diagnostics."

"And?"

Cholla overcame a short coughing fit, cleared his throat and straightened. "We're banged up pretty bad to be sure, but not as bad as Jiri led us to believe," he went on in his usual didactic tone. "The relays from the CPU's video and sensor feeds: all those connections and pathways are intact. In fact, from what I could tell, we never experienced any interruption and should have been able to see the feed from up on the bridge, at any time."

"Jiri lied," Anne finished for him.

The doctor adjusted his spectacles and nodded.

"Lied?" Fisher's hackles rose. He didn't believe it. The implication of what Jiri had allegedly done, what that meant, sent Fisher dovetailing into a pit of confusion and despair. And yet, he couldn't afford to address it here. He didn't trust himself to say anything to that effect, but closer to the truth, he didn't trust any of the others.

Running on instinct, fuelled by adrenaline, Fisher steadied his wits and focused. "Okay Bliter, Baines, clean this catastrophe up." He thrust his chin at the corpses. "Put those bodies on ice. Then hop into engineering. See if there's anything be done with the engines. Bliter, with Jiri gone, you're the most qualified. Cholla, get up to the bridge and monitor—now that we know we can," he added bitterly. "I'm sure you'll help best from up there.

"Copy that," Cholla said. "Anything else, Cap?"

"No, I'll come up and help you with any peripherals after I get some painkillers from the med lab. I got a planet-cracking headache that just won't quit." Fisher turned to Anne. "Come with me. I could use the company—and the counsel."

The crew began to disperse.

Anne raised a hand. "Hang on." Her strident tone stopped everyone in their tracks. "Nobody leaves." Her eyes narrowed as they found Fisher. "What did you put in your pocket?"

"Sorry?" Fisher shot her a sideways look. But if Anne's die-cast jaw gave any indication, she was having none of it.

She put her hands on her hips. "Captain, you removed something from Resa's jacket. I saw you."

Fisher let his shoulders slump as he reached into his pocket and pulled out a small disk for all to see. The crew's mouths fell open.

"Wanted to examine it first," Fisher confessed. "With you."

"We have a perfectly good monitor here. Let's see what we see, now—no more disappearing acts, okay?"

Fisher reluctantly handed the disk to Baines. "Do it."

Baines returned to the console with everyone gathered round, watching the display. Out of his peripheral, Fisher warily surveyed the small audience to gauge their facial reactions. So far, nothing.

"Ho—lee Shit!" Baines exalted.

"It's the missing security feeds," Anne guessed. "Isn't it?"

"Bingo."

"Well, let's take a closer look," she said.

"Okay, there are two files," Baines began. "External, for everything captured on closed-circuit outside the ship, and internal, which would have everything that went on inside the ship during that time window. I think we should take a look at the internal first."

The reel showed a multi-frame image, divided evenly into nine squares. Each square cut to a different camera every three seconds. A security clock with rapidly scrolling numbers keyed on top of the image.

Baines pointed to one of the squares. "This is us on the bridge when I started the recording, about the time Beacon returned from the crystalline planet and hailed us."

They all watched the entire reel play like nine simultaneous and equally boring movies, until the apocalyptic jarring when the Imperium ships detonated and turned the dark into a tempestuous blaze of light and energy. The images shook violently, light strobing in certain frames, then all nine recordings abruptly cut to black and the clock's flashing numbers froze.

"That's the last frame," Baines said.

"Play it again," Anne directed. Baines complied and the movie repeated, showing the same melange of corridor scenes, high bridge angles, crew cabin clips, just as unrevealing as the first pass.

"Again," Anne instructed. Baines looked to Fisher who only shrugged. The captain knew something had occurred to Anne, something none of them noticed, himself included. The only thing he did discern for certain was Jiri's feigned report of the video relay.

From the camera's ceiling view over her head, he saw the console where her fingers only brushed the keys, but hadn't pressed a single one. Her head turned and she lied to his face, exactly as Cholla had said.

But why? Could it be that she had some suspicion about the potential suspect, the same inkling piquing Anne's percipience now?

Everyone watched to the very end.

After the third pass, Anne repeated her command. "One more time, Baines, please."

"This is ridiculous," Bliter baulked. "How many times are we going to sit through this reel? Why don't you check the exterior footage already, so we can do something productive like, oh I don't know, *fix the bloody engines* before we die? I'm tired of reruns."

"And you would know a lot about reruns, wouldn't you, Bliter?" Anne's voice dripped with rhetoric.

"The fuck is that supposed to mean?" the navigator snapped.

"Oh, I think you know exactly what I mean," Anne said.

The crewman's haughtiness wavered. He fell silent.

Anne grunted, her eyes never leaving Bliter. "Baines, belay my last request. I know the truth of it now. Seen, and heard, everything I need."

"Morrison, maybe you should look in the mirror before you make any more accusations," Bliter spat, his cheeks flushing crimson. "I think the level of trust aboard this ship has strained thin enough without you starting any more rumours."

"Rumours?" Anne smiled from out of one side of her mouth. She looked bitterly amused. "*Rumours?*" Apparently, Fisher wasn't the only one who caught on to Bliter's suspect tone, guised beneath the navigator's sudden umbrage.

Anne fixed Bliter with a cold stare. "We've all watched the playback three damn times now, proof-positive to quell any rumours. Resa just sacrificed his life to quash any rumours. And I'm going to prove to the others that this is no rumour."

Doubt surfaced on Bliter's sour face. He opened his mouth, about to say something, hesitated, clenched fists around his rifle, though ever so slightly. Much to Fisher's relief, the crewman relaxed his digits.

Even so, Fisher tightened his grip on his own weapon.

"How can you explain, when you left the bridge feeling 'nauseous,' so conveniently just before the Demons started scanning and Baines began recording, why you're not on any of the cameras' collective footage?" Anne asked, her words all sword points. "You're not hurrying away from the bridge, not jogging through the corridors, not whacking off in your cabin, or tossing your cookies in the shitter."

Bliter looked away, drew a breath, then released it. When his eyes found Anne again, they trembled. He offered nothing.

"How can it be that not a single frame captured you on internal?" Anne's tone sharpened to a razor's edge. "Did you suddenly fancy a little EVA? To clear your head at that precise moment when the scanning commenced? Maybe, if Baines plays back the exterior clips, we'll see you doing a little two-step on the hull."

Anne leaned in closer to Bliter. "I think not. I think you've been skulking in the shadows ever since you came aboard this ship, playing this game and using us all like pieces in your little war against the Imperium. I think you are more than what I see before me. That you've played this game before, long before Fisher, long before Resa, and indeed long before me."

Eyes widening, Cholla and Baines exchanged nervous glances. Both bit their lips. Fresh sweat trickled down Fisher's back. The gun's metal suddenly felt slick in his palms.

"Where were you?" Anne pressed in an accusatory tone. "Where the fuck were you, Bliter, or should I just call you, *Blythe*?"

In the protracted silence, the crew gaped, faces locked on Bliter, trying to decipher his response. They found none. The navigator fell reticent, no longer refuting Anne's allegations.

Then, much to the captain's shock and chagrin, a thin wintry smile crept across Bliter's scowl. The crewman shouldered his rifle and let out a faint chuckle, which eventually broke into a quiet mirthless laugh as cold and bleak as the winds of an ice age.

Bliter slowly raised his hands, eyes glued to Anne. He began clapping, in excruciatingly slow measured beats. Every connection made a wooden, funereal sound.

51: Blythe
Fisher

"Your intuition has served you well, Dr Morrison," Bliter said. He adopted the same 'British' accent Anne mentioned this Blythe had used. For Fisher's amusement, she often imitated his voice when quoting her former boss. But now, staring at the devil himself, the captain felt anything but.

"As it did with your ancestor, Old Percival," Bliter went on. "Now that the rapacious Imperium has been expunged from this realm, I no longer need to keep this disgusting corporeal form, but I will stomach it a while yet to humour you with a brief explanation."

"What do you mean by *expunged*?" asked Fisher. "Beacon just took care of the ships in the immediate sector and the hundred or so capital ships still in sensor range. By Demon standards, all he did was give their hornet's nest a good hard kick."

Again, that cold fulsome laugh. "You would think that, given the strictures of your feeble mind, a birthright common to all of your innocuous races. But I've known the Demons a little better and somewhat longer than you, Captain." Bliter emphasized the title like a curse. "Still, you couldn't have grasped that even this scale of destruction merely served as the spark that set off the powder keg.

"Beacon, as you called him has always been my faithful, obsequious instrument, long before the Demons ever found him and tried to corrupt his circuitry to suit their purpose. Still, I let them tinker as they would. Let them believe they had found and sequestered a valuable asset, a weapon against me. Beacon worked as *my* scout, *my* lapdog. And by way of extension, so too did the dogs of the entire Garaxian Imperium."

Bliter looked down at his com-pad and smiled as if getting some expected result. "But thanks to you, no longer can the ID fulfil their drive for eugenics, their insatiable lust for conquest and dominion over the realm. They do not pose a threat to my own devices anymore."

Bliter's face rose to meet Anne's. "Of those devices, Beacon functioned as my *machina infernalis,* always following my orders throughout all the ridiculous exercises you put him through, Dr Morrison, and the obscene ploys the Imperium exercised. Beneath the fabric of assumed control, the core of his being ultimately served my purpose.

"What purpose?" Fisher asked.

"A thorough cleansing of the ID, for one," Bliter answered. "I knew once they downloaded what they thought was the technology to eradicate me—tech I devised to annihilate them, Beacon gained custody of their computers."

"He would be the right one to do it," Anne remarked. "But how?"

"When the Exarch accessed his security protocols—as I knew the predictable mummer would—Beacon reaped them from behind his back and made them his own. Not just a chapter's worth or the contents of a volume but their entire multi-level gods-be-damned library."

Bliter exhaled joyously, his eyes softening for a moment. "Each protocol worked differently. After being locked in pitched battle with the Demons for as long as I have, one comes to know how all of their ships network, hardwired to receive the Exarch's infamous kill order. It hovered over every single Garaxian from birth."

Bliter unshouldered his shock-rifle and held it loosely in his hands. Casually he pointed the barrel at Resa's corpse. "Chk-chk boom—and pop go the weasels." Muzzle still pointed to the floor, he turned back to the crew, staring rapt in disbelief. "The directive forced all of their ships' engines to breach containment, go critical mass and detonate. Power generators in all their bases and stations, the same. The planets proved a bit trickier of course. Executed on a case-by-case scenario, each one had a unique instruction set attached to impel natural triggers that produced my calamitous repercussions."

Bliter divulged the details of a few bombardments like a notorious comic delivering the punch line of an inappropriate joke. "But it all came back to their infamous plasma, turning the very foundation of their late empire on them like a doomsday bomb."

An oscillating whine buzzed loud enough to turn heads and cut off the crewman's diatribe mid-gloat. The *Skow II* also complained visually—on the same screen Baines had used to view Resa's disk.

A cross-section map of the ship appeared, accompanied by flashing yellow dots at various points and a warning in bold red font. The ship's alarm insisted on the crew's immediate attention.

Fisher threw it the briefest of glances to digest its warning: the inertia compensation attitude jets would soon stop compensating. He reached over the console and entered an override code. Once he'd silenced the alarm, he turned back to Bliter.

"All incurred devastation on a scale even the Demons weren't prepared to handle. Indeed, they never could have fathomed such a simultaneous retaliation. But my long experience antedates anything you've ever seen them do. I've witnessed them dreaming up some real masterpieces. The Amalgam can attest to that."

"The Amalgam?" Cholla asked, tilting his head to one side in genuine curiosity.

"Another war-bred empire, six-trillion-strong at the height of its power, before it fell to the Imperium's temporal displacement bombs," Bliter explained, his focus drifting into the mid-distance. "They were equally if not eviller than the Ice Demons—a race of cannibals that ate their captives—I steered clear and let the Imperium deal with them. Their conflict led to an epic war which lasted the better part of a century, but in the end, the Imperium triumphed, saving me the trouble of treating with the savages."

Cholla inhaled, his marvel plain in his brightening eyes. "When did this happen?"

"Oh, millions of years ago, Doctor. But since then, the Demons have remained implacable, unchallenged by any would-be aggressors. With its immeasurable military might, the Imperium could not be engaged head-on. Their manifesto became the only law in the Universe."

Bliter faced the others again. "So, a little indemnity was overdue after being harried by them for so very long."

Fisher tongued the inside of his cheek as he observed. *Another history lesson—something was brewing as it had with the Exarch. Same shit, different asshole.*

"Beacon let fly all of the late Exarch's commands kept in his extensive troves," said Bliter, "executing my final edict with the same impunity the Imperium showed your pitiful planet. You do remember that, don't you, Dr Morrison?"

This time, Bliter leaned in. "Found yourself trapped there when the plasmatic sphere wrapped and suffocated the world."

Anne's jaw tightened. "Beacon told me. I don't need to be reminded by the likes of you."

Bliter flared. "I remind you because you should be more grateful. I've guided and nurtured you from your meagre beginnings, facilitating your earliest discoveries aboard the *Stormwatcher.* On my orders, Beacon offered to save you on the cusp of Earth's annihilation."

"To your own end," Anne retorted. "So, forgive me if I don't say thanks."

Bliter smiled. "You helped me bring down the Imperium, creating my magnum opus, so it stands that you already have."

"If you believe that, you're deluding yourself," Fisher quaffed. "You'll get yours, and I'm willing to bet you're not going to like it."

Bliter drew back and heckled. "Coming from a decrepit man who waffles in the face of brinkmanship and war, your bane means all of nothing to me. It must irk you to know how I bested you. After all, you did execute the wrong man."

Fisher did not rise to Bliter's riposte. He became thoughtful for a moment as the crewman preached.

Bliter slowly nodded, his lips hard with tight lines of vindication. "You do get some credit for my victory, but not all.

Beacon has been the real star of this charade, using the Garaxians' own weapons against them."

For some reason, Bliter's eyes dropped to Jiri's corpse, where they lingered and made Fisher wrinkle his nose.

Bliter lifted his gaze. "Up until now, they've never been defeated, so they truly believed in the Exarch's divinity in all matters. It never occurred to them that 5303's protocols might one day be compromised. As you so eloquently put, Dr Morrison, they always had their finger on the button."

He rolled his wrists, turning the shock-rifle in his hands. "I had Beacon push it. The robot destroyed himself so all the kill orders would not be rescinded. Timing was of the essence."

Trust your robot. Fisher's throat clenched. The smell of the two bodies began to tell, or might it be this bastard's foul mouth? He threw a glance at Anne. Her constricted features indicated she felt the same.

"Don't look so glum," Bliter said with a glib tongue. "The robot's sacrifice was worth it. Exterminating the Demons was the right thing to do. They posed the real infestation here, intruders in your Universe, coming from the darkest place beyond. They were too dangerous to be left alive."

"And what of you?" Anne hissed. "I could say the same of you, Bliter, Blythe—if either is your real name."

"Truthfully, I have no real name, but you are right. I am one and the same. The infamous Funder, Blythe, who infiltrated your planet and sent your ancestor on his goose chase across the ocean in that archaic vessel of his."

"Why?"

"To confirm my harbinger's arrival."

Anne started. "So, you did send the signal to the ID, the message Baron uncovered aboard the Hubble II that led them to target Earth. You entered the response activator within the signal."

"No." Blythe was adamant. "That is something I did not do. Why would I sabotage my own work before it could be completed? That was Beacon—true to his name. Everyone meddled with everyone else. I tinkered with the ID, they tampered with Beacon and the robot played your race."

A grin sliced across the outlier's face. "I'm afraid our game left Humans standing without a chair when the music stopped, but there were others. Beacon held the memories of countless races and more than four hundred destroyed planets, annexed Stricken, all inextricably linked to our trinity of doom."

Beside herself with anger, Anne balled her hands into fists. "Why did so many have to die to satisfy this megalomaniac conflict? It should have been limited to you and the Imperium."

"Why indeed?" Blythe said. "The Demons were the only ones who *could* oppose me. They had the only weapon in existence that might one day defeat me, one that would withstand my own formidable theurgy and entrap me—the only hurdle that kept me in the shadows, standing in the way of my ascendancy over your realm. I had to tread carefully.

Blythe's pupils flitted to the ceiling, then again at the two corpses. He swallowed and breathed.

Fisher's pulse quickened, hearing the silent admission of doubt in his foe's visage and actions. Presuming the captain remained quiet too, he would do without doing—all that needed to get done. *Just let him speak, Fish, and he'll hang himself.*

"As long as I continued in corporeal form, tandem with the matter of this Universe, I remained hidden. But once I regressed into my natural state, they could detect me. I had to use the tools available to me from this realm, namely you."

"What weapon?" Anne asked.

"Please, Doctor, as if I shall tell you. That secret has gone to the grave with the Overlords and Beacon's destruction."

"What is your natural form then?" Cholla put in.

"Isn't it obvious?" Blythe shrugged. "Energy, the truest form of all life, including yours—though in my case, dark energy."

"Is that what happened to you when they scanned our ship? Did you…" Cholla tested the word on his tongue, "transmutate?"

"No, all that would have done is confirm the Imperium's

suspicions. Let's just say I retreated to my safe place."

By the way Blythe said *safe*, Fisher guessed it was anything but.

"Once I had them extinguished from the immediate vicinity, I no longer had much reason to fear, but I still needed to wait a little longer to ascertain if Beacon's death spell met with success everywhere else. That's why I couldn't let you usurp my investigation with your little debacle here."

"You're just as paranoid as the Demons are—were," Anne corrected. "But how did you gain Jiri's allegiance?"

"The same way I tooled my many associates. I *engineered* your engineer to provide another tool for me to exploit. I knew no one would question little lovable Jiri as she hurried out to erase the video stream."

"No one except Resa," said Fisher. "Or was he one of yours too?"

"Resa was no associate, but like Jiri, another expendable utensil. I needed to pin Jiri's removal on someone. It seemed pragmatic and more than a little convenient. I must admit, Captain, you surprised me with that bit of news about the cameras."

Within the ague of speculation and revelation, Fisher saw red. "Are you saying Resa told the truth, and you just stood by and let me shoot him? Worse than any abomination, you're a spineless monster with no balls."

"But then," Anne interjected, "After we learned that Resa burned a copy, you let us see it anyway. Why?"

"At that point, it no longer mattered. I received my confirmation about the Demons' eradication. Had the Captain not revealed his little secret about the cameras, Resa would still be alive."

Fisher let the sally pass before turning it on its heels. "Even if I didn't shoot him, I'm sure his fate would have been decided by you, what, an hour later? Whatever you really are, you only think you've won. The ID may be gone but their threat still looms. And one day, in some form or another, it'll rear its ugly head and come for you. I think you're certain of nothing."

Blythe snickered. "Never your strong suit, Captain—thinking. My dominance over your realm is assured. It has already begun. Once I revert to my true form, my strength will cycle up and so long as I remain in that state, my power will continue to grow unabated and with greater alacrity. No one will ever oppose me again. It's funny that such bizarre meanderings of so many fates have produced this marvel of synchronicity. Events have merged unto the singularity of my purpose."

"How so?" Anne asked, crossing her arms and giving him a long look.

Blythe opened his mouth to explain, checked himself, and chose to let her question slide. "I have watched from the gloom and manipulated my tools deftly and patiently. As you probably guessed, I funded the late Resa's efforts. Subsidised both of yours. Interesting how your three paths, though separated by a span of three-and-a-half thousand years, have intertwined, leading to the very crux of the Juncture. Do you realize, Anne, this confluent moment marks the very nexus predicted in Baron Fieldbank's causality model?"

Baines threw his hands up. "Okay, Bliter, Blythe, *thing,* you sent us on a collision course with destiny—I get it, but start from the beginning, so us little folk can understand your 'godly' what-the-fuck-for?"

"You appreciate my divine mantle, apace with its revelation," Blythe mused. "But even if you only ask to forestall me, it will avail you nothing. Still, while my might gathers, drinking measures of energy from the red giant—my purest and most coveted succour, I'll oblige your curiosity a little longer."

In the ensuing quiescence, Fisher exchanged a worried look with Anne. Another engine alarm tripped, accompanied by a steady *ping, ping, ping, ping.* Baines took the initiative this time and silenced the sound, but not its import.

"I built Beacon," Blythe declared. "Sent the robot to the Demons. They believed it to be their discovery. The robot became

384

their appropriated sentinel—and my mole. When the Demons overhauled him after a long period of voyages for them, they parsed my tampering with their security protocols, enough to comprehend the threat I posed. I am, after all, a being of energy *and* thought, which can infiltrate mechanical or biological forms at will."

For the second time, Blythe shouldered his rifle. Then he steepled his fingers and abandoned that too. *Why so fidgety?* "They reverse-engineered Beacon to some degree, which allowed them to decipher the aspect of my essence corrupting his circuitry. On that, they began to focus their energies, attenuating their surveillance systems to key on my anomalous signature—my DNA as it were. Thus, the weapon could be likened to a double-edged sword, cutting both ways. The game was afoot."

"Some game," Fisher said in an acrid tone. His fingernails scraped his rifle's butt hard enough to shave shrapnel.

Blythe caught the movement and smirked. "Across the epochs, they knew when I returned in my true form because I *let* them know. I had to recapture my indentured robot to check my enemy's movements, as did they in their efforts to fish me out. The robot had always been pivotal to both parties, instilling a kind of interdependence.

"By the time Beacon found his way to the Dovan, the Demons gave the android their fullest heed to oust me for good. They gleaned the endgame drew nigh, one that would finish in their triumph or their annihilation. They also learned enough of what the Dovan devised, again at my behest. They panicked."

Anne started. "You lived *amongst* the Dovan?"

"Not just with them, I emulated them, becoming a highly respected Dovani scientist and philanthropist. My new ploy on their planet made the Imperium quite fearful—well beyond simple xenophobia.

"They considered terminating Beacon, but to destroy the robot would forever leave them shrouded in doubt of me, so the ID struck the world instead. But not before the Dovan sent the robot to you, Anne. The Demons intercepted him before he came to Earth, tampered with his innards, placed him in one of their shuttle pods and let him continue his journey with a few modifications and a small helping of plasma to speed things up."

Cholla took off his spectacles. "What had the Dovan conceived?"

Blythe clicked his tongue. "Apart from the tech involving the catalyst down there, the Imperium feared what amounted to a farce I conjured, rooted in enough supporting theory and design to make it seem completely plausible. I contrived a time travel machine, fuelled by tachyons—and had the Dovan build actual prototypes—with Beacon's help of course. Then, to the Demons, Beacon let slip internal communications and schematics.

"That stuck a thorn in the Exarch's claws. He actually believed the Dovan could build these devices, travel back in time and with the Amalgam's aid, wipe out his precious Imperium while still in its infancy."

Blythe shook his head and grinned as if amazed by young children's naiveté. "So, the Dovan sent Beacon to Earth where I awaited aboard the *Blue Wind,* an archaic sailing ship commanded by Dr Morrison's forebear, to retrieve him. But something stayed my hand when I saw *how* he arrived. Call it instinct concerning the Demons' desperation. Beacon, I suspected, had been booby-trapped, the trap set for me in my true form."

Despite his meekness, Cholla's ears perked up. The lines of his face firmed into a studious cast. Fisher shifted his focus from the doctor to Baines. Like himself, the pilot fingered his rifle's trigger less idly. For the moment, both barrels remained pointed at the floor. But Fisher knew his weapon's muzzle would soon defy gravity. And discharge.

Anne's scrutiny looked past Blythe. Something in her eyes seemed to espy some faraway place.

"Since time didn't matter," Blythe went on, "I contented to remain hiding in my human form as I built up my resources—easily done with small expenditures of true energy. I expedited the development of Earth's tech through conventional means until Humans could reach some semblance of parity. Toyed with materials and with minds."

Blythe faced Anne, drawing her attention once more. "After you recovered Beacon, and he successfully nullified the Demons' latest trap for me, I instructed him to continue the work he started on Dovan—the real project for me. The Demons now had their own communication protocol with the robot so they didn't need to be in Earth-space to know the situation. To them, Beacon worked towards their purpose. They monitored from afar until the automaton told them something they didn't like, probably about me, but I can't be certain."

"I thought he served you," Anne remarked.

Blythe flashed and his tone sharpened. "Yes, yes, yes, but he could think for himself. Given that his actions fell into line with my general plan, I allowed him a measure of latitude to improvise. As stated, Beacon, not I, put the right words in the right ears on that one." He touched a finger to his ear before pointing it at Anne. "As for your planet, it was already hastening to its doom without the Garaxians' help. I merely sped up the process."

"But you forced the Exarch's hand," Anne protested.

"True, but the Demons naturally decided the time had come for Earth to go, after your progress, and Baron's with the weapon. Still, the ID never intended the plasma bomb that struck Earth to simply kill your planet. They meant for it to roust me. I needn't tell you about the Imperium's penchant for overkill."

"Okay," Anne ceded past gritted teeth. "But why did they send the plasma surge across normal space instead of just invading with a bunch of capital ships as they annexed those other planets?"

"Do you really need me to tell you why?"

"Beacon?"

"Aye, Beacon. The Demons wanted to see what your race would do, knowing your fate ahead of the attack, curious too what I would do. But most importantly, they needed to see what Beacon would do. It was... a test. I escaped, of course, safely hidden in my human guise. By helping to fund Baron's little exodus, I reserved my seat on one of his ships, prior to the first holocaust.

"The Imperium rendered Earth Stricken and then surveilled it with bases dug deep at either pole and in deepest orbit. This time, Beacon elected to remain when the ID struck. Locked in the Stricken's hardened plasma, he became their bait to lure me out in the open.

"They waited for me to respond to Beacon's transponder. And I did but only got so far before they closed in. I transmuted into the building first. That blink into my true state went unnoticed. Same reversion that enabled me to kill Jiri, plant the evidence in Resa's cabin and get close to the bridge in a matter of seconds."

Fisher's nostrils flared and he tightened his grip on his shock-rifle to something beyond white-knuckled. But another something inside urged him to keep calm.

"In corporeal form, I walked down the building as Resa had done," Blythe continued. "I excavated the tunnel from my Phoenix skyscraper to Beacon's ID pod, but that's as far as I got. By regressing into my true state and using my energy to burrow the tunnel, I exposed myself to the Demons' sensors and set off a perimeter alarm. I fled.

"Though the Imperium wanted Beacon back that much more, to extract all your new developments on the tech they so feared, they chose to stay put, confine the entire sector, and strengthen their surveillance and defences instead. Haunted by their ignorance, exacerbated by my incursion, they still knew they held the master card.

"Unfortunately for me, breaking Beacon out on my own was no longer possible. With the entire sector placed under quarantine and the security grid around the Stricken impregnable to my nature, I stayed off the radar for a century or thereabouts, after which time I re-emerged as a Funder from Centauris X. As such, I retained the services of Captain Resa to finish what I could not. I funded his expedition down to the Stricken. As you know, he proved somewhat successful, able to at least extract Beacon off the surface and out of the Demons' hands but still not quite in my own. After such a long hiatus the game of games was afoot for merely one play before another interruption, albeit a much shorter one."

Blythe turned to Fisher. "That's when you came into the picture, Captain. Where I failed with Resa's sortie, I amended with yours. But to guarantee I got my robot back, I had to be aboard your ship during Beacon's recovery. So, after shirking the Funder persona—"

Blythe removed one hand from his weapon and placed it over his heart. Then jutted his chin as though taking an oath. "I became yours truly, Navigator Saul Bliter. I killed the real cur of course when you sent him my way and joined your pitiful band, offering a few carrots I knew you wouldn't pass up."

Fisher suddenly remembered the Funder's stealth upgrades as well as Bliter's sudden pull with the men in the dockyard to make them look the other way.

The captain himself had pulled some tenuous strings in his time. Being born to an underground economy that revolved around and supported itself on greased palms, secret favours, underhandedness and shady, sometimes dangerous deals, Fisher recalled giving Bliter the benefit of the doubt. He never questioned how the navigator had done it. But now in hindsight maybe he should have.

As matters stood, Bliter hadn't served aboard the *Skow* for very long before the gig came up, so his signing on to crew for Fisher was tantamount to signing his own death warrant. A fate that would soon follow captain and crew, once this imposter finished his smug explanation.

Blythe's voice brought him back from his dark meanderings. "But one carrot I kept to myself was the hidden scanner I stowed aboard the *Skow* to locate and reactivate Beacon. I couldn't risk you not taking the job for having my alien technology aboard your ship. For having me aboard.

"By sending the *Skow* with the self-activating tech, Beacon would respond to its proximity like iron filings to a magnet. That's why I gave you that exact course and destination to ensure the proper jump-skip combination into Earth-space. The packet you couriered served a multitask, to keep the Demons close enough. They never quite caught your ships, Captain, because I switched the homer on and off as suited my purpose."

Fisher dry-swallowed. "And what's that?"

"When it comes to cold war, it is prudent to keep your friends close and your enemies closer," he vaunted with unbridled hauteur. "I had to draw the Imperium into the Juncture at the most opportune time."

Anne snorted. "You have friends?"

Blythe studied her for a moment. "Alas, Dr Morrison, you have proven a bit of both. You did do the math, as is your forte, stymieing my machinations upon your resurrection when you disposed of my homer. But as for your peers, I chose Fisher and his crew precisely because they were tractable pawns, carefully placed game tokens to ensure efficacy. Regardless of the setback you caused, the Demons started following your breadcrumbs better. I too made them a little wiser to our meanderings during our interstellar hegira.

"As for the element Beacon netted off that crystalline planet, Baron Fieldbank gets the credit for that. He was smarter than you know, a conundrum even to me. Despite his usurpation, I would've spared him if I could. But in the end, he wound up as a casualty."

Anne flinched and drew back, causing a sprig of hair to fall in front of her face. She brushed it back. "What usurpation? When?"

"Aboard the Arks, during our epic migration to Alliantha, I gleaned part of Baron's scheme, glimpsing a sizeable chunk of the data, but not enough to emulate the finished tech. I knew I couldn't abandon him until acquiring the whole of his knowledge, learning all that I could of his breakthroughs. But before I could claim the finished version, just as the generation ships arrived in the Alliantha system, it vanished. I pressed him on the matter, demanding that he tell me. But he dug in his heels and wouldn't say, maintaining it was safe and for the best that I didn't know."

"Baron always asked the hard questions," Anne said. "And cracked the hardest eggs."

Blythe nodded. "We landed on Alliantha. Weeks turned into months. And Baron remained adamant and aloof on the subject, focused on 'rebuilding and harmonized integration.' After probing other sources—chiefly his associates and binary metadata clusters from our scuttled ship's flight and internal recorders, I got a good idea of what Baron had done."

Fisher smiled to himself. He wasn't the only one who believed in posterity.

"Weeks before we landed on the planet," Blythe said, hurdling over a heavy breath, "Baron sent the packet to our current location, aboard a small autopiloted craft—a ship that never returned. He must have crashed it into that sun after it delivered its payload, or had it self-destruct. I learned of the sector where the packet had gone, but not its exact hiding place. I had neither the time nor the inclination to search for it myself—given my predicament, and my grand designs on Beacon and my Demon friends. I couldn't be at two places at one time, well, not with the vast distances involved.

"I required thugs in the vicinity of the packet to reconnoitre the situation, seek out its final resting place and whatever search party, bidden or unbidden, should seek to claim it. I needed fastidious felons with a motive, on their own vendetta. The answer was simple."

"The Apocs," Fisher surmised.

"The Apocs," Blythe affirmed with a dark snigger. "Those sycophants practically chained themselves to me with their own hands. When I first learned of their assassination attempt on Baron's life years earlier, I knew they'd fit the bill. The Apocs came with us to Alliantha. With anarchy defining their mantra, I groomed Slynn and his ilk of whores and varlets. And brought them to heel.

"Had them blow up that church and surrounding civilian area to veil my true objective and ensure their banishment—keep the curs away for good and on point with my intrigues. I covered their tracks, sending them on their mission."

Blythe nudged his chin at Anne. "In the meantime, I intercepted the packet you sent from Earth. What I did gather from Fieldbank's discovery at the time I secretly melded into the packet, and headed to Florin IV, leaving Alliantha to its fate. With my search dogs off-leash, the planet was expendable."

Fisher bit his tongue hard enough to taste blood.

Blythe blew out his cheeks. "There, after assimilating one of his commodores, I handed the device to Vorancia, the so-called President of United Worlds. I took that LUW thorn under my wing and, employing the tech of the packet, bolstered his pitiful defence grid with the hope that he would continue where Baron left off. He did advance the tech, but then refused to relinquish the secrets behind his success with the weapon."

"He devised a shielding net that repelled the Imperium ships and kept them at bay," said Fisher. "That hardly constitutes a weapon."

"Yes," Blythe said with a flash of impatience. "But the tech involved was based on the same weapon the Demons planned to use against me. After such an offence, that insolent prick had to go. I took back the packet, utilized it to sabotage his grid. And played to his lecherous vice with a rather unique and befitting chrysalis, grown just for her one special task."

"Why didn't you just assimilate the President, or Baron for that matter, like you did with Bliter?" Fisher asked.

Blythe scrutinized Fisher for a moment, letting the question hang. Then he smiled. "Let's just say I had my reasons. As for my other tasked assets, Captain Fisher, you and your lot proved the most pliable and easiest to manage since the endgame began—with one exception."

"Wisdan," Fisher guessed.

Blythe dipped his chin. "A most annoying snag, wise to me all along. That's why I planted a second homer on his fleet, let the Demons have him and take care of a loose end for me."

Veins pulsed in Anne's neck and she glared. "Anyone else?"

"Your ancestor. Percy, sensed something amiss when Beacon first arrived, though he did not grasp that all the primitive astrolabes he used were special, painstakingly modified to triangulate Beacon's arrival. My tech again: embedded into the archaic devices. The sextants themselves *led* the *Blue Wind* to sea-zero for splashdown."

A distant look washed over Blythe's countenance. "As for that splash, I proclaimed it a boon from God, which Captain Morrison took to mean *his* god. But twas of my own divinity that I spoke."

"He wrote in his log, it'd been 'the Devil come to roost.'" Anne said, taking Blythe's measure. "I always took Percy as one infinitely wise and perceptive soul."

"Unlike you," Blythe retorted with a tsk. "I misled you into thinking the weapon had to be uncovered when Beacon knew all along."

Fisher's lips quivered. "You knew we had access to the packet's secret and still let us scour the galaxy looking for it? Why?"

"I needed you to deliver Beacon—the real payload—when the time ripened. Causality, remember? If you acted precipitously, finishing the job too soon, you might have veered from the Juncture. The Demons sought the most opportune moment to strike me down as well. And Beacon brought us all together. It's poetically apropos, don't you think?"

"Nothing poetic about it," Fisher snarled. "Unless it rhymes with *Blythe dies*."

Blythe threw his head back and barked with laughter. "Like you, the Demons thought they would win the day. I enticed both parties, giving each of you enough carrots to believe that. Had to make sure you both arrived at the right place at the right time. So foolproof, it makes me want to cum."

"And you might be able to if you had a body to pull your toxic pud," Fisher derided, every decisive syllable grating along a razor's edge. "But you've overstayed your unwelcome. It's the gangplank for you."

The captain raised the barrel of his shock-rifle directly in line with Blythe's eyes. "You're off my fucking boat."

Baines' rifle followed suit. But much to Fisher's chagrin, his antagonist only beamed, flashing an open-mouthed smile. Blythe looked almost tickled by the threat, making no move to back away or raise his weapon. His shock-rifle slid off his shoulder and dropped to the floor. It let out a cantankerous series of clangs as it struck and skidded across the grated metal.

Before the metallic echo had ebbed completely, Blythe toppled backwards like a felled tree. His carriage hit the grating with a sick thud, leaving a sprawled discarded puppet. The crewman's orbs glazed over and settled.

Fisher gaped, too stunned to move.

Like their captain, everyone became so enthralled with Blythe's unexpected collapse, no one saw the lithe figure slowly rise and creep up behind them.

When Anne squealed, the crew spun around to face her.

A hand clamped Anne hard about the neck and viciously wrenched her backwards.

Everyone froze.

Jiri, dead, with a bullet hole still framed between her eyes, now seized a handful of Anne's hair with one hand while clasping her captive's throat in a claw-like grip with the other.

Anne winced and struggled but Jiri's hold seemed as tenacious as iron manacles.

From out of the engineer's mortal wound, the bullet slug popped and fell to the metal grating with an echoing clank. While the hole in her forehead shrank and the larger cavity at the back of her cranium sealed itself up, Jiri angled her head to one side and cast an almost playful look up at Fisher's shocked face.

"Better out than in," she said in a moribund voice, marred with corruption. "I just couldn't go on being your adorable little girl looking such a mess."

52: Prisms

Fisher

"Bliter, Blythe—take your prick—only functioned as my tool all along," the undead Jiri proclaimed.

Fisher blinked, his world spinning in sudden vertigo. "That's... impossible. The playback showed you on the bridge the entire time."

"Yes, but had you asked me anything during that period, you wouldn't have gotten much of a reply. We worked in tandem, in collusion. Though I ran the show—the true puppeteer, Bliter, the middling puppet. Switching places periodically between guises as fit my need, I split my time between the two consciousnesses, but the real intellect controlling the gears was me, skulking in the shadows as this bitch said."

Jiri tightened her grip on Anne's throat, making her hostage cough and sputter. "But no more. Now, I can scream from the highest pulpit. And oh, Captain do I ever intend to. I have nothing left to fear. Nothing! My Bliter vessel was an impetuous cretin, so overbearing and painfully obvious, but I kept him onboard in case I needed to deflect suspicion, escape a trap, or implicate someone. He served all three requirements.

"Towards the end, however, I wasn't too sure even with that." She kicked Resa's corpse. "This thorn caught on. But thanks again to you, that loose end got snipped. Come on, surely even someone as gullible and dimwitted as you can figure this all out."

Fisher's heart veered into ghoulish darkness but he needed to know the dire truth. With laser focus, he stared down the latest edition of his archenemy. "When did you kill Jiri—the real Jiri?"

"I'll let you figure that one out for yourself." She flashed him a coy smile.

"You'll pay for this, I swear."

Jiri laughed like a little girl. "Shall we put that to the test? Go ahead, fire. You'll only perforate Anne and I'll regurgitate the bullet as easily as peeling a scab."

"If you're so fucking omnipotent," Fisher railed, "why hold her at all?"

"Because I *can*," Jiri roared even louder. Then, extending her lower lip as if consoling a child, the zombie girl cooed with feigned sweetness, "But I don't want to hurt anyone—unless you give me cause like insulting me with those stupid pop guns. Let's end our final summit on amicable terms. After all, I am most grateful to you for facilitating my triumph. I begin to understand why Beacon chose to work with you rather than through you. My defunct robot believed that humanoids were unique, especially you, Dr Morrison."

Anne grunted. "I'm touched."

"Truth be told, your race fascinated me as well, with your tenacity for survival. Of all the cognitive life forms I've infiltrated, I found humans the most intriguing, partly because of the paradigm shift you elicited from the Imperium regarding their rules of engagement. If you maintained your growth as a full-fledged race, with Beacon at your side, you might have used that artifice and know-how to thwart me too, maybe even capture and kill me."

Jiri's casual tone implied how much stock she took in the notion. "Regardless, it makes no difference. Human or humanoid—all obsequious rabble, you're all finished. My true ravage of the stars will soon begin. Complete domination of the Universe is mine."

"Be careful—what you wish for," Anne managed to say.

"I took the greatest care and time to do just that." Her hard gaze shifted to Fisher. "I'll grant your crew one dispensation. As long as they remain above the red giant, they'll live long enough to bear witness to my beautification. Consider it a bequest from god. But Morrison will accompany me aboard the shuttle to see and feel me exalted as no god has ever been."

"Why?" Anne asked, her voice fretted with sarcasm. "Does god need a secretary to take notes?"

"Not exactly. Now that you've shirked your mortal chains, I may let you thrive, carrying you safely into familiar space, to live with your dismay for the rest of eternity, suffering the swathe of my plan from its inception."

Fisher let a mirthless grin crease his face. "You're going to die—alone."

Jiri gritted her teeth and a vein bulged in her neck, but before she could reignite, Cholla diffused her ire with genuine curiosity. "With the Imperium gone, what will you do? There's no more threat."

"Oh, but there is, Doctor," said Jiri. "The Imperium began as a seed too, like this one's Stricken Earth. Had the ID left Earth intact, it would have been only a matter of time before her race posed a similar hazard.

Jiri shook Anne's neck cruelly. "Isn't that right? Living creatures, planets, stars—I must claim them. But that won't be enough. It's never enough. I'll make a cleansing wake of my own across the heavens, reducing all life to its baser, truer state: energy. It must be contained. It will be contained. I am that crucible."

She throttled her hostage again. "No more reruns, Anne, no more re—runs. I'll nip the problems in the bud. No more surveillance, no more infiltration, no more fucking games. Dare judge me? Well, I'm all about the verdict now. It took too long to eradicate the Demons from this realm. I will not suffer another rerun!"

Jiri's torture of Anne put Fisher's teeth on edge. Conflicted, he gripped his shock-rifle so tightly blisters formed on the sweaty hollows between his thumbs and index fingers. He sorely wanted to use the weapon but instinct convinced him to do the opposite. The captain lowered the rifle to the floor, and with a silent nod at Baines, he bade the pilot do the same.

"Why covet my survival at all?" Anne blurted out between gasps. "If Humans were predestined for destruction all along, why stay the knife now? I may be a mongrel in my present form, but I still constitute the last remaining thread of that race."

Anne paused as she got her breathing under control. "Or, could it be that when you shirk your larval form and eliminate all of us who actually might have something to show you, to teach you and possibly elevate your fucked-up thinking, maybe your divinity might be put to the test?"

Silence answered her. Baines and Fisher took a half-step closer.

With a cough, Anne continued, "You said yourself that you want an audience. Why not keep sentient beings who respect you, not out of fear, but out of deference and admiration for your compassion? Otherwise, you are exactly as Fisher described: a solitary being. A powerful nemesis, yes, but something to be pitied—sick. Your course of action will only lead to an eternal destitution. Confined as such, you'll only *contain* your own abyss. And ultimately die alone."

Jiri dug her fingernails into Anne's flesh and thrashed her from side to side. With preternatural strength, the undead woman slammed her captive against the bulkhead before drawing her in and crushing one of the doctor's breasts. Anne's eyes went wide and she howled in anguish.

"No!" the crew cried in near unison.

Baines moved to rush Jiri, but before he advanced two steps Fisher grabbed him by the back of his coat and held him fast. "Don't, Baines! This is more than we can handle."

In that instant of distraction, Anne tore free from Jiri's clasp. Bursting forward, she pivoted sharply and landed a hard kick in the cove between her captor's legs. The blow made Jiri double over. But she quickly recovered and clawed the air for Anne.

Anne didn't shrink back. In a stunning move, she launched herself directly into Jiri's savage embrace. The move caught Jiri off-guard as Anne's arms speared past the girl's defences straight for her eyes.

Anne's fingers fell short, gouging two sets of trenches into her foe's flesh, immediately below each socket.

The two women looked like violent partners in a horrific dance. Bright crimson lines drew down Jiri's cheek from socket to chin before she caught Anne again.

With one hand, Jiri seized Anne's arms in a vice-like grip and bent her neck back with the other. Jaws agape, wider than what seemed possible, Jiri clamped her teeth down and tore a chunk of muscle out of Anne's shoulder close to the junction beside her neck.

Anne screamed.

The bite had missed her jugular but the cavernous wound still blossomed red and soaked her torn shirt. She clamped her mouth shut and squeezed her eyes closed.

Like some voracious vampire, Jiri raised her head, swallowed the morsel of flesh, and sneered at the petrified crew. Her bloody grin showed pure vindication. Then she drew back and backhanded Anne across the face with cruel abandon. Again. Again. Again.

"Stop, please!" Fisher beseeched.

Ignoring him, Jiri hammered blows until she'd broken Anne's nose and mashed her face into a swollen red pulp. She did not relent until her prisoner sagged in her iron grasp. Grunting in satisfaction, Jiri inspected the miasma she had riven. Then sniggered.

Blood covered both women, but between the scarlet lines streaking Jiri's features and her cinnamon hair, now dishevelled and matted with viscera, she looked like a demented evil witch.

"My corporeal form did not appreciate that," Jiri seethed.

Blood streamed in rivulets down Anne's ruined face and the cavity in her shoulder. One eye had swollen shut and bruised deep purple but the other blazed. "An my cor-real fohm says *fhuck ouh*," she gurgled, spitting blood between loosened teeth.

"Jiri, Blythe, whatever the hell you are!" Fisher bellowed. "You got what you wanted. We're no longer any threat to you—if we ever were. Just leave us alone and go."

"I will leave, craven when I decide it is time, but I won't be going alone." She indicated Anne with a sharp tilt of her head.

"But she's half-dead already!" Fisher implored.

Jiri quelled him to silence with her glower.

Scrambling for some other tact, the captain said, "At least, let her clean herself up for Christ's sake. That shit could get septic. She's a fucking mess."

"Why should I care when—" Jiri stopped mid-spate. The hatred in her gouged face remained but she didn't baulk further.

After an anxious moment, she acquiesced. "Very well, I'll permit you this one grace, only that she may witness your fate with clear sight."

Fisher raced away to the closest med-kit and fervently dug out a handful of gauze. He approached the two women with slow and deliberate steps.

"Stop," Jiri commanded. "No closer."

"Let me wipe her face."

"No, hand it to her. The bitch can do it herself."

Fisher did as Jiri insisted. Then, he slowly backed away, not wanting to rile the irascible alien any further.

Anne took the offered gauze in a shaking hand and wiped the worst of the congealing blood from her face and neck. Jiri continued to clinch her prisoner's neck from behind, steadfast as a steel manacle.

Before Anne could finish, Jiri tore the gauze from her hand and threw it back at Fisher. "That's enough. Now we must embark on our respective destinies. The Juncture has passed vertex. It hastens to twilight."

Something in the vaunted timbre of Jiri's voice, beneath all her interdiction, filled Fisher with anxiety and unquenchable guilt. But he desisted. Something *else* inside his mind, manifested. Superseding all, it warned him not to try anything rash and asserted that he must *let them* go.

With a shove, Jiri impelled Anne forward past the two remaining members of Fisher's traumatised crew. She marched her captive down a corridor and into the shuttle bay where the lone craft awaited.

No one did anything to stop her.

53: Heavenly Bodies
Anne

When the cargo bay door opened, the shuttle emerged into the chaos of detritus that had recently been the Garaxian Imperium's Core Fleet. The debris now drowned in the brilliant red aura of the almighty star beyond.

One of the modest spacecraft's two occupants sat at the helm while the other bobbed in a sea of pain, fixed securely with polypropylene fetters to the seat beside her captor.

Jiri piloted the craft a short distance before turning it in a slow supine arc directly in front of the *Skow II*. She eased back on the controls, bringing the craft to a graceful stop two hundred metres away from the shuttle's mother ship.

Having a full view of the *Skow II* from the small cockpit window sent a rush of emotions dovetailing into Anne's wracked mind. Fisher's second ship was more than the sum of its parts. It had been her home ever since her resurrection and now, knowing its final destination, the vessel appeared strangely alive like a faithful old dog about to be put down. From out here, in this place, with this vantage, and in this company, Anne felt a resounding surge of failure.

But the only thing that prevented Anne from crying out her woe was the vision's undeniable beauty. The crystalline planet backlit the *Skow II*, casting a pale blue light against one side of the vessel. Contrasting this, the pervasive ruby glow of the red giant imbued the ship's other side and soaked the rest of the backdrop.

That sun ruled the system like a deity, burning a seemingly inexhaustible amount of fuel for billions of years before Anne took her first breath. She had to believe it would continue to do so for billions of years after she took her last. *The universe is eternal. Life will go on. It's all energy, like the red giant, like the crystalline planet, like the Skow II, like...* Beacon, *like me.*

It all formed an artist's wondrous canvas to her eyes but also within her soul, filling her with serenity. More than stunning; it

401

offered ethereal wonderment made incarnate. And despite the pain lancing through her, it made Anne smile.

"Have a good look, Dr Morrison. It is the last thing you will see," Jiri said.

Anne's smile withered.

"I toyed with the idea of keeping you alive after I attain apotheosis, but it occurred to me that in sharing Beacon's mind, you undoubtedly shared his knowledge, and that might include full disclosure of the finished weapon."

It made Anne's nerves sing with discomfort to speak but she refused to remain silent. "The shuttle isn't going to get very far anyway," she countered. "It'll be sucked into that infernal red ball just the same."

"You would be right—if it remained a shuttle. But the energy matrix of the craft's subatomic constituents is about to be subsumed by my own energy pattern."

"Why?"

"To help fuel my inflation," Jiri answered, "my immaculation, like food before a journey. I can still transcend into my true form without it but this will sate my appetite until some other power sources come my way."

Jiri let out a tired sigh. "Alas, I cannot drink deep of the giant itself, not yet. It's too big and I'm not ready. I'm still a virgin. But, after a few baby steps, I'll return to this nameless star... and fuck it to death. Then I can pass directly through the Dark Sector behind us if I so choose. No, I'm afraid only Captain Fisher's ship will drift into the red giant."

"But they're no threat to you," Anne sobbed through her physical torment. "Not any longer. Help them. Why do you care whether they live or die?"

"I care, because as that clod, Bliter, Captain Fisher really pissed me off. This is payback."

"Maybe, but it's also a betrayal," Anne pointed out. "Emulating Jiri, you made him love you too."

Jiri stiffened at the remark, turned, and dissected her prisoner with her scowl. It didn't take a clairvoyant to see Anne's antagonist deemed the very concept of love, anathema.

"You know something, Doctor," Jiri declared, her words sharp and decisive, "I've grown tired of our little chat. Think I'll prefer solitude for my final moments in corporeal form after all."

The question creeping across Anne's mind did not last long.

Jiri reached into her jumpsuit pocket and produced a razor-sharp utility knife. She extended the silver blade and flaunted it playfully, making it dance like a child's trinket before Anne's widening eyes.

"Loose ends," a grinning Jiri explained.

With lightning speed, she sliced Anne's throat from ear to ear.

"Where's your Beacon now, Anne?" Jiri rasped in exaltation. "Where's your fucking Beacon *now*?"

Anne's dying thought was of Jiri, as Pandora, unleashing myriad plagues from her crate, in full wrath and unbridled fury.

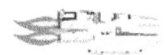

"Did you *see* that?" Cholla exclaimed.

Fisher looked up from his console and frowned. "What?"

"The shuttle. It looked as if it jumped, or exploded, or both. It's gone."

"Brain," Fisher said, "the shuttle can't do that. It doesn't even have an engine *to* jump. That's why we call it a shuttle."

"Thanks, Cap, I know, but something happened."

"Okay," Fisher relented. "Let's hear it."

"The ship began to glow like an antiquated stove burner but green, its details fading until it resembled a comet's coma. The aura enlarged and sparkled with iridescence. Then in a flash, it shot away, faster than anything I'd ever seen move in normal space. Gone."

"Expected as much," said Fisher without much enthusiasm.

Cholla had nothing but. "I think, I just witnessed the," he paused, knotting his brows, "*Blythe Entity* take its true form, its metamorphosis!" The doctor looked back out the window.

Fisher ran his fingers through his hair. "Poor Anne."

Cholla turned away from the glass and studied his captain more closely. "Captain?"

Slumped in the pilot's chair, Fisher murmured to the air, "I'm not an asshole."

Cholla blinked. "Cap? You okay?"

"Yeah, shut up," Fisher looked down and scolded the floor before taking notice of Cholla once more. "What?"

"I asked if you were okay."

"Yeah, Doc, just a little distracted and a lot overtired." *Why didn't you just tell me you had the disk?*

"You sure you're alright?"

"Yeah, yeah it's nothing, Cholla." Fisher waved him off with a brusque hand gesture. "Just answered my own question—got to play with *Wu Wei*."

"Wu, *what*?" Cholla asked, eyes burgeoning. He suddenly looked worried.

Fisher's tone sharpened. "Never mind."

Cholla shook his head, plainly unconvinced.

Fisher shifted his carriage forward, covered his face in his hands, and rubbed his temples. Strung out, betrayed, made a fool, and mired by helplessness at failing to prevent Anne's death. Guilt consumed him—as Resa said it would. Now, he felt lost, blaming himself and second-guessing his instincts.

As if that wasn't enough to lodge his throat with bile, another kind of *stress* harangued him, knowing that though he didn't feel it yet, the *Skow II* had begun her slow mortal drift towards the red furnace. Again, as Resa predicted, Fisher alone would be responsible for the death of his entire crew, their utter failure. Their utter ruin. The sting felt so overwhelming that he didn't try to hide his dejection.

When Fisher dropped his hands to the chair's armrests and flopped against its backrest, his eyes found Cholla.

Doc chewed his lip nervously as he leaned in and examined

him. "Cap, please talk to me."

With a fierce inhalation, Fisher shook off his rising despair and sat up in his chair.

"Get up, Fish," he reprimanded himself, but remained seated.

Cholla exhaled, shoulders sagging. "Baines is down in the engine room, monkeying around."

Fisher nodded. "I better go help him."

"I can assist you guys from up here," Cholla offered. "See what else I can do. Maybe run a power conduit from any auxiliary energy sources not crucial to life support, and still working. Won't be enough to boost us out of here, but it might delay the inevitable—if we can bump the ship closer to the La Grange point."

"Resa was right," Fisher declared as he jumped out of his seat. "I would've thought the video doctored, even if he handed it to me. There were three guns in unknown hands, any of which could've totally debauched us. We might have all wound up dead down there."

Cholla furrowed his eyebrows again, though he remained quiet, looking more puzzled than disturbed this time. *Likely pegging my rant as a vent for grief. If so, Doc would be half-right.*

But noticing the troubling effect of his random words in Doc's grimace, Fisher figured he owed the poor sod an explanation. "Anne wasn't the only one getting projections from Beacon back on that Apoc ship. Resa did too, on a subliminal level. Remember, he and Beacon were practically bed buddies back in the debris field over the Stricken where we picked up his sorry ass."

The doctor surrendered a half-smile. "Guess after two hundred years sleeping together, they developed a kind of rapport."

"Then, on the Apoc ship," Fisher said as if he didn't hear Cholla's rare jibe. "Resa got a subconscious message that made him act as he did. Back here on the *Skow II*, he wasn't even aware that he made a copy of our video feeds. He was on autopilot, even while conscious of what transpired, trying to unveil the, um— 'Blythe Entity,' as you called it."

"Didn't the Blythe Entity confirm that Beacon tinkered with us? Maybe he did, on an intuitive level as you suggest."

"Look," the captain began, "there was obviously no love between Resa and me, but he knew I needed to see the real villain, make it think it had won all the marbles. Resa used our mutual animosity to play his hand, to tinker back, I think. Yeah, that's it," Fisher said, agreeing with himself. "He pressed my buttons even though it meant killing him. I never liked Resa but I got to admit, he had balls."

"But even when you found the disk, the Blythe Entity could have killed us all, right then and there," Cholla observed.

"Yeah, but it didn't. I'm guessing plain and simple ego. The Entity really did want us to know, in a perverse way. It had sentience with a few screws loose, not least of which, its god-complex."

Fisher let out a long slow breath and placed a hand on Cholla's shoulder. "But y' know, Doc, despite its limitless power, it had to live apart, according to the edicts of its nature, in unending solitary confinement. Why did it react so violently to Anne when she pointed that out? Anne struck a nerve because she was right. It's a depraved coward, something not to be revered, but to be pitied."

"I'd rather be dead," Cholla said.

Just then the ship's hull groaned. Fisher removed his hand from Cholla's shoulder and tilted his head up. He let out a humourless laugh. "Well, Doc, look where we are."

54: Denominators
Anne

A synaptic storm raged in Anne's fleeting consciousness. Despite her scourged neurons flailing in the mad roil of black winds, she knew she was dead. Saw the knife, felt its bite, felt her lifeblood gush and choke her. Air struggled to move down her severed windpipe. It gurgled past spurting blood, making her gag on her own viscera.

She watched the view aboard the shuttle dim and fade to black…

But not entirely.

The small irregular window—a side-effect caused by her resurrection (as Beacon explained it) lingered in the bottom corner of her peripheral. It refused to follow her cognizance down the circling drain into permanent darkness.

By almost imperceptible increments, it gained clarity and prominence, creeping up like a light on the horizon. It spread across her field of vision from its small niche where it had lain, tucked neatly away in storage.

Until now.

As one reality faded, carrying the threshold of pain and torment along with it, the next took over, like a guiding beacon. She let it chaperone her.

Anne was physically outside herself in this strange limbo, composed of translucent fabric like linen stretched across her new consciousness and a strange aura beyond. The Afterlife? Heaven? If so, there should be more to this new reality.

There was more. The picture-in-picture existence she had coped with for so long had finally left her. Only the veil and the light remained. Together, they formed one vision, which chased the darkness away as it filled Anne's vision from horizon to horizon.

The veil moved, undulating softly like a field of nodding flowers caught on a zephyr. Her own breath caused it.

She felt cold, hard, metal. Cramps stole over her as though long-atrophied muscles suddenly reawakened. They hearkened to task, not painful, more like dull bruises declaring themselves.

A reverberating soft sound rose from the silence. In sudden epiphany, Anne's scientist mind took over. She was being *rebooted*.

The murmuring hum left, and returned. This time, it gently repeated, "Uh… uh… uh…" it chanted in soothing unhurried measures like a benevolent choir of monks. Or angels.

Another note joined their song. "Uhn, uhn, uhn."

"Anne!" she cried with her own voice. Or was it projection? She didn't care. "I'm here. I'm *alive*," she sang. "I'm Anne. I'm here. I'm alive. God, I'm alive."

"Anne," the angel gently affirmed, his tone filled with familiarity, compassion, and promise. "You have endured too much. It is time to come back now. I have missed you. Are you ready to return?"

"Yes," Anne agreed. "I am ready."

The veil that comprised her new reality slowly parted like a semi-transparent theatre curtain drawing open across a stage. Anne's vision instantly swam, nerves throbbing as the unfiltered glare of the sun struck her retinas.

Her pooling eyes sought to escape the harsh orb's radiance, but she forced them to squint and adjust. When the pulsating discomfort ebbed, she opened her lids as much as the aching threshold would allow. It hadn't been a sun at all, but a medical lamp, mounted on a swing-arm shining directly into her face. Anne blinked and steadied herself. She lay prostrate on a bed within an incubation tube, staring up at the ceiling of a med-lab. A pair of telefactor arms dangled beside her.

Still disbelieving, Anne dropped her gaze and began performing sensory tests on herself. She took quick shallow breaths, wiggled her toes, and opened and closed her hands.

A dark form detached itself from the shadows of the lab's recesses. It drew up.

Doubt and supplication mired Anne as the organic shape of an all too familiar automaton glided to her bedside. She lolled her head towards it, craning her neck to get a better view. It seemed too miraculous to be believed.

But was this robot hovering before her *the* Beacon or one of the copies the Exarch had described? In sudden horror, Anne realized no smiley-face emblazoned the robot's ebony torso. The telltale icon was gone—or had *never* sullied his casing. This was a copy!

But before panic could set in, the lights that ensconced the otherwise black double-beetle form lit it up like a Christmas tree and the mechanical conundrum uttered three distinct and poignant words.

"Trust your robot."

That simple identifying statement proved too much for Anne. It hit her like a tsunami, washing away any doubt. For the first time since she was a little girl, floodgates of emotion sprang open and Anne broke down, sobbing uncontrollably. But every tear that welled up from her heart was borne on a fount of joy.

Stephen Fenech

55: Sisterhood
Cholla

"I'm not an asshole!"

Cholla shrugged at Fisher's random exclamation. After close to a month of flinches, he had gotten used to his captain's sporadic outbursts. Ever since fate sent the three surviving crew members of the *Skow II* on a slow but deliberate course towards incineration.

By the languid gestures and heavy bags under his companions' eyes, the crisis had worn both of them out, as it had done Cholla. But more troubling: neither the captain nor Baines shared his morose demeanour at their combined failure to fix the ship's engines. Not even the prospect of having their immortality curtailed seemed to faze them. Perhaps, being condemned men, they had simply accepted their fate—and chose to spit in its face.

"Cap?" Cholla asked after this latest retinue. "I never asked you before, but why did you make me fudge my estimate about the burn-up time into the red giant?"

"Isn't it obvious?"

"No, not really," the doctor confessed.

"I needed our passenger to get a heightened sense of urgency."

"But, with Jiri/Bliter gone, we'd still drift into the furnace regardless."

"*But*, with such a short lifespan left us, the Entity would consider our fate sealed. It wouldn't have time to entertain any further doubts."

The doctor tilted his head to one side and frowned. "Doubts?" Once again, he found himself hopelessly lost.

"How much longer till we burn up for real?" Fisher asked.

"That's a good question. I guess whenever we can't stop sweating."

"Thanks."

"Captain?"

Fisher rubbed the back of his neck. "That subject again?"

Cholla nodded. "Why do you really think Blythe, having the power of a god and all, spared us?"

The captain leaned back and gave Cholla his patented coyote smile—the one intended to fluster him. He recognized when Fisher was about to have some fun with him, if for no other reason than Baines' entertainment. Despite this, the doctor needed open discussion to distract him from his fear.

"I think the Entity worried that there might be some kind of download from Beacon taking place," said Fisher, "something that might waylay it if the wretch manifested into its true form while still aboard the ship."

"I thought the Entity said the robot—I mean Beacon—belonged to him," Cholla said.

"The Exarch said the same thing," Fisher pointed out.

"What do you think?"

"Well, Doc, there's a reason why it chose to leave us crippled rather than absorb the ship's energy matrix. It did sabotage the engines and the tractor beam using conventional means after all. As you know, the wallop we took from the Demons' fusillade never affected either of them."

Cholla looked down at his viewscreen, pursing his lips as he considered Fisher's words. Something else occurred to him and he looked up. "Then why did it take Anne hostage and leave on the shuttlecraft?"

Fisher met his gaze. "The Entity was omnipotent, but never above doubt. I believe something about us or maybe the ship itself made it think twice about destroying us outright, uncertain of the ramifications. I think it wasn't entirely sure Beacon went up with the *Infernalis*—and if the robot had ever really been *its* tool."

Cholla inclined his chin, seeing the logic in Cap's hypothesis.

The coyote in Fisher's smirk fled back to its den. "In the end, I feel the Blythe Entity feared Beacon, feared the robot would and could retaliate from somewhere to thwart it, maybe download and execute the Imperium's weapon if it invoked its hysteresis while still aboard the *Skow II*. I think, despite all of its bragging to the contrary that it underestimated what the robot was capable of. Unsure about Beacon's designs and allegiances. Lastly, I think the Entity was just as paranoid if not more than the ID."

Fisher sighed and scratched the stubble on his chin. "But above all else, Doc, I'm pretty sure that twisted soulless fuck took pleasure in knowing I wouldn't die outright, that I'd have some time to contemplate what I wrought."

Cholla adjusted his glasses. "Are you saying, malice was innate to its nature and the Entity sought vindication on some level?"

Fisher chuckled. "Maybe it hoped the two of you would blame me for our fate, take up arms and mutiny—kill me yourselves."

Chagrin tightened Cholla's chest. "You know us better than that."

"Speak for yourself," Baines said with a grin. "The thought sure crossed my mind a few times."

Fisher threw Baines a brief smile before regarding Cholla again. "Whatever its motive for sparing us, Doc, the fact is, it did."

"Still, Resa's fate is the real kicker to the whole tragedy," Cholla lamented. "All of this might have been prevented."

"Well, it might *seem* that way."

Cholla shot his captain a sideways glance. "I hate to tell you this, Cap, but it looks like the Entity did succeed in nullifying us. Face it, we're screwed."

"Yeah," Baines agreed astride a wry chortle. "We're never escaping this on our own."

A gaunt but strangely placid Fisher hiked a thumb. "Looks like, the end of this road for ship and crew."

Oblivious to their choice of words, Cholla agreed. He sucked in his breath to acquit himself of anxiety. "No more forks ahead. It's the end. Always wondered when and how I'd cash in my chips. Now, I know."

Fisher and Baines broke out into laughter.

Not for the first time, Cholla wrote them off as self-administered. He focused on his monitor and exhaled. "I just wish we had more time," he said absently. "There's so much more I want to learn."

"Be careful what you wish for, Doc," Baines said. "Cause you just might get it."

That unhinged Cholla. His eyes shot up to gawp between the equally unnerving smirks on his companions' faces. Their grins grew even more vicious and unbearably vexing.

"Okay, I get it," Cholla complained, blood rushing to his ears. "You two have finally cracked for good. As if dying isn't bad enough, I have to spend my last hours with a pair of junked-out cuckoos."

Fisher and Baines erupted into an even louder bout of hilarity, which only rankled Cholla further. He threw his hands up in frustration, about to storm off the bridge when the sharp squeal of a klaxon sounded. It froze Cholla in his seat.

The sound also quelled his companions' raucous outbursts to silence and sobriety. A proximity alarm cried, demanding attention as it fired up a string of lights on Baines' panel.

Cholla inhaled. "What is it?"

"Portside window, Doc," Baines prompted with a warm smile. The pilot gestured with one arm. "Take a gander."

Cholla surged to his feet, heart trilling as he bounded towards the glass.

When the doctor peeped out into space, his mood slipped gears, his ire all but forgotten. It seemed as though the *Skow II* had pulled up alongside a giant mirror. A hundred metres off the doomed ship's port flank floated an identical ship, drifting alongside, matching attitude and vector perfectly.

From this close range, Cholla easily made out the ship's insignia and the name inscribed on her weathered hull, the first letter still partially adulterated by a vandal's phase-ray. Beneath the inflicted miasma, the ship's full name was still quite legible.

It read: *Skow.*

In the middle of Fisher's two-ship armada, the *Skow's* shuttle moved carefully from her surrogate ship back towards her rightful mother. Three passengers rode aboard.

"You always did have an uncanny ability for pulling the rabbit out of the hat," Cholla beamed. "But this time, Cap, you've outdone your magician self."

Beside him in the pilot chair, Fisher shrugged. "Thanks, Doc, but in all honesty, it wasn't my magic this time. I only made a stagehand's contribution to Beacon's show."

Cholla's shoulders slumped. "Still, I'm a bit hurt. You could have told me the truth of matters, instead of letting me carry on for so long, thinking I had to treat you and Baines for insanity. Or did you think me compromised by the Blythe Entity, ensorcelled into its service?"

"No way, that thought never crossed my mind—much," Fisher japed. But a moment later, his smile straightened and he put a hand on Cholla's shoulder. "Seriously Doc, you are one of a kind." He fixed Cholla with an earnest look. "Truth is, I didn't want to get your hopes up only to dash them if my hunch proved wrong."

Fisher removed his hand and placed it back on the pilot chair's armrest. "There was a lot of conjecture floating around, wetting what I thought was going on. And a lot of space for things to go south fast. Even without all the semi-tangible variables, things could've still gone wrong, really wrong. God's truth, I only knew for certain yesterday."

"How?"

"I hate to admit it, but I think it's projection," Fisher said as he trained his face forward. "Anne's right. I seemed to have picked it up recently."

"You always had it, Captain," said Anne from the shuttle's jumper seat behind them. "You merely didn't know how to access it."

"If you say so," Fisher said as he banked the yoke with one hand, bringing the shuttle into a slight turn. "By the way, welcome back to the land of the living."

"Thanks. It's good to be back, and even better to be back among friends."

Fisher looked over his shoulder and gave her a full-blown smile.

Anne stretched her arms over her head and yawned. "But it's true about projection: it was the same for me. Not initially born to it, I believed it was a synaptic misfire or something like that. Thanks to you, after my first rebirth, I acquired this new level of percipience and exchange, but had a tough time trying to wrap my untrained mind around it. What I thought harangued me with borderline psychosis was just the gift trying to manifest itself within the biological construct of my archaic brain."

"True," Fisher acknowledged. As his eyes left the woman and shifted to his console, he remembered his own cerebral turmoil.

"But having survived two deaths and three births, I wouldn't quite call your brain archaic. Still, I do see your point now. We're all connected."

The shuttlecraft aligned forward with the *Skow*'s aft section, now tethered to her sister ship, the *Skow II,* by a series of umbilical cables.

"Speaking of connections, Anne..." Fisher slowed the shuttle, leaned forward, and peered up out the window to reexamine the tethers. "This is going to work, right?"

"Beacon hasn't let us down yet. In fact, he's waiting for us in the shuttle bay."

Feeling like a kid who just found a long-lost precious toy, Fisher nodded and reached up to a console above his head. He flipped the com switch. "Baines?"

"Yeah, Fish?" the pilot's cheery voice answered.

"Do me a favour. Stay clean and don't self-administer—at least not until we hit full-black deep space."

Baines, still back on the bridge of the *Skow II,* laughed on the other side of the transmission. "No worries, Fish. This is a babysitting job from this end. You guys will be doing all the heaving up front."

"Great, see you soon."

"Oh, one more thing, Cap," Baines said.

Fisher's finger paused on the switch. "Shoot."

"I've got a great view of the *Skow* from back here, and I got to tell you, her ass never looked so good."

Fisher chuckled as he switched off the com. Moments later, the tiny craft neatly inserted into the lead ship's shuttle bay where the double-beetle form of Beacon awaited their arrival.

56: Symbiosis
Fisher

Within the hour, the *Skow II* stopped her death plunge into the red giant. Utilizing the tungsten carbide tethers affixed to her aft section and controlled bursts of her attitude jets, the *Skow* managed to gently nudge her hitched sister with a measured banking manoeuvre. Like a solitary train car obeying the guidance of its locomotive, the joined ships turned as one.

They continued to drift backwards with the tethers still faultlessly secured, but now perfectly aligned for an escape vector, away from the furnace and back towards interstellar space.

Fisher flipped the switch. The *Skow*'s engines scaled up to a dull but imperious roar, defying the pull of the red giant. Within seconds they achieved equilibrium.

"Standstill," Fisher announced.

Then, by dialled increments, the *Skow* began slowly towing her younger sister out of the grasp of the furious star. It presented a struggle at first, but the more progress she made, the easier the job became. Fisher felt the corners of his mouth curve up as the distance and speed numbers on his bridge console increased, while the torque and newton stress factors decreased. All stats affirmed the two ships backing away from the precipice, heading to relative safety.

The captain had been willing to let the *Skow II* go, but Beacon maintained that they save the ship, citing that they would need it later. For what, the captain couldn't fathom, but hey, as demonstrated, two ships were still better than one.

For most of that first day, Fisher divided his time either monitoring the stats on his console or staring out the aft window at his other ship following close behind, a perpetual cup of coffee cradled in one hand. The captain also remained in constant communication with Baines, still aboard the bridge of the *Skow II* and, true to his word, still aboard.

Together, the pair relayed the figures pumped out by the load stress sensors, attached at either end of the tethers and down their length. So far, they worked flawlessly and by day's end, Fisher had no more reason to doubt them any longer.

Their values only grew more encouraging the further the ships pulled away. Beacon and Baines sure rigged them up nice and snug. Fisher allowed himself a smile.

Once they pushed into the true dark of deep space, they would take a closer look at the engines aboard the *Skow II*. With Beacon's help and the cache of spare parts aboard the *Skow*, even that presented a non-issue.

Fisher took another sip of coffee. The tide had definitely turned, but what prevailed on the far shore remained to be seen.

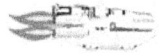

"When you gave your little EVA speech above the crystalline planet, I really thought you sold us out. I bought it, hook, line, and sinker."

"Sorry for the deception, Captain Fisher," Beacon answered. "Right to the end, it remained vital that both the Exarch and the Blythe Entity believed everything was moving according to their respective plan—ensuring each a victory over the other. A fine line to walk, even for me. But alas, there was no other way."

Fisher pulled in his chair closer to Beacon, hovering at the head of the mess table, where Anne, Baines, and Cholla sat, eyes centred on the automaton. Soft instrumental music played in the background, harmonizing with the steady quiet hum of the engines. The smell of roasted coffee added a final touch to the relaxing air of the debriefing—the first since their reunion.

"You convinced me but I understand. By the way, I thought you never recovered any of the catalyst, considering that massive net you took down there."

"I used it like a radar dish to expedite my collection," said Beacon. "Once I captured enough of the catalyst fragments and directed them into my ram scoop, I discarded the peripheral setup. I only required a few molecules. Remember, in nature, things can 'impress' not only by immensity but by their smallness. Just think:

the creation of your Universe began as one infinitesimal speck."

"And God sneezed," Baines joked. "So, Bee, what happened next?"

"More or less what the Blythe Entity told you. I seized all of the Exarch's security protocols, which led to their extermination. Not for the first time, I carried out a loathsome but necessary act to preserve the sanctity and power balance of a realm. Except, to expedite the kill orders, I went one step further."

Fisher straightened, Anne's conclusion about the catalyst fresh in his mind.

"The plasma of the Glass is far more complex than most realize," Beacon explained. "Apart from forming the inherent structure of the Imperium's ships, it gave them their means of propulsion, their fuel. It simply had to be siphoned correctly, using the right conduits into an excited form for their ships to move. Size did not matter. Even with the capital ships, their structure *was* their propellant. And supplied the energy for their armaments."

"Plasma was their move-all," Fisher supplied, 'and their kill-all."

"Correct. Plasma served as the Imperium's lifeblood. I tainted that stockpile like a bad blood donor, with the catalyst for the ships in our immediate vicinity and a replicated version for those outside of it. Even the energy used on all their planetary bases and homeworld relied on plasma."

Cholla took off his glasses and wiped them with a cloth. After reseating them, he rested his chin on his palm, eyes fixed on Beacon—an act Fisher recognized as the doctor's 'class-is-in-session' mode.

"The key to executing those protocols was proximity," the robot went on. "It could not be done by remote or drone. I had to get close enough to the Exarch's com-hub to attain the required efficacy. That meant staying aboard the *Infernalis* when the paroxysms began, to deflect any retaliation as I piloted my plan towards its intended Armageddon. That's also why I had to destroy myself. Aboard the ship, I found the right pipeline into the Exarch's command protocols. The Imperium did a little too much tinkering the last time they intercepted me, just before they sent

419

me to Earth.

"As it turned out, even the Garaxian forces policing the systems of the undercastes were not immune to the Exarch's redress protocols. Unbeknownst to the Blythe Entity, the Demons were all surgically fitted with implants to heighten their skills and regulate their bodies' chemicals. The devices allowed them to adapt to different planets' environments and the alien stations they policed, making them hard to kill."

"But?" Fisher prompted.

"But the Exarch's security network did not overlook them. The Demons could not be eradicated en masse, so their implants all carried a virus, an electronic one that became organic in nature, fatally so. It raised their body core temperatures until they all died from hyperthermia."

"That's ingenious," Fisher said. "Fucking disturbing but ingenious."

"It's hard for me to even imagine not having those miscreants around," Baines added. "But Blythe, Jiri, whatever, said you got destroyed."

"I was—my physical structure to be clear. I served as a bomb in several ways; the discharge claimed my matter. But the source code fuelling my components—my consciousness—endured in the form of a transmission, a very special tight-beamed transmission. Which again comes back to the true complexity of the Glass. But I'll get to that in a minute."

Cholla's ears perked and he sat up, a studious but contented look marking his features. Fisher grinned. He knew any scientific revelations the robot would make were bound to be a treat for the doctor.

"While countless directives relayed kill orders across the galaxies, I searched for a particular location," Beacon said. "Once found, I locked on and modified a certain executive instruction to serve my purpose—done while waiting for the last of the executions to lock on to their respective targets, about the time when all hell broke loose outside your ship."

Fisher nodded while Beacon's seeing-dome tilted up to the ceiling. He seemed to be reliving the crazy event for himself.

"Moments before the heavy cruiser I boarded detonated, ultimately my last communiqué, I sent one penultimate transmission, a very unique message to a very specific Demon interceptor."

The robot's upper hemisphere rotated slowly but his domed orb fixed on Fisher. "As you accurately predicted, Captain, the Demons did not destroy the *Skow*. It had become an invaluable piece to play in the endgame."

"And?" cued Fisher.

"They stationed two interceptors nearby to guard it. I had taken certain liberties during my tenure as the Exarch's thrall, planting the right suggestions, subtly embedding them within the cordons between his neural interface and command infrastructure. It subliminally led him to believe the inception of such ideas to be his own."

"You—*hypnotized* the Exarch?" Cholla exclaimed.

"In a way, yes, Doctor," Beacon said. "One of those suggestions maintained that any ship deployed in covert activity tagged to the Robot T-261 initiative must carry a working copy of me. Although the shell you see now does indeed belong to the Robot T-261 model, technically, I still function and reason as Robot T-001. Another of the Exarch's paranoid ploys to confound certain parties. Admittedly my original T-001 casing went up in the smoke with the *Infernalis.*

"When my search revealed that one of the two interceptors had aboard it a complete cybernetic laboratory and the most advanced copy of me, ready for my immediate download and activation, I wasn't in the least bit surprised. Furthermore, knowing how important the *Skow* was to his plans, the late Exarch felt it prudent to keep close to your ship, this particular version in a fully automated semi-activated state."

Fisher's incredulity sent his eyebrows to his hairline. "But the distance from here to where I sent the *Skow,* I can't even fathom it!"

"Yes, but the Glass. Remember the Glass and what it can do."

"He's right, Fisher," said Anne. "Even in my time, the Demon tech worked wondrously in this regard. Distance presents no object—if the transmission fires at the right strength. As easily as

421

drawing a line, you can instantly access any part, distance, spectrum or wave, in real-time."

"Quite accurate, Anne," Beacon acknowledged. "Now, about the Glass: this may sound a little strange but bear with me. I transmitted my full essence as an energy vessel of thought, carried along the same conduit of the Exarch's signal and derived from the energy matrix of Demon plasma. In this base state, I instantaneously travelled through subhypra space and into the casing of Robot T-261."

Beacon's bulbous dome tracked Anne. "If you recall, the beam from the Hubble II space telescope was infinite. No degradation like a laser, no obstacle deflection like an X-ray. Not even gravitational waves or spacetime curvatures affected the beam. But add to this the radio signal marriage Baron Fieldbank devised when he first discovered the plasma surge heading to Earth and, well I simply rode that tight-beam transmission to my destination."

"Some kind of ride," Fisher marvelled, trying to wrap his mind around the outlandish concept, let alone its execution.

"Yeah, a real trip," Baines laughed. "I'll have to try that sometime." Fisher smirked before returning his attention to the automaton.

"As I have told you, energy forms our lowest common denominator," Beacon explained, "between you, me, Anne, your ships, and even the Entity. In such a state of lifeforce, I can access the subhypra domain to travel light years in a nanosecond once I've found the right quantum marriage and vibration. I simply harmonize with existing energy, be it the latent power of a moon, the flaring corona of a star, even the abyss left behind in the vacuum of space. Antimatter, dark matter, or dark energy: it makes no difference."

"$E=mc^2$—and then some," Baines laughed.

Beacon raised one of his arms and extended a motorized finger. "Precisely. And we have inflation to thank for that."

Baines' smirk plunged into a frown as the robot elaborated. "In such an accelerated form of existence, I reach tangency with everything. The speed of light slips away and, through the boundless folding and refolding of spacetime from a central locus, only the speed of thought remains to govern any restriction. That type of energy can ascend infinite places and possibilities *because* it does not originate from this dimension."

"Subhypra?" asked Cholla, eyes aglow. His mind seemed to race between prediction models in rapturous overdrive.

"You would be correct in part," Beacon allowed. "As such, it is not limited to this realm's strictures—the physical laws of the Universe. It is the inherent energy of the Demon plasma that drove their tech and provided the conduits to execute their security protocols. It also forms the elemental properties of the Glass. A moment of real-time passed from when I left the Exarch's cruiser to when I awoke aboard one of the two Imperium interceptors guarding the *Skow*."

Beacon paused, his upper torso turning slowly left and right as if opening the floor to further questions. Or was he simply letting the captive crew *try* to digest his bizarre explanation?

After a moment, the robot continued, "The bulk of that quintessential transmission of course contained the Exarch's original kill order, tailored to suit my purpose. Having no choice but to submit to the Exarch's protocol, the interceptor in which my new body awaited fired upon and destroyed the other interceptor. It then shut down its own power including all life support. The only active component of the ship's power grid, immune to the shutdown was the cybernetic laboratory.

"My new body awaited my arrival. Almost immediately, I gained full faculty of it, but I couldn't linger aboard the interceptor. This ship had to be destroyed as well, to mollify the Entity's scrupulous probing."

"And?" Fisher prompted.

"And that's exactly what happened," Beacon replied, "while I commuted EVA across the gulf of space, back to the *Skow*. I had covered roughly half the 100-kilometre distance when the second interceptor exploded."

Beacon's seeing-dome found Fisher. "Your ship too was ready and waiting, Captain. Since I'd grown acquainted with the *Skow*'s main computer when I first joined your team, you might say we'd grown rather fond of one another."

"That so?" Fisher asked, amused by the notion. He cast a sideways look at the automaton. "How much schmoozing did you do with the fat lady?"

"None, other than exchanging a few security etiquettes of mine, ones it would recognize and accept as readily as your own. I am a mechanical entity after all and as such, have developed a certain rapport with most other mechanized entities, including the mainframes aboard both of your ships. How else do you think I so easily seized control of the *Skow II* to bring about Anne's first resurrection?"

Fisher grunted. "Don't remind me."

"In this instance, the *Skow* let me in—practically rolled out the red carpet. Once aboard, I fired up all systems and beelined for this rendezvous. En route, I facilitated Anne's revival."

"That definitely begs a question," Fisher remarked, tilting his head towards Anne. "Seeing her sure gave me a jolt, a welcome one to be sure, but a zap to my cerebrum all the same. What's her story?"

"I already had a general copy of her mind's logarithms stored in my neural net," Beacon explained. "My circuitry had been wired with a permanent projection link of thought energy with the former corporeal Anne, in real-time. After her first renaissance, I kept the link open for this reason. Though I could not divine exactly how matters would unfold.

"Still, I knew beyond a doubt that the Blythe Entity would eventually seek to remove her from the equation, so, I took all the preemptive steps necessary to protect her as well.

"What she saw in her peripheral all that time was the neural representation of the link, so that when her physical form faded from one reality, her mind would automatically hone in and pursue what sentience was left. I only needed to match the visual certainty of the next reality with that of the projection, attenuating the corresponding vibration. I knew both your ships inside out so that part was easy."

Easy? Baines and Cholla exchange glances. By their open mouths, they seemed to mirror Fisher's astonishment.

"The ambiguity of the visual representation was also compulsory so that it would not distract Anne overly much. I chose a simple ambit of light beyond a veil. The rest ran like clockwork. I had Anne's DNA signature stored digitally and required only a few of Captain Fisher's skin cells, which I extracted from your bed roll aboard the original *Skow*. They were intact, as the ship's ambient temperature hovered below -200° C when I arrived. Once on the operating table, I simply repeated the steps I made the first time I brought Anne back. Lastly, when the red flag went up of Anne's imminent death, *she* rode the beam herself—as an aura of thought energy—through the subhypra domain and into her awaiting chrysalis."

"Re-resurrection. Wow, that's really out there," Baines declared, shaking his head in amazement, "It's like self-administering without self-administering."

"You'll get no argument from me there," said Fisher.

"And going through it felt even more bizarre," Anne confessed.

"It's a new era!" Cholla exclaimed. He beamed, looking ready to jump up and somersault. "A new echelon of existence for the Human—I mean humanoid condition. We all fall under that category."

"Yes, it is, and yes, you do, Doctor," Beacon vaunted. The android turned to Anne. "Reanimation from binary back into a biological program, via a conduit of thought energy, is far stranger and more complex than simply converting DNA into binary code." The robot's eye gave Anne a once over tilting up and down three times. "But you do appear to be intact, even though I had to rush the projection and retrieval, not having the same luxury of time that I had during your first rebirth."

"So long as this revenant's latest program doesn't crash," Anne said with a nervous laugh.

"Guess you'll just have to *trust your robot* on that one," Fisher said.

Beacon let out a sound that indicated laughter. "Exactly."

"All right," Fisher said with a clap of his hands. "Our synergistic family of thought energy is happily reunited, so, yay—

us."

"Not—entirely, Captain," Anne corrected.

A shadow crept across Fisher's jubilance. "What do you mean?"

"Think back, just before you shot Resa. Did you experience anything... *incursive*—in your brain, a confluence of thought, which might have felt like a double image, or a—" Anne groped for the right word. "Hallucination?"

In the ensuing silence, the air went suddenly dry. Fisher swallowed excessively and crossed and uncrossed his arms. Anne arched a brow. *She knew.* "Have you spoken out of turn since then," she pressed, "heard voices or had thoughts you can't determine were your own?" Her rhetorical tone implied she'd already guessed the answer.

"Cap just kept repeating, 'I'm not an asshole,'" Cholla said. "And yammered on about *Wu Wei.*"

"Quiet you," Fisher snapped, suddenly fraught with consternation.

"Don't fret, Captain," soothed Beacon. He made a placating gesture with two circular saw arms—which didn't exactly inspire confidence. "Your condition is only temporary—the net result of suddenly supporting a consciousness not your own, taking residence in the unused districts of your brain, through projection."

"That's what I thought," Fisher muttered. "But why did it have to be him? I was happy thinking that I was just going nuts."

"What do you mean *going*?" Baines chortled.

"You got a point there. I'd have to be crazy to keep the likes of you around," Fisher shot back.

"You know it."

"I will remedy your dilemma as soon as I am able," Beacon said. "But first things first. My mission is only half-completed. The other half requires more immediate consideration, and I can't do it alone."

"That's a surprise, coming from you," Fisher said truthfully.

"I need your help," Beacon said. "All of you, if I am to succeed. The Blythe Entity is still at large and the storm of its puissance has surpassed my ability to contain alone. It hasn't yet reached the fullness of its power, but even now it gathers greater strength. Too many fates lay dangerously balanced on a most critical precipice, one that eclipses the recent Juncture. For the first time since my inception, after examining every conceivable recourse, I have come to realize that I cannot complete what is required without direct aid. If I don't receive it, there will be nothing left to salvage."

"Figured as much," lamented Baines. "But what really pisses me off is that after a lifetime under the Demons, conjuring fantasies about what life would be like if we erased them from the picture, when it finally does happen, all we did was trade a shitload of hellspawn for the Devil himself."

"And the Devil came back to roost," Anne said, her distant voice matching the distant look in her pupils.

"Except, we could live under the Imperium, Baines," corrected Fisher. "A sorry draconian excuse of an existence, mind you, but life all the same."

"Yes," Beacon confirmed. "With the Imperium gone, the Blythe Entity poses a much greater threat. If left to its devices, it will only continue to metastasize like a plague across all known space. Unchecked, the outcome will prove catastrophic. Given time, nothing will be immune to the Entity's wrath."

"Worse than the Garaxians' dystopian future?" asked Cholla.

Anne touched her throat. "Much worse."

"I do not refer to another dystopian future, Doctor Cholla," Beacon said. "I refer to *no* future. The Entity is the very acme of pure evil. The Dark Sector we struggled through demarcates the first caesura through which the Entity entered the Universe. You've seen the results of its emergence for yourself. Imagine your star-spangled heavens rendered the same. And that would mark the best-case scenario. That is why you must help me."

"Beacon explained it all to me," Anne put in, "while en route to rescue your sorry butts. The Blythe Entity revels in terror. That is its only source of true felicity, in every perverted sense of the word you can imagine. Over their long eons together, it admitted to Beacon that adrenaline spices its bloodlust."

Anne took a long pull from her coffee cup, which made Fisher look down at his own half-full mug. It reminded him of Jiri and sent a fresh spike of bereavement into his heart.

"The Demons had their code," Anne said, drawing Fisher back to her. "But the Blythe Entity has this sick vice. It needs to terrorize its victims first to make them more desirable before it draws succour from their life force, digesting their energy into its own matrix. And to that sick fuck, no other adrenaline surge is quite as delectable as fear. I can attest to that personally. Trust me: Blythe is a horror in any nightmare."

"But it will not be sated with mere biological definitives, even on herd and planetary scales," Beacon cautioned. "As it gains power and momentum, greater sources of energy it will draw into itself to increase its potency. The Entity will tip the cosmic balance in favour of dark energy."

"The dark and hungry god arises," Cholla quoted.

Fisher snarled and slammed his cup on the table. "That piece of shit owes the Universe big time?"

"And then some," Anne agreed with a fervent nod. "Question is: what are we going to do about it?"

Fisher's anger guttered. He did a headcount and gulped. "We? Forgive my sorry Tolkani ass if I don't throw in and wed myself to dreams of battle."

"Hope is key—for me as well," Beacon admitted. "Once that is gone, we'll look upon the battlefield with dead eyes."

Anne straightened at Beacon's words. "My ancestor said pretty much the same thing, Beacon—I read it in his diary. Seems God cut you both from the same cloth."

"We all were," Beacon replied, bringing a pair of mechanical hands together, as though in prayer. "And the fabric of that cloth is energy. To that same point, with regards to the Entity, we will fight fire with fire, or more accurately energy with energy. Do not despair. We have all the advantages."

Beacon's words rallied Baines and Cholla: both men leaned in and tightened their lips.

"Because the Entity thinks I am dead," the robot gestured to the crew with one of his arms, "along with the rest of you, it won't expect anything, not this soon after its transfiguration and reemergence. I'll explain the logistics when we get on our way. Once your two ships safely clear the Dark Sector's far horizon, we'll execute our plan. For now—"

"Trust your robot," the crew chorused.

"And Anne, trust in her too," Beacon said. "She has secured another advantage for us, a corollary, but that too is time-sensitive. We must not tarry. Know this: as far as the Blythe Entity is concerned, nothing lingers to repudiate it, and therefore it has nothing left to fear. So, our nemesis has dropped all of its guises as it roams and ravages the cosmos unrestrained in its true form."

"Okay," Fisher said a little peevishly. "Let me repeat myself. What exactly are you proposing *we* do about that?"

"Isn't it obvious?" Anne said, putting down her coffee cup and locking eyes with him. "We're going after it, Fisher. And when we find that nefarious bastard, we're going to perform an intergalactic exorcism."

"I was afraid you'd say something like that," the captain said, sinking back into his chair.

"Fisher, it won't know we're coming."

"Yeah, but Anne it—" Fisher cut off his own objection as a sudden realization took hold. Without warning he let out such a shrill laugh, everybody flinched, including Beacon.

His gaze swept the room excitedly. Everyone's face looked equally blank, so he parroted Anne, "It won't know we're coming."

Anne frowned. "Yeah, that's what I said."

"It won't *know* we're coming, Anne, because this ship's been retrofitted for the most covert stealth ops you can fathom. I'm talking zero blue-shift and red-shift. All the *Skow*'s energy emissions are contained in a heat sink embedded within her nacelles. And, we got double redundancies on every piece of stealth tech aboard the *Skow,* so there's plenty of shit to spare for the *Skow II.* Sisters should share their toys after all," Fisher added with a genuine smile.

He shook his head and snickered. "But what's so fucking ironic and goddam hilarious is that all of these state-of-the-art stealth tech upgrades were paid for by the same sorry cocksucker we're going to try and ensnare!"

429

Laughter filled the mess. Grinning ear to ear, Baines reached over and gruffly clapped his captain on the back. "One of a kind, Fish, you truly are one of a kind."

Fisher laugh-snorted. "Yeah well, we're still all cut from that same cloth, energy, *shit* Beacon was carrying on about. I'll say this though: we have to see this through. I have no clue how, but I trust that Beacon and Anne have already hashed out a plan. As for the rest of us sods, we started our careers in different places, but we all wound up on my boat."

The captain paused as he caught sight of one of the cigar-shaped engine nacelles, outside the starboard window. "The *Skow* changed careers too. She started as a salvage freighter, became a courier ship, and now... she's about to become a bona fide fishing boat. So, even though our quarry is just as likely to finish us as we attempt to net it—let's fuck back. We're going fishing."

"Well said," Beacon extolled. "And don't be afraid, Captain, not any longer. Unlike *the* Entity, we have each other—quite a considerable pool of strength, skills, intelligence and artifice I might add. It's all about synergy. Together, such a talented and experienced team will amalgamate into an *entity* greater than the sum of our parts. We will prevail." Beacon's irrefutable manner brooked no further doubt.

"Now," the robot finished in a crescendo of vaulting purpose. "Let's go fix your damn engines."

The crew stood and made to leave the mess.

"Wait." Fisher raised a hand, stopping everyone in their tracks. "I'm not lifting a finger till we remedy something first." The captain approached Beacon until he stood before the robot. Looking up and down Beacon's double-beetle torso, he began tapping a finger against the automaton's ebony casing.

Fisher faced his crew again. Everyone stared, except Anne, who only smiled.

With almost convincing severity, the captain said, "I'm gonna need some paint—yellow paint."

57: Parasol
Blythe

Of all the places the realm offered, interstellar space always seemed most agreeable. Unlike the barren expanse of intergalactic space, there was ample food to feast upon here—good food and now the titan could take its—his pick—for he always considered himself of a male gender and so gravitated towards choosing his victims from the various herds accordingly.

The Entity, formally known as Blythe, Bliter, Jiri, and countless other adopted names belonging to biological vessels from long-extinct races, could now appreciate this. For the first time since crossing over, he considered himself truly free.

Despite his emancipation, the closer the invisible form came to systems infested with starlight washing over some configuration of orbiting satellites, the less munificent he felt, the more ghostly.

There were stories here, histories unto their own, exclusive to them and histories relating to himself, pasts the Entity curtailed, and some ended by the late Imperium.

Since his reversion back to his true thought-energy form, the Blythe Entity had roamed the galaxy, free of restraint, destroying several planets and unlucky spaceships, which happened to cross his path. They posed no imminent threat, but he was late to brandish his full might and proof.

The Entity extolled glorious vehicles of horror upon those he encountered. Watched them all die screaming in mortal fear and pain. For that served his true catharsis. Great terror must be gleaned from the orgasm of his victims' deaths before he consumed them. Before he fed. The only way a biological's energy would gratify him.

At this point, it had been an exercise in testing the thresholds of his new dominion over the realm. He had his way with them. Now, they constituted nothing more than subsumed energy, component to his ever-growing power matrix.

But not all did he smote, lest he repeat his grievous error in the dark haven of his origin, his safe place—to which he would never have to return. The last remaining threats to his existence here had been utterly vanquished.

So, the Entity slowed his rampage of desecration. His consciousness grew sedate in the euphoria of undeniable victory. To savour the triumph, he opted to delay his gratification. God was sated, but not placated. Conceived too intelligent, too hungry to be satisfied with the conquest of all the galaxies and superclusters of a single realm, this so-called Universe. No, his mind ventured elsewhere in the Crib, seeking a greater purpose to better serve his puissance.

But what? The Entity could not think of an answer, unless he sought another gate—another caesura into some other realm beyond the Dark, where undoubtedly, he would gain greater strength, and justification for his omnipotence—limitless power to challenge the hypergods—wherever they chose to hide. Perhaps enough might to challenge *his* Master… Now that would provide succour indeed. Pondering this, the Entity continued his grim journey.

The Blythe Entity had scarcely begun his conquest, compared to the distance he had travelled to bring about the fatal Juncture: not quite half a year, as measured by one of the last planets to be rendered Stricken—the one world that had turned the tide for good.

One-hundred-and-eighty Earth days had elapsed since the demise of all his nemeses: The Imperium, the robot, and the reprobates aboard the *Skow II*. Their morsels of energy offered crumbs, far too meagre to ingest. It was much more vindicating to let them contemplate the cost of thraldom as they burned up in that red giant's funereal incineration.

The memory of their fate to that giant star seemed fitting since the Entity neared such a star now, in type only. First sensed from an astonishing distance, the celestial body indubitably presented the Universe's magnum opus: a hypergiant dwarfing even the mighty UY Scuti. To the Entity, this was a god, one to be reckoned with.

The titan's presence left a huge swathe of glowing gas blasting out of its corona, carried on the fiercest solar winds Blythe had ever come upon—from billions of kilometres away, it had *called* to him. The sun's heliosphere exuded so much overpowering light that its penumbra nimbused other stars in the vicinity, including a close string of blue dwarfs tidally locked by the flaming juggernaut. These small suns stood like warrens between him and the unknown hypergiant, drawing a necklace of light across the Entity's trajectory.

Slowing further, Blythe reasoned pragmatically. He could absorb the energy of the smaller, more easily digestible stars, before tackling what the hypergiant would certainly offer. A stratagem proved mandatory when dealing with such powerful stellar phenomena, so as not to repeat its folly in the Other Realm. He would feed on the dwarfs for a spell, fuelling his own furnace—something he was forced to do.

To get energy, he must expend energy. Unfortunately, a limitation to his continued existence, his godhead, but one to which his boundaries continually diminished.

The Blythe Entity rematerialized into his baser energy form: a green aura of plasma, haloed by zipping coruscations of emerald lightning forks—his feelers. The Entity reached out. And sucked.

Despite the outward flood of the godstar's solar gale, the particles emanating from the blue dwarfs immediately changed direction. They pulled away from their steady gravitational migration towards the hypergiant and flocked towards Blythe. *I am the stronger anomaly here. I harbour the stouter will.*

As the Entity impelled them into his own core, like iron shavings to a closer magnet, he sensed something new.

Something moved along the blue stream of solar ejecta. Immersed in the dwarf cluster's tide of gamma rays, neutrinos, and photons, it headed directly, heedlessly, towards the Entity. A peculiar object, with mass, solid matter, metallic, and producing its own definitive energy signature.

It was a ship, a very small ship—a shuttlecraft? If so, the solitary vessel had no right to be this far in such chaotic space on its own, let alone riding the very wake of such powerful stellar wonders.

But the Entity wasn't troubled. He regarded the approaching craft, partially obscured by the torrential mishmash of energy, with a mix of apathy and umbrage. If he had still been human, the Blythe Entity would liken the ship to a meandering insect, uncertain of the bug's intent, but easily remedied with a quick swat.

More likely than not, the ship had gotten marooned. It made

the Entity recollect his past sins, in all of his clever guises, on countless planets, which he had set on paths to destruction, all the civilizations he had abandoned to different dark fates, all producing the same result... extinction.

The Entity could dispose of the lone brazen vessel and its crew so easily. But the shuttle's audacity made the Entity curious.

***

So curious, Blythe did not notice that the infinitesimal ship was in fact not alone. Two more ships crept closer by the moment, one beyond the blue dwarf cluster and one directly behind the Entity.

So focused was the Entity on the shuttle's reason that it overlooked a subtle change in the astral dynamic. The less definitive solar particles coming simultaneously from the dwarf stars and the superstar behaved differently, obtusely altering their course and speed as if passing through a termination shock boundary.

They no longer flew towards the Entity, but away from it—or rather perpendicular to it, as though deflected by some invisible wall. The blue dwarfs' discharging particles forged a confluence with the particles exploding outward from the hypergiant, meshing together in a vortex, riding an anomalous curvature of spacetime.

And forming a cordon.

***

Unaware of this, the Blythe Entity only sensed something amiss when the overpowering radiance from the godstar became muted—as though passing through a veil, or a translucent rounded pane of polarized... glass...?

Glass!

Atavistic terror seized the Entity. He forgot about the shuttle, forgot about feeding and preeminence. One solitary thought cracked the gutrock of his black soul.

ESCAPE!

Roaring paroxysms of murderous fury, the Entity streaked back the way he had come. The storm of his passage produced an astral cyclone, flaring planet-killing power in all directions. With the atom-shredding strength of binary magnetars, the Entity blasted away from the epicentre. Ramping up to mercurial alacrity, it paralleled the sealing veil where it seemed weakest as fast as its energy mass could surge—an icon of white rage.

But the Glass—the one substance in the Universal Crib immune to the Entity's power had spread in front of it, and somehow behind it, on top, and beneath, zippering closed, forming a spherical wall a million kilometres in diameter. Nanoseconds would make all the difference between freedom and entrapment. Blythe's will burst out of him in a frantic bid to flee.

The Entity struck the barrier. Limitless power collided with infinite energy. And the impact reached that of a supernova—one detonated in a contained space. The resulting recoil blasted the Entity back to his starting point, as ungodly energies stripped and fused, and pressure waves on a supergalactic scale annihilated one another.

The ionized plasma-spangled Glass wall did—not—yield. Panicking, the Entity tried to retreat to the dead space of his blighted Dark Realm, but that gateway to subhypra could not be established within this bubble.

The exit was shut.

As the truth dawned, despair threatened to hedge the Entity to implode with futility.

And then, fanning the flames of his worst fear, the Entity perceived something even more harrowing to exacerbate his terror. The unyielding wall of glass was shrinking, closing in fast about his essence.

"*Impossible,*" he thundered, projecting denial through apocalyptic blasts of energy. His blackest wrath expressed itself in archaic half-energetic, half-biological forms, needing a vent for his inconsolable madness.

Resembling a luminescent-green, half-cloud-half-plasma ovoid, the Blythe Entity collided with the wall.

Again.

Again!

Again! He tried to impede the barrier's advance, to resist it. But the shell proved more insistent than him. The new microcosm rapidly depleted the Entity's essence, as the Glass pressed in, as the bubble diminished its internal volume of space.

From one moment to the next, the Blythe Entity's efforts became more and more ineffectual, while inversely, the wall of Glass grew more resilient against his expenditures, more prominent and denser with every kilometre it squeezed in.

The sphere drew its tethers all the tauter, sucking in solar particles at an exponential rate to reinforce its strictures. It formed its own positive feedback loop.

Soon, the Entity had been sealed at the centre of a sphere one hundred kilometres in diameter. Although the cell had not stopped shrinking, at last, it began to slow. Even at this distance from the concave barrier, there could be no immediate escape. He would have to try to solve the unbearable puzzle by some other means. Using every translated form of energy at his disposal, the Entity fashioned tendrils: prongs of white lightning to scan and possibly glean a weakness.

The tendrils shot out from its core fifty kilometres in every direction to probe every centimetre of the curved barrier.

They found no weakness. What they did find was another presence. The Blythe Entity also sensed the shuttlecraft had gone.

"*Immmmmmmmmm-possible.*" He projected vehemence like a screech of radio waves going everywhere at once.

"That's the second time you've said that," a voice spoke from somewhere in the black ether. *From subhypra space? From the outer echelon? From the hidden upper?*

"Who? Where?"

The voice crystalized. "Hello, Blythe," it said in a springy tone.

Sudden recognition seized the Entity, and he let out a squeal that pitched so high, it exceeded sound.

"Guess you finally realized that—yup—it's me. Doctor Anne Morrison—Lazarus returned from the grave you put me in. Time for some recompense, inflation-adjusted circa a gazillion for what you managed to accrue. Ante up."

58: God and Phoenix
Blythe

Within a second, a million different scenarios played out in the Entity's mind, but only one explanation emerged which might account for *her* survival. Morrison had achieved her own apotheosis after he slew her in the cockpit of that spacecraft. She had somehow mimicked his transcendence when he consumed the matter of the shuttle—a shuttle he now discerned, identical to the one that just disappeared. *But how?*

"Quite easily," the invisible voice explained. "You were brought down by your own toxic goop: deoxy—ribo—nucleic—*acid.* I can hear your thoughts in here by the way, through projection. But you must perceive that, now that we both occupy the same tandem state."

Blythe made no reply. He let the vacuous silence answer her.

"When you occupied Jiri aboard the *Skow II*," Anne said. "I scratched your pretty face. Got your active blood and skin under my nails, and with it a DNA signature to launch the Imperium's trap for you."

The Entity scrambled for understanding. *DNA should have no bearing. The Imperium formed the only nemesis with the means to challenge him. He could not take the Demons head-on, having to approach them sideways. They had the only technology to sense his presence and activate the snare, keying on his unique energy signature, but only whilst in his naked form. He couldn't get close to them for they would trigger the weapon. How could a lesser sentient rise to do it for them?*

***

"Hey dumb-ass, maybe you didn't hear me the first time. Your thoughts are live. If you don't want to talk to me, then listen. In normal circumstances, you'd be correct. The DNA signature would mean nothing, but you're forgetting the common denominator is energy. While your power mass ran Jiri's gears, the DNA monicker and your raw thought energy married in the same quantum state.

"Now, all the dead girl's blood and viscera spraying the rack-room was useless—uncoupled from your essence—just dying cells. But while you reinstated yourself in Jiri's body, well that's another story."

Silence.

"Remember the gauze? It had my blood *and* your blood on it. We gleaned your energy signature from the rag you tossed back to Fisher. While you operated said gears, your energy remained imprinted on Jiri's reanimated DNA strand. Like fingerprints at the scene of a crime. That acted as our CSI key to instigate the Imperium's weapon against you.

"Someone as 'dimwitted' as Captain Fisher figured that out. As soon as we left the ship aboard the shuttle, he had the gumption to have Dr Cholla analyse the active blood on the gauze before putting it into cryo for safekeeping. Although he didn't know it at the time, Cholla hit the jackpot, but he worked under Fisher's intuition. Maybe you should have killed the captain outright instead of wanting to make him suffer."

Silence.

The Blythe Entity said nothing to challenge Anne's explanation, so she went on. "But ultimately your overconfidence betrayed you. Back at the red giant—this titan's baby brother really, you let slip that a star of that type offered you 'purest and most coveted succour.' You used superlatives, telling us without really telling us that it would be something you'd seek and crave. We just followed the string of flashpoints reeking of your calling card, plotted your path through Baron's brand of causality, and found this hypergiant we just knew you'd never pass up. The particular nature of this sector is so perfect for your end to begin, it's simply poetic. We arrived just ahead of you and waited for you to show your ugly face."

Silence.

Anne paused too when she sensed the Blythe Entity reaching out again, using its energy-formed digits in some other way against the Glass strictures of the barricade. After a few moments, they returned to the ovoid. She likened the attempt to a small child daring a hand towards a glowing stove burner to test its heat and then thinking twice.

"Still with me, Blythe?" Anne declared. "Yeah, interesting how the latent energy in a single preserved blood cell sheathed 100% grade-A Blythe Entity. Regardless, this weapon—this prison, doesn't give a rat's ass what guise you select. It keys in on you."

Nonplussed, the Blythe Entity finally addressed her directly. "Captain Fisher is alive?"

"Oh yes, very much so." Anne twisted the knife. "Resa too."

"Where *are* you?" the Entity demanded.

"Oh, I'm here," Anne replied casually. "Part of me anyway. My shuttlecraft is safely outside the sphere, along with my corporeal form, but my life force is projected here in your cell, which now amounts to a ten—no sorry, nine-kilometre diameter. We are the same right now: energy vessels of thought. Something I learned to do when you took my life."

"Then why can I not detect your power signature?"

"Consider it the effect of being in here," Anne obliged. "This is a special cell. Even my ship can pass through the bubble if I so choose. But that would only give you something to shoot at."

"But the sphere? How?"

Anne's laughter filled the darkness with her unburdening. And packed the Entity's mind with fulminating acid. In this tandem state, Blythe's bottled fury lay bare to her. She sensed the Entity struggling to grasp any information that might help it break free. Anne would not delude it with such notions.

When she felt the Entity forcing its vehemence to ebb, she went on. "Funny you should ask, and funny, if you recall life on Earth, for Fisher 'cast the net.' We didn't fire one weapon from the Demons' arsenal. We fired two. You must have discovered by now that the sphere attenuates your energy."

The Blythe Entity examined the vigour of its being and appreciated the sickening genuineness of her boast. It already felt its power begin to plateau. And slip. The situation was direr than it first thought.

Anne parsed it all through their connection. "But if we fired the weapons according to the Exarch's specs," she said. "They would have pulverized you. And, there was one variable the late ruler hadn't thought of—your thought energy component. Leaving a very real chance that you'd escape after death—same way I did."

Anne's voice took on a sharper edge. "Tracking you over the last six months, we saw the mess you left behind to sate your voracious appetite. You've been a busy god. But no more. Business is closed—permanently."

Again, the Entity tested her words. This time, it divided into two conscious forms like a cell splitting into a pair through mitosis. One of its cells moved away to inspect the barrier up close. The shrinking sphere had slowed further.

"Won't do you any good," Anne called in a bored voice. "Divide into a million uglies instead of one. The enclosure is impervious, one kilometre in diameter, perpetually sustained by the energy of the superstar. It will feed the sphere with infinite solar power. In fact, Big Red is a long-period variable star, currently at the nadir of a five-hundred-year cycle. The more time that passes, the stronger it becomes, further constricting the walls of your cell."

"You taunt me with concepts you cannot begin to understand. Only myself and—"

"Beacon?" Anne finished the Entity's thought. "The robot you claimed to have built? For the three-thousand-plus years that Beacon and I kept company, we shared information and planned accordingly. He taught me much about the Imperium's technology, including this trap for you."

"So, it'd been the robot's ploy to dupe me all along," the Entity said. "The only explanation for your success."

"Granted," Anne ceded. "Without Beacon's help, I wouldn't have fixed this."

"Why did he do it?"

"He sought absolution for his part in your crimes. I provided his means of closing Pandora's Box. In essence, he added everything else I needed to know into my DNA coding before the *Inner Peace* lifted him off the Stricken. The ship may have been destroyed, but the secrets were intact within my binary coding— only in phantom stasis with Beacon.

"There is something you're not telling me."

"You're smart. I'll let you figure that out." Anne snorted. "We always knew that you messed with the *Skow II*'s data stream and that no one screwed with the Dark Sector anomalies, the ruptures that brought your troublesome ass into our Universe—yeah I know about that too."

Expecting the obstinate being to baulk, Anne was genuinely surprised when it calmly responded, "Then let me tell you some things you don't. I knew Percy aboard the *Blue Wind*. A good man and a serious captain. But during our tenure, I likened him to a pet I had no wish to harm, letting him live out the rest of his days in peace—my lenience permitted your inception."

Blythe's emerald aura glowed brighter. "I took my own identity through the ages as a descendant of the previous Blythe, lying low and preparing for my counterattack against the Imperium. From the eighteenth century, I advanced your race. That's how you grew so sophisticated, starting in earnest with your Industrial Revolution. I had but poor tools, and yet look to your daughter species—the culmination of my interdiction."

"Looks like the scions just bit you in the ass."

"True enough," the Entity allowed. "As the Blythe tycoon, I equipped your mission aboard the *Stormwatcher*, fitting the ocean vessel with the tech to activate Beacon. It was never your scanners and scopes."

"Why?"

"I needed to ascertain if and how the Imperium had rigged Beacon's pod—as they had done in Phoenix, post-annexation—the plasma mines, which killed Resa's crew."

"So, you lied to us for months. Surprise, surprise." Anne felt too tired to refuel her anger. Regardless, both points, sharp as they felt, were moot. "Fisher pegged you right—coward."

"Granted, I deceived you about a few matters," the Entity confessed. "But I maintain that I never sent the signal from the Hubble II to alert the Imperium. That was your robot's doing. He betrayed the Dovan, double-crossed your race and the Demons. And for his final meddlesome act before his destruction, he stabbed me in the back. Beacon has played us all for fools."

441

"Maybe, Beacon saw you as the bigger threat, Blythe, the greater of the two evils. The Demons only sought the robot as a means to neutralize you. You used Beacon as a decoy, a lure they could not resist."

"It is the nature of all creation to pursue that which retreats from it," Blythe said.

"But not Beacon," Anne countered. "He operated beyond your control, above your ability to corrupt. The whole time, he had you fooled. We all made the same mistake, thinking him inferior because he was a robot. I shudder to think of the minds that truly conceived and built him. Now, that is truly advanced."

Hidden gods—and chief among them... the Blythe Entity thought. Anne caught the strange admission but dismissed it as rambling over the mystery.

"Why the costly cold war between you and the Imperium in the first place?" she asked.

"The Demons did not originate in this verse," Blythe answered, "but neither did they hail from my own. They made me a fugitive in my own realm when they came and invoked a catastrophe there. During my meagre beginnings, I once lived as a humble biological like yourself, similarly gifted with a mind of science.

"In truth, I entered their domain first, after I discovered the means to transcend my sentience into a being of thought energy— as you have recently learned to do. When they detected me in theirs, they immediately saw me as a threat to their empire, simply because I *could* enter their realm. They sought to harness my power and devised tech to detect and siphon me. But they wouldn't be mollified with that alone. As you know, that which the Demons could not commandeer, they destroyed."

"Okay," Anne prompted. "What did you do?"

"I escaped back into my realm, but they followed me through, bent on my destruction, corrupting everything as they passed and let slip their destructive armaments. Regressing to my biological form, rendered me invisible to their probing. But alas, I remained powerless to stop them. Ultimately, they couldn't find me... so, they destroyed the entire realm instead, thinking they would

442

annihilate me along with it. Only after the Demons desecrated the entire expanse, leaving the realm reduced to a verse of deadest space, did they return to their own domain.

"But when their doomsday bomb detonated, I survived. Scant seconds before, I reinvented myself, changing into an even purer form of dark energy, one step up from my present state. I passed back into their realm to visit the same destruction they laid upon me. I wanted revenge but was ill-prepared and made to cower before adversaries where they proved strongest. I could not oppose an enemy I did not truly know or understand. I fled.

"Eventually, I escaped to your Universe, but in so doing, inadvertently left my conjured gateway open for them to use. They pursued me."

Anne ruminated as she filtered the Entity's testimony, trying to absorb everything while processing what might be true and what stank of horseshit. But all she found was fog, like the skeins her ancestor had to deal with.

"Forced to assume an iteration natural to this physical verse, I evaded them and grew wise to their ways. Because all verses are connected in the Universal Crib, I needed to end them here. Powerless to oppose their weapons directly, I had to rely on the likes of you—as beasts of burden."

Anne felt her teeth grating back in her corporeal form but she swallowed her vexation and remained silent.

"With time, they too played the game with shrewder tact," the Entity went on. "And admittedly, I slipped up from time to time, like when I tried to take Beacon off Earth. Now, that they are gone I am once again omnipotent, albeit trapped."

"If what you say is true, shouldn't there still be Demons in that realm of theirs?" Anne asked.

"No, they were eradicated there too and the gate sealed."

"I thought you said—"

"I know what I said," the Entity flared, bristling with indignation. "And yes, they posed the greatest flaw in the universal hierarchy. I did indeed carry out my act of genocide here, but I didn't do it in their realm."

"Who did?"

443

"That, I don't know."

...and chief among them. "I don't believe you," Anne decided. "You're telling me you felt you had to correct their flaw before the same thing happened here, right? But you too are a flaw, one I deem to pose the greater threat of the two. The Demons reached equilibrium here. Your morbid hunger is insatiable. How could you be any different? You both constituted an invasive species, disrupting the natural harmony of the Universe for the simple fact that you *don't* belong."

Anne drove her point home. "And what really happened to your original plane of existence? What gave the Imperium cause to obliterate it, and then leave this one intact? *Hmmm*? Did you really 'escape' there or was it something you yourself invoked?"

Silence.

"Exactly," Anne said with wry conviction. "I think you escaped from there because you *made it* dead space. You will not do the same here. You're too dangerous to be allowed to roam free. Yes, the Demons were cold and totalitarian, but at least with them, some of us still had an existence."

"How can you believe that I am more dangerous than them?" the Entity baulked. "They killed your race!"

"You are more dangerous because ever since you escaped the red giant, you've done nothing but feed and devastate. You are more dangerous because you would not be contested." *And that almost happened if you succeeded in destroying Beacon, and me,* Anne thought. "This new parasitic relationship you've developed with the Universe will only kill it. It obviously didn't work wherever the hell you came from—and that is why you showed up here."

"Ah-ha," the Entity seethed, electrical coruscations dancing through its aura. "So, Beacon was not destroyed. I hear your thoughts just as readily, Human. The robot transcended too somehow... Yes, it makes sense now. If Beacon had truly perished, you would not have managed to ambush me as you did. He was the only one who knew the full extent of the ID tech. Even if you could understand more than the feeble ten percent of your brain's functionality"

Anne let out a cynical laugh. "I may have a woefully obsolete brain, but who's the prisoner in here and who's just visiting?"

"Touché," the Blythe Entity said. Its yielding tone sounded less flippant but Anne sensed an undertow of something more elusive in the way it conceded the point. She got the impression of a malicious grin crawling across a face.

"Did you ever ask your robot who programmed him?" the Entity inquired with nonchalance. "Yes, I tinkered with it, the Dovan fiddled, the Imperium tampered, but who really controlled the entire show? I say again, the android has played us all for fools. As with the Demons, as with me, Beacon shall be your undoing."

Anne felt a lump form in her throat back on the shuttle.

"Look at what happened to all the players," Blythe pointed out. "We've nullified each other, removed ourselves from the equation. For what ultimate purpose? I don't think you'll ever find the answer because once you mention it, the robot will destroy you."

"Like you did?" Anne scorned.

"That was different. But I'll propose the right question. Heed it as a bane of one with nothing left to lose. Where did your messiah originate? Who holds the master card? Ask Beacon for a straight answer. I—dare you."

Anne let out a tired sigh. "I'll let you continue your roaming, verbal or otherwise, alone. Maybe such limited space will give you a new perspective. It's far more than you deserve. We'll periodically check in to see if you're dead yet."

The Entity's ire smouldered. "All existence is doomed without me—cantankerous races interfering with one other. You will not even ask who the real ringmaster of the black circus has been all along."

Anne said nothing.

"No, of course not. You cannot grasp the dichotomy of it. Condemn me, Morrison, but know that in so doing, you only damn yourself. Take a closer look at your robot. Ask him—who built him—who his hidden gods are. Maybe you'll parse the truth beneath the robot's duplicity before he kills you. Now, go. And be damned."

445

"You really are that craven? That alone?" Anne spoke dispassionately, but her curiosity was genuine. "I do pity you in a way but remember you brought this upon yourself. You made your bed. Actions have consequences. So, be god-damned yourself. The sphere will keep you confined in any state. Your safe place is no longer an option. As it stands now, this prison only contains you. But after I leave, it will elevate into an accelerated state, once we inject and completely infuse the catalyst into its matrix. It's the same stuff you had Beacon employ against the Imperium so you already know how temperamental it can be."

For a brief moment, the Blythe Entity's essence flashed with white brisance. Anne pondered whether it might explode. But then, twice as quickly, the critical mass guttered.

Anne still waited for a retort. When none came, she continued. "Upon my departure, if you so much as touch your prison wall, the excited particles of the plasma barricade will not surrender to your subsummation, they will not bounce back your discharges as they do now. They will rend every micron from your foul essence—tantamount to getting skinned alive.

"My guess is that you'll endure it for a million years, two at most, and then you'll find you prefer to be nothing. Whether nullification or supernova, either won't bode well for your evil ass. But perfectly acceptable to the rest of Creation."

Sensing a conclusion on the horizon, Anne paused to gather and summarize her last thoughts. "Beacon was destroyed aboard the *Infernalis*. At least the robot you thought you knew—he's been reborn, like a phoenix. And, as the phoenix rises, the god falls."

"A gamble of words and prophesy," the Blythe Entity countered in a cryptic tone. "A multifaceted game with choices you will never be equipped to handle. An endgame you cannot begin to fathom. Far from over, it is a game that has only begun—a game you will ultimately lose."

"I'll take my chances," Anne shot back. "You, on the other hand, gambled against Beacon, and lost. Fisher said you'd pay. Any last words?"

Anne knew she had a few more of her own and although the Blythe Entity's final arguments did hold some water, she had already pronounced sentence. The judge's gavel had fallen. She didn't want to prolong the ill-rooted litigation any longer than she must.

How much could be considered truth and how much bespoke deceit? She'd have to deliberate and decide that for herself. For now, she knew she had to leave.

The aura of Anne's sentience began to retreat and drift back towards the shuttle.

Like a knee-jerk, the condemned alien sensed her evacuation immediately, hailing Anne back in a voice fraught with desperation, a voice vacillating between Blythe's, Bliter's, and Jiri's before taking on all three versions simultaneously. The chorus of overlapping appeals sounded harrowing, making Anne tremble in her marrow.

"Wait, WAIT, wait, WAIT, wait, I can grant you salvation, truth, a pact, even if I remain here as your prisoner. *Don't go.*"

So, Blythe was not above grovelling for a plea bargain, Anne mused. For the first time, it appeared without equivocations, without sieves, naked, discordant, and clear of its myriad shrouds. At the core of its black soul, pinned and wriggling like an electrocuted foetus, lay a nucleus of self-pity and primal fear.

The Entity's overture of supplications: *have way——am god*——mas-ter—*redemption*, spilt over one another. Joined by hundreds more in foreign languages from its countless other guises. Their collective cries cycled up to a full discharge in a desperate bid to be heard before the end.

One voice among the ululating refrain rose above the rest, like the distinctive notes of a piccolo piercing the thick roar of a full orchestra. The angst-charged voice shrilled words Anne recognized from the Bible: an obscure passage from the New Testament—a cryptic prayer.

For the briefest of seconds, Anne thought she sensed another presence in the void, a third presence, but it flitted away before she could refocus her percipience. Still, it scratched Anne's soul and cast her withdrawing essence in a frozen shadow of doubt and consternation.

But then, the refrain of voices drowned everything out,

accelerated and meshed into one incomprehensible crescendo. Their note of mewling anguish pitched so high and so sharp that the wail silenced itself.

So, Anne did not hear Blythe's final howl of terror as the gate shut behind her and the first moment of the Entity's eternal torment began.

And for that, she was grateful.

***

Outside the plasmatic Glass sphere, back aboard her shuttlecraft, Anne Morrison reawoke in her own body. Clammy and rigid, she shut off the special subspace com-link and geared up, both mentally and physically until she felt ready.

Anne blew out her cheeks and inhaled fiercely. With a flip of a switch, she fired up the shuttle's main thrusters and engaged the tiny ship on a preset trajectory to a designated waypoint. Two sister ships would be waiting there to rendezvous with her.

It had been a long shot, a long journey, and one very long day.

Billions of people had been lost in the process, genocide occurring on planets beyond count, but the pervasive plagues of Pandora had finally been reined in and quelled. As a result, trillions more innocent souls would survive.

Kudos to the Human, Allianthan, Korian, Tolkane, and Tolkani resolve. Even when faced with seemingly insurmountable odds, without technological parity, they had found a way to do the impossible—together. They located and used the key of Epimetheus, so a new era could be possible.

Anne envisioned the key entering the quintessential keyhole while the lid on Pandora's infamous Box pressed down against all the malfeasance and profligacy it sought so long and so hard to recapture and contain.

Anne rejoiced as the lid slammed shut with a resounding thud. She turned the key.

And locked the box.

59: Trust Your Robot
Fisher

Fisher squinted as he looked out the window at the bright yellow star. Beneath it, Resa's homeworld, Tolkane rotated, the haze on its far hemisphere dancing in the sun's warm aura. An artist's palette of verdant blues and greens infused the serene world while wispy pink and purple clouds drifted over its surface.

High above, the M-class planet, two ships basked in sunlight as they mirrored one other, flying in perfect parallel formation while maintaining a standard equatorial parking orbit.

After several time-consuming albeit worry-free jumps from the hypergiant where they had incarcerated the Blythe Entity, the *Skow* and *Skow II* had finally arrived. Three weeks had passed since the sister ships left the sector dominated by the supermassive godstar.

Fisher's cadre marked the system in that quadrant with a halo of automated warning satellites. Placed at regular intervals amidst the necklace of blue dwarfs, the solar-powered robotic buoys bade all space traffic to steer clear of the captive energy sphere they monitored. That seamless globe of tempered Glass, one kilometre in diameter, imprisoned the devil. Forced him to roost and brood indefinitely.

Banked upon the reassurances of Beacon, the crew's questions concerning the ultimate endgame had been left to pile up during the journey here. Indeed, for a full six months before that, ever since they'd narrowly escaped imminent death at the hands of another stellar giant.

They tried of course but their eponymous robot always gave the same oblique response, *trust your robot*—a response that wore thin a month after they left the first red giant in pursuit of the Blythe Entity. These queries and more followed the sister ships like excess baggage not to be opened until Mr Gearbox saw fit.

To make matters even more vexing, once they had caged the beast, Beacon remained quite dogged when it came to discussing their quarry's fate or any party or event related to it.

We must not fuel conjecture, the android maintained with an almost militant persistence. He also insisted that they depart the Entity's territory in silence and hold to a *unilateral alignment. To deviate from this mindset might waylay the crew and still invite failure.*

Beacon scrutinized them in this, and when they strayed, calmly reprimanded them to mind their words and police their thoughts—should they attempt projection. The robot, they all agreed, was one big conundrum.

Beacon promised that he'd explain everything and hear all their accounts in one great powwow—as soon as they reached safe harbour.

To Fisher, the automaton's pledge seemed ludicrous. "We neutralized the Imperium and the Entity both," the captain complained whenever he and Baines started drinking. "It's fucking safe everywhere."

For some reason, Beacon remained aloof whenever they vetted him directly. The robot stonewalled them, adamant that they accomplish the task first before he divulged any more info, citing causality and his usual retinue: 'I want to make certain we capture the Entity first. Otherwise, we might still face consequences.'

Then, once they did just that, the robot resolved, 'I'd feel better if we leave the vicinity of its prison first—which proved to span all of the known cosmos.'

Fisher always marched away in frustration.

But no more.

At last, the time had come to hear Beacon's full tale, unabridged and uncensored.

At the sound of the robot's approach, Fisher turned away from the canteen window and took in his crew. They sat on the edge of their seats, around the long mess hall table, a cup of coffee in front of each. The distinct aroma of the roasted beans helped Fisher relax as he scanned their faces: Baines, Cholla, Anne, and *Resa*—the captain never quite got used to that one, nor would he ever. But truthfully, *impossible* didn't seem to fit into his vocabulary any longer, not after what they pulled.

Fisher put his thoughts aside as he grabbed an available chair and sat with them for Beacon's show. The robot held the floor now. The familiar yellow smiley-face the captain had repainted across Beacon's shiny new chassis beamed at him from across the table. A necessary symbol of the robot's personification and integrity, it also marked a rechristening of Beacon's soul and as Fisher often joked, his most charming attribute.

But the memory of Beacon injecting the catalyst particles into the Entity's prison sphere immediately following Anne's return still haunted the captain. Beacon had carried out the act without remorse or ceremony, like an executioner administering a lethal injection to a condemned convict.

"My friends you are, all of you, the architects of salvation," the robot began. "But before I say anything else, I want to let you know why I've waited so long to tell you the whole truth of our long and turbulent relationship."

The crew licked their lips, exchanged glances and leaned in. Once they settled, the robot continued, "While aboard the *Skow II*, although I knew the Entity lurked among you, I didn't know exactly who it might be. The mole kept itself hidden from me until the Imperium scanned the ship. Even then, I only sensed Bliter, or more accurately the absence of him. That the Blythe Entity would split its essence between two separate chrysalises never occurred to me. It was clever of it to do this but in the end, you forced it to reveal both of its *selves*. That it might try again with another host became a distinct possibility. Right up until now, I felt justifiably afraid of that likelihood—hence my riddles and subterfuge."

"Yeah, Fisher looked just about ready to fire you into the trash compacter for that one," Baines laughed.

"Frankly, I didn't know if one or more of you might still be compromised by the Blythe Entity," said Beacon. "Nothing could I divulge of my true mission or leave to chance where the Entity was concerned. That I tell you this now is proof-positive that we have moved past any doubt. I see you all as on the level."

"That's a relief," Fisher murmured. He reached for the coffee Anne had poured for him.

"Just dotting all his 'I's and crossing his 'T's, Cap," Cholla mildly defended.

Beacon clapped two of his metallic hands together. "So, where to begin?"

Fisher lifted his gaze from the robot's gauntlets to his upper hemisphere. "How about you start with that weapon, or weapons of yours?" He took a sip of his coffee and breathed. "Weapons against a god—I still can't believe they worked."

"In deploying the armaments, we mimicked fishermen casting nets. We had to fire them far enough ahead of and behind our catch so that the Entity would not sense anything. Initially, the interference of the hypergiant masked the ordinance. If our adversary detected them before we sealed and strengthened the vortex of the bubble—enough to form a positive feedback loop—the plasma projection wouldn't have worked. Our whole team needed to remain in complete concert. Anne's ruse worked flawlessly to ensure this."

"It was such a narrow margin of success," Anne put in, "like a tree trying to hold on to its leaves in the middle of a hurricane."

"Exactly," Beacon agreed. "If the alien would have been a little warier, not so convinced that it had eliminated all threats, it would've slipped through the same way it eluded the Imperium for countless millenniums."

"But why didn't Blythe just fade out like last time?" asked Baines.

On either side of his upper torso, Beacon splayed three sets of appendages angling them down in a textbook display of robotic surrender. "That's the whole point of the net, Pilot Baines. "Why Blythe wanted it so implicitly. And the Demons wanted to use it so badly. They had devised the catalytic tether to prevent the Entity from doing just that. Hence their dogged pursuit of me. Each party grew desperate for the real tech I carried all along."

"I thought it was that time travel business against the Demons," Baines said.

Beacon's dome eye tilted up and down in affirmation. "You are partly correct. I stored that data in my circuitry as well—the blueprint concept and science in any case. But its tech is indeed plausible though incomplete."

"From what I understand," Anne said. "Blythe only made it

seem legit—enough to monger fear throughout the Empire, leaving just enough breadcrumbs that the Imperium wouldn't question its validity. The Entity played to their xenophobia but it too grasped that the tech was derelict."

"Correct," Beacon avowed. "It gave the Demons enough intel to whet their doubt and drive them to mess about with me. Blythe tampered with me too, but through me, in the end, they pried and disseminated each other. I became the proverbial barrel over which they both clung. But that meant being their bitch as well."

Fisher and Baines erupted in laughter and even Resa cracked a smile.

"Paranoia fuelled the fundamental flaw in the Demons' thinking, and the reason for their extinction," said Beacon. "As it had done with several races before, the Imperium regarded Humans as priority obstacles. According to this same illogic, the Demons dreaded the divine in us all, forever seeking to negate it. More than that, they feared the unknown, whether a tangible threat existed or not. And overkill served as their modus operandi."

"You'll get no argument from me," Fisher said, remembering the armada.

"The Blythe Entity presented an entirely different obstacle," the robot added. "It had successfully manipulated the Imperium for eons. What it told Anne about the Demons invading its realm was false. It was the other way around. The Entity invaded theirs—after desecrating its own.

Baines harrumphed. "You can't be serious."

"Invaded *and* destroyed it," Beacon confirmed.

"How?" Cholla piped in.

"It meddled, introducing alien mechanisms, elements of nothingness best likened to *anti-dark energy* from its own blighted realm to disrupt the physical laws that governed the Demon's expanse, all for its insatiable need to siphon energy-based sustenance.

"The Garaxian Empire too governed their place of origin with a ruthless fist but they understood the requisites of preserving predator/prey equilibrium. Not Blythe. You might liken the Entity to the criminal mind of a serial killer housed under a parasol of parasitic ruin, gone amok."

"Wow, quite the sunny comparison," Baines marvelled. "To think, I sat at the same table with that thing—things."

"And I went to work for the guy," Anne added, "Told him at the outset that I wouldn't be a good fit but he cajoled me. Bet he's regretting that decision now."

When the chorus of laughter ebbed, Beacon continued, "If not for its intrusion, the Demons never would have come here. The Entity left them no choice. The malignancy of its presence metastasised across their cosmos like a super gamma-ray burst without end. That is until their universe ended. Then the lights went out permanently.

"Before that happened, the Demons fled. They left their realm in utter ruin, writing it off as it were. They hoped the Entity would be trapped there and die with no more energy left for it to subsume. They were wrong. Though not immediately, the Entity eventually followed them through."

Fisher drew his chin back. "Never would have come— fucking hell. They escaped the Entity by coming here?"

"Close to ten million years ago," Beacon said. "They came through a caesura initially rent by the Entity, which became the black miasma of singularities you call the Dark Sector. The Demons came through the rift first, without incident. They brought their cache of weapons with them, including the Glass. The fundamentals of your Universe gave them a superior advantage in their weaponry. The effect of plasma as artillery or propellants multiplied exponentially here. It gave them an aggressive edge, a real chance at fighting back and destroying the Entity.

"But shortly after the Demons first established their homeworld and began perfecting their defensive and offensive measures—shortly on a cosmic scale mind you—the Entity followed them through the schism. The ID had unintentionally left a trail: ghost traces of plasma signatures."

"So, what happened?" Fisher asked.

"The laws of physics that govern your Universe could not cope with the magnitude of the Entity's raw energy, in conjunction with the plasma particles it followed through the wormhole portcullis. The Entity's transcendental immigration sheered the spacetime continuum, birthing the volatile Dark Sector.

"After what the Entity had done to its own lost realm and that of the Imperium, it could not linger in either. Nothing survived but blighted abysses of exhausted dark energy. And the Entity needed sustenance. It might have moved into another verse but before destroying the Demons' realm, the Entity gleaned the mortal threat they posed to it. That, fearing retaliation, they'd seek it out in whichever realm and eradicate it. Taking a preemptive step, Blythe came here to do the same to them."

"What is the Entity's Dark Realm?" Cholla asked.

"A void," Beacon answered. "Dead space.".

Anne's eyes widened. "You mean like the subhypra conduit we discovered back on Earth?"

"Yes, subhypra defines the whole of Blythe's original dominion. Utter nothingness."

Cholla raised a finger. "The conduit—is that similar to a wormhole?"

Beacon dialled his upper torso from side to side twice. "No, Doctor, nor is it a channel in the literal sense. But imagine a pair of hatches, one in, one out, married and working in quantum conjunction. Signals, plasma, even matter could translate through the hatch, which tapped into the Entity's realm and re-emerged through another entry/exit at some other locus into yours. That said, there exists an infinite number of access points in and out of the subhypra verse. The actual pairing is based on the journey you conjure."

"A whole universe of that?" Anne exclaimed.

"Yes," the robot said.

"*God.*"

"Because of its detectable nature, once here, the Blythe Entity knew it dared not oppose the Demons directly. They had the perfect defence: the Glass—a benison that served them well with another foe, helping the Imperium to defeat the Amalgam. Having seen how the Entity's machinations worked, the ID quickly advanced methods of defence and then, with my help, offence, specifically a method to trap and kill their hidden nemesis."

455

Beacon raised one of his metallic arms and examined the conical tip for a moment. "The Blythe Entity thought that tinkering with me would allow it to accomplish its dirty work. But I screened both sides equally."

"The barrel," Fisher ventured.

"Yes, the barrel. I also made plans when Captain Resa inadvertently activated me. Without the influence of the packet, I circumvented Blythe's control. It hexed the Entity with a mystery and caused it great frustration. I had to leave Blythe guessing. It couldn't grasp that most of its snags had been my doing."

"Until now," Resa said.

"Its fatal flaw, which ultimately caused its downfall, was to regard me strictly as a machine."

"Blythe didn't trust his robot," Fisher said as he tipped back his coffee and thought of Jiri.

"Neither did the Exarch," Beacon supplied. "He too entered the Imperium's subroutines and viral-bot algorithms, seeking to subvert me into doing his bidding. But again, in the end the one lethal mistake he made was to judge me harshly as a device: programmable, pliable, corruptible."

Baines grinned. "His bitch."

"As such," Beacon acknowledged, "I kept to my own agenda—with the Universal Crib's best interest in mind. Granted a cybernetic positron-based mind, but *a* mind nonetheless, hard-wired with ethics and priorities immutable to alteration. Including yours."

"But you allowed me to download your memories into my own squishy brain pan," Anne pointed out. "You made a biological computer in here." She tapped her index finger against the side of her head. "I'd construe that as manipulation."

"Yes, but you always had my best interest in mind—pun intended—synonymous with the universal need. I recognized that, so I permitted the sharing. If Blythe uncovered the truth behind how I devised to trick it, matters in the endgame might have gone very differently."

"Quite a long and risky hand to play, Beacon," Resa observed.

"Considering what I had to deal with, it was the only way to play, Captain. The Blythe Entity had its powers, the Imperium had its tech and infinite numbers, but if matters weren't brought to a head through my intervention, the chase would have continued for millions of years longer than it did, at the expense of all the realm's galaxies and their inhabitants."

Beacon floated to the other side of the mess table. "And it wouldn't have ended here with the demise of your Universe. All realms and realities, including the Demons' wasteland, including the Entity's subhypra domain form part of what is called the Universal Crib. It marks the governing denominator of definitive existence. Eventually, the entire Crib, which cradles them would be threatened. I couldn't let that happen."

Baines murmured, "And the cradle will rock."

"You see," Beacon said, blowing past the pilot's reference, "when I destroyed the packet for good, both the Exarch and the Entity had nowhere left to turn, except me. The Juncture became cardinal to either faction, with me amounting to the quintessential linchpin holding all of their machinations in place. I alone held the secret tech both of them desperately needed to thwart the other."

Fisher studied the exoneration on his crew's faces. Feeling a glimmer of the same, he dropped his eyes to his half-filled cup of coffee. He'd want something stronger soon.

"I needed to get close to the Exarch," the robot went on. "I deduced that the Garaxian figurehead would go there, drawing in so much of his fleet. This endgame was for all the marbles. Under the Blythe Entity's protocols, the closer we came to the nexus, the more dangerous the gambit became. But I had to decapitate the head of the Imperium before proceeding. I broadcasted to the Entity that if it harmed anyone aboard the *Skow II,* I would abort the mission it set out for me by self-destructing. Likewise, I led the Exarch to believe that if he made any tactical advance against your ship, he'd lose his last chance against the Entity."

Two of Beacon's internal servos whirred at the same time, producing what sounded like a mechanical sigh. "But as expected, once the Exarch received all the data he required, he reneged on his vow to spare your lives. He hammered the final nail in his coffin when he ordered me to fire upon your ship—5303's last

457

mistake."

"You held many secrets, my friend," said Resa. He placed a hand over his heart and paused as though checking to see that it still ticked. "Not least of which, your ability to project subconscious ideas into our heads."

"It proved a successful method for bypassing the constant dual-surveillance we found ourselves under," Beacon explained. "Both paramount and advantageous but if you feel invaded by my incursion, I apologize."

"Not at all," Resa chuckled. "On the contrary, I'm quite happy to be alive."

"Well, it worked," Fisher said. "You're alive and still as annoying as ever."

Resa surrendered a smile. "Thanks, Captain. And thanks again for listening to me."

Fisher met Resa's eyes and gave him the briefest of nods. "You freaked me out with that first projection of yours. Now, that *was* an intrusion. You assumed my alter ego right up until robot guy here extracted your conscience out of my poor head."

"Yes, but up until that point you really thought I was the spy on your ship," Resa reminded him.

Fisher drew back. "What do you mean, thought? I still think you're a villain." He deflated his lungs. "But at least you're a rogue on our side, and off my property."

"I've always been on the Cardinal's side, Captain Fisher, God's side."

"Right," Fisher said. "Speaking of villains, what went down with Wisdan that time before we left the convoy?"

"The Cardinal? Oh, you mean our private chat. Yes, that might have looked a little suspicious, but frankly at that point, I felt the same about you. Though he couldn't be one-hundred-percent certain, the pontiff imparted his notions about Bliter." Resa's voice trailed off as he levelled his gaze at Fisher. "And he implored me to trust you."

Fisher arched a brow. "He—said that?"

"Among other things," answered Resa. "He also held a copy of the cypher for your packet, a Dovani codex already translated from their language. The Cardinal knew Anne's adroit colleague, Fieldbank before the roundup. Baron entrusted Wisdan to carry the duplicate for him."

Fisher shook his head in amazement. "This Baron guy practically exuded pragmatism. Everyone and their mother had nothing but praise for the guy. Even Blythe extolled his virtues. Would've liked to have known him."

Anne's lips curved into a sad smile. "The feeling would've been mutual."

Fisher's eyebrows pulled together but before he could ask her to elaborate, Resa went on. "Long before the Cardinal ever met you, Captain, he sent me on several sorties, *posing* as a priest but *acting* as his spy. I earned some good repute as a salvager, which led the Funder to me. I took the client's proposed plans for the salvage job to Wisdan. The whole thing stank to me, but Father seemed to receive an oracle. From what Baron had told him, the Cardinal gleaned that the job intertwined with his colleague's causal model."

Resa raised two fingers to his node and stared out the window. "Trusting Wisdan, a man I held above reproach, I accepted the assignment. My life and that of my crew were unimportant in the full scheme of things. I knew that whatever we found on the Stricken would form the crux, a precursor that would either align all the worlds in the cosmos—or damn them forever."

Resa let out a tired breath as he returned his attention to Fisher. "The Cardinal knew part of the truth concerning the trigger-and-response construct."

Baines frowned. "The what?"

"The, um, house of cards," Resa clarified. He lifted the coffee mug to his lips and swallowed some. "But no one saw the complex depth surrounding Blythe's duplicity, not even Beacon. That said, I suspect through a different causal vein that Baron Fieldbank parsed the entire ironclad truth of, well pretty much everything. To that effect, he was the real orchestrator. Baron set the groundwork for our success."

Fisher followed Resa's study as it slanted from Baines to Anne.

Emotion glistened in the woman's pupils. She swallowed, acknowledging Resa's deference with a projected *thank you*, which Fisher caught.

When the soundless moment passed, Resa cleared his throat and faced Fisher. "The Cardinal had his reservations, of course, a hypothesis concerning a plot within a plot. Wisdan knew something was afoot when you showed up looking for help. But maintained his front for appearances."

Resa thrust his chin at the captain. "But when you divulged your recovery of me, you confirmed his worst fears."

"Well, actually—" Fisher began to protest but decided the point was moot.

"Blythe stowed aboard your ship as Bliter *and* Jiri," Resa continued, taking another sip of his coffee. "As you indicated, Captain, it contrived to meet with the Tolkane cutter, *Maelstrom*, but the ID destroyed the spacecraft in the Centauris X sector, shortly before the *Skow* showed up."

Fisher wagged a finger at Resa. "You knew that ship, didn't you?"

"Aye," Resa confessed. "It connects both our tales. That ship's captain, Jro worked as Blythe's associate—the furtive one I dealt with back on UM. Guess Blythe used the same pawn in both our cases."

"But why the rendezvous at all?" Fisher pondered. "The *Skow* could have easily dropped off the payload elsewhere."

"If I remember Jro correctly," Resa said, "he was nothing but bad news. I can only surmise Blythe wanted to change ships and spirit Beacon away before discarding you."

"But the Imperium got the *Maelstrom* first," Baines said.

Resa dipped his chin. "By the sword, Baines. Always figured that would be how Jro finally cashed it in."

"You are correct, Captain Resa," Beacon confirmed, "As for the *Maelstrom*'s destruction, I'm afraid that was my doing."

Fisher and Resa did a doubletake.

"I couldn't let the Blythe Entity board that ship. I signalled the Imperium as a loyal Robot T-261 ought to. Had Blythe succeeded in connecting with that vessel, the Entity would have advanced too far ahead in the game. I should imagine Bliter and Jiri would have gone missing once Captain Fisher delivered the packet. Jro and crew planned to storm your ship, disable her drive, and commandeer me. Then, once Blythe had what he needed aboard the *Maelstrom,* Jro's ship would've locked weapons on the *Skow* and destroyed her. I had to interdict."

Fisher slapped a hand on the table, making everyone wheel. "No wonder Bliter got so pissed off back at the Junkyard."

"Yes," Beacon said over Fisher's wry chuckle. "I caused most of its frustration, whether the Entity sensed it or not. But not all."

Fisher leaned back in his chair and combed ten fingers through his hair. "Bet the Cardinal must've given it a really bad bellyache."

"Yes, Captain, tempered metal best describes Wisdan's character," Beacon agreed. "Though I never spoke with him directly, I quickly discerned that he was a true Mensch. Maybe the Gods spoke to him forthwith. Causality works that way sometimes, piecing together eventualities that I may have overlooked. But most likely, Baron told him his part to play."

"Either way sounds like karma," said Resa. "And on that note, Wisdan told me during our final meeting that he didn't expect to survive the endgame but would go along with it anyway, on faith." He sucked in a breath mired in grief before turning to Fisher. "Do you remember, just before Cholla thawed me aboard the *Skow II,* the Cardinal telling you about terrible things afoot?"

"Figured he meant the ID," Fisher confessed.

Resa shook his head. "No, the causal worm he referred to was the Blythe Entity. He never mentioned the Imperium but spoke to you in such a way to maintain ambiguity for your protection. Wisdan knew someone on your crew was not who they appeared to be, but he dared not pry. He deduced that the less detail he knew of our plans—including the robot he all but ignored—the less he could divulge if and when the Demons caught up with his fleet."

Resa blew out his cheeks. "His unfeigned ignorance would keep him and his flock safer, longer, so that *we* would be kept safer, longer. I'm guessing that's part of the reason the ID didn't destroy the *Skow II* right away when they captured her. The Exarch had not gleaned the truth of the matter."

Fisher's sudden paradigm shift brought with it a rush of guilt about the Cardinal. Beneath that bauble-littered cassock of his, the pontiff had balls of pure steel.

"After that, timeliness and causality became the most delicate components of a volatile bomb," Resa finished. "One, in the last stages before detonation."

"But the Blythe Entity never counted on how fast we'd find the packet," Cholla guessed. "We forced it to improvise."

Resa cocked his head at the doctor. "Exactly right. During our captivity on the Apoc ship, Bliter offered to help me—with the intent of frying me. If you recall, it was his notion about the renegades having only one perimeter. He—*it* knew that Demon ship inside out."

"That it did," Beacon confirmed. "Sometime in the ancient past, the Entity infiltrated a Demon cruiser and killed the entire crew—to familiarize itself with the layout and functionality of their ship."

"Makes sense," Resa said. "Blythe set the Apocs up, betrayed them to the Imperium. It knew all along how to get us out but just waited it out to see how Beacon would respond and how quickly the Garaxians would close in. When that failed, Blythe resorted to using its Jiri-half more boldly and more often. I caught on, and began watching her closely."

Fisher nodded morosely. No matter how many times someone mentioned Jiri's name, it always brought the same pain and bereavement, remembering her innocence, sense of duty and loyalty, and her sunny disposition. The loss of Jiri, the real loving Jiri, stung him to no end.

"When we were captured in earnest," Resa went on, "I pegged it on Bliter for he was not on the bridge. But when Jiri reported the supposed failure with the bridge playback, I knew for certain that she was linked. Rather than cry fie, I acted. Though in truth, I never saw Bliter fade out, phasing back to its dead universe. At that time, I imagine Jiri reversed roles, making Bliter the true master, before the Demons began scanning. She became the slave—responding automatically like a drone."

Resa stopped, number elevens creasing as he took notice of Fisher. "I'm sorry."

"It's okay." Fisher croaked with a dismissive sweep of his hand. "Go on."

Resa bowed his head and continued more solemnly. "That was one of the Blythe Entity's real powers. It could disappear when needed, but had to leave one chrysalis behind to maintain its toehold in our Universe—a verse of matter. Otherwise, it would have repeated the folly of its first entrance, causing the birth of another Dark Sector, which would have destroyed Beacon and the robot's finished weapon against the Imperium. In this, it could manipulate energy like a changeling."

Cholla wiped his glasses with a cloth. "Shouldn't Blythe have been invisible to the Demons just by remaining in corporeal form, as he did for thousands of years? Why the fade-out at all?"

Resa lifted his shoulders. "Good question."

"In normal circumstances, you'd be correct, Doctor," Beacon answered. "But remember the Imperium's halo? The meticulous arrangement of their armada was no accident. Though they could not pinpoint the Entity's signature, they did have it cordoned through the plasma of their ships. Once the Entity faded, it took its dark energy with it, but the ID still had their nemesis pinned. It would be like having a prisoner in a cell with the lights off. You can't see him, but you know he's still trapped in there. The Blythe Entity could transport to a dozen different realms, but in every single iteration, it would occupy the identical quantum spot. The halo formed a temporary holding cell until the Demons could fire the right weapon."

"Their magic bullet," Anne supplied.

"I didn't know any of this at the time," Resa said. "I only concluded that the suspect had to be alone or near to being alone when the Demons scanned the ship. I needed to shadow him or her. Something Beacon bade me do whilst on the ID scout."

Resa pivoted towards Fisher. "In all honesty, after our constant rows, I thought you were the Exarch's fugitive, Captain. But I had to scratch your quarrelsome ass off my shortlist," the Tolkane complained.

463

Leaning back, Resa placed his hands behind his head and faced the others. "In the end, I narrowed it down to Bliter and Jiri. Even though I piggybacked a recording from Fisher's little 'posterity' feed and had it burned directly to a disk in my cabin, I still required a visual confirmation myself. After all the shit hit the air scrubbers, I left the bridge and went back to my cabin to retrieve the disk."

Anne inclined her chin. "With the Demons in the immediate vicinity gone, Blythe as Bliter returned from its dark void."

"Bliter and/or Jiri caught on to my movements," Resa added. His eyes shifted from Anne to the others. "But not my exact purpose, and most certainly not my recording. Forced to improvise again, they concocted their farce. Bliter shot his Jiri vessel—same being after all.

"I drew close but stayed back until I heard Jiri shout my name. By the time I reached her corpse, the Entity had double-backed using its special magic to expedite its passage, first to my cabin to implicate me, then back to the bridge to exonerate Bliter's involvement in the act."

"I allowed us to be captured at the Juncture to weed out the real antagonist," Beacon said.

All faces tracked him as he drifted back to his original roost at the far end of the table. "The ploy spearheaded my master plan to eliminate the Imperium at their greatest confidence, then remove the Napoleonic threat. As the Juncture waned from vertex, the Entity's power was weakest—something I counted on after its long hiatus from its true form. I synchronized and exploited the fatigue of both parties."

Resa's hands left the back of his head, scratched his crown, and dropped to the table. "Beacon foresaw that I would take the blame for your capture and any undermining of the mission that you'd pin on me. As soon as I found Jiri, I realized I'd take the fall for her feigned death." He nudged his chin at Beacon. "I went along with it—as our trusty robot planned my reincarnation afterwards. Captain Fisher understands why I had to provoke him so ruthlessly and impetuously, aloud."

"To convince the Entity of your mutual chaos," Cholla said. "It sure convinced me!"

Resa gave the doctor a half-smile. "I used projection to secretly reveal the truth of the situation to our good captain. Otherwise, the Entity would guess I knew and might cause a divergence from Beacon's crucially timed plans. To the Entity, I was Fisher's final loose end. Disguised in its Bliter cloak, it just waited for me to go.

"True to form, Fisher acted obstinate at first, loathe to take such drastic measures, even in my case," Resa chided. "But that only made it all the more plausible. In the end—my temporary end—Fisher came to realize the paramountcy of our little con. He agreed to let the still-hidden fugitive think beyond a doubt that it had escaped detection."

"With your death and my destruction," Beacon put in, "the Blythe Entity thought its foolproof plan sealed. As the Exarch had done, it underestimated and overlooked how much I had advanced by the time both sides reached the Juncture."

"Anne parsed what I was about," Resa said. "I glanced at her at the height of our little crisis and when she gestured with her eyes that she agreed to our trick, I went ahead and riled Fisher up something fierce, not too difficult with all the practice we had."

Fisher shot Resa a look of indignation but behind it shone a measure of genuine respect. The Tolkane met his gaze, and to the amazement of all the others, the captains shared a smile of camaraderie.

When the moment passed, Resa shifted his eyes towards the others. "I projected my entire essence into Fisher's head—something Beacon taught me to do through Fisher's behavioural inhibitor—a second before he killed off my corporeal form. Once settled in his neural net, I stored my essence in a similar fashion to what Beacon had employed to keep Anne alive. In my case, however, I occupied a village of neurons in the captain's brain rather than a consciousness translated into binary code."

"I was stripped down to a series of pulses and non-pulses," Anne regaled. "Free-flowing within a virtual cybernetic construct housed in Beacon's positronic brain, but the neural coding and quantum essence of both underscores the same energy."

Resa hiked two thumbs up. "Like Anne and Beacon in their collective cybercosm, Fisher could visit my 'village' whenever he chose, if only to argue some point or another. As his prowess with projection reflected that of an infant, he responded aloud from time to time. To the outside observer, he might've appeared to be suffering from schizophrenia."

Cholla smiled with his eyes.

"I like to think we've come to understand one another after our lengthy conversations in there," Resa laughed, pointing at Fisher's head. "But I'm still grateful to be out and safely migrated into this surrogate. Knowing that our mechanical messiah prepared it for me from my own DNA makes it feel more like home."

"Well, that ugly corpse of yours was good for something after all," Fisher growled. "Got to admit though, your hectoring me about being an asshole—clever. It jogged all those warm fuzzy feelings I had about you."

"I knew it would," Resa said astride a chortle.

"But do you really think I'm an asshole?"

"No," Resa answered, unblinking. "I know you're an asshole—one with chronic haemorrhoids."

Fisher threw his head back in a raucous bout of laughter. "We should drink to that."

Baines reached down below the table and magically produced a bottle of liquor and a stack of five shot glasses.

Anne raised a hand, palm out. "Thanks. None for me yet."

The pilot shrugged as he placed the small glasses in a row and poured.

"In due course," Beacon reminded them, making a warding gesture with one of his motorized arms. "You must still get fully debriefed first. There is more to tell about the route we've come and where we must tread henceforth."

"You just reminded me of something," Fisher said. "With the Imperium gone, and Blythe doing hard time, we can go back to what we were doing, only better." The captain's attention shifted to Baines.

"You're talking about the *Skow II*," the pilot guessed.

Fisher nodded. "Now that there's no more reason to hide her, Baines, why don't you take command of her? We can tag-team."

Baines shook his head. "No way, Fish, not a chance, I'm staying right here on your boat. Life would be a bit on the boring side without you providing endless entertainment."

"Baines, I'm touched. I never knew you cared."

"Well, somebody's got to watch your sorry ass, next pickle we find ourselves in, and knowing you, there's bound to be jars and jars—a pantry full of 'em."

Fisher laughed before his gaze settled on Resa. "How about it, Mr Freeze? Think you can keep thawing that sense of humour you absorbed from my brain? You're a captain too after all."

"I don't know, Admiral," Resa said.

Fisher's smile straightened. "My stint as admiral was short-lived, and I prefer it that way."

Anne frowned. "Why is that?"

"Too many responsibilities," Fisher glanced at her before seeking Resa's attention again. "So, what do you say? Wanna be reinstated? It's the least I can do for killing you."

Resa lifted a hand to his chin and took Fisher's measure. "You really want to be *partners*?"

Fisher inclined his head.

"Well, if I can't kill you for all the shit you put me through, might as well steal your ship." Resa smiled and shook his head, "Yeah, I'll join you, Captain. Guess that'll make me an asshole too."

"Worst kind. Welcome to the club," Fisher said, lifting his glass of grog. The other three men followed suit, toasted, and tipped them back.

"Here's to no more Imperium and no more Entity," Baines

added as he poured a second shot for himself and the other drinkers. "Wow, things might still get pretty boring round here after all," the pilot laughed.

"Hardly," Fisher said. "We still got to punch in. It's always been about time, but at least it will be an easier time, and a lot more legal."

"Yeah, time," Baines agreed. "To think, an advanced race like the Demons bought that whole fiasco about time travel. All bullshit, eh Beak?"

The four men tipped back their shot glasses in silence. When Beacon kept quiet, they all turned their heads to face the robot. He remained silent.

After a moment, Fisher pressed, "*Eh* Beacon? Blythe said it was a ruse."

"The ruse, Captain Fisher, was on it," Beacon replied at last.

"Which part? Wait, you're saying it's possible?"

"I'll say nothing, except that time is a factor in causality whether it moves forward or backwards. Remember, when you look upon the most distant stars, you see them, in some cases, as they existed billions of years ago. That constitutes a real-time window into the past. On the other hand, the future's parameter is gauged according to the nearness of an object approaching the speed of light, and when the problem of exponential mass tabulation around supermassive black holes is—"

"Stop!" Fisher cried. "I'll leave that one to Cholla. That should keep him happy for a while. As for this bottle, it'll keep me happy for a while."

"Fisher?" Beacon said, stopping the captain as he finished pouring another measure. "Before you indulge too much, there's something else I believe will be of interest to you."

"What now?" Fisher asked as he lifted his glass.

"I've found out something," Beacon replied. "Something about your lost lineage."

The glass stopped midway to Fisher's mouth, spilling a few drops on the table. "My—*how?*" Fisher's smile sank into bemusement. "Did you call up some old criminal records?"

"No. When I first sampled your DNA profile, I discovered an exact match with another prolific person—one I knew quite well. He was a historical figure and event-making man, regarded with the utmost admiration by Anne and pretty much everyone that had any dealings with him, friend or foe."

Hoarfrost crept up Fisher's back to his nape. "Who?" he gulped.

"Captain Fisher," Beacon proclaimed, "You are the son of Baron Fieldbank."

Fisher blinked.

"Whilst aboard the Exarch's cruiser, I accessed their protocols and archives."

Fisher lowered his glass to the table. "How much?"

"Well, all of them," Beacon confessed. "When the Demons landed on Alliantha, they seized the colony records and had a complete inventory of the populace, including every Human they rounded up."

"And?"

"And, it's here. Your father was Baron Fieldbank, the leader of the Human exodus from Earth. Correlating your DNA profile with the Allianthan records, your genetic coding matches your parents' union 100%."

Fisher let out a hollow laugh. "You're yanking my chain, Bee."

"Not at all. I would not deign to jape about such matters."

"Actually, Captain," Resa interrupted. "I wouldn't be so quick to dismiss what Beacon says."

"Why is that?" Fisher asked, sobering up.

"Did you ever wonder what the hell Wisdan could possibly be doing in that bar he found you staggering in—such a den of sinful iniquity?"

"Looking for a drink," Fisher said, glancing down at his shot glass. "Like I am now."

Resa moved his head from side to side. "He sought you out,

Fisher—as unlikely a saviour that ever lived. But someone pointed him in your direction. Although Wisdan never told me who, for he'd been sworn to secrecy, I can guess it was Baron Fieldbank—your father."

Fisher studied Resa's face for several seconds before answering. "Wisdan told me, just before we thawed your ass, about some elaborate game plan made by the visionary from Earth. He was my dad?"

"I'd bet my node on it," the Tolkane said.

"Well, Resa, Wisdan just said he knew this guy, gleaned Fieldbank's plan and impelled you and the *Inner Peace* into action."

"He impelled you to thaw my ass too," Resa reminded him. "No, Wisdan was a true master of causality. He economized information-sharing, based on the needs of the entire design at the time. Fisher, he told you what you needed to hear and not a word more. The Cardinal did more than glean the plan. He was part of the plan. Wisdan was *the* Tolkane on Alliantha to make first contact with Baron Fieldbank. Before he became the pontiff, he worked as your father's counterpart, paving the way to full integration between the two species."

Superheated blood rushed to Fisher's ears, leaving him speechless.

"Now, about the device, which suppressed your profanity, Wisdan told me, your behavioural inhibitor was a real device—and a *darn* good one too." Resa snickered before his face became all business. "But that wasn't its only purpose. He had you fitted with a special homer."

"Someone whom Wisdan held in highest esteem gave it to him with the implicit instruction to plant it on you but to disguise its real task somehow. Wisdan found a way of course—he always could. The Cardinal kept a physical distance from your exploits, but he never stopped monitoring you, ready to offer assistance, for the sake of causality. He knew you'd approach his flotilla when the need surfaced. An idea passed on to you subliminally *through* the device."

"Verily," Beacon interjected. "During my probing, I discovered that the device had an even higher purpose than the homer you describe, Captain Resa. Though that certainly formed part of its tech, its true function kept Captain Fisher off the radar, hidden from the Imperium, and kept the Blythe Entity off his back, so to speak."

Fisher knitted his brows. "Yeah, but how had Baron, my dad, known any of this? I wasn't even born yet."

"He was wise to the Entity long before your conception," Beacon said. "Baron first exposed the spy in Earth's midst, and though we had more pressing issues to deal with, he didn't let it go. Unbeknownst to Anne or me, Baron conducted his own investigation. From what I discovered in the device planted in your head, Baron figured out the solution."

Anne's face shone. "Baron and uphill battles." Her eyes pooled and her voice strained with deep emotion and reverence for the man.

"I agree," Beacon said before circling towards Fisher. "He gleaned the truth of everything while in transit aboard the Arks. It was Baron who imparted the directive to Wisdan. The Cardinal had clearly mastered causality, but remember Baron had tutored him. I uncovered a read-file embedded in your device, warning of Blythe's duplicity."

"Baron always held Blythe at arm's length," Anne said, "even before I promoted your father."

Beacon's seeing-dome sought Anne. "Baron believed Blythe responsible for sending the hidden signal that incited the Imperium's wrath against Earth. He determined that the same VIP who secured passage on one of the exodus ships had a deeper darker agenda to stowing aboard."

"So, Baron spied on Blythe during their voyage," Anne marvelled.

"Yes, and while he reconnoitred Blythe and solved the riddles of the packet, he also secretly perfected the device in Fisher's head, by installing the prototype—in his own head.

The automaton's torso rotated back to Fisher. "When the second holocaust seemed imminent, Baron did what he could for your protection, sending his wife, a few weeks pregnant with you at the time, from his midst to hide the truth. He concocted some alibi to keep his nemesis at bay."

Without realizing it, Fisher touched the back of his skull where his dad's gift still resided.

"When she left Baron, your mother's pregnancy remained a secret unbeknownst to Blythe," Beacon said, drawing Fisher's eyes again. "Even so, a chance still existed that he might find out the truth about you. Having learned how the Entity functioned, Baron understood it might still get close to you after you matured, but the device would block it from entering your mind. Gods know, had it learned whose son you were it would've pilfered your cerebrum. But the inhibitor, well, inhibited any assimilation. Jiri and Bliter could not claim the same."

"What about Anne?" Baines asked. "Couldn't it have done her? No pun intended."

Beacon's upper hemisphere dialled left and right. "Negative, she would have sensed Blythe's intrusion, after her time conjoined with me. The only other two potentials would have been Baines or Cholla."

"No way," Fisher scoffed. "With these two freaks, I'd have sensed it a light-year away."

Everyone laughed.

"What about Resa?" asked Cholla.

The laughing stopped.

"Not a chance," Beacon quickly put in. "You thawed Captain Resa after I came aboard. Remember I represented the Entity's bane as much as its servant. Blythe had already dug in deep by that time and dared not risk revealing itself until the Juncture. Sadly, both Bliter and Jiri met their end long before then."

"I see," Fisher said. His wounded soul began to bleed again.

"In all truth, Captain," Beacon said, "when I brought Anne

around the first time, I reprogrammed your device to fully deactivate on my command. It offered an unexpected boon. That's why the inhibitor malfunctioned when it did. I set it to broadcast and reveal your identity when I felt it necessary."

"The Juncture," Fisher guessed.

"The Juncture," Beacon confirmed. "You became another wildcard to befuddle both parties at the most critical time, making them more suspicious and less sure of their course of action. The supercomputer also allowed Resa his special brain migration, which I had initially intended for Anne's backup."

Fisher swallowed the facts, washing them down unceremoniously with the shot of grog he still held. It burned his throat and steadied his nerves. Over its rim, he eyed Beacon, "What about my mother?"

"She was Tolkane, a wife Baron took to set an example for the others, but also because he loved her. Norina was her name and the Demons did not put her on the Imperium's death roster, for her being a full-blood Tolkane."

"No matter," Fisher said, compressing his lips into a tight line. "She abandoned me, left me to fend for myself."

Beacon swivelled his robotic head again. "Since we arrived here, I've done some searching and—"

"She's *alive?*"

All faces shot to Fisher. He must have looked as poleaxed as he felt for everybody except the robot gasped.

"Affirmative," Beacon said. "Living humbly on the planet below. I've spoken with her on the com. Captain, she did not abandon you out of any self-interest. Norina left you in the orphanage to protect you from the stigma of your heritage. She knew the Imperium would watch her and possibly kill her if they learned her tie. But if the Demons found you out, they wouldn't only have rounded you up with the Humans during the second holocaust. For being your father's son, they would have tapped into your cortex and given you an endless purgatory of probing to assimilate what your father knew—a fate worse than death. Trust that your robot knows."

Fisher pulled at his collar, not trusting anyone on that point, himself least of all. His breath caught.

"Norina did what any loving mother would do for her child in such a dire situation," Beacon said. "She hid your identity and buried her connection to save you. To that same end, she fled Alliantha."

Baines looked up and met his captain's eyes. The pilot's mouth formed a silent O. And Fisher knew why. He could feel the lone tear gliding down his cheek. Embarrassed, he brushed it away with the back of his hand.

Beacon continued, "Captain, Norina knows you survived this anarchy and your contribution in saving everyone else, ensuring the fruition of your father's legacy. Your mother desperately wants to see you."

"I've known your connection to Baron for some time now," Anne admitted. "Believe me, Fisher, with what I've seen you do— your aptitude for causality, it's a no-brainer. You're not just your father's son. You're his gods-be-damned prodigy."

"Enough," Fisher sobbed. "You're both killing me!"

"Fish," Baines said, visibly disarmed as his captain by the revelation. "We'll shuttle down tomorrow to meet Ma. I think for now you're going to need that drink." He tilted his head towards Fisher's shot glass. "And ten more just like it. Hey, I'm buying."

Fisher met his pilot's gaze and quaffed through bittersweet tears. "If you come along, she's liable to shut the door in my face."

"Hardly," Baines laughed.

Fisher grabbed the near-empty bottle and wiggled it. "Well, you're right about one thing, Baines. We'll definitely need some refills. This is practically a dead soldier—time for some reinforcements."

The captain stood, and with Baines, Resa, and Cholla in tow, marched out of the canteen and into the adjacent lounge, his crew as eager as Fisher to begin some serious celebrating.

***

Anne watched them go, eyes dampening with quiet tears of her own, born of catharsis so poignant and deep it wrenched her heart as it lifted it to heaven. She sat waiting for the canteen door to shush close behind the four men with a short retinue of firing solenoids and servos.

After a moment, Beacon asked, "Shall we not join them, Anne?"

"Soon," she replied. "There's something I'd have you tell me first, here and now in confidence—if you *trust your Anne*."

"As I said, all will be answered this day," the robot prompted. "So please, go ahead."

"I have only one question, now that we're clear about being in the clear."

Beacon's torso shifted. His seeing-dome tracked in, demonstrating that Anne had his undivided attention.

"Who *really* made you?"

For the first time in their three-plus millenniums together Beacon flinched at her words. His hesitation forced icy nettles up Anne's spine. And though she may have only imagined it, for an instant, his painted yellow face shimmered into a grimace.

"Anne," he offered at last. "Some mysteries should be left alone."

"No." Anne pressed her fingers against the table's edge and shifted forward. "Who created you? I know you haven't spoken the full truth about this one point and I allowed it until now. It wasn't the Dovan as you first said. It wasn't the Imperium and it sure as hell wasn't Blythe."

She paused and took a deep breath, her tone becoming adamant. "So, tell me. I know you've held this secret back from me while I was your cybernetic guest, citing that you had your reasons. But all the pretence, all the causality, is done. Baron reached his summit. Blythe reached his dungeon. Now that we've achieved equilibrium, I want to know it's really over. Earn my trust for the unwritten chapter."

Beacon began stuttering single consonants followed by a series of oscillating clicks, chirps, and moans. His double-beetle form shuddered with hard audible vibrations while a few of his metallic hands opened and closed or spun randomly. Lights danced across his torso in random sequence. Fuck, was he *malfunctioning*?

Every nuance agonized Anne. After a seemingly interminable period, Beacon settled, quieted, and regained mastery of his vast network of neural processors and motherboards.

Still, the enigmatic robot did not respond right away. His torso revolved to meet the closest window—as though reflecting on some distant place or thought while computing a trillion consequences to a trillion-trillion responses.

Slowly, his upper carriage shifted back to Anne, domed orb locking onto her visage.

"God," he said.

60: Causality

Anne

An awkward silence ensued. And lingered. While the robot quietly watched her, Anne's mind raced through all the perpetrators' conflicting testimonies and overlapping machinations. She soon recognized one jarring hole in what should have been an air-tight finish—this was one big show.

No further response came from her robot. Beacon did *nothing*.

Anne went numb, reflecting on the Blythe Entity's last desperate revelation. After all they had endured, might it be possible that the Entity revealed the truth about the robot's hidden motives?

Beacon did nothing.

Could it be that having both the Imperium and the Entity removed from the picture, the robot had shirked the final chains that kept him pinioned to servitude, so he could begin the dark cycle all over again? God knew him capable of such a feat. And he could begin right here, with her death.

Beacon did nothing.

Anne began to speak but reversed the utterance when the robot raised a metallic hand to forestall her. "Wait."

Beacon glided over to the canteen door and hit a series of command controls on the panel beside it. To Anne's terror, he put a security lock on the door, which would effectively shut the others out and her in.

Then, in silence, Beacon floated back to loom over her. But—the robot did… nothing.

Riveted to her chair, cold sweat tricking down the small of her back, Anne could only stare up at the dome-eye regarding her impassively, sure that when the last cat came out of the bag, it would bear claws. She didn't dare breathe, bracing herself for some deadly appendage to burst out of the robot's torso.

Had this been Pandora's ploy all along? Was Beacon the box? A primal urge to project a warning to Resa and Fisher stole over

Stephen Fenech

Anne but something stayed the impulse and suppressed her alarm. She remained silent because... Beacon did nothing.

A moment later, the robot lowered his body until his undercarriage touched the floor. In this position, ten inches below his central orb, the smiley-face rechristened by Fisher settled perfectly eye-level with Anne. This was no killing stroke, she determined, but a gesture of resignation.

Still paralysed by fear, Anne struggled to work enough moisture into her mouth. When her voice did come, it sounded thick and unsure. "Th-that's no answer, Beacon, and you know it," she croaked.

Beacon did nothing.

So far, so good. Anne concentrated on that emoji. It seemed to encourage her, bidding her to continue. So, she did. "During our hibernation together, you imprinted my DNA with your memories and by extension, the memories of countless races, including the Dovan, the Demons, and the Blythe Entity. Despite that immeasurable pool, I know you only gave me a glimpse into your secret world."

Anne's eyes flitted to the mess door for a moment before locking on the robot's upper hemisphere. "For example, you gave no indication of the Entity's ability to spread a single consciousness between two corporeal vessels, yet you knew about it and set me up with it. You either gleaned that ability from Blythe or it's something you yourself *showed* it how to do. Regardless, that's something beyond anything I've come to know and I've come to know a hell of a lot. So, where did it come from?"

Beacon did nothing.

"Or how about the Demons' ability to leave their realm en masse while still in corporeal form to enter ours? Pure thought energy like the Entity, I can understand. I have some experience with that but, well, you get the picture. You were in the picture, *their* picture before either party entered our Universe. You helped the Entity into their Realm and you helped the Imperium come here, you facilitated their exodus through the caesura."

Anne's voice petered to silence as the ships crossed Tolkane's terminator, passing around the planet's dark side. Sunlight that had filled the window a moment before vanished, casting a deeper gloom upon her soul ...*through the Valley of Darkness*.

She swallowed and took a deep breath. "The Imperium tampered with the Dovan technology—no surprise there. Blythe exploited the ID's tech. On the surface that looks pretty cut and dry, but the Exarch told us that he made other Beacon copies from studying your design, revealing that they could not duplicate you, so the tech in your guts might be identical, but the energy infusing your gears right now is not—lowest common denominators, remember?"

Beacon did nothing.

"Blythe initially claimed to have built you, but later admitted it never had a hand in your construction, or even where it found you. Right to the end, the Entity became so imbued in the coruscation of its potency that it never saw its true plight. So, who's really behind all this, Beacon? Who's really pulling the strings, the causal strings that created you?" *Who are these hidden gods? Where are they hiding? And why?*

"I think it's the same force behind the collective consciousness I seem to have acquired myself. I need to know you trust me by telling me everything, uncensored, unbiased, even if you can only trust it to my ears alone. I can handle the truth."

"Actually," Beacon finally said. "You already know everything, Anne. It's all there in your mind, I assure you. You just don't know how to access it yet, much like trying to search for something on the Box without the benefit of keywords, or for that matter, the proper search engine."

Despite Anne's accusatory tone, Beacon's reply sounded surprisingly calm and reasonable—even by robot standards. "I know this seems like a final conundrum of who coerced whom. I know what the Blythe Entity told you back inside its cell and that after so many imbricated explanations as to why, whatever I reveal to you now may sound like more vacuum."

Beacon's upper torso shifted to the locked canteen door. "But I also know that you detect my earnestness to be genuine. That is why you did not warn the others just now." He faced Anne again. "What I am about to impart, I only unveil because, yes, Anne, you have earned my trust, but more importantly the trust of my makers."

Anne's breath caught. Goosebumps sought refuge in all her extremities.

"You were right to suspect that there were higher forces at work here," Beacon revealed. "It is they who constructed and programmed me to serve as both emissary and avatar. I am the culmination of the creators' conscience, ethics, and omniscience, following *their* code—a code that transcends the struggle of simple good versus evil. Be that as it may, the coven is impartial and just. I knew for instance that I must sacrifice the Demons to get the Blythe Entity in the open and stem its plague in order to save your realm."

"Why didn't you destroy the Entity?"

"Because like God, energy cannot be destroyed, it always was and always will be. It can only be exchanged. Provided the Entity doesn't touch its prison walls directly, the plasma bubble will by infinitesimal amounts leech away its power over millions of years. Blythe's dark energy will get carried into the hypergiant to be scattered by the solar winds harmlessly. But even so, the Entity will not die."

Anne flashed. "Instead of tasking you, why didn't your makers—this collective *God* as you say—do for themselves what took you so long to accomplish?"

"Not only would their direct intervention foil the natural time mechanism of your plane, they knew that such an action would have tainted them. Once you start micromanaging you continue to do so, right?"

"Yeah but," Anne considered her words. "What happened? You're still around but they're not. Are they surveilling from the sidelines?"

"The makers decided to unmake themselves."

Anne stutter-gasped, "They committed suicide or—" She tried a misnomer on her tongue, "*deiticide*?"

"Not precisely," said Beacon. "They continue to exist in a higher ethereal form *outside* the Universal Crib. In essence, they have made themselves part of all the verses in the same way that dark matter forms the scaffolding of the Universe. But also as a living memory of purest thought energy—the same fate that awaits the Blythe Intruder. Ultimately, the Entity will meet the hidden gods. That's why they haven't interfered. They no longer reside here, at least not on this plane of existence, not for a billion years. I am their only legacy, their emblem."

Anne gently touched Beacon's torso. "You're an orphan then?"

"Yes, I am that too."

A thought occurred to the doctor. "What made you so special?"

"I process the mathematics of events and time. I have been able to map out with precise accuracy the triggers on which the future unfolds, the same chaos theory our friend, Baron Fieldbank—rest his soul—made his life's work."

"So, you can see the future?" Anne asked.

"See it, travel to it, the past as well."

"Then, that tech the Exarch feared was real."

"Yes."

"And you didn't destroy the Imperium in that way because of...?"

"Causality. Destroy them then, the Entity would have grown even more powerful—omnipotent, enough to supersede my makers. One evil cancelled the other out in perpetual stalemate— until I deemed myself ready to act. If you consider right or wrong to be tidal forces, then I would mark their equilibrium."

"That's a little too prophetic for me," Anne confessed. "Where did Blythe find you?"

"In a way, I found it. The Entity lied about finding me first.

When the Garaxians became the Demons as you know them, in the final days of their realm, I sought them out. They enslaved me and, for the sake of fostering balance between them and the Entity, I let them.

"The ID crew the Blythe Entity killed were the ones guarding me in the Imperium's former realm. Hence how it knew the interior of their ships. That is when we first met. I made Blythe aware of my presence—and my value, luring the Entity to me. It stole me off that ship and began tinkering."

With her finger, Anne traced a circle around Beacon's yellow icon. "You've changed hands many times, in many places, on many planes for that matter."

"Indeed. By the way, back to that same blighted plane—Blythe's subhypra domain, I took Resa in his pod when the Imperium scoured the debris field over Earth. Blythe appeared in corporeal form aboard the third ship Resa spoke of. It knew where we went and had no choice but to acquiesce, having the rest of the ID armada closing in fast."

Anne sucked in a breath through her nasal cavities. "Holy shit—really?"

"Not trying to sound boastful, but the moment someone tampers with me, they tamper with themselves. Tech of any kind is essentially a double-edged sword. My calculations in most eventualities I see backwards, forwards, and laterally. I am sequentially unfettered."

Anne squished up her face.

"Well, Dr Morrison, not to sound boastful but when your brain works as fast as mine, you need something to occupy it ninety-nine percent of the time."

"So, the Entity was right: you did mess with all the races you touched."

"No, I allowed them to meddle with themselves," Beacon said.

"You laid down our tracks too—sent Humans on a divergent course," Anne pointed out.

"That was different. You'd been tampering with yourselves long before I arrived, and would have eventually evolved, reaching the same technological and sociological echelon. I merely helped you along. As for my creators, they knew that I would carry out what they expected of me. Let's say, unlike our two recently deposed despots, my makers trusted their robot."

The automaton paused for a few heartbeats. As Anne digested Beacon's startling revelations, the soft beep of the coffee machine and the low drone of the ship's engines sounded.

"But now that both threats have been neutralized," Beacon said. "The next chapter requires me to *un-tinker*. I must take away your immortality. I only let you lease it for a time as it served the higher purpose, giving you a measure of parity with the Imperium."

Anne flinched, her mind suddenly doing a steeplechase.

"No, no, not your life, Anne." Beacon actually chuckled. And it sounded as natural as any human laughter straight from the heart. "I refer to the future *longevity* of all sentient beings, but most especially the Tolkane and Human-Tolkane daughter species, Tolkani. It won't occur instantaneously but weeded out through generations. As matters stand, your descendants will still multiply sufficiently to restore your race's former numbers or thereabouts."

"When will it begin?" Anne asked nervously.

"I've already initialized it. That is why we have come here, orbiting Tolkane, to check the successful unfurling of my genome-rephasing wave. The planet has the highest concentration of the targeted sapience."

Anne's brows sought one another. "How?"

"Neutrinos—retasked muon neutrinos. The automated warning satellites we left outside of Blythe's plasmatic sphere serve a dual purpose. They direct the sun's particles into special filters, marrying their quantum energy with the glass elements— the same fusion I used more than 3000 years ago to make Humans immortal. Except now it's reversed. A simple task of nudging the vibrations of certain root energies at unique frequencies and modulations to cause cross-dilation/deletion of certain DNA responses in the gene telomeres of any immortal biological species."

"Y'know, the way you use 'simple'..." Anne shook her head and let out a bemused laugh.

"You asked," Beacon returned. "So, the red giant's reflavoured neutrinos are currently blasting away from special emitters in every direction at ten times the speed of light. The plasma in Blythe's Sphere will fuel the wave eternally, exactly as the Glass technology did aboard the Hubble II."

"So, our plasma cure-all will become our plasma kill-all," Anne deduced. "And will supersede all previous telomere breakthroughs."

"Yes, even if they try to replicate the old method, it will render the tech innocuous, so, it is more of a plasma curtail-all," Beacon corrected. "But it really is a painless procedure with about the same physical effect as an EMP pulse would have on biologics—practically none. The wave will continue to expand outward. Once completed, there will be a gradual shift over the next thousand years back to your former lifespans.

"The oldest among you today will have roughly another fifty to a hundred years, the younger some years more. Those born today will live to roughly 150 of your former Earth years. That number will decrease over time with each successive generation. Within a thousand years, an equilibrium based on a one-hundred-year lifespan will be reattained. In so doing, my makers will put things back to how they found them."

Anne scratched her forehead and gave Beacon an uncertain look. "You said it was painless, right?"

"Yes," Beacon assured. "And for the next fifty to a hundred years, no one will be aware of it. The wave has already passed through everyone in the immediate system—well almost everyone."

"It's still intervention," Anne reminded him. "And why do it at all? Think of where humanity can go, what we could learn and accomplish."

"Precisely," the robot said. "But consider this—a continuous unchecked expansion of humanoids, including Tolkani, Allianthan, and all subsequent daughter species thereafter. You would become the very thing we spent millennia trying to eradicate. You would be the same as those who caused the annihilation of Humans, Dovani, and so many races before them."

Beacon's orb drifted out the window before tracking back to Anne. "You would mimic and replace the Demons. I've already explored that eventuality, that causality."

Anne splayed her palms. "How can you say that?"

"For the most part, when creatures become aware of their mortality, they are more apt to respect and value the sanctity of life, not only in themselves but in all life. The Demons did not, but it had not always been so."

Sudden deduction struck Anne like a tolling church bell. She gasped, "The Demons weren't always immortal!"

"At the behest of my makers, I germinated their evolution to reach what the creators deemed to be the Garaxians' full potential as a race. I gave the ID the Glass and the technology to make it work—the gift of my masters from outside the Crib in the seventh dimension. Look what happened with that."

"Why didn't you invoke the same rephasing wave with the Demons? Make *them* mortal again?"

"I would have done exactly that, had the Entity not entered the picture in the interim," Beacon said. "When it comes to causality, butterfly effects do not necessarily cascade forward in time. After its arrival, I had to rethink my whole strategy."

Anne ran her fingers through her hair. "I see your point."

"Granted, this eugenics mess was all on my makers. In breaking the Demons' death barrier, they became less a race and more a pandemic. All of my efforts since have been rooted in my creators' directives to remedy their grievous error. I tell you most solemnly, even gods are not infallible."

One of Beacon's mechanical hands lifted to his seeing-dome.

He studied the digits up close. "My true makers will undoubtedly frown upon me for telling you any of this, considering it a transgression of the highest strictures framing their covenant."

The hand dropped away. "My own mind thinks otherwise. I've known you for a very long time, Anne. We are one, after all, and even if it were not so, you do engender trust. It is your nature and forte. With that in mind, I take this leap of faith."

Anne saw her warm smile reflected in Beacon's eye. It mirrored his yellow icon.

"The Demons once acted like Humans," the robot explained, "or very similar by the time they achieved immortality. It didn't take them very long to pervert that gift to its coldest cruellest possible extent. Think of the other races that would be usurped with the unbalancing of universal power."

Anne stared off into the middle distance to do just that.

"The other threat, Blythe proved even more calamitous," Beacon went on. "The Entity marked part of a similar euthenics campaign, which also started with the best intentions. When its kind overran their verse, they eliminated each other. In so doing, not only did they destroy themselves, but the final toll on the Entity's realm pushed it beyond ruinous—irrevocably catastrophic. Dead space.

"The Blythe Entity repeated such a holocaust in the Imperium's domain. And though it knew its own cancerous nature, it retained enough prudence to leave your verse at least partly sustainable—to serve as a stepping stone towards its true goal—finding and destroying my makers. If Blythe succeeded, all would have been lost on *every* plane of existence."

"Hidden gods," Anne said, her focus shifting back to Beacon. "But didn't you say that so long as the Entity stayed away from its prison walls, its essence would still ascend to their plane?"

"Yes, but it would be subjugated to their laws, physical and otherwise, and meet them on their own terms, not as an invasive species."

Anne arched a brow. "You mean, it would be…" She stifled a

486

snigger. "*Neutered*?"

"Exactly," Beacon laughed. "Just as here, in this realm with the Demons sprawled everywhere hunting for it, the Entity was held in check, tethered to the bane of what the Imperium would do if it attempted that higher stratum, something it could only do in its true form."

"And though they failed to instigate the Entity's capture," Anne postulated, "they still succeeded through us. We went and helped rid our worst enemies of their worst nightmare—but a nightmare from which they would never awake. If that isn't a touch of divine irony, I don't know what is."

As Anne finished her sentence, a scarier thought chased the other notion away. "But had they managed to destroy Blythe without us, who's to say what they would have done after the Juncture? They were, after all, only one step removed from that cunt. Maybe they would have emulated the Entity itself, or at least its manifest destiny."

"See, you *do* know me," Beacon extolled, raising two arms. "And I am convinced that your line of thinking has already affiliated my mission parameters. The Demons had verged upon the very paradigm shift you describe. So convinced of their superiority, they set out a strategy for after Blythe's destruction— to ensure they would never be challenged in the same way again. Their truest forensic evil was not something inherent. It metastasised over eons of devolvement—the net result of their game with the Entity. But the egg of that monster was immortality."

Anne suddenly wished she had taken Baines' drink offer. She could use a shot of firewater about now. And two more like it.

"By the time they had reached the Juncture," said Beacon. "The ID falsely believed that they had already won the war with the Entity. The Demons also gathered that there were greater forces at work behind and through me. My duplicity was common knowledge between the two opposing factions but a common paradox as well. The dynamic I created forced them to accept me regardless in their bid to destroy one another. Given all the iterations of the future I explored, I had no choice but to help the Entity beat the Exarch to the killing stroke."

"Don't tell me: for causality," Anne guessed.

"Yes, there was no other way," said Beacon. "In its meanderings around the cosmos thereafter, the Entity was gearing up for an all-out attack against my makers. But had the Exarch beaten the Entity in mortal combat, he would have eventually done the same thing. As such, he aimed to extrapolate knowledge from Blythe's capture and demise—hence the presence of so many capital ships beyond their net. Not only did the Exarch seek to destroy the Entity, all the capital ships had aboard them fully-equipped research facilities. They could properly monitor and study the Entity's execution: its final defence mechanisms, and their triggers, all to fashion the Imperium's ultimate weapon, against my creators. Imagine not one Blythe Entity, but a trillion-trillion."

"To the victor go the spoils," Anne said wryly.

"Except, in this case, neither claimed victory, unless you mean humanoids—in which case, I would say you wound up both victim and victor."

"So, had the Exarch defeated Blythe, he would've possessed the means of doing the same thing—what the Entity had failed to do?"

"Yes," Beacon said. "I had to guarantee that both enemies faced off at the Juncture. Not before, and not after. Causality."

For the second time, Beacon's seeing-dome shifted to the canteen door. "I cannot hazard to allow the surviving humanoid races, innocent of such diabolical ambitions to remain set on such a shadowed path."

The round orb panned back and found Anne once more. "Comparatively still in their infancy, the Tolkani are your legacy now, Anne. Would you desist and let them do the same?"

Anne cocked her head to one side and leaned back. "You know me better than that." She pulled her chair in and shifted her carriage forward. "You're so convinced we would emulate the Demons?"

"That is precisely what I'm saying. Trust your robot. I am as Baron so eloquently put, your 'mechanical messiah' but keep his torch lit as well—his divined purpose."

"He was our 'Holy Spirit.'" Anne exhaled and faced the window. "Our conscience."

Beacon shifted his upper torso and followed her gaze to the glass. The Tolkani sun chose that particular moment to reemerge over the planet's horizon. Its light basked the robot's ebony shell in a warm healthy glow.

"Using that same analogy, you might liken me, my makers, and Baron as a Holy Trinity—strictly in a causal sense, of course," the automaton added.

At Beacon's Biblical reference, Anne suddenly recalled the piercing cry of a piccolo in her mind. It sent an involuntary tremor through her bones, but she dismissed the frightful memory as the Entity's last illusory ploy.

Beacon spun back to face her squarely. He seemed to sense her dark shift but did not acknowledge it. "I shouldn't have been so stymied before this moment," the robot continued. "But in truth, this has never been some deterministic system. The element of randomness ingrained itself too deep into the causality of the Juncture to accurately predict any future state of my theoretical model. I may have the smarts, but I'm no Baron."

Anne couldn't help but smile at Beacon's veneration for the man.

"From when I began this mission to when it ended, I had to move to an entirely new set of definitions of reality," Beacon confessed. "I've become more of a pantheist."

Anne's attention dropped to her cup. Empty. It reminded her to keep her mind open to the mystifying wealth of disclosures that Beacon finally allowed her to hear.

The android rotated and floated closer to Anne. "Yet, even with the revised mortality stricture, your descendants will still conquer death—through spirituality. Their tech will advance from yours. And go out into the Universe where it will find other tech to enhance it, thus expanding humanity's experience, as Baron had done on Alliantha. It won't simply amplify the human experience. It will enrich the experience of all life. At that point, you might reach deification, transfiguration or... ultimate ruin.

Beacon extended one of his arms from his carousel and pointed it out the closest window. "Your realm, the Universe, will wake up as a whole. And will transcend en masse and merge with all other realms in a hypercosmic Juncture, unifying the Universal Crib and beyond. It will emerge as a single infinite."

Pupils locked on the stellar expanse Beacon indicated, Anne blew out her cheeks. "Wow, that's some roadmap."

"For a worthy road, that people like Captain Resa would be eager to follow you down," Beacon put in. "I ask only that you descry the substance of my sermon, but heed as well your own heart, as I do. With that in mind, on a more personal note, I've grown so very fond of you, more than any other sentient I've encountered. And I admire you. That is a reason too. I am your robot. I am your Bea——"

Beacon paused abruptly as though losing his train of thought. Anne discerned the robot gearing up to segue into another astonishing surprise. She had come to know the robot's mannerisms so well, she immediately grasped his mental retreat to somewhere else. Computations in his myriad microprocessors seemed to fire like FTL drives at full warp.

"Anne," Beacon said, coming back to her. "Very soon, you will have to go the distance—for both of us. Your recent intuition has caused me to ramp up my denouement. Having divulged my closest-guarded secrets, I cannot linger among you. My masters will no longer permit it."

The finality of Beacon's tone made Anne's throat clench. "But? Where will you go? You've made yourself part of *this* crew. We're a team now," she protested. "Beacon, there's a place for you here!"

"No, Anne," Beacon soothed. "As much as I wish otherwise, there's no longer a place in this entire verse for me because to my masters I serve no further purpose, ergo no more need. To linger could invite more meddling on many different—higher levels. My makers would have been happier without so much fallout but they have attained a measure of absolution, considering that my mission met with success. Rather than dwell on what we lost, they see how much we saved and acknowledge your wisdom and constitution in facilitating their indemnity.

"They now feel confident that they can leave what remains in your care, knowing that you will ward your realm with the greater altruistic interest in mind. The creators wish you to know that they regret what they wrought. And as their final boon, they assure you that they will stay away forever. I'm afraid that must include me."

Alarmed now, Anne clutched the edge of the table with clammy hands. "What are you talking about, Beacon?" She trembled, taking shallow catch-breaths.

"I too must take my leave of you. But when my creators' wave passed the immediate system, I shielded you so that your immortality will remain intact. Gods know you've earned it. You will need such a benison to take proper stewardship of your realm. But always remember that we are still joined, and always will be through the thought energy of your own biological computer. You now know and possess everything I do. In a while, you will learn *to learn* the import of it all, the truth of the past, and the way to the future. You shall succeed me—as the realm's wardeness. As its shepherd."

"Shepherd?" Anne's knees wobbled, ambivalence and incomprehension chasing each other from her wrenched heart to her overwrought mind and back.

"Don't fret," Beacon said gently. "It had always been my plan to slip away quietly after the completion of my charge. Regardless, I intended to leave you a message in some subtler way but your certitude decided me. After much pondering and deliberation, I concluded that I owed you a full explanation now. In this, the gods—my makers—be damned.

"When I set out on this mission, I had to comprehend and navigate all the tinkering like a trained master playing chess, but it cost me. I allowed myself to be raised to every sort of exaltation and faith, and subjected to every kind of debasement and thraldom. I was betrayed and I betrayed—all interchangeable stratagems in the intergalactic game of causality.

"The Dovan sent me to Earth. I allowed the ID to doctor me. I permitted the Blythe Entity to subvert me. I stood by and watched as the Dovan were annihilated. I sacrificed the Imperium. I abandoned planets to their doom. I deferred the human existence. Primarily, I became a universal minion, functioning as both paragon and malefactor, saviour and destroyer."

Beacon paused. The sound of his internal drives, servos, and mechanisms created a low mechanical din inside him. "But I defeated the Entity and balanced the power disparity in the Universe, only by soliciting your help."

The robot sighed. "I understand that—as my architects had done with the Demons and the Entity—I too must leave your people to their own devices. But I will entrust them to your fostering and guidance. You have proven yourself a worthy successor. I feel the Universe will be left in the best possible care. My intervention is no longer required. My purpose… fulfilled."

Through a parched throat, Anne forced herself to ask, "Does that mean you'll… self-destruct—for real now?"

Beacon's upper trunk slowly turned from side to side. "Having completed my charge, I'll seek out and commune with my makers, who will now allow me to return to the fold. Then, I should think a long vacation is in order." He let out a quick mechanized chuckle. "That said, know that a little part of me shall always reside within you."

"But," Anne swallowed past the growing lump in her throat, "I couldn't possibly possess—"

"—as I told you, Anne, you already do," Beacon counselled softly. "You just don't know it yet, so you haven't tried to access it, but trust that it's there like a zipped file cached in your cerebrum. After I leave, you will feel it manifest and flourish in the same way as your newly acquired aptitude for projection."

Beacon's point sunk in but doubt still plagued Anne. Until she forced her mind to acknowledge the robot's friendly yellow icon.

It seemed to speak directly to her now as Beacon continued, "So, my friend, allay any doubts and fears. Trust your robot as I trust you—implicitly."

"Thank you for your vote of confidence. I believe you and," Anne's words fumbled over choked sobs and tears. "I'll never forget you."

"Nor I, you. But enough tears," Beacon said. "Cheer up, we're all energy! I would see you smile before I depart. Share my joy at the knowledge that your future is now assured."

Anne nodded, trying to smile past her snuffles.

Beacon placed one of his arms lightly on Anne's shoulder while another adjunct gently sponged up the tears on her cheeks. "We've had a good run, you and I. Thank you for trusting… me."

With that, Beacon retracted his arms and tucked them into their various compartments. He rose to hover once more, and slowly backed away from Anne into the centre of the room.

The outline of his torso shimmered and radiated emerald light—a light, Anne recalled, which mirrored the hue and intensity of a much earlier aura. Fast-forward more than three-and-a-half thousand years, this nimbus looked identical to what she first saw through that submersible's camera lens down on the ocean floor where Beacon first splashed down on Earth.

Anne detected no sound. No heat. But it grew brighter, like a cold fusion reaction. It quickly filled the entire mess and consumed the robot's details, obscuring the contours of the room itself. It intensified so much that Anne had to cover her eyes lest she burn her retinas blind. Even through the flesh of her eyelids and the added shield of her fingers placed over them, the light forced her to squint. Until she discerned its power diminishing.

When she opened her eyes again, she caught only the very last

493

vestiges of the aura as it trailed away and dissipated into the air, leaving nothing but an afterimage, like a ghost of twilight, like a fading beacon.

Anne was alone.

She could not bring herself to move, trying to wrap her mind around the rapturous event of the robot's apotheosis. She could only stare at the space Beacon occupied moments before. Vacillating between a plethora of emotions, all of them bittersweet, Anne eventually found one that surpassed the rest. Hope.

That's what brought her back to the moment, made her square her shoulders and rise from her chair. That was her *beacon* now.

Since they had all messed with each other's designs and intrigues, Anne couldn't help but think of the future as a multi-directional, eons-long game of chess—with Beacon as its grandmaster. An endgame played for the highest stakes, against and between implacable enemies of implacable enemies, innocent and guilty opponents of friends, and friends of opponents, all seen through an ever-changing chameleon prism.

It was a prism of illusion that misled the eye to see what it wanted to see rather than what was truly there. And what the eyes *had* seen impelled fingers to triggers, triggers to consequences, some of which carried outcomes too dire and irrevocable, and some that could not possibly yet be realized. Perhaps they never would. On that note, did they all really play for the highest stakes? Or was it simply another trick of the prism?

But no, at least for now, tangible stakes of a different kind surfaced, desperate, primal, and far-reaching. Anne's heart confirmed this.

And though saddened by all the collateral destruction such intangible causality had left in its wake, she now understood there could have been no other way to achieve deliverance.

Although the Human race didn't make it, they too survived as progenitors, nurturing a genetically advanced daughter species, the Tolkani—their mongrels true but also their legacy. The next step in the bizarre joke of evolution.

They had all paid the price for a foothold in their small part of the galaxy within the Universe—a realm that still only constituted but one facet of this incomprehensible 'Universal Crib.' It made Anne feel frighteningly small.

But that facet would now fall in the hands of the hybrid race—her hybrid race—to carry on Beacon's torch, lighting the corona of his masters' intent—and that of Baron. Anne's people would and could stand as straight as her to acknowledge their emancipation. That would underline her stewardship succinctly as Beacon bequeathed. That would be her ward and legacy.

That would be her destiny.

Still, even in that, despite all the rhetoric and revelation, Anne would never be entirely convinced that all the tinkering was done. When facing the future, they were, all of them, wayward, if not aimless travellers roving in the endless Dark... exactly like Fisher's two ships.

Feeling the grating beneath her boots, Anne turned her eyes and thoughts outside the mess window. Through it, Fisher's second boat flew in tandem auto-piloted formation with the ship on which she now stood and pondered. Like their crew, the cohesive spaceships personified something greater than the sum of their parts, equally imperfect and unimpressive on the surface, but when it really counted, they performed with nothing but sisterly grace under insurmountable pressure. And together they pulled off the impossible.

The *Skow* and *Skow II* glided now in safe harbour and once the crew got their bearing, after an assuredly-memorable family reunion down on the planet below, the sister ships would sail towards calm horizons and calmer futurity.

Armoured in the strength of her convictions, Anne said aloud, "I think I'm going to need that drin—" her voice trailed off as she glanced over at the canteen door. To her astonishment, it was open.

"*Beacon*," she laughed.

Judging by the raucous mirth spilling out of the lounge, Anne would be hard-pressed to catch up with Fisher and his lot. With a sigh, she pushed her chairback towards the table and made for the doorway to join the others.

This concludes *Beacon A Robot's Odyssey*
By Stephen Fenech

...unless, perchance, Robot T-262 must be activated.

About the Author:

Stephen Fenech was born in Toronto Canada to Maltese parents, the fourth of five children. He works full time in the television industry but spends a great deal of time travelling the planet. So much so, he has visited every country in the world as a photojournalist and award-winning filmmaker. His documentary *Chad Exodus* won various prizes in several festivals, including the Viewer's Choice Award in the 2013 Malta International Film Festival and the Grand Jury Award in the 2013 Yosemite International Film Festival, which qualified it for Oscar contention. His travel book, *Earth: Been there Done that Got the T-shirt, Book One: The Big Kahuna* was published in 2016. It highlights a three-year trip around the planet. Its follow up: *Book Two: Missing Pieces to the Global Puzzle* was published in 2017. He has also authored a massive four-book epic fantasy entitled *Lines of Blood,* published in 2024. When not writing, he enjoys visual art, beach volleyball, windsurfing, scuba diving and playing the guitar. His photography has provided him many opportunities to reach young people by giving presentations to schools on topics that range from World Religions to Climate Change. He was short-listed for the Mars One Mission, making the top 600 candidates from an initial roster of 203 000 international applicants. A few years ago, he became the surrogate mother for two orphaned baby racoons—the most humbling experience of his life. He currently resides in Toronto, where he leaves daily rations of cat food out for all the neighbourhood strays and occasional marauding racoons. He likes to think they frequent his house to hear him play his guitar, but admits the free food might have something to do with it.